Shadows of the Stage

Fae & Glamour #1

Patience D. Schoene

Pentacle Publishing Group

ISBN: 979-8-9945654-3-8 (Hardcover)

ISBN: 979-8-9945654-4-5 (Paperback)

ISBN: 979-8-9945654-5-2 (eBook)

Library of Congress Control Number: 2026905750

Edited by Spellbound Publishing House and Alyssa Munch

Printed in the United States

10 9 8 7 6 5 4 3 2 1

To my mother, Joanne, who taught me how to succeed.

To my husband, Tyson, who was there for every high and every low, your support gives me the audacity.

To Joleen, for reading every iteration of this book, especially the terrible ones.

To Robin, for cheering on every insane idea that pops into my head.

To Ozzie and James, and all the dogs that came before them. There is nothing like the unconditional love of a furry family member to help you reach for the stars.

To the readers who have picked up this book, I don't have the words to thank you.

Acknowledgements

Shadows of the Stage is the culmination of support from a wide variety of people. First, I must give credit to the amazingly vibrant burlesque scene in Seattle. Numerous shows and local theaters went into shaping the world Jolie moves through. This book would also not exist without a team of talented editors who held my hand throughout the entire process and helped me craft a story that I could be proud of. Also, you would never have heard of this book if it weren't for the marketing talents of Solymar Valdez at Canned Bread Productions.

CHAPTER ONE

Setting the Stage

The music throbbed through her, a physical vibration that was timed perfectly with the deliberate sway of her hips. Her pale hand moved with glacial slowness up her thigh. Each crimson nail seemed to etch itself into her skin, as her fingers traced the delicate curve of her hip. Her hand lingered on her lower back; the silken touch barely disturbed the shimmering green sequins of her bra. Thousands of tiny emeralds caught the stage lights and exploded into bursts of glittering light that danced across the theater's darkness.

She unhooked the clasp at the back. Her head tilted, her gaze lingering over her bare shoulder as the bra slipped down her arms. The green fabric fell like a discarded whisper, leaving her momentarily bare before she crossed her arms protectively across her breasts. Gasps and whispers rippled through the crowd. The atmosphere thickened with anticipation; the protective shield of her arms had the audience leaning forward in their seats. Her performance was a tantalizing game of give and take. Her hips rolled gently, mimicking the languid ebb of water.

Even in the dim light, the unique character of The Black Cat House was evident. Plush black velvet booths hugged the walls, worn smooth from years of soft conversations and clinking glasses. Smaller, more intimate café tables were scattered across the center of the room, their surfaces marred with the stories of countless nights. Vintage gold wallpaper, faded yet undeniably opulent, showcased a bygone era of glamour. A short set of stairs wound toward the back bar. Security maintained a watchful presence, clad in sleek black uniforms that emphasized their imposing physiques. Servers wore costumes that were as much performance art as uniform—plumes of feathers dyed in vibrant shades of red, gold, and purple swayed gently with their hurried movements and added splashes of color to the dark theater.

The dancer turned to face the audience. Her arms still crossed over her chest, hiding herself yet always remaining in the spotlight. The music swelled as she continued to roll her hips. The audience anticipated the reveal; whistles and cheers echoed around the theater. Her ruby-red lips stretched into a calculated smile, more show than genuine warmth, and she offered her final reveal: rhinestone pasties sparkling in the stage lights. The lights cut out, and she slipped into the darkness of the wings.

Finally shielded from the electric energy of the stage, she slumped against the concrete wall. She took a deep breath and pressed her eyes shut, savoring the coolness against her skin. The hallway that connected the dressing room to the stage entrance contrasted sharply with the lavish atmosphere beyond. It was brightly lit and smelled faintly of damp concrete. The walls were layers upon layers of spray paint, scrawled messages, and crudely drawn images. The floor's uneven surface bore the imprints of countless scuffed shoes and spilled drinks; visceral history carved into every surface.

The heavy metal door at the hallway's end hung open to the alley; its rusty hinges groaned softly in the draft. It remained stubbornly unlatched, defying the owner's repeated attempts to keep it shut. A sliver of cool night air carried the distant sounds of city traffic as it snaked through the gap.

Though the hefty wooden door between the hallway and the theater was padded to muffle noise from inside, the boisterous sounds of the audience still seeped through. It created a frantic thrumming that pressed against her. The audience's pulses throbbed visibly beneath flushed skin and dilated pupils; it enveloped her in their excitement. Laughter leaked through in raucous waves as inhibitions melted like ice in the warmth of camaraderie. It was a potent siren song she fought to resist.

She could see the darkness in their eyes, the fear they drowned out with bravado. They chose to ignore the danger that lurked in the shadows. They regarded themselves as masters of their world; they hid their prey instincts deep. Alcohol only dulled that instinct further.

Images flickered behind her eyelids like warning signs. Memories of her Maker surged forward. The concrete walls of the club faded, swallowed by the weight of her past.

His long fingers traced lazy patterns down her bare shoulder. A shiver raced up her spine. His touch was a reminder of his unwavering control.

He surveyed the sea of faces and landed abruptly on a young woman near the bar. Her laughter was a little too loud, her eyes a little too wide. A subtle shift in his posture, a tightening around the jaw. Then his thoughts brushed against her mind: her.

It wasn't a request.

Her own smile was practiced and held no warmth as she approached the object of his desire. She reached out with her mind, and her thoughts became a gentle brush against the woman's, a thread of curiosity with a promise of something exciting. The woman met her eyes, and her initial apprehension dissolved. It was a delicate dance, a subtle redirection of will. Within moments, she was theirs.

The suffocating confines of their nest were a place of velvet and shadows, where the air stank of shared hunger. There the feast would begin. He would lose himself in it, days blurring into a symphony of torment.

Terror was his sustenance, the spice that made the blood sing on his tongue. Sometimes he allowed her to partake; other times, when her efforts were too slow or her quarry too elusive, his displeasure manifested in a crueler game: he would force the victim to bear witness as he turned his attention upon her.

That memory, and a hundred others like it, formed the stones that built the wall between her and her instincts. The wall that kept her from acting on her forbidden nature. A silent battle raged against the urge to abandon her self-imposed constraints and to let the protective shell crack and release the power simmering beneath. But tonight, like every other night for these long, weary years, duty prevailed.

Without opening her eyes, Jolie felt the tentative approach, the wariness. Maddy, the stage kitten, stood just within her peripheral vision. The backstage wall dug into the girl's shoulder blades as she edged sideways like a mouse inching away from a predator. Her arms, heavy with discarded costumes, trembled. Jolie could smell the sweat and hairspray that clung to her, along with the delicate scent of fear. Some humans were oblivious to the danger she presented; others were more attuned.

Maddy shifted her weight from one foot to the other. The worn heels of her shoes dug into the cracked floor. Her words softly mumbled. "Miss Jolie Mason." The name sounded more like a plea than a greeting. She gulped. A desperate flutter of her hand nearly caused the precarious pile of clothing to slip. "Jolie? Um . . . Miss Mason?"

Jolie finally looked up. Her features softened into a smile as she met the girl's eyes. "Oh, Maddy, I'm sorry. I didn't hear you."

Maddy was an anxious knot of short, choppy blonde hair and startlingly bright blue eyes. Her body was a coiled spring, ready to flee. She held the discarded silks and sequins out to Jolie as if offering a venomous creature. She kept a careful, almost comical distance. A tremor ran through Maddy's slight frame. "It's . . . it's all right," she stammered. "You . . . you were amazing. Absolutely incredible. The audience went wild. You'll be back on in forty-five minutes." The words tumbled out in a rush. With a sudden, jerky movement, she threw the clothes into Jolie's arms. The silks landed with a soft rustle.

Maddy recoiled instantly, eyes wide and pleading. The space between them seemed to expand. Jolie's lips curled into her friendliest grin, but the young woman appeared to possess a keen sense of self-preservation. She would never realize Jolie was a vampire, but she might tell her friends about the odd woman at work who gave her the creeps.

"Thank you," Jolie offered.

Maddy turned with a swish of her purple bustle and scurried back toward the stage. A dull ache grew behind Jolie's eyes, mirroring the hollowness in her chest. The familiar pressure settled like a leaden blanket. Her shoulders drooped slightly as she absentmindedly twisted a loose strand of hair around her finger. The longing wasn't new; she'd worn it for years. Resignation settled in her gut. She lived on the periphery, watching from the edges.

Jolie walked with purpose down the dimly lit hallway, heels clicking against the worn floorboards. Muffled laughter and playful banter filtered through the dressing room doorway; each burst of sound clenched her heart with longing. The dressing room was a flurry of activity—sequins and feathers flying as the dancers hurried to prepare for their performances. Jolie wove through the chaos, between suitcases and costume pieces, until she reached her vanity in the back corner.

The club's luxurious front of house didn't match the backstage area. Little had been done to upgrade it. Realizing the need for improvements, the owners had hastily provided a vanity for each dancer, a rolling rack for costumes during shows, and a locking trunk for overnight storage of costumes and makeup. While helpful, these additions only added to the clutter on busy nights. There was only one bathroom for all the dancers to share and no heating system. As a result, many resorted to sneaking in space heaters to keep their feet warm during cold nights.

The web of shimmering silks and feathers, the bell-like laughter punctuated by the sharp click of heels, echoed a past she thought was buried deep.

She remembered the early days: the cramped dressing room of her first theater when she was only a chorus girl. She would press her eye to a frayed hole in the heavy velvet curtain, unbothered by the rough fabric scratching her cheek. The stage lights had transformed the already dazzling dancers into goddesses. The yearning had been a physical ache, a hunger that gnawed at her insides.

She remembered the sting of stage lights and the dizzying rush of a thousand eyes fixed upon her, the days when her deepest anxieties revolved around a chance to be on stage. She could almost hear the raw, unvarnished conviction in her own voice. A rueful smile slowly grew over her features. Immortality, once a shimmering promise, now felt more like a prison. It had been the agonizing life with her Maker that dispelled her clinging delusion that this was anything but a curse.

She stood and moved to her clothing rack. She stripped off the remaining pieces of her green costume and slipped into her red ball gown with its flowing rhinestone train. Every decade brought a new city and a new focus: singing, dancing, or costumes to rival Vegas showgirls. In the early years of burlesque, taking off a glove could send the audience into ecstasy. Today, you had to work much harder. Competition for jobs was fierce, and the dancers were as cutthroat as ever. Excessive publicity would be bad for Jolie. She happily took the worst shifts, never made trouble for management, and stuck to the same style she had maintained throughout her career.

The mirror reflected a fleeting glimpse of Jolie's pale face. Her eyes darted to the riot of colors swirling around her. The other dancers' laughter tinkled in the air. Each tug of her corset laces felt like a tightening knot in her stomach.

Two months. She'd spent two months in The Black Cat House, two months of observing their effortless companionship from the edges. At first, their glances were sharp and assessing. Now they were simply absent. They moved around her like a lively current that flowed seamlessly around a submerged stone.

Her reflection showed a meticulously crafted facade, a perfect imitation of elegance and darkness. She imagined herself as a character from those pulp novels: a brooding, aloof vampire eternally waiting for her human prince. But Jolie knew better. The books romanticized solitude and inherent otherness. They didn't capture the gnawing ache of isolation.

Yes, vampires were creatures of shadow and silence. Yes, she embraced that part of her nature. But the darkness she felt now was the cold, suffocating gloom of loneliness.

Her gaze drifted across the laughing group. Their voices formed a melody of inside jokes and shared references. A familiar chill settled in her chest. The air itself seemed to vibrate with their connection, a tangible energy that left her feeling increasingly isolated.

"Jolie, we're on in ten minutes," Charles's voice boomed through the dressing room as he poked his head in. Charles, the stage manager and the owner's cousin, was known for his tough exterior and his role as the unofficial security guard of the theater. Tonight, his black T-shirt strained over his muscular frame. His beard had grown longer, and the intricate maze of tattoos on his arms was visible beneath the sleeves.

"Thank you, ten," Jolie replied.

Her reflection was eclipsed by the memory of a woman she used to know, the last person she had considered a friend before the betrayal. Jolie could still see the way her impossibly bright eyes crinkled at the corners when she smiled. The woman's face was a snapshot burned onto the back of her eyelids: a cascade of platinum blonde hair sculpted into perfect, gravity-defying waves. Jolie could almost feel the cool silkiness wrapped around her fingers. The memory of her perfume tightened her throat.

A phantom pang rippled through her chest as the memories threatened to overflow. Each year that passed deepened the void between who she had been and who she had become. The flash of betrayal burned in her memory and left only emptiness.

"Jolie, five minutes," Charles called out, jolting her from her thoughts.

She forced her lips into a semblance of a smile before responding simply, "Thank you, five."

Chapter Two

The Tease

Jolie carefully packed away her elaborate costumes and makeup into her lockable trunk. She pulled an oversized sweatshirt over her head. The fabric swallowed her silhouette, offering comfort as she blended into the night. A glance at her reflection brought a small smile to her lips. She released her hair from the tight pins and rolls that had held it in place during the show, then gathered it into a messy ponytail. She didn't bother brushing out the stiff hairspray yet. Instead, she reached for a soft cloth scented with lavender and gently removed her makeup.

The thrill of performing still lingered in her veins, a pulse echoing the final notes from the stage. She could feel a faint tremor even as the soothing lavender began to quiet the frantic thoughts in her head. Her face slowly materialized from beneath the thick layers of stage makeup. The crimson blush, meticulously applied, now looked like a mask—faintly comical against the pale skin peeking through at the edges. Her dark eyes, amplified by liner, were softened now.

Jolie wrapped her worn jacket around herself, grabbed her purse, and slung the strap across her body. She headed down the hallway toward the back door, slipped out into the cool night air, and left the lingering applause and ongoing show behind her. Squinting up at the night sky, she took in the dark gray clouds and the steady drizzle of rain. She could smell renewal in the air; longer days were approaching. Although she didn't mind the temperature fluctuations, in the peak of summer, the sun wouldn't set until nearly ten in the evening. Those longer days robbed her of the cover of darkness.

Farther down the street, a pale-yellow light spilled from an apartment window; it illuminated a single, slightly crooked bookshelf. A tall silhouette moved behind it. Jolie wondered what kind of book he was reading: a gripping thriller, a weighty tome of philosophy, or a dog-eared collection of poetry? Did he have a mug of tea warming his hands? Was he alone, or was someone else curled up in a nearby armchair? A faint melody drifted from a cracked window across the street; it wove itself into her story of imagined lives. The silent tales unfolding behind windows were a refuge from the ache of isolation.

Pedestrians stepped aside, their eyes glued to the ground. People avoided her gaze as if her presence might disrupt the fragile peace of the evening. This was the way of Seattle: everyone accepted one another, but in a distant and indifferent manner.

Jolie made her way toward her building, her steps quiet as she approached the back entrance. With each step, she traced the cracks in the pavement, circling the block to avoid the other tenants. It was easy to slip through the unlit, broken back door.

As she entered the building, she climbed three flights of stairs to the top floor. Flickering light bulbs cast shaky shadows that danced along the peeling wallpaper, making the old building feel alive in its decay. She had claimed the top floor like a crow perched on the highest branches. The musty air pointed to a level of neglect that made her feel hidden yet free. The peeling paint and general dysfunction were simply part of her world. Jolie shrugged off the complaints of other tenants, content in her solitude. She had used the building's dire appearance and limited water pressure to bargain with the landlords, skillfully negotiating the right to knock down walls and claim multiple apartments as her own.

An old sensation coiled in her gut, a visceral echo of her time in the nest with her kin. Unwelcome images flickered behind her eyelids: her Maker's other creations were a constant, suffocating tide. They had slept entwined in a knot of limbs, waking to the same gnawing hunger and desperate scramble for their Maker's favor, and for the privilege of sharing in his blood-soaked hunts. Their pale faces seemed to loom closer, pressing in with overpowering intimacy. Had something fundamentally fractured in her own making? Was a crucial element missed and replaced by a wild, untamed spark that set her apart from the others of her kind?

The chipped paint of her dilapidated apartment building seemed infinitely preferable. The vast space was filled with a different kind of energy. Tonight, as on most nights, Jolie followed her routine. She lit a fire in the hearth; the flames cast flickering shadows across the books stacked haphazardly on a nearby table. She grabbed the one on top and curled up on the sofa.

Hours later, Jolie set the book aside and moved to the balcony. The city stretched out before her; streetlights glittered in the darkness. She stretched her arms wide and savored the absence of watching eyes. The stillness wrapped around her. Here she could indulge in the simple human luxuries her kin would never even consider: the soft caress of a wool blanket, the soothing warmth of a long, perfumed bath, a moment of quiet contemplation before dawn broke. These were the comforts that truly nourished her soul, a soul that seemed to have strayed from the rigid confines of its vampiric origins.

She opened the refrigerator door. She scanned the neatly stacked blood packets, each one a promise of survival in a world where she didn't belong. She had learned the unspoken rules: a quiet nod to the right person, a small payment exchanged for her hidden needs. Money was a great equalizer and far more effective at guaranteeing her anonymity than violence ever could be. She often wondered what her contact at the blood bank thought she did with all the blood packets, but she never asked.

Carefully, she emptied a blood packet into her mug, held it up to the light, and watched the crimson liquid swirl sluggishly. It wasn't the brilliant scarlet of fresh blood, but it would do. Unlike the others of her kind, who gulped blood as if it were water, Jolie treated it as a culinary art. Tonight's offering would be a symphony of flavors.

She produced a small mortar and pestle from a mostly empty drawer. Nestled in the mortar's worn grooves lay a few pinches of finely ground cinnamon. She added it to the blood in her cup, then poured in aged brandy. The scent intensified; the cinnamon's warmth mingled with the brandy's sweetness, subtly altering the underlying metallic tang of the blood. She breathed in the concoction's fragrance, her body responding with a shiver of anticipation. With a small, reverent sigh, she raised the mug to her lips.

Jolie clung to the remnants of her human life, pushing the boundaries of what vampires would consume. She still relished the fiery burn of alcohol and the occasional bite of spicy curry. As a vampire, she couldn't taste the nuances of flavor, but the simple act of eating soothed her soul. She could digest food, but she could not absorb its nutrients. Only blood would sustain her.

Jolie turned and took in her apartment. The old sofa in front of the fireplace was one of her favorite pieces, not because of its appearance, but because of the memories it held: cozy nights spent by the fire reading books, memories that reminded her of a simpler time before she became a vampire. The dark burgundy drapes that hung on the windows had come from her first apartment after she had split from her Maker. While deeply sentimental to her, they were beginning to show signs of fading from the sun.

Mug in hand, she made her way to the bathroom and turned on the faucet. The spigot squealed as it filled the vintage claw-foot tub with steaming hot water. Metal shelves mounted on the wall held her collection of bath salts, a luxury she couldn't live without. Jolie had always been drawn to the floral scents of lavender, lilac, and her absolute favorite, rose.

She placed her mug on the stained table next to the tub and began to undress. Carefully, she added a spoonful of rose bath salts to the water, watching as the tiny pink crystals dissolved. She slowly lowered herself into the tub. The warm water enveloped her. She closed her eyes and let out a small moan as the scent of rose filled her senses. As the water reached her neck, Jolie turned off the faucet and settled deeper.

Her eyes, usually closed in serene contemplation, snapped open. The corners of her mouth dipped. A slow, reluctant frown cut into the smooth skin between her brows. As the warm water engulfed her, a weight settled in her gut. The rose scent swirled around her, but instead of blissful surrender, a knot formed in her neck and tension settled into the hollows of her shoulders. While she always feared her Maker would find her, she didn't sense him now. This was something else entirely. Something tugged at the edges of her consciousness. The air prickled with an unnamed tension that made her skin crawl. It was as if the shadows themselves were watching, and something was wrong.

CHAPTER THREE

Milk the Audience

Jolie pulled back the curtains, exposing her small balcony. She squeezed her eyes shut. The pressure was a small comfort against the insistent light. Contrary to cinematic depictions of fiery explosions and ash, sunlight seeped into her skin like a slow poison. It drained her energy and left her feeling empty. Her limbs would feel leaden, her thoughts sluggish and slow. The strength she usually possessed would be muted and replaced by bone-deep weariness that demanded rest. A hollow ache twisted in her gut, sending a ripple of discomfort through her. This wasn't the pleasant, anticipatory hunger of a healthy appetite. This was the same hollow dread from the bath.

The familiar scent of wood and spirits greeted her as she approached The Black Cat House, arriving early she decided to enter through the front door instead of the alley entrance. She gracefully made her way through the theater. Front-of-house staff scurried around, making sure every detail was perfect for the upcoming night. Small lamps were placed on the tables to cast a warm glow throughout the room.

Jolie appreciated the meticulousness. This wasn't just a bar; it was a carefully crafted stage set for a life less ordinary. Usually it was a blur of dark wood in the periphery. Tonight she halted mid-step, the bar was covered in intricate carvings: snarling wolves leered from the wood grain, interspersed with symbols that looked suspiciously ancient. The prickling unease from the night before crawled up her spine.

She was so absorbed in deciphering the unsettling patterns that she almost missed him. A newcomer. Behind the bar stood a figure entirely foreign to the familiar faces of The Black Cat House. The staff here was legendary; composed of veterans who'd poured drinks for the pervious owners and countless patrons throughout the decades. Turnover was practically unheard of. A chill crept through her and settled in her bones.

Dark hair was slicked back from his high forehead, accentuating sharp cheekbones. His frame was tall and lean, suggesting an intensity that went beyond mere physicality. But it was his eyes that stopped her breath: ice blue and startlingly bright against his dark features. They weren't merely looking at her, they were seeing through her, piercing the carefully constructed mask she wore like a second skin.

The way he held himself was poised yet restless. He scanned the room, assessing vulnerabilities. His hands moved skillfully, polishing glasses with a dancer's grace that drew the attention of the nearby waitresses. They couldn't help but sneak glances at him, their curiosity bubbling just beneath the surface.

Jolie turned to the lead waitress, Lina. Her rich, dark skin glowed under the low light, and her tight, curly hair cascaded over one eye. Lina was the embodiment of charm and resilience, cool and distant to Jolie, but always professional. If anyone could keep the waitresses in line, it was Lina.

"Lina, who's that?" Jolie asked, gesturing toward the new bartender whose presence dominated the room.

Lina glanced over her shoulder. Her eyes lingered on him as if he were a rare book she couldn't put down. "Oh, that's the new bartender," she replied, her tone layered with a hint of both admiration and annoyance as her gaze remained fixed on him.

Jolie's brow furrowed slightly as she scrutinized Lina's reaction. She was keenly aware of the tension thickening the air between them. "But why is he here?"

"Boden thought we were getting too busy," Lina explained with a flicker of irritation. She brushed a wayward curl from her face. "So he brought in some help. I think his name is Mikhail." Her tone shifted slightly, an edge of protectiveness creeping in as she watched the other waitresses momentarily abandon their duties to fawn over the newcomer. "He's far too flirty for my taste. He's annoying, but he'll work out fine."

Lina was making note of the way the staff languished in their tasks, completely distracted by Mikhail's effortless charm. It wouldn't take long before jealousy and competition gurgled to the surface unless Boden treaded carefully.

Jolie leaned against the scuffed backstage door, her gaze fixed on Mikhail. He was a gravitational force. His smile was meant to dissolve any resistance, a practiced gesture, an invitation.

He moved through the organized chaos like a king surveying his court, offering a soft touch to anyone who lingered in his orbit. As he passed a cluster of waitresses, his hand brushed the shoulder of one, a seemingly accidental contact that lingered just long enough to register.

Jolie sighed and pushed the door open, stepped through, and let it close behind her. The scattered chatter of the other dancers rushed to meet her. Some were already in full costume; others unpacked their trunks and set up their stations. Jolie watched them with lazy indifference as she twisted and pinned sections of her hair into an elaborate updo. Dancers shouted their orders to the waiting waitress. Laughter sparkled amidst the clatter of heels on hardwood, the atmosphere electric with anticipation. Jolie caught the disapproving look on Boden's face as he entered the dressing room.

Boden's scowl spoke volumes. His shaved head gleamed under the lights. The intricate spiderweb of tattoos twisting across his arms seemed to writhe as he crossed them. He stood rigidly by the door, a granite statue guarding against the energy within. Boden's jaw tightened. Disapproval radiated from him in waves.

Rori leaned casually against the door frame, unmoved by the mounting tension simmering from Boden. Her warm laugh rang out. With her shoulders squared and a slight tilt to her head, Rori exuded a calm self-possession. It was the kind of grace Jolie remembered from the ladies who'd once owned the stage of the old smoky clubs. There was an elegance in the way she moved, a subtle ease that showed the years spent controlling her body on stage.

"Jolie, darling," Rori's voice cut through the chatter, "care for a little something to take the edge off?" She gestured toward the waitress who was busy taking the other dancers' orders. Jolie understood the need for that liquid courage, a pre-show ritual, the way a seasoned performer might prime their instrument. Rori, with her knowing smile, clearly understood too.

"Bourbon, neat. Thank you," Jolie replied.

"Oh, that sounds good. Change my order," came a high-pitched, overly sweet voice from behind her. Jolie turned to see yet another new face standing in the doorway. The comfortable rhythm of the dressing room dissolved. Determined to maintain her composure, Jolie forced a smile, her lips stretching thin as she mentally shook off the creeping doubt, a maneuver learned over years of keeping her feelings tightly leashed. This was not the time nor the place to let insecurity show. Jolie took a breath and released it slowly, but the unease continued.

Her gaze locked onto the newcomer. Every movement drew her in, a mix of fascination and wariness swirling in her chest. Her style was striking: a black mini skirt rode high on a pair of vibrant orange tights that shimmered with a metallic sheen. A simple black tank top, cut low, complemented the outfit. The boots were worn with buckles that gleamed dully under the lights. It was a look that screamed individuality, a contrast to the carefully coordinated uniformity of the other dancers. It wasn't just the clothes, though. It was the way she carried herself: a quiet confidence that seemed to emanate from within. Jolie found herself inexplicably drawn to this unapologetic self-assurance.

Jolie took another long breath, then exhaled as she counted to three. She extended her hand, feeling clumsy and inadequate beside the other woman's elegantly manicured nails. "Hi," she said, her voice a little steadier than she felt. "I'm Jolie. Welcome to the club."

The newcomer clasped Jolie's hand with hers and smiled broadly as she started to speak. Jolie's initial smile solidified into a grimace. The new girl's words tumbled out in a breathless waterfall of syllables, each sentence spilling into the next without pause. The room swelled to hold the new girl's unceasing monologue.

Jolie's eyes dimmed under the weight of her annoyance, focus blurred as she attempted to filter the incessant flow of information. "I'm so excited to be here. I've known Rori forever, but you know... Miss Zaire." Jolie pictured Miss Zaire, a vision of shimmering silks and hypnotic movements. "Well, she's sick." The new girl informed her. "Well, not exactly sick. More like had to go away for her health." The newcomer paused. "By health I mean rehab."

Jolie's jaw clenched tightly, a pulse of tension radiating from her shoulders as irritation flared within her. How, she wondered, could anyone possibly possess such lung capacity? It was inhuman.

"I suppose I should introduce myself," the new girl said, finally taking a breath. "I'm Wynter Wilde, with a Y, but you can just call me Wyn."

Wyn's cherry-red hair was cropped close to her head. She stared at Jolie with a wide, toothy grin. Her curves were accentuated by a narrow waist and voluptuous hips. Heat rushed to Jolie's cheeks, igniting her skin as a wave of self-doubt crashed over her. Wynter's hands, warm and surprisingly strong, remained clasped on hers. The contact sent a jolt of awareness coursing through Jolie.

With a sudden, jerky movement, Jolie extracted her hand. The friction of skin on skin was momentarily jarring. She tucked her fingers into her lap, her palms pressed against the cool fabric of her skirt, a small but defined barrier between herself and Wynter's encroaching warmth.

Wyn raised an eyebrow, a mischievous glint in her eye. "So, Jolie. Real name or burlesque name?" she asked. Wyn was leaning against Jolie's vanity, blocking access to her supplies.

"I don't use a stage name. I'm just Jolie," she replied, rubbing her hands together.

Wyn chuckled, her focus lingered on Jolie. "You're not just Jolie, now, are you?" she asked with a wink. Jolie's fingers fidgeted. She avoided eye contact, her eyes darting nervously around the room. The smile she attempted felt strained.

Jolie leaned away from Wyn and sighed. "You should probably get ready," she said, trying to change the subject. "Boden doesn't like late dancers."

"Ahh, Boden," Wyn said, a sly smile forming on her lips. "Handsome one, isn't he?" She leaned closer to Jolie, her voluptuous curves pressing against the vanity, causing it to sway.

Jolie pushed past Wynter to grab her supplies. "Can we focus on getting ready, please?" she asked. Her shoulders tightened. Her hands, clasped tightly on her vanity, whitened at the knuckles.

Wyn shrugged. "Just trying to get to know my new coworker," she said with a mischievous grin.

Jolie's shoulders slumped, frown lines etched between her eyebrows, a momentary disruption from the flawless composure she usually maintained. Wyn was already getting under her skin. She had made a mistake; she shouldn't have started a conversation. It was already too personal. "Look, I really need to get ready. I think I'm on first," she said, gesturing toward the stage.

"Nope. The ballet girl is up first. I've heard that Rori isn't too pleased with her," Wyn whispered. She leaned in close as Jolie tried to pull away, her voice low, as if sharing a juicy secret. Jolie cringed inwardly; the prickle of unease was back. But even as her exasperation simmered, a reluctant fascination pulled at her. Wyn's words were a curious blend of bizarre and useful.

"How do you know that?" Jolie asked, trying to keep her tone neutral.

Wyn's eyes gleamed mischievously as she leaned back, a knowing smirk on her lips. "I saw the lineup list in Boden's hand, and you know how Rori is. Her least favorites always go first."

Jolie furrowed her brow. She tried to remember the last time she hadn't been chosen to go first. She was flushed with a sudden wave of insecurity. Did Rori dislike her? Their conversation was interrupted by the arrival of a waitress, who carefully balanced a tray full of drinks as she maneuvered around dancers.

"Booze!" Wyn exclaimed excitedly, causing a few nearby dancers to chuckle.

"House is opening in five minutes, and the show starts in thirty-five. Be ready," Charles announced briskly before turning to leave. But then he popped back in, remembering something. "Oh, Jolie! The order has changed. Your acts are now in the second and third set."

With that, he was gone, leaving Jolie with no time to respond. She slumped in her chair. The time waiting backstage with nothing to do was going to be torturous. She let out a long, slow breath, the air hissing between her teeth. She counted to ten. She could sit backstage and pout, or she could meander out to the bar and watch the evening unfold. Jolie wrapped herself in her silk robe and headed out of the dressing room. Anxiety followed her.

Each step through the theater was a tiny battle against the rising tide of unease. It wasn't just the changes. There was a prickling at the back of her neck, a sudden awareness of the people around her. The scent of perfume and pheromones wrapped around her as the theater started to fill.

The muscles in her shoulders coiled tight. It was a familiar feeling, a hyper-awareness that came with her abilities. This time, though, it was amplified. She was floundering in a sea of overwhelming sensations. Ignoring it felt reckless, like ignoring a storm brewing on the horizon. But what could she do? She pushed the unsettling feeling down.

Boden had been right, as he always was. The theater was getting busier by the minute. The Black Cat House normally didn't do marketing; word of mouth was enough. A few weeks back, a local celebrity had attended a show and posted about it on social media. Now they had to add additional tables and a long line of eager patrons waited to be seated. Jolie smiled as she took in the fashion choices of the crowd. This was the kind of audience that would truly appreciate their entertainment. They spared no expense for a night of glamour.

Her thoughts were interrupted. She turned to see Mikhail leaning on the bar, his shoulder-length hair falling out of position and over one eye. He flashed Jolie a grin as he spoke. "Shouldn't you be hiding backstage?"

She shrugged playfully and replied, "I'm mostly ready, and I'm bored. I have a long wait ahead of me."

Mikhail reached out and ran a single finger down the length of her arm, sending pules of heat along her spine. "Well, the crowd should be good tonight," he said with a cold smile.

Jolie moved her hands away from Mikhail's warm touch. His hand remained outstretched. Its stillness was more unsettling than any overt movement. She studied his face. The smile lines around his eyes seemed less charming, more calculated. The faint scent of his expensive cologne, moments ago a pleasant aroma, now felt suffocating. A prickling sensation crawled along her skin. It was a visceral warning: people were dangerous. She couldn't get close to anyone; it wasn't safe, and Mikhail was pushing against the boundaries she had to maintain.

Jolie slid off the barstool, the smooth wood gliding beneath her as she created distance. The corners of her smile faltered. A flicker of tension flashed across her face before she masked it again. She caught the cold gleam in his eyes, an unsettling sharpness that sent a warning signal straight to her core. "You're right," she said, her words tight with tension that vibrated in the air between them. "Backstage is... safer. I should go."

Jolie weaved her way back through the growing crowd. She occasionally turned around and looked at Mikhail. A good bartender knows how to work the crowd for tips, but there was something different about him. Both men and women were drawn to him. He had an effortless charm that seemed to captivate everyone, more unease danced on Jolie's skin and settled in the pit of her stomach.

Jolie settled into a chair behind the stage, hidden in the wings by the curtains. She listened to the room's growing buzz of conversation. As she prepared to watch the show from her secret vantage point, she began to relax, forcing her unease to melt away. She rolled her shoulders and tilted her head from side to side. She closed her eyes and raised her arms above her head in a long, slow stretch. Just as Jolie began to settle into a sense of calm, she heard a voice from the other side of the curtain. It was the opening dancer. Her voice rose to a fever pitch as she exclaimed, "I left them right there! You were the only one around." Jolie's eyes snapped open.

"I didn't take them," Cherry Stems' voice rang out, dripping with disdain. "Why would I want your pathetic pasties? You couldn't set a rhinestone if your life depended on it." Cherry was a visiting dancer from Canada, but already she was a crowd favorite. While the club had a regular set of performers, there was always a spot or two available for traveling dancers. Some stayed longer than others, and Cherry kept extending her stay.

"You're a liar," Falyn Fatale hissed. Falyn was the resident ballet dancer and well-known drama queen. Jolie hurried to the dressing room just in time to see Falyn launch herself at Cherry. Her hands reached for the other dancer's wig. But instead of pulling Cherry down, the wig gave way from its pins and tore from her head. Falyn, caught off guard by the sudden loss of balance, stumbled sideways and crashed into the wall. She landed hard on her hands and knees, her body trembling from the force. Seeing an opportunity to strike, Cherry moved to deliver a glittery high-heeled kick to Falyn's stomach. But Charles arrived just in time. Maddy had tracked him down at the first sign of trouble. Maddy really had a strong self-preservation instinct, Jolie reminded herself to keep her distance. The more aware a human was, the more dangerous they were.

Charles quickly wrapped his arms around Cherry and dragged her away from the chaos. Cherry cursed and struggled against Charles's hold. Falyn curled herself up into a ball on the floor and seemed to retreat into herself, her back heaving with silent sobs. The other dancers clustered around her and murmured words of comfort, their hands fluttering near her slumped shoulders. Jolie kept her distance. A conviction as hot as molten glass grew within her, Falyn's distress felt staged. Too perfectly timed. Too dramatically rendered.

The memory of Falyn's previous transgressions ran through Jolie's mind like a slideshow of petty conflicts and calculated maneuvers. There was the incident with Isabella when Falyn had "accidentally" tripped her backstage, resulting in a sprained ankle and Isabella's desperate last-minute replacement. Or the time she'd subtly sabotaged Monique's costume, leaving her scrambling just moments before her act. Each incident was a carefully crafted miniature drama, all designed to shift the spotlight back onto Falyn. Tonight was just the latest act in her ongoing production.

Wyn bent down under Falyn's vanity. She reached for something in the far corner. Her hand emerged with two shiny purple nipple covers with rhinestones in alternating patterns of light and dark swirls.

Wyn showed the pasties to Falyn and smiled sweetly. "Are these what you're looking for?" Falyn stared at them blankly before snatching them from her hand and storming off to the bathroom. She slammed the door shut.

Wyn turned to Jolie with a large, mirthful grin on her face. "This place is so much fun."

"Where is Falyn?" Charles asked, his dissatisfaction evident. Jolie pointed to the bathroom. She purposely avoided Wyn's gaze. If she met it, she would burst out laughing. Charles banged his meaty fist on the peeling paint of the wooden door. "You have ten minutes to get it together or get out," he shouted sternly.

As the minutes ticked by, the tension in the room grew. The door to the bathroom finally opened, and Falyn emerged. Her makeup was perfect. Her eyes were not even slightly red from crying.

Jolie moved back to her seat in the wings and watched the show unfold. The dancers glistened under the stage lights. Each movement was a spell that captivated the audience. As she watched the dancers, a hesitant calm settled over her. Perhaps her instincts were merely overreacting to a phantom warning triggered by Falyn's antics. The tension in her shoulders eased fractionally. For now, at least, she would push the worry aside.

The stage lights dimmed, and a spotlight shone as Wynter Wilde glided out, every move oozing sensuality. She walked and dipped to the slow beat, her glimmering gown hugging every curve. Jolie couldn't tear her eyes away. Wyn removed a glove from her left hand and let the accessory hang with a sly half-smile on her lips. With a flick of her wrist, she snapped the glove on a hard beat. The tempo increased, and Wyn wiggled out of her gown, revealing black leather and lace underneath. The audience erupted into a frenzy of cheers as she twisted and turned around the stage. Her dance became a beautiful flurry of acrobatics and skin. A jolt electrified Jolie. The nervous flutter in her stomach morphed into something fierce and exhilarating. Her fingers tingled with a vibrant energy that pulsed through her arms and legs. The world sharpened. Sounds became crisper.

The dance came to an end almost as quickly as it had started. The tempo dropped off suddenly as Wyn sauntered off stage, swinging her lush hips. The audience erupted into applause and cheers. The room once again filled with talking and laughter.

There was something mesmerizing about the way Wyn held herself, shoulders relaxed yet radiating power. It wasn't just talent, it was an aura; a captivating magnetism that held the audience spellbound. Jolie's senses swam as she watched Wyn walk into the dressing room.

Jolie moved to get ready. The silk of her gown was cool against her skin but did little to soothe the tremor in her hands as she fastened the delicate clasp at her back. The mirror reflected her carefully crafted face. She dabbed at a smudge of crimson lipstick and a stray strand of dark hair escaped its pins. She smoothed it down with shaking fingers.

It wasn't just the new faces or the nervous energy buzzing from the other performers—though those certainly contributed to the prickly feeling crawling up her spine. This went deeper. It was the same unsettling premonition that had warned her of Falyn's clumsy attempts to sabotage the previous performance. The feeling intensified, a chilling certainty that something far more serious was about to happen. The warning bells were clamoring.

Jolie immersed herself in the logic of the situation. There were just too many changes, and Falyn had been up to her old tricks. That was it. Slowly she was able to calm herself and occupy herself with rehearsing her routine. She buried the warning bells deep within herself, so deep that she failed to notice the growing commotion in the theater. A woman's yell suddenly pierced through the air. Glasses shattered. Instructions were shouted. The house lights suddenly snapped on. She could feel tremors in the floor beneath her, a subtle shaking of panicked footsteps and hurried breaths.

Chapter Four

The Slow Reveal

Jolie tilted her head as she stood in the doorway to the theater. She closed her eyes for a moment and leaned into the panic. Her mind sifted through the clamor. Her muscles tightened as her hunter's instinct flickered to life. She stretched her senses, filtering through the mayhem. Boden's voice finally broke through. "Stay seated! Wait for the police!"

His words did little to quell the rising panic in her chest. The faint scent of fear curled around her, mingled with the musty smell of the hallway. A low, guttural groan escaped her lips. "Damn it," she muttered. She kicked the floor with her heel. Splinters of wood gave way in a futile act of anger against her own carelessness. "I should have trusted my gut," she whispered.

She moved toward the stage, where Charles stood rigid. His complexion had drained of color, and shadows deepened beneath his eyes as he stared ahead. A quiet fear was painted across his features. Her fingers clamped onto his arm. She gripped him so fiercely that her knuckles turned white.

She leaned in close; the words strained with urgency. "What . . . happened?"

She clung to Charles with an iron grip. His shoulders bunched up as if he were trying to shed a heavy coat. But Jolie's fingers dug into his arm, leaving white crescents on his skin. He stopped. His body stiffened. He slowly turned to face her. The warmth in his hazel eyes dimmed, replaced by a wary glimmer. He didn't speak immediately. Instead, he stared at her, a silent challenge in his gaze. Then he reached down. His hands were surprisingly gentle at first, as if handling something delicate and easily broken. But the gentleness quickly evaporated. His fingers pried her clinging ones loose.

His voice came out harsh and hurried, each word punctuated by the tightness in his throat. "There's a body. In the men's room. Probably . . . overdose." Charles gave her one last withering look before turning and walking away.

She blinked rapidly. A surge of frustration bubbled within her as she focused on the empty space he'd left behind. "Damn it," she said again. The pressure she had put on his arm was an involuntary reflex in her panic.

Years spent mastering the subtle nuances of human interaction, the careful crafting of a believable persona. She was fraying at the edges. "So stupid, Jolie," she whispered to herself.

Through the chaos, her gaze found Boden. His imposing figure was a beacon of calm. He was talking on his cell phone. When she approached, he gave her a reassuring pat on the shoulder. A warmth bloomed in Jolie's chest, a feeling at odds with her usual cool detachment. Her default setting was a locked door. Yet with Boden, the latch seemed to click open on its own. The air around him was heavily scented with a blend of untamed wilderness and something primal. His stillness acted as a silent assertion of strength that loosened the stubborn knots of tension anchored between her shoulder blades. It wasn't attraction, just an undeniably potent peace.

Jolie crossed the room and settled onto the edge of the stage. Her gaze swept across the sea of upturned faces, each one covered in unspoken grief.

A weight settled beside her: Wyn. Jolie barely needed to turn her head. The scent of spice and hairspray wafted over. Wyn let out a theatrical sigh, her legs splaying out before her, toes pointed in a surprisingly elegant gesture. Jolie turned and took her in. A sparkling white corset squeezed her midsection like a vise. Wyn had paired it with the baggy comfort of charcoal sweatpants that pooled around her ankles. Her fiery red hair was ruthlessly subdued, plastered to her scalp beneath a tight wig cap.

"This place is awesome!" Wyn exclaimed, looking around with a grin on her face.

Jolie spun around to face her, exasperation evident in her voice. "You can't be serious!"

Jolie could see the smirk on Wyn's lips as she spoke. "I get it. Someone died. It's all very sad. But how many times in my life am I going to see a catfight and a dead body in one night?"

Wyn hummed a tuneless melody and idly flicked a stray crumb from her pants. Then Jolie recognized them, her sweatpants. Soft, gray, with the faintest trace of lavender still clinging to the fabric. Undeniably hers. For a long moment, Jolie simply stared, the silent accusation burning in her eyes.

Jolie raised a single finger and pointed to Wyn's legs. Wyn's lips curled into a Cheshire grin. Delight in her eyes as she caught the silent accusation in Jolie's stare. She gestured to the sweatpants she was wearing. "Yes, they are yours. But I was naked and needed something to cover up."

Jolie blinked in disbelief. She couldn't believe Wyn had the audacity to wear her sweatpants without even asking. "I prefer my nights quiet and peaceful. You should just keep the sweatpants."

"Thanks!" Wyn continued. "You mean you like your nights dull and boring. And I'm not sure you really prefer it that way."

Jolie's shoulders tightened, and she turned her back on Wyn. She watched the churning sea of faces, their eyes darting frantically, their hands shaking as they grasped purses and coats. She licked her lips. The taste of fear and apprehension coated her tongue. She was lost in the swirling energy of the room. Her hunting instincts were growing stronger.

Wyn's arm settled over Jolie's shoulders. Jolie braced against the contact, but let it happen. "Didn't mean to upset you, love." Wyn's voice was soft and apologetic. "Do you really think it was drugs? I don't. The security here is too good for that."

"Then what?" Jolie asked. Why hadn't Wyn decided to sit beside someone else? The stage was now full of waiting dancers. There were plenty of other people for Wyn to talk to.

"Foul play? Do people say foul play? It has a nice ring to it," Wyn mused, completely unfazed by the gravity of the situation. "Anyway," she continued. She leaned back and stretched her arms. "I think I'd like to take a look around and see if I can find any clues." Wyn let out a contented sigh as she slid to the edge of the stage. The old wooden boards creaked beneath her. Wyn pretended to gaze up at the ceiling as her eyes darted around, looking for an opportunity to make her way toward the men's room.

Jolie reached out and grabbed Wyn's hand. She leaned in close, her voice low and urgent. "You can't do this, Wyn."

Wyn rolled her eyes and pulled her hand away from Jolie's grasp. "Oh, stop it. Of course I can. No one's even paying attention." She leaned in even closer, her face just inches from Jolie's. "Come with me?"

Jolie turned away and faced the other dancers. They huddled together in small groups with their backs turned. She could feel their hearts race with anxiety. What if it wasn't drugs? What if there was another vampire lurking around? If that were the case, she could easily be blamed for this death.

A metallic tang bloomed at the back of her throat. She needed to see it for herself. Was this a human failing? Or something far older, far more sinister? The thought sent a fresh shiver down her spine. If it were just a case of bad drugs, a simple overdose, she could finally let the tension leech from her bones.

Jolie hopped off the stage and followed after Wyn. She caught up to her just as they reached the men's room. Their path was blocked by one of Boden's men, another intimidating figure with a hairless head and a full body of tattoos. His arms were folded over his broad chest. He glared at them. Jolie knew him well enough to know that he was all bark and no bite. He was a gentle giant, always fussing over the dancers. She remembered the way his kind eyes sparkled when he offered her a glass of ice water or a plate piled high with his wife's legendary oatmeal raisin cookies.

A pang pierced her, a sudden, unexpected stab of remorse. She halted Wyn's forward movement with a subtle touch of her hand. Jolie's eyes narrowed. Energy swelled within her, willing itself out. "Excuse us," she said politely. Another push of her will. "Boden says he needs to see you over there." The security guard's expression instantly softened. His eyes went blank. Then he walked away in the direction Jolie had pointed.

"Wow, that really worked." Shock flooded her voice. She turned to Wyn. A slow smile spread across her face. "Well," she said, her voice laced with the thrill of a gamble that had inexplicably paid off. "Let's go."

Wyn smiled. "That's a neat trick. Are you some kind of mentalist?"

Jolie ignored Wyn and reached for the door. It groaned inward and was cold beneath her fingers. A wave of antiseptic lemon freshness hit her as she stepped into the men's restroom. Rows of pristine white and pale blue tiles caught the soft lighting. The bathroom reflected a surprising level of upkeep. But even the sharp citrus scent couldn't mask the subtle, unfamiliar spice that tickled her nose. It hinted at cinnamon but was warmer and earthier.

Her gaze swept across the bright fixtures. She crouched low, her keen eyes tracing the line of the stalls. The faint, spicy aroma seemed strongest near the last one. Peering beneath the gap, she saw the outline of a man, his form slumped against the toilet, his head lolled forward.

Straightening, Jolie met Wyn's gaze. "He's in the last stall," she said.

Wyn's face had gone pale, and she was trembling slightly. "You go. I'll wait here," she said. Her voice shook as she wrung her hands.

Jolie sighed, a deflated sound that mirrored the sinking feeling in her stomach. Wyn's eyes widened. The color drained from her cheeks as she pressed herself against the cool tiled wall. "This was your idea," Jolie ground out. "But fine, I'll go . . ." Her voice trailed off. How had she allowed herself to be swayed into this ludicrous idea?

"Yes, and the first thing you should know about me is that I am full of bad ideas." Wyn had shuffled as far back against the wall as possible.

"Great, looks like I am totally on my own," Jolie muttered under her breath.

She made her way to the end of the stalls. With a gentle push, Jolie opened the door to the last stall and peered inside. The sight that greeted her was far from normal. The man lay crumpled on the floor like a discarded rag doll. His chin rested on his chest, and his hands hung limply in his lap. His shirt buttons were misaligned, hinting at a struggle to redress.

His dark hair stood out against his pale blue skin. His eyes, lips, and fingernails had all turned silvery white. Even in death, bodies did not turn this color.

Jolie's fingers trembled slightly as she brushed a stray strand of hair from her face. Vampire killings were usually messy. This wasn't that. No wounds. No blood. Thoughts of her Maker sliced through her like a cold wind. Memories flooded back.

The crimson mist hit her face and dripped into her partially open mouth. Her Maker, a shadow cloaked in night, was a whirlwind of motion. The young man in his grasp gurgled. His eyes were now glazed and vacant as his head rolled to the side. His heart pulsed a final, desperate rhythm before going still.

Her Maker stood, a liquid sheen of blood decorating his pale face. He turned, his eyes locked onto the fleeing figure of a woman. Her footsteps were a frantic scuttling against the stone floor. A blur of speed, and she was no longer running but a limp heap in his arms. A sickening tearing of flesh, and the light drained from her eyes. Then, he tossed her toward the waiting figures emerging from the gloom—his children, hungry and already fixed on their prize.

Jolie shook her head and willed herself back to the present. The pristine bathroom betrayed no signs of struggle or chaos.

Her thoughts scattered at the sound of the bathroom door creaking open. Jolie turned to see Boden standing in the doorway with his arms folded. His brow furrowed deeply. A muscle twitched in his jaw as he stared at her with fierce intensity. His guard stood sheepishly behind him. "Are you fucking kidding me?" Boden's voice was low and menacing. "Get. Out. Now."

Jolie grabbed Wyn and rushed out of the bathroom. They avoided Boden's gaze as they pushed past him. They took a seat in an empty booth, and Jolie slumped forward, resting her head in her hands. Wyn leaned close, her breath hot on Jolie's ear. "Wow, Boden has a temper. What did you see?"

Jolie spoke into the table, not raising her head. "I don't know. A body. But it's not normal." A wave of nausea twisted in her gut, and a muscle spasmed near her temple. "It's just . . . I don't know," she mumbled.

Wyn's body pressed against Jolie's. "Well, was it drugs?" she demanded. Jolie could feel her breath on her skin, the feeling tugging at her resolve. There was no way she could answer truthfully.

"Must have been." The corners of her mouth pulled into a barely held-together smile. It wasn't drugs. She knew it with a certainty that chilled her to the bone. She didn't want to be there. She didn't want to unravel the thread of this mystery. All she wanted was to melt into the anonymity of the night, to erase all this from her memory, to pretend it had all been a bad dream.

Wyn rested her head on Jolie's shoulder, and warmth seeped into her. "All of this has made me sleepy," Wyn mumbled. Her voice grew heavy with exhaustion. Jolie closed her eyes and let herself relax into Wyn's embrace. It was the most physical contact she had experienced in years. She thought she would detest it. Instead, it was oddly comforting.

The scent of Wyn's perfume enveloped her. The steady thump of her heart echoed in Jolie's head. She was drawn to it, her body responding before she was even aware of it. She breathed in deeply, savoring Wyn's spicy scent. Her desire increased with each passing moment. Her thoughts wandered to Wyn's body, to the two of them alone, and the metallic taste of fresh blood on her tongue. She felt her teeth extending.

Jolie's eyes flew open. She scrambled back from Wyn. The air grew heavy, the near miss thickening the space and tightening her throat. "I . . . I need to change," she stammered. Her voice was a little too high, a little too rushed.

Wyn's sly smile only fueled Jolie's embarrassment. "I'll keep your spot warm," she teased and patted the vacant space beside her.

Jolie wrestled with the drawstring of her backup sweatpants. The flimsy cotton felt alien against her skin, and the sweatshirt offered little comfort. It smelled faintly of laundry detergent and the musty corner of her trunk.

Frantic energy pulsed beneath her skin. Focus. She had to focus. Questions would come from the police. She needed to be ready. She quickly locked up her belongings and made her way back to the theater. The police were questioning the other dancers and sending them on their way. She took a seat as far from Wyn as possible.

Boden strode toward her, his brow furrowing as he neared, the tension in his shoulders hinting at his disappointment. A sudden tightness knotted in her stomach, a wave of regret washing over her as she met Boden's disappointed stare. Boden shook his head and gave her a small smile. "It's your turn to answer questions," he said. "Try not to get us into any more trouble, please."

"We didn't mean to . . ." Jolie stopped. It didn't matter.

With hesitant steps, she trailed behind Boden. The detective sat surrounded by a clutter of papers. His rumpled shirt hung loosely against his wiry frame, his tie askew as if he kept adjusting it. Jolie's expression shifted ever so slightly as she took in the detective's weary demeanor and the shadows under his eyes. His jaw was a blunt, strong line with three-day stubble. Short, dark hair was styled into a shaggy curtain falling across his forehead. A constructed pretense of incompetence, it was all there in his eyes. They were watching everything in the theater, and her too. The way she sat, the way Boden watched them from a few tables away. She took a deep breath. The detective would notice if she didn't breathe. Caution threaded her thoughts. The echo of old lessons reverberated in her mind like a mantra, reminding her to keep her secrets close.

The detective stood up to greet her. He wiped his hand on his pants before extending it to shake hers. "Detective Danny O'Neil," he introduced himself with a friendly smile. He motioned to the chair across from him. "Please take a seat." He smiled broadly and returned to his seat. "I'm just going to ask you a few routine questions, and then you can go," he said. His voice grew soft and soothing.

Jolie strained to form a smile. Her lips stretched tightly as she willed her expression to mask the tornado of anxiety brewing inside. She kept her eyes locked on him, assessing as he rummaged through his pockets. "It was right here," he muttered, his hands moving from pocket to pocket. He patted himself down. "Where is that pen?" First, his jacket. Then his shirt and pants. It was a frantic search for the elusive implement. "I seem to always be losing things," he said with a abashed smile.

She settled into the uncomfortable wooden chair, leaning back to create some distance between them. Her hands lay folded in her lap. She squeezed them tighter in forced stillness. The way he tilted his head just so grated on her nerves. It was a deliberate, infuriating performance. She could feel herself starting to fray. The games he played. His transparent attempts at manipulation. She wanted them to be useless on her, but they were maddening.

"Ah-ha, found it!" He retrieved his pen from under a stack of papers and clicked it open. "Okay, then, name?" His eyes scanned her face.

Jolie hesitated for a moment. Her voice level, she replied, "Jolie Mason." He had the most amazing blue eyes, deep and bright. Her eyes grazed his strong hands and solid forearms.

"Is that your real name?" he asked. He followed her gaze as it roamed over him.

A nervous tic began at her brow, then her eyelid fluttered. "Yes," she replied curtly.

"How long have you been working here?" His eyes never left hers.

"Two months." Determination lined her voice as she spoke. Only a slight quiver betrayed her. Under the weight of his scrutiny, she felt her skin prickle, warmth rushing to her cheeks as she shifted uneasily in her seat. "I was backstage all night. Either in the dressing room or in the wings. I never saw the victim." She hesitated, biting her lip before adding, "Except when we snuck into the bathroom afterward." The words slipped out before she could stop them. Her rule about sharing only what was necessary shattered in an instant.

The detective's presence pulled her in with a magnetic intensity and left her teetering on the edge of uncertainty. The scent of him was crisp, like fall air. She caught herself brushing her dark hair back and tilting her head ever so slightly.

"I don't know anything," Jolie finally said. The reality of the moment crashed over her like a tidal wave. "I just want to go home." The words slipped out softer than intended. Desperation caught in her throat as she missed the comfort of her own space.

"Why did you go into the bathroom?" His voice was stern as he abruptly stopped writing and leaned back in his chair. His piercing eyes bored into her, searching for any signs of deception.

"I . . . I didn't mean to interfere." The words stumbled from her lips, a feeble defense of her impulsiveness. Curiosity had rarely boded well for her. "I've never seen a dead body before."

A flicker of understanding crossed his face, yet the skepticism still danced in his eyes. "Is that so? And you didn't touch anything?"

Frantically, she shook her head, a wild gesture born of a need to flee. "No, I swear. I wouldn't even know where to start. I just . . . I wanted to see what was going on. It's not every day that the police show up at my place of work. In an official capacity, that is."

He studied her for a moment longer before getting up from his seat and pushing the pad and pen toward her. "Your address and phone number, please. Then you can go." The pen, a cheap ballpoint, scratched across the notepad. Each character seemed to take an eternity to form. She extended her hand. The slight tremor betrayed her nerves as her fingers grazed his, an electric touch that sent a jolt through her. As he accepted the pad, a wave of relief washed over her. The urge to flee pulsed within her; every instinct screamed for her to cut ties and retreat into safety.

"Thank you for your cooperation," he said. His voice softened, and concern knitted across his features as he leaned closer. "We may need to follow up with you in the future."

Nodding absentmindedly, she stood. Her fingers fumbled slightly as she hurriedly gathered her belongings. "Of course. I'll do whatever I can to help."

The night's turmoil clung to her skin like a sweaty garment. Her mind reeled at the absurdity of it all. "I'm trapped in a detective novel," she muttered under her breath.

Chapter Five

The Immortal Understudy

Jolie entered her apartment and wrinkled her nose at the musty air. She moved to open the door to her balcony. Her limbs felt leaden. She collapsed onto the bed; the mattress welcomed her like an old friend as she let out a ragged sigh. Beneath her fatigue, a restless energy churned. It coiled in her gut and amplified every creak of the building. Two months. Two months she'd spent in Seattle, chasing a promise of stability. The rhythm of inevitability gripped her. For almost a century, this had been her life: she would drift into a new city, seamlessly blend in, and stay low until she pulled too much attention. An old ache twisted in her chest. Memories flooded in of places she had long abandoned, each one tinged with bittersweet regret. "Fuuuuccckkk!" she yelled.

An unwelcome longing settled in her chest, pulling her thoughts back to days spent in his shadow, where comfort came at the price of freedom, where decisions were made for her. Her world had revolved around her

Maker's every whim. She had slowly grown tired of living as a predator, a mere animal. The memory of his rage pulsed behind her eyelids. Jolie squeezed her eyes shut, a desperate plea for the past to recede.

The crypt smelled of dust and the metallic tang of fear. Her Maker, Viktor, was a tempest of barely contained anger. His eyes blazed with fury; the blue veins at his temples throbbed. The figures of the other vampires were cloaked and hunched in the shadows, their eyes fixed on the epicenter of the storm.

"Why did you let him escape?" Viktor's voice roared. He picked up a table and tossed it across the room; it landed in a group of huddled vampires, the crack of breaking wood echoing against the stone. "Did I sculpt you from the very essence of power only to birth a brood of sniveling, witless worms?"

A younger vampire opened his mouth, a silent plea forming on his lips. Viktor's rage didn't grant him the courtesy of a word. He surged forward, gripped the vampire by the neck, and lifted him into the air. "You are a blemish, a pathetic miscalculation in the grand design of my creation!"

Viktor flung the trembling vampire away. He landed with a crunching thud against the stone. The surrounding vampires remained frozen, statues carved from fear. Viktor's eyes glowed with a hunger that promised annihilation.

Each violent episode was a raw scar on her mind. It had taken her a year of running, a year of constantly seeking a way to break the psychic bond tethering them, before she found her freedom.

Hope sparked when she heard rumors of a woman who could sever ties with the past. Desperate for a solution, Jolie made her way to a seemingly abandoned shack by a fetid lake. There, a stooped old woman forced her to drink a concoction of foul blood and stale herbs while chanting incomprehensible nonsense. Jolie was sick for what seemed like days. But when she woke, the shack, the woman, and her connection to her Maker were gone.

His face haunted her: sharp and menacing features, cold and cruel eyes, long blond hair always pulled tightly at the nape of his neck, a reminder of dominance and control that echoed in her memory. The scent of blood always seemed to linger around him.

Propelled by a surge of frustration, Jolie propped herself up on her elbows. The familiar contours of her apartment no longer felt like a sanctuary as anxiety clawed at her. She curled her legs beneath her and sank deeper into the mattress. She clicked her tongue against her teeth, mentally chiding herself.

She looked at the clock on the wall, a reminder that there was still plenty of night left. After a moment's hesitation, she decided that a walk through the city might be the antidote to the turmoil swirling within her. A chance to reclaim herself.

The streets lay still and quiet; shadows stretched beneath the glow of streetlamps. Faint strains of laughter and music drifted from nearby apartments; voices mingled with the night air and crafted a fabric of life just out of reach. The crisp aroma of pine mingled with the briny freshness of the water. She inhaled deeply, letting the tranquility seep into her chest.

Jolie turned her gaze to the staircase leading to Pike Place Market. Once the coast was clear, she burst into motion, legs propelling her forward. She reached the top of the stairs and launched herself at a nearby wall, then used the momentum to thrust herself into a rolling flip. She hit the next flight of stairs with ease, her feet barely making a sound as she crouched low. Her eyes constantly scanned her surroundings for signs of life. With a burst of energy, she grabbed the roofline and pulled herself up. These fleeting moments of agility were a refreshing reminder of the freedom that came with nimbleness.

She attempted to leap to another roof, but her feet slipped out from under her. She landed hard on her butt, skidding to a stop. With a frustrated huff, she brushed the dirt from her backside. Dark hair fell from her bun as she shook her head. "Graceful as a newborn giraffe," she murmured. The corner of her mouth twitched upward as she began to laugh. Luckily, no one had witnessed her clumsy landing.

"Damn," she muttered. "I used to be so much better." The admission barely touched on the well of regrets and the skills lost to time and neglect. Not that she particularly needed to fight, but it would be nice to know that she could defend herself if necessary. Stepping to the edge of the roof, she looked out on a breathtaking view of the city below her. Seattle might not have had the same bustling energy as cities like Boston or New York, but it had a unique pulse of its own. The history and life that had passed through its streets left a subtle mark that only a few could sense.

Jolie made her way along the rooftop, her movements growing more agile as she leaped from one building to the next. Once she reached the far side of the block, she jumped off and landed gracefully on the street below.

Jolie would have to pass through Pike and Pine to reach her apartment. During the day, this area was filled with tourists. But at night, it attracted a different kind of crowd. Crime was growing in this area, much of it perpetrated by drug addicts and their dealers. Unfortunately, that also attracted the creatures that fed on them. At the bottom of the vampire hierarchy were the Bitzers, vampires who fed on drug addicts to get a high. They were aggressive, violent, and always hungry. Jolie had no desire to encounter any of them tonight. She crossed the street as she approached an alley.

She halted mid-step. The scent of damp cardboard seemed to surround her. A subtle rustling emanated from a shadowed alcove choked with discarded boxes. Her fangs extended and pressed against her lower lip. The alley yawned before her, a black, empty mouth gnawing at the edges of the weak streetlight's reach.

Beyond those lights, absolute darkness reigned. But Jolie could lift the veil. A stray thread snagged on a rusty drainpipe. Rats skittering from crack to crack. She could see it all with piercing clarity. She narrowed her eyes and looked for the source of the unsettling sound. Slowly, a tiny shape detached itself from the jumble of boxes. A whimper accompanied the emergence of a scrawny puppy. Its ribs were visible beneath its fur. Hesitant steps moved it toward her.

Her fangs retreated, a deliberate easing. The tension that had knotted her shoulders and tightened her jaw seemed to melt away. It was replaced by a surprising softness, as if a tiny sun had ignited within her chest, spreading outward and thawing the icy exterior she normally presented to the world.

Her affinity for animals was a source of confusion, a peculiar anomaly among her kind. Where other vampires found sustenance, she found kinship. The puppy wagged its tail tentatively as it approached.

Jolie extended her hand. After allowing the puppy to sniff her, she gently scratched behind its ears. This earned a delighted yelp and an enthusiastic lick on the hand. A low hum vibrated in her chest, a sound she didn't realize she was making. The small creature tilted its head. Its large, amber eyes were unwavering in their focus. A wave of protectiveness washed over Jolie. Anger, hot and sharp, replaced the comfort. Who, she raged silently, would abandon such a vulnerable creature in this place?

Jolie sank to her knees, carefully getting closer to the puppy's level. The rough concrete dug into her jeans. Her own frown mirrored the small creature's anxious expression. "Good goddess," she breathed. "You shouldn't be alone here."

The puppy whimpered, a tiny, pathetic sound that tugged at something deep inside her. She met the puppy's wide, innocent eyes. The tiny creature tilted its head, its wet nose twitching. "Look," she said. Her voice was tight with a struggle she wasn't quite sure she was winning. She pointed a finger. "I appreciate . . . the . . . uh . . . company," she stammered. "But you're not coming home with me," she finished, the firmness wavering slightly.

A single, mournful whine escaped the puppy's tiny throat. It nudged her again, its wet nose brushing against her skin. Jolie's resolve crumbled. The puppy's persistence was a silent plea threatening to drown out the voice of reason. The dog let out a small whimper and sat down. It looked up at her with big, pleading eyes.

The weight of her night pressed down on her; she had yet to figure out if she had to flee Seattle, but she couldn't leave the puppy here. She also couldn't take him home with her. His pleading eyes refused to leave her. Jolie turned and looked down the dark alley. She pictured the Bitzers, and a cold wave of revulsion washed over her.

"Damn it." She bent down to pick up the dog. He eagerly licked her face in gratitude. "You're going to make my life a lot more complicated, little guy. I don't even know what to feed you."

Jolie had never had a dog. Once when she was a girl, she had a fish, but she had forgotten to feed it, and it had quickly died. Vampires had no use for animals, so she had no frame of reference, no idea what to do next.

The dog snuggled deeper into her arms. He was small, no more than five pounds. His eyes, dark and bright, assessed her every movement. Most animals reacted with wary distance. But this dog held her gaze. A quiet understanding flickered in the depths of his eyes.

Jolie cradled the painfully skinny dog as she walked. As they neared her apartment, Jolie remembered a fast-food restaurant a few blocks away that was open twenty-four hours. She altered her course and made a detour to the restaurant. The little dog still snuggled in her arms. She entered and approached the counter, eyeing the menu for appropriate options.

The clerk behind the counter glanced up and immediately shook his head, opening his mouth to speak. "No dogs allowed."

Jolie arched an eyebrow. The movement was laced with an unspoken command. "Fill my order quickly," she said. Her voice held the promise of impatience. ". . . and it won't be a problem." She internally debated the quantity. Twelve double cheeseburgers seemed excessive. But the thought of him going hungry gnawed at her. Two large fries, she reasoned, were a reasonable addition to the burger mountain.

The walk home was a symphony of rustling paper bags and the rhythmic thump of Jolie's boots against the pavement. The little dog was a wriggling mass of fur tucked securely under her arm. He strained against her, his tiny body vibrating with barely contained excitement. His nose twitched and repeatedly nudged the burger-laden bags. A low growl of anticipation rumbled in his chest.

"Almost there, buddy," she murmured. Her voice softened further as she adjusted her grip. "Just a little further." The dog let out a small, ecstatic yelp.

"You need a name," she said softly. "I can't keep calling you 'dog,' even though this isn't a permanent arrangement." She reached down and stroked the soft fur behind his ears.

She tried to think of a sweet name for the little dog. "How about Calisto?" she suggested, her voice gentle. "Because you're so pretty." But the dog simply snorted and turned his head away.

Taken aback by his distinct disapproval, she tried again. "Okay, how about Felix?" But the dog continued to ignore her, his head turned away in disdain. Jolie cackled at his pickiness. "Fine, then what about Caleb?" she said. "It means bold, and that definitely describes you." The dog settled his head back on her chest. Jolie took that as agreement and smiled down at the little creature in her arms.

When they returned to the apartment, Jolie set Caleb down to explore on his own. His curious nose led him into every nook and cranny of the space. With a groan, Jolie kicked off her boots. The heels clattered against the floor and landed with a thud. The leather jacket followed; she shrugged it off and draped it carelessly over the back of a chair. Its weight seemed to lift a layer of the day's fatigue with it. Her bed called to her, but she fought against its pull.

Her eyes fell on the ever-growing Everest of clothes by the front door—a jumble of jeans, sweaters, and scarves creating the appearance of a small textile avalanche. "Seriously?" she muttered to herself. The words were more of a lament than an accusation. A fleeting thought of tackling the pile wrestled with the overwhelming urge to simply collapse. The battle was short-lived. Relaxation won decisively.

Jolie opened her cabinets and pulled out one of the two plates she owned. She unwrapped a few burgers and placed them on the floor for Caleb. While he ate, Jolie took the opportunity to change into her cozy sweats and slippers.

When she returned to the kitchen, Caleb was pawing at his empty plate. "Okay. More food then," she said while plating the remaining fries and one more burger.

Caleb was already looking healthier and stronger. How long had he been on his own before she found him?

"I'm going to bed now. Make yourself at home; just try not to pee on anything."

Each muscle ached; fatigue ran from the soles of her feet to the crown of her head. Caleb bounded onto the bed, burrowing into the blankets near her feet. "Caleb," she whispered, her voice laced with affectionate exasperation, "not on the bed."

There was no telling what he had dragged in from the alley. Jolie moved toward him, trying to budge him off the bed, but he wouldn't move. He just looked at her with those big, pleading eyes, then curled himself into a tighter ball on the bed.

"Fine," she mumbled. "You can stay, but don't get used to it." She ran her fingers over his fur, yawning and fighting against her drooping eyelids. She focused on the warmth from Caleb's small body and the way it melted the tension and smoothed the frayed edges of her thoughts.

CHAPTER SIX

The Emcee Calls Your Name

Jolie stood alone in a dense forest. Mist crept between the towering trees, gnarled and ancient, adorned with hanging moss. The cold, damp air wrapped around her like a heavy cloak. The scent of cold earth and thick moss filled her senses. She swiveled her head slowly. Each rustle of leaves, each snap of a twig, was amplified in her ears.

"Is someone there?" Jolie called out. She strained her eyes to see through the thick mist, but all she could make out was swirling vapor. She squeezed her lips together tightly. Coldness seeped up her legs from the frost-covered ground beneath her feet. Jolie pressed her back against a large tree behind her. Its rough bark scratched against her skin, grounding her against the mist.

Shapes emerged from the mist, blurry and indistinct at first, but becoming clearer as they approached. A majestic gray wolf stepped into the clearing. Its piercing yellow eyes scanned the area. Its thick fur rustled in the cool breeze. The wolf paused, its head cocked sideways. But Jolie no longer watched the wolf; she was riveted by the child who trailed it with slow steps.

Jolie whispered, more to herself than anyone else, "What in the world?"

The wolf seemed to understand her question. It let out a low, almost musical whine. The wolf nudged the girl's hand with its nose.

The girl's long, dark hair cascaded down her back in waves. She brushed it back from her face, revealing features that seemed to glow, power radiating from every pore. Her skin was as pale as the mist surrounding them. But her eyes . . . they were a striking shade of gold that glowed in the dim light. The girl wore a simple white dress that blended seamlessly with the fog. She gently stroked the wolf's fur. Her eyes never left Jolie's.

A shiver, half fear, half fascination, moved through Jolie's body. The girl leaned so heavily on the wolf that its breath mingled with the girl's own. "Aren't you going to ask," the girl murmured, her voice echoing through the woods, "why you're dreaming about me?"

Panic clawed at Jolie's throat. This didn't feel like any dream she had had before. Dreams didn't smell like decay. They didn't leave this metallic taste coating her tongue. She swallowed. Her throat was dry as dust. Finally, Jolie found her voice. It was a thin, reedy sound. "Um . . . who . . . who are you?"

She shifted her weight from one foot to the other, her eyes darting nervously around the swirling landscape.

"I am Sikrele, god of all gods, ruler of all from the dark who dwell on the earth," the girl replied, running her hands through the wolf's fur lazily.

Slowly, a hesitant smile tugged at the corners of Jolie's lips. She chuckled. "Vampire dreams are so vivid."

But the girl's gaze told her otherwise, an intense, unwavering stare that seemed to pierce straight through her. A strange conviction grew in her chest. This wasn't a dream; it was utterly insane, but she believed it. The girl's presence emanated a power that defied logic. It wasn't just the intensity of her eyes. It was the stillness and an aura of ancient, untamed energy.

Sikrele's voice was low and steady. It cut through Jolie's astonishment. "And this," she said, gesturing to the imposing wolf that stood silently beside her, "is Caleb's spirit."

"Whoa, wait. You're telling me this is the spirit of Caleb? The Caleb in my bed right now?" Jolie asked, still in disbelief.

Sikrele's smile widened, revealing rows of sharp teeth. "Yes, my dear. And you have a chance to make things right with his help." She reached for Jolie, her fingers closing around Jolie's arm, digging in with surprising force. She squeezed until dark prints formed on her skin. There was no jolt. No jarring transition back to her bed.

"Oh, goddess," Jolie whispered.

Sikrele drew her attention back with a gesture. "I know you may be confused right now, but trust me. This is real. You have a purpose." Sikrele reached out and twirled a lock of Jolie's hair between her fingers.

She opened her mouth to object. "I . . ."

Sikrele's hand closed over her wrist. The pressure was a subtle but undeniable assertion of control. Jolie's choked gasp was replaced by a silent, desperate struggle against a force far greater than her own. "Do not underestimate me. My power is what granted you your freedom in that Louisiana swamp," Sikrele recounted with a knowing smile. "And now, I am offering you a chance to use that power for good. Caleb will help you."

Jolie blinked. The world shifted, its blurry colors like a badly tuned television. Fragments of images flickered through her mind: bone-chilling water, foul-smelling herbs, a blinding flash of light, a heavy, suffocating pressure on her chest. The ground tilted beneath her. Nausea clawed at her throat.

Sikrele's face swam into focus, impossibly close. An unnerving smile stretched across her lips. The goddess's yellow eyes held chilling amusement. She inclined her head, the movement feline.

Sikrele leaned closer. Her breath was warm against Jolie's ear. "Don't forget our little agreement." Sikrele's finger, long and elegant, traced a slow line along Jolie's jaw. Her touch lingered just a moment too long. "We have . . . a very important task ahead of us," Sikrele purred. "Awaken."

Jolie's eyelids, heavy as lead, fluttered open. The harsh morning light scorched her eyes, forcing a groan from her throat. She squeezed them shut, trying to recapture the fragmented nightmare. The lingering taste of bile was the only physical reminder of its unpleasantness.

A rhythmic, low rumble vibrated through the mattress. Caleb. His chest rose and fell in a steady rhythm. He snored with the abandon only deep sleep could allow. The sight of him only intensified the unsettling remnants of her dream.

She burrowed deeper into the pillows. A silent scream trapped her chest. The sheets felt clammy. It wasn't just the dream itself. It was the lingering feeling of violation, a sense of being trapped and helpless, that still made her stomach churn.

CHAPTER SEVEN

Bump, Grind, and Bite

Jolie's eyes opened to the warm rays of late-afternoon sun spilling through the small cracks in her drapes. She took a deep breath and stretched her limbs. Finally, a day without the humdrum of responsibility. Caleb had curled up next to her in the night and was still snoozing peacefully, his warm body pressed against her back. The feather duvet cradled Jolie. The lingering echo of her dream, however, was anything but warm. It wasn't the fuzzy, half-remembered sort. This one clung to her.

A groan rumbled from beside her. Caleb stirred. She rolled over to pet his head and paused. Something felt off. She ran her hands over his snout and ears, feeling the differences. Jolie's hand paused mid-stroke on Caleb's fur. She recoiled, eyes widening as she retraced her touch. She lifted the covers and saw that he had easily doubled in size.

Caleb gave her a sleepy yawn and licked her face. She lifted him off the bed and tested his weight and size difference. "You are definitely much bigger," she said into his sleepy face.

Caleb gave her a playful bark. He wiggled out of her arms and bounded toward the balcony. He paced back and forth in front of the door, his claws clicking with impatience on the wooden floor. He let out a low growl.

Jolie raised one eyebrow. "Do you want to go out on the balcony?"

He responded with a more insistent scratch at the door. Jolie unlocked it for him. The cool breeze of the fading day rushed into her apartment. Caleb eagerly bounded onto the balcony. He sniffed in wide circles. Lifting his leg, he proceeded to relieve himself with the nonchalance of a seasoned outdoorsman.

A slow smile played on her lips, laced with a hint of exasperation. "Caleb," she said, her voice smooth but with an underlying strain, "don't let anyone see you do that, please." She gestured vaguely toward the edge of the balcony before turning and heading to the kitchen.

Once they had both eaten, Jolie changed into a pair of faded sweats and curled up on the couch with her book. Caleb settled on the floor beside her, occasionally snapping at dust dancing in the fading sunlight or finding a loose thread from the rug to chew on. Jolie turned the pages of *The Shattered Moonstone* as hours melted away. The scent of paper and ink wrapped around her like a blanket as she devoured chapter after chapter. She didn't notice the deepening twilight or the shift in shadows across her apartment. Then a grumble came from deep within her own belly. It jolted her back to the mundane.

Jolie went to the refrigerator. She carefully poured blood into her chipped mug, then opened her spice cabinet. Cinnamon reminded her too much of Wyn, maybe ginger? She pulled down the jar, added a bit to her mug, stirred it in, and let the scent rise around her. The ruby liquid shimmered as she raised it to her lips. Caleb peeked over the back of the couch to watch her.

"Looks like we both need a snack," she murmured.

Jolie grabbed her cell phone and began browsing for a nearby pizza place. With one hand scratching his ears, she placed an order. She settled back onto the couch and retrieved her book, content until the dog's low growl broke her concentration. He stood in front of the door, head lowered and tense with anticipation. Jolie sank to her knees. Another low rumble vibrated through the floor. "Easy, boy," she murmured. "Caleb, it's just the pizza. Relax," she reassured him.

Jolie jumped at the rap on the door. "See? Just . . . just the pizza," she mumbled.

She hesitated before finally turning the knob. A sliver of the hallway was visible beyond the slightly ajar door. She peered out cautiously, her eyes wide and questioning, before opening the door the rest of the way. Detective Danny O'Neil filled the doorway, backlit by the sickly yellow hallway light. He was taller than she remembered. His shoulders were broad and powerful, straining against his jacket. The leather itself was a roadmap of creases and scuffs.

His scent permeated the apartment, a familiar cocktail of sharp, spicy cologne mingling with the smell of his skin. It clung to the air and lingered on her senses. Her hand instinctively went to her mouth to cover her fangs should they extend without permission.

His expression was carefully neutral, but the softening of his usually steely gaze hinted at something more than professional courtesy. He held a worn notebook in his hand, its pages dog-eared and creased.

"Miss Mason," he began, his voice deep and resonant, "I apologize for disturbing you. I know you've already given a statement, but . . . there are a few more details I need to clarify."

He paused. His eyes met hers. The scent of his cologne intensified—a sudden, overwhelming wave that threatened to drown her.

A resigned sigh escaped her lips. "I suppose you can come in. But please make it quick." She stepped aside to let him enter, her eyes lingering on him a little longer than necessary. Caleb followed them, his head still low. His eyes held a note of wariness, and his tail drooped slightly.

Jolie led the detective to the kitchen. "Please have a seat. But I must warn you, I've already told you everything I know."

Once seated, Detective O'Neil leaned forward and met her gaze. "I appreciate your cooperation, Miss Mason. But I have a feeling there might be more to this case than meets the eye. I believe you may have some valuable insights."

Caleb had positioned himself protectively between her and the detective. His weight shifted in a subtle but noticeable flinch as the detective leaned closer. A low growl rumbled deep in his chest. He didn't outright block the detective, but his stance, legs braced slightly apart, formed an invisible barrier.

Jolie reached out her hand. Her fingers scratched behind Caleb's ears. A soft sigh escaped her lips as she murmured, "Easy, boy. It's alright." Her voice was low and soothing. Caleb's ears flicked back slightly. The growl subsided and was replaced by a soft whine. He leaned slightly into her touch, a small concession.

The detective watched the exchange with narrowed eyes. "Miss Mason, I apologize for intruding on your evening. I'll get right to the point. I have some follow-up questions regarding the incident at the club."

"Of course, Detective. Please, go ahead," she replied. Her voice was steady despite the turmoil of emotions swirling within her.

Detective O'Neil leaned forward, his gaze sharp as he tapped his finger against her kitchen table. "You mentioned being backstage all night. Can you be more precise? Were you alone?"

Jolie shifted in her seat. She smoothed a stray strand of dark hair behind her ear. "Not really. Backstage isn't big enough for a more precise location," she replied, her voice carefully neutral. "I wasn't alone. There were the other dancers. Security. Waitresses. Same as any other night." She subtly glanced at Caleb. Shared anxiety passed between them.

The detective raised a skeptical eyebrow. He steepled his fingers. Jolie swallowed. Her throat suddenly felt dry. "There was a . . . a rather large crowd. It was noisy. I was preoccupied." Detective O'Neil's silence was damning. He simply watched, letting the tension build.

Finally, he spoke. "Miss Mason, I can't help but notice your unique choice of pet. He seems to be very interested in our conversation."

Jolie's eyes darted to Caleb. "I'm not sure a dog counts as unique, but he does have a distinctiveness about him," she replied, her tone light and casual.

Detective O'Neil's gaze narrowed. "I just meant that . . ." But before he could press further, the sound of Caleb's low growl filled the room. After making his displeasure with the detective's comments known, Caleb nestled at her feet and closed his eyes. Detective O'Neil let out a weary sigh. "I'm not here to give you a hard time. But I have a feeling you know more than you're letting on."

Amusement danced in her eyes. She tilted her head. "Really, I don't," she said. Her voice was low and steady, emphasizing each word. "I keep to myself mostly. Focus on the job. You know . . . the usual. Dance. Then home. Straight home."

His eyes lingered on her for a moment too long. He didn't break eye contact, but the slight upward curve of his mouth betrayed a hint of skepticism. "What's the management like?" he finally asked. His voice was smoother than before, a subtle shift that suggested a change of tactics. He leaned forward, his elbows resting lightly on the table. His eyes mesmerized her; the blue was so clear and bright. She wouldn't be surprised if they glowed in a dark room. The corners of his mouth lifted further now. A genuine smile replaced the earlier, more guarded expression.

He wasn't just pleasing to look at. He was captivating. For a moment, neither of them spoke. Then he tilted his head, a questioning eyebrow raised.

Jolie remembered her words. "They're like family. They treat us dancers with respect and have a strict zero-tolerance policy for any shady behavior. If that guy had drugs, he must have brought them in himself."

The scent of his cologne hung in the air, and the faint hint of soap barely masked the saltiness of his skin. His questions blurred into an indistinct drone. Her eyes kept drifting, drawn irresistibly to the corded muscles flexing beneath his shirt as he gestured. The casual movement, and the strength it implied, sent a surprising shock of heat through her. She cleared her throat. "I don't know why you're here, honestly. I don't know anything."

He flashed another smile and chuckled softly. "I highly doubt you had a hand in this." He shifted in his chair. She rested her chin on her hand, gazing over his shoulder at the wall behind him. His words continued to flow despite her lack of attention. "But the color, there's no rational explanation for it. Nothing in his system could have caused that."

Jolie chewed the inside of her cheek. She tapped a restless finger against the table. The possibilities were a chaotic swarm of bees buzzing around her head. Were there unknown entities lurking in the world? Or perhaps a newly concocted toxic substance that had yet to be discovered by authorities? Did Sikrele want her to act against this killer? She pushed the ideas away.

The detective's eyes bored into her. Beyond looking, they were cataloging, dissecting. A muscle twitched in her jaw as she met his stare. It felt less like an interrogation and more like an unveiling. Each word she offered seemed to create one more crack in her carefully constructed persona, leaving him with a knowing tilt of his head. He knew she was a puzzle, and he seemed to enjoy fitting the pieces together even if he hadn't found them all yet.

Detective O'Neil leaned forward. "What about the victim? Did you notice anything unusual about him that night?"

Jolie hesitated. "No, nothing comes to mind. I didn't interact with him at all."

A sudden knock on the door broke the tension. She glanced at Caleb. He was already on his feet, barking excitedly. He wiggled and twisted in anticipation, his tail wagging furiously. As Jolie opened the door, Caleb ran toward it; she had to put a leg out to keep him from body-slamming the startled delivery boy.

Once she had paid and collected the pizza, Caleb followed her into the kitchen, his nose in the air, trying to catch a whiff of cheese and bread. He jumped around her legs, his tail now wagging in a circular motion. Jolie immediately gave him a slice of pizza.

"That smells amazing." She turned to see Detective O'Neil standing behind her, hands in his pockets, eyes fixed on her.

Jolie shifted uncomfortably as Detective O'Neil's eyes roamed over her body. She held his gaze. Her teeth ground slightly as she fought the urge to look away. "Yes, it does. Are we done?" she asked.

He simply nodded once before turning and backing away from her. "Almost," he replied. Her eyes kept snagging on the sharp angles of his face.

He cleared his throat. "You're not eating?" The question was a velvet glove over an iron fist, less a genuine inquiry and more an observation he expected her to confirm.

She hesitated, a tiny frown pulling at her lips. He was digging. She could feel it. But the reason for his interest remained maddeningly obscure.

Should she keep up her character and eat? Or offer him a glimpse behind the mask? She lifted a slice and took a slow, deliberate bite. She chewed with exaggerated care, her eyes locked on him, challenging him to find fault. The remains of the piece she tossed to Caleb, who caught it midair with a leap.

Something flickered across the detective's features before it was expertly masked by a placid smile. "Have you seen anything like this at the club before?" he asked, the words carefully measured, his eyes roaming her body.

Jolie's cheeks flushed a warm, prickly red. She'd forgotten to brush her hair that morning. The strands had escaped their haphazard knot at the nape of her neck and fell around her shoulders in a chaotic halo. Her worn-out gray sweatpants suddenly felt like a public proclamation of her disheveled mental state. She shifted uneasily and tugged at the frayed cuff of her sweatshirt.

With a heavy sigh, she broke eye contact, then tossed more pizza to Caleb. "I've never seen anything like this at all, ever," she replied. Her tone was serious again.

"Do you really feed your dog pizza?" he asked, a soft teasing in his voice.

Jolie frowned. "Well, he seems to like it. What else would I feed him?" She tossed another slice to her furry companion, who eagerly gobbled it up.

He chuckled, shaking his head in disbelief. "Dog food, from the pet store?" he suggested with a raised eyebrow.

She shrugged. "I like to mix things up for Caleb. Keeps things interesting for him." This earned a fresh laugh from Detective O'Neil.

Then the lightness in his eyes vanished. Deep lines etched themselves around his mouth, pulling it into a thin line. "I don't quite get you, and I think there's something you're not telling me," he said. "But I should probably leave before it gets dark." His calloused hand extended toward hers. She hesitated for a fraction of a second as a flicker of something unreadable crossed his eyes; she offered her own hand. His fingers enveloped hers in a surprisingly gentle grip. As their fingers brushed, a spark passed between them.

"Goodbye, then," she said. Her voice was a little shaky. He turned. Her shoulders relaxed as he finally stepped over the threshold. The door clicked shut behind him.

Jolie listened to his steps retreating down the hallway. Her mind still buzzed with his voice, his scent, and confusing thoughts about why he was so focused on her. Mechanically, she tossed a slice of pizza toward Caleb, who caught it with ease. Caleb, oblivious to the internal storm raging within her, munched contentedly.

She shook her head and snapped herself back to the present. Caleb, pizza crumbs clinging to his muzzle, looked up at her expectantly. She smiled. Before tonight, the idea of finding a man attractive had seemed as obsolete as a rotary phone. Detective O'Neil was a striking exception. His intensity. His quiet strength. A thrill, unexpected and exhilarating, pulsed through her. There was also the danger, she couldn't deny it. Despite the inevitable grilling that awaited their next encounter, she found herself eagerly anticipating his return.

CHAPTER EIGHT

Before the Curtain Rises

The next afternoon seemed perfect for exploring the city with Caleb. The sky was overcast and accompanied by the gentle pitter-patter of soft drizzle falling from the clouds. The air was filled with the musky scent of wet pavement. Jolie got out of bed and stretched her limbs. She yanked back the duvet.

A gasp escaped her lips. Her hand flew to her chest. "Caleb?" she whispered. Gone was the compact frame of a large Chihuahua. His body had elongated, ribs expanding to fill out a powerful torso. His legs were long and muscular, corded with the kind of strength that hinted at explosive power. A low whistle escaped her lips. This wasn't growth. It was a metamorphosis.

The transformation was both horrifying and utterly fascinating. His fur had deepened in color. His head had lengthened, his muzzle was more pronounced, giving him the powerful, square head appearance of a bully breed. A low rumble vibrated from his chest, not the yip or whimper of a small dog, but the growl of a predator.

Caleb rolled onto his back with the power of his newfound size. His tail gave a playful swipe at the air before settling with a thump. Jolie reached out a hesitant finger, tracing the line of his muscles. "Caleb?" she whispered. He let out a soft, almost purring rumble. His eyes had moved from innocent pools of amber to reflect the spark of ancient wisdom. Her disbelief was all-consuming. "What are you?" she asked, half expecting an answer from the canine.

Caleb's head tilted. A small roll of his eyes conveyed an exasperated sigh. He silently communicated: *Seriously? Still haven't cracked it?*

The trouble at the club. Detective O'Neil's relentless, accusatory tone. And now this: Caleb seemed to have sprouted an extra six inches overnight. "You . . . you're quite something, aren't you?" she murmured.

Caleb thumped his tail lightly against the bed. He was a furry enigma. She had to unravel the mystery of this bizarre creature. "I'll figure out what you are. But first, breakfast, and then a walk," she declared.

When they reached the pet store, she felt herself get carried away by the excitement of pet ownership. Her fingers traced the plush texture of a squeaky frog. The scent of new rope and leather drifted from racks of leashes. A wave of contentment washed over her. But a flicker of self-consciousness followed.

The feeling of childish delight morphed into something more self-aware. Her selections became practical and efficient. A bright red leash felt reassuring in her hand, its nylon sturdy and supple. Next, an adjustable harness to accommodate any more growth spurts. Finally, she chose a collar: sleek and black, with a shiny tag engraved with a crisp, elegant "Caleb."

Caleb responded with a joyous bounce, his tail a blur of delighted wags. He pranced, a little dance of eager anticipation. His eyes shone with an almost human understanding of the adventure that lay ahead. He looked, quite simply, magnificent.

They meandered through the city streets, Caleb leading and Jolie following until she lost all sense of direction. With his nose to the ground, he sniffed out scents that even Jolie couldn't detect. Finally, he led her to a seemingly abandoned bookstore.

The bookstore wasn't just old. It was ancient, a crumbling brick behemoth clinging stubbornly to the corner. The faded red paint on the door peeled in ragged strips. Layers of color popped out between the crimson.

"This," she murmured, "is exactly my kind of place." Caleb pulled her toward the door. She followed him down the steps and pushed the door open. As they stepped inside, a bell chimed to announce their arrival. Jolie was hit with the heavy scent of dust and old paper. She felt transported back in time as she gazed at the shelves upon shelves of books that seemed to hold a lifetime of stories within their pages. The front room was cramped with overstuffed shelves and a large antique desk. Small lamps were scattered throughout, casting a soft light that would make it difficult for anyone without Jolie's keen eyesight to see. Rooms were partitioned with heavy drapes in faded reds and golds, adding to the cloistered atmosphere of the shop.

Jolie's curiosity grew as she explored the rooms branching off from the entrance. Each held its own treasures, from rare first editions to antique trinkets and knickknacks. She felt as if she were discovering a secret world hidden within the bustling city. As she perused the shelves, Caleb tugged at her arm, eager to pull her further into the shop.

Following Caleb, she entered a small room just behind the main entrance. A small figure emerged from one of the doorways behind a desk. He was no taller than four feet, but he walked toward them with purpose, his eyes narrowed in a scowl.

"No, no, no . . . Dogs are dirty animals," he said in a gruff voice. He was dressed in a tailored three-piece suit of dark blue. Each stubby finger was adorned with a gold ring. A band of gray hair covered the sides and back of his head, sticking out in tufts over his ears and leaving the top gleaming bald. The man stopped in front of them, his gaze shifting from her to Caleb and back again. He seemed taken aback by their unexpected presence.

His expression slowly changed as he stared at Caleb. "Intriguing. Your companion can stay." He gestured toward a nearby elevated desk and climbed a short set of stairs to a platform behind it. "Come, let's talk."

The worn desk seemed to loom as Jolie approached. The strange little man's presence filled the small space. He leaned forward, his bushy eyebrows wiggling with unspoken questions. The air crackled with anticipation. "Well, what do you want?" he asked expectantly.

Jolie fiddled with Caleb's leash. She avoided the expectant eyes across the table, then quickly blurted out, "I'm not sure. I just wanted to browse. I like books." The man frowned, making her answer feel foolish. Caleb, sensing her discomfort, pressed into her leg reassuringly.

The bookseller's sharp eyes pierced through Jolie as he spoke. "No browsing allowed. You ask, and I supply." His voice was stern, almost daring her to challenge his rule. Jolie shifted nervously on her feet, unsure how to answer. The bookseller's eyebrows furrowed as he awaited a better response. His small, thin lips and large, hooked nose gave him a stern, serious look. His bright green eyes glowed in the gloom. She glanced at Caleb, hoping he would come to her aid. But he simply panted in reply, clearly unimpressed by her handling of the situation.

The bookseller let out a scoff, his disappointment clear. "Did you bring her here?" he asked Caleb, his tone annoyed. Caleb tilted his head and pawed at the air as Jolie's mouth fell open slightly.

The bookseller let out a sigh. "Follow me," he said, turning and disappearing behind the curtain he had emerged from earlier. Caleb tugged Jolie along, and they entered a room that was reminiscent of the cramped rooms of the shop. However, this one was rich in color and space, with dark red rugs lining the floor and overstuffed chairs arranged in front of a roaring fire. Jolie's eyes widened in wonder as she took in the intricately carved table made of polished dark wood between the chairs.

"Sit," the bookseller commanded, pointing to one of the chairs. Jolie obeyed, feeling small and insignificant. Caleb curled up in front of the fire and dozed off, clearly comfortable with what was about to unfold.

The room felt like it belonged in a different time, perhaps even further back than her own years. The only windows were narrow and dirty, located close to the ceiling since the room was below street level. But the warm glow of the fire and numerous lamps made up for the lack of natural light. The wallpaper was in varying shades of red, but with mismatched prints. She was drawn to the shelves lined with a plethora of knickknacks, from antique bells to troll dolls. The scent of dust mixed with herbs surrounded her, the herbs likely from the roaring fire. And upon closer inspection, she could see a thick layer of dust covering the lamps and mantel. It was clear that whoever this man was, he was not the best at maintaining a tidy home.

As her host returned with an abundant tray, Jolie caught a whiff of a familiar metallic tang. He placed her cup on the table next to her: warm blood, AB negative. She couldn't believe it. How did he know her true nature? His bushy eyebrows furrowed in annoyance. "What did you think? That I wouldn't know?" He sounded almost insulted.

Jolie watched in awe as he placed a large plate of sweet cream scones, jam, butter, and a pot of strong black tea on the table. He even threw a scone to Caleb, who eagerly devoured it. Pouring himself some tea, he explained, "I always like to add a shot of amaretto to my tea. Would you like some in your cup?" Still too stunned to speak, Jolie could only nod.

He proceeded to add a second shot to his own cup before casually placing the flask back into his coat pocket. "Now, let's do introductions and then we can get to your questions," he said, taking a sip of his tea. "I'm Sebger Rockvein, but I go by Dimitri among humans. You can call me Seb."

Jolie stared at him; silent questions danced through her mind in a frantic jumble of possibilities. No words formed. No questions coalesced into coherent thought. Seb didn't break the silence. Instead, his impatience became a palpable thing, radiating outward like heat. With an almost theatrical flourish, he set his teacup down on the saucer. His jaw tightened, the corners of his mouth pulling down into a thin, unpleasant line. His annoyance had a physical presence, as distinct as the scent of woodsmoke clinging to the room.

Gathering her courage, she finally spoke. "I'm Jolie Mason."

"What name did your Maker give you?"

Seb's question caught Jolie off guard. She cleared her throat, trying not to annoy him any further. "Lisette," she replied hesitantly. As a product of the old world, her Maker had given her a name that reflected his traditional values.

"Um . . . how do you know what I am?" Jolie finally mustered the courage to ask, her curiosity getting the best of her.

Seb let out a laugh, his eyes sparkling with amusement. "Well, most nonhumans can pick out other nonhumans from the crowd. Not sure what's wrong with you, though."

Jolie shrugged off the insult. "Okay, then, since we're being rude. What are you?"

Seb laughed heartily. "Well, that's actually quite rude," he said, taking a sip from his cup. Jolie had never met anyone quite like Seb before. "I'm a dwarf," he continued, noticing her surprise and narrowing his eyes in playful annoyance. "I take it your Maker kept you in the dark about a lot of things."

Jolie nervously tucked a strand of hair behind her ear. "That's very true," she admitted. As their conversation continued, Jolie quickly found herself trusting Seb. She gave him a brief synopsis of her life, including the incident at the club and her dream of Sikrele—trying to remember as many details as she could. When she had finished speaking, she took a deep breath and asked, "What is Caleb? I've figured out that he isn't a dog, but I'm not sure what he is."

At the mention of his name, Caleb lifted his head and turned to look at them expectantly. Seb tossed him another scone. "Caleb, as you've chosen to call him, is actually a barghest. A spirit dog. Although they are sometimes depicted as cats, it is rare. In human mythology, they are often portrayed as shapeshifting beasts that would attack and kill travelers. However, they are protectors. This truth has been altered by humans, as is often the case with mythology. Barghests have been linked to legends in almost all cultures. I'm sure you've heard of Anubis."

Caleb snorted, crumbs from his scone falling to the ground as he chewed.

The rich scent of butter and warm pastry drifted from the platter like a caress against Jolie's enhanced senses. She stared longingly at the golden-brown domes. A memory flickered in her mind: the yielding crumb, the burst of sun-sweetened berries against her tongue. A sensation so alien now that it felt like a dream of another existence. She didn't need food, not in the way a human craved it. Yet an insistent tug, a whisper of something lost, pulled her toward the plate.

Her vampire palate, a finely tuned instrument for blood and the subtle pulse of life, would find the scone bland and tasteless. Still, the longing persisted, a stubborn ember refusing to be extinguished.

Her hand extended, and she broke off a piece of scone. She lifted it, the texture rough against her fingertips, and brought it to her lips. The expected burst of flavor was muted and flat. A soft, almost imperceptible sigh escaped her.

Across the small table, Seb's green eyes, alight with amused curiosity, traced the movement. He tilted his head. "You're a peculiar creature, Jolie," he drawled. "Truly one of a kind."

He leaned in closer, his voice taking on a more serious tone. "Caleb has come to you for a reason. He believes that you have a purpose, something that you need to do, and he is here to help you do it. You've also met Sikrele, and it seems she has a plan for you as well."

Caleb wagged his tail in agreement, his eyes meeting Jolie's. Spirit dog? Goddess? The words were absurd, fantastical, and utterly unbelievable. They painted a scene so wildly improbable that it felt like a cruel joke. Yet Seb's voice resonated with an unshakable conviction that pricked at her disbelief. There was an inexplicable pull she felt toward Caleb. Jolie finished her cup of blood and settled back into the comfortable, yet dusty, armchair.

"Wait, so Sikrele is a real person?"

"Well, in a manner of speaking, yes. She exists beyond linear time and space. My best advice is to do as she says," Seb replied.

Jolie tried and failed to stifle her laugh. "I'm sorry, I'm just having a hard time believing all of this. A goddess and a spirit dog? It's a lot to take in."

Seb raised his bushy eyebrows, a small smile playing on his lips. "Is it any easier to believe in a vampire?"

Jolie shrugged. "No, I guess not." She turned her attention back to Caleb. "So, you're saying he can transform into something other than a dog? He can change at will?"

Seb shook his head. "No. Once barghests choose a form, they typically stick with it for a while. However, he will grow larger and stronger." As if on cue, Seb tossed another scone to Caleb, who eagerly caught it.

The entire situation gave her a pounding headache. Jolie could feel the pressure building behind her eyes as she tried to make sense of everything that had happened. She pressed her fingers into her temples, trying to massage away the pain, but it only seemed to intensify.

Seb calmly buttered a scone for himself. "Oh, come now," he said, biting into the scone with a satisfied look on his face. "You've been through a lot. You felt the darkness of magic when you split from your Maker. Surely you can handle a bigger worldview than just humans and vampires."

Jolie sighed, feeling discouraged and out of her depth. "It's not just that," she confessed, her voice strained. "I'm not sure what I'm supposed to do now. Where do I even begin?"

Seb leaned over the arm of his chair, his gaze fixed on her. "Perhaps you should start small," he suggested. "Figure out what's going on at the club and trust your instincts."

She mimicked his posture, leaning toward him. "How is that starting small?" she asked, her tone incredulous.

Seb stared at her, his eyes serious. "Your instincts are a powerful tool. They will guide you in the right direction." She wasn't entirely convinced, but she conceded that Seb might have a point.

She needed to trust herself and her own abilities. "Do you have any ideas about the death?" she asked, hoping he would have some concrete answers for her.

Seb's lips curved into a small smile. "I have plenty of ideas," he replied cryptically. "Possibly a cursed object. Did he have anything that looked old or powerful on him?" Jolie shook her head, and Seb continued. "Ah, well, that would have been too easy. Could be a banshee, but you would have heard the call, so probably not. There is a Black Shuck, but again, you'd hear the bark. Taqriaqsuit? Hmm, no, they don't leave a body."

Jolie's eyes grew wider with each listed option. How many could there really be? Seb continued, "Pukwudgie? Nah, that would involve a cliff. Considering we're in a city, it could be a succubus, though I haven't known modern ones to kill. I'll gather some information that may help." With that, he exited the room, leaving her alone with her thoughts.

Caleb got up from his spot and rested his square head on her leg. She absentmindedly stroked his fur, grateful for his comforting presence. At least she now knew what he was, so this trip hadn't been entirely fruitless. But she couldn't shake the nagging worry about Caleb's size. Seb had mentioned something about him getting bigger, but how big exactly? Would she find herself living with a horse? She pushed the thought away, not wanting to think about the logistics of it all.

Seb walked into the room with a bag of books in his hand, a thoughtful expression on his face. "A gift for the vampire who likes books," he said with a playful smile. "Maybe you'll find some answers in these." Jolie's face lit up as she took the bag from Seb.

"You didn't have to do this, Seb. You know I appreciate it, but you could always just tell me what I need to know."

Seb shook his head. "No, no. You need to learn and understand for yourself. Plus, dwarves can be quite difficult and ornery. I'm sure you'll find some useful information in these books." He chuckled to himself before adding, "I don't have all the answers you need, but I'll help as much as I can. Now, let me show you out."

A wave of relief washed over Jolie as Seb's reassuring words faded behind her. She'd have to find a way to properly thank him. A simple "thank you" felt insufficient.

On the way home, they stopped by a local food truck, and she ordered a dozen burritos, a mountain of foil-wrapped goodness. Each one overflowed with rice, beans, and a generous helping of whatever mysterious, intensely flavorful meat they used. Surely that would keep Caleb's hunger at bay for at least a day.

Jolie finally settled in as the evening wore on, slipping out of her street clothes and into a cozy pair of sweatpants. She could hear Caleb happily chomping away in the kitchen, and she was soothed by the sound of life in her apartment. She couldn't resist flipping through the books Seb had given her earlier that day. He had carefully chosen four titles: *The Complete Fae Encyclopedia*, *Charms and Chants for Warding and Protection*, *A Fae History of the World*, and *Myths and Legends of Vampires*. Jolie chortled in surprise when she read the title of the last one. *Myths and Legends of Vampires*? Was Seb playing a joke on her? She opened the book and was surprised to find that it was written almost like a children's book. There were vampire versions of popular fairytales such as *Snow White*, *Cinderella*, and *Sleeping Beauty*. She paused her reading, trying to figure out who would possibly read these stories. Were there vampire children? It seemed like a cruel fate.

Shaking her head, Jolie put down the book and picked up *The Complete Fae Encyclopedia* instead. She slid under the covers of her bed and made herself comfortable. Caleb jumped up and burrowed next to her. Jolie flipped to the section on dwarves and scanned the first page of the entry.

She learned about their short and stocky build, unruly hair, and ability to withstand extreme temperatures. She chuckled at the paragraphs dedicated to their love of food and drink and their distaste for cleaning. But as she continued reading, Jolie's interest was piqued by the mention of noble and lesser houses among the dwarves. She learned about the wars that had been fought over land rights and power, but she couldn't locate Seb's surname on any of the lists.

Turning to the section on succubi, she carefully combed through the text, searching for any nuggets of useful information. Though often portrayed in human myth as solely female beings, succubi could also manifest as males. These seductive creatures preyed on humans through sexual intercourse and physical contact, their allure proving equally potent for both men and women. Despite their human-like appearance, succubi possessed incredible strength and the ability to regenerate themselves. Jolie was disappointed to discover that, other than an aversion to silver and iron, they had no known weaknesses. Irritated and feeling no closer to understanding, Jolie placed the book on her chest, her thoughts swirling. It appeared she was learning nothing fast.

Picking up the book once again, she flipped through the pages in search of any mention of Sikrele. The entry she found was disappointingly short, offering little insight into the mysterious being that had visited her. According to the text, Sikrele was the creator of all things, existing before the heavens or the earth. Humans had mistakenly associated this powerful entity with creatures like gorgons or harpies, often blaming Sikrele for issues such as infertility and miscarriage. But their limited knowledge prevented them from seeing the true nature of this being, encompassing both benevolence and malevolence.

Jolie furrowed her brow in dissatisfaction. There was no mention of Sikrele's strengths or weaknesses. No indication of why she may have chosen to visit her.

Jolie turned to the back of the book, looking for the Vs. Dust lifted off the pages as she flipped through them, each one feeling brittle and making her slow down and take more care.

A stark black heading slashed across the page: VAMPIRE HUNTERS.

Viktor's face flashed in her mind, a memory of his rage whenever she ventured too far from their hidden enclaves. He'd drilled into them the necessity of silence, of vanishing like mist, of retreating at the first sign of trouble. But vampire hunters? That had never been part of his dire warnings.

She devoured the passage, the words a sudden, cold wind. "Vampire hunters are the unwavering protectors of humanity. They are trained in secret to be the shadows' keenest observers, with the precision of assassins and the cunning of spies."

She slammed the book shut, the sharp crack echoing in the silence of her apartment. She licked her lips as unease crept up her spine. Had she ever been hunted? Even now, could a human be tracking her, stalking her? The question settled in her stomach like a stone.

Chapter Nine

Pasties and Shadows

Jolie looked out on the city from her balcony; the distant hum of life stretched out around her, but her shoulders sagged under an unseen weight. The world was so much bigger than she had ever imagined. She was filled with a gnawing certainty that this immensity held teeth she hadn't yet encountered. Fear pricked at her composure, tangling with the bewildering confusion that had become her constant companion.

A rough, warm presence nudged her hand. Caleb whined softly. Jolie turned, her fingers finding the familiar groove of his skull, tracing the soft fur behind his ears. "Look at you," she murmured. "Getting so big, friend." A contented sigh rumbled in his chest. His amber eyes fixed on hers, as though he truly understood her unspoken anxieties. She had to push down the wave of doubt. She wouldn't let recent events and revelations shatter the life she had painstakingly pieced together.

Turning from the beckoning abyss of the city, she stepped back into the warm, lamp-lit interior of her apartment. "Just promise me," she called out, her voice gaining a sudden, unexpected firmness, "you won't go around peeing on people in the street, alright?"

Jolie made her way into the kitchen and plated the last of Caleb's food before setting it on the floor. "I don't know about you, Caleb, but I'm not really in the mood to go anywhere tonight," she said as she watched him devour his food. "I have costumes to mend, and more reading to do before work tomorrow." She could see the disappointment on Caleb's face and felt a little guilty.

"But how about a nice walk once the sun goes down?" she suggested, hoping to lift his spirits. Caleb responded with a reserved tail wag, and she knew she would have to keep her promise, or he would become unruly. She made her way toward her closet to retrieve her old silver gown. Nostalgia washed over her. She had worn this gown in many performances, and it held a special place in her heart. But over time, the snap tape started to come loose, and the beading had begun to unravel. She couldn't bear to part with it, so she took it upon herself to repair it.

Caleb took a break from chewing on the warped floorboards to circle the kitchen table, watching her intently as she sewed. "We'll go for a walk soon, Caleb, I promise," she reassured him with a smile. She continued to work on her gown, admiring the elaborate design and beading. Caleb barked, his patience wearing thin. She looked down at him and smiled. "Okay, okay, let's go for that walk," she said as she put away her sewing kit.

Before she could gather his leash, Caleb stood and let out a soft, low growl. She followed his line of sight to the door, waiting for someone to knock. "Please, Caleb, tell me it isn't him," she whispered.

Just before the knock came, Caleb blocked the door. "Caleb, you're quite a bit larger than the last time he saw you. Maybe you should hang back a bit," she said, trying to protect her beloved canine companion.

Caleb's ears drooped, his usually commanding posture wilted. He took a hesitant step backward and tried to look as small as possible, but his loyalty tethered him to her side. Protective energy radiated from him like heat waves off asphalt. She drew a shaky breath, her lungs expanding as if to absorb some of his strength. With deliberate, almost agonizing slowness, she opened the door. "I thought it was you," she said, her voice laced with a hint of playfulness.

Detective O'Neil's eyes crinkled at the corners as he smiled, his lips curling up in a mischievous grin. "Been missing me, have you?" he teased, his voice deep and smooth.

Jolie felt a rush of attraction toward him despite her anxieties. "Not exactly," she replied, trying to keep her tone light and casual. "But you can come in anyway, Detective." As he stepped inside, his scent hit her, making her mouth water. She quickly regretted her choice of clothing as she pulled at the fabric, trying to hide the stains.

For a moment, his eyes lingered on her, taking in every detail of her appearance. "You look beautiful, Jolie," he finally said, his voice low and sincere.

She tilted her head as her eyes mapped the contours of his face. A ripple of something akin to regret seemed to cross his features. His pupils dilated, then contracted, as if trying to retract the compliment. He cleared his throat, and his gaze darted, skittering away to fix on some invisible point on the far wall. "Oh," she breathed, a tiny puff of air. "Thank you," she finally managed. The words felt clumsy on her tongue. She felt a prickle of unease, her senses on high alert, trying to sift through the tangled signals his body was sending.

Jolie hastened to move past the building tension. "Let's get down to business." She gestured for him to follow her into the living room, where they both took a seat on the couch. Caleb immediately jumped up next to Jolie, his head resting on her lap. "So, what brings you here tonight, Detective?" Jolie asked, trying to steer the conversation toward the reason for his unexpected visit.

Tonight, Detective O'Neil was dressed more casually than usual. His face was clean-shaven, revealing his handsome features. He held a dark gray pea coat in his hand, draped across his leg. Caleb rolled over and crept toward him. "Well, hello, buddy. Is this the same dog? What happened?" he asked, taken aback by Caleb's growth.

"He's a special breed. They grow a lot," Jolie explained, biting her lip nervously. She knew it wasn't the best explanation, but it was all she could offer.

The detective chuckled reluctantly. "Must be the pizza," he teased, giving Jolie a sideways glance. She could sense his confusion, but he didn't push the subject. Instead, he rubbed Caleb's neck and behind his ears, noticing his tag. "Caleb, huh? Good name," he commented with a smile.

"I'm assuming you've come to double-check my story," she said, testing the waters.

Detective O'Neil absentmindedly stroked Caleb's side as he continued to speak. "Not really. The club is about to reopen, and it's probably going to be packed." His tone was serious, his eyes betraying his concern.

"I was worried about that. I don't want the staff to suffer because of this." Jolie experienced a brief wave of guilt. Her heart sank at the thought of Boden and Rori possibly suffering because of the club's newfound infamy. There was a part of her that assumed this was all her fault. Logically, there was no reason to feel that way, but currently, logic didn't matter. She tucked her feet under her and tried to focus on anything else but how close he was.

"You know, it's going to be hard for me to find answers at the club," Detective O'Neil spoke up, finally getting to the reason for his visit. "They know I'm a cop, and it's been nearly impossible to sort out what's going on."

"Do you really think the killer will be back?" Jolie asked, her voice laced with concern.

Detective O'Neil's expression hardened. Darkness filtered across his features as he let his eyes roam over her. "I do. It's an opportune hunting ground, and I believe the killer is back every night." His words were like a curtain that had dropped and revealed a landscape she hadn't anticipated. Would the killer be back? It prickled the hair on the back of her neck.

"An employee?" Her stomach twisted at the thought. She couldn't imagine any of her coworkers being capable of such deceit.

"Maybe. It's hard to say for sure. I haven't been able to get close enough to anyone there." He paused, his hand thoughtfully stroking his chin as he locked eyes with her.

"What do you mean?" Jolie tilted her head. His voice dropped a register and sent a shiver, not entirely unpleasant, through her core.

The attraction was undeniable. It was a current beneath the surface of their conversation. A spark that had ignited from their first meeting. He was sharp, witty, and possessed a confident charm that drew her in. But the way his eyes lingered, the hint of possessiveness in his smile, made her stomach clench.

"My point is, you have access to information that I don't. You see and hear things that I never could." His tactics were maddeningly vague. She wished he would just come out and ask her already so she could say no without feeling guilty.

"You want me to spy for you? That seems a bit underhanded." Her voice wavered with uncertainty. She had learned so much from Seb about the supernatural world. Could the detective handle the truth? The thought of explaining succubi and dwarves to him made her smile, but the thought of telling him she was a vampire quickly disrupted that notion.

"I'm not asking you to spy. I just want you to keep your eyes and ears open. If you see or hear anything suspicious, I would appreciate it if you let me know." The sincerity in his eyes did little to combat the grime clinging to the edges of his proposal. It wasn't just the violation of privacy, but the feeling of betrayal that repulsed her.

She met his eyes. "I won't betray the trust of my colleagues." The leather of the couch felt slick under her palms. She wiped them on her pants and silently willed this conversation to end.

"I'm not asking you to betray anyone, Jolie. I was just hoping that if you happened to stumble upon any useful information, you would let me know," Detective O'Neil said, leaning against the armrest of the couch.

Jolie shifted her position, resting her elbow on the back of the couch and propping her head up with her hand. "You know, I don't really mingle with the other dancers," she replied with a small shrug. "You'd probably have better luck asking one of them."

A chuckle rumbled in his chest. "There is something about you, though, something that makes me think you could be useful in all this."

Her scoff was sharp. Jolie couldn't shake off the feeling that this was all a trap. Detective O'Neil's words may have sounded sincere, but she couldn't ignore the hidden agenda lurking behind his eyes. She could sense his wariness. It was clear that he didn't fully trust her, and she couldn't blame him. Despite her reservations, Jolie couldn't turn her back on the situation. Rori and Boden were involved, and they had always been kind to her. They were worth the risk.

She took a deep breath and mustered her courage. "Okay, Detective. I'll do what I can to help," she said, trying to sound confident.

As Jolie watched the detective nod, a sense of apprehension washed over her. His guarded expression made her question if there was more to this case than he was letting on. But she brushed off her suspicions and focused on the task at hand.

"Thank you, Jolie. I appreciate it. Also, please call me Danny." He pulled out his wallet to hand her his business card. Jolie's eyes lingered on him. "Here's my number, just in case," Danny said, his voice breaking through her thoughts. "If I don't hear from you, I'll track you down in a few days."

Jolie thanked him and saw him safely to the door, her mind still spinning. As she closed the door and turned to head back inside, she felt a nudge at the back of her knee. Looking down, she saw Caleb looking up at her with pleading eyes. "Looks like we both need a walk," she chuckled, giving Caleb a pat on the head. As she changed into fresh clothes, Jolie tried to push Danny from her thoughts. Against her better judgment, she still found herself wanting him. Shaking her head to clear her mind, Jolie scolded herself for getting so caught up in this stranger. But as she closed her eyes, her thoughts returned to the handsome detective.

Caleb and Jolie walked the quiet, dark streets. The barghest kept pulling her, willing her to increase their speed. Jolie gave up fighting him. "Fine, Caleb, you asked for it." She unhooked the leash from his collar, eager to let him run free. His tail wagged excitedly as she gave him the signal to go. With a burst of energy, he took off down the street, buildings and street signs whipping past in a blur. She followed close behind, thrilled by their speedy run. As they made a sharp turn, she admired the grace and agility of her furry companion. She had expected to leave Caleb far behind, but to her surprise, he was right by her side. His tongue hung out, panting with a wide, floppy grin.

Slowing down, she looked at Caleb with a mix of awe and amusement. "You're quite the runner, aren't you?" she chuckled, admiring his boundless energy. She couldn't resist the urge to challenge him. "Let's see what you've got!" she exclaimed, taking off down the street once again.

Amid their run, she spotted a nearby balcony and couldn't resist the opportunity to show off her own agility. With a swift push off the ground, she sprang into the air, reaching for the railing. In a graceful arc, she swung herself over the ledge and onto the next balcony, and then the next. Through a series of enthusiastic leaps, she made her way up to the roof.

Stretching out in the moonlight, she relished her sense of freedom and accomplishment. But as she looked around, she realized Caleb was nowhere in sight. Leaning over the edge, she searched the street below, but he was nowhere to be found. Then her senses flared, and she felt his presence behind her. Before she could react, Caleb was on her, knocking her to her knees. She laughed as she hugged him tightly. "You never cease to amaze me," she exclaimed, showering him with affection.

They ran through the dark streets, jumping from rooftop to rooftop. But as the hours passed and the moon began to set, Caleb's panting grew heavier, and his steps slowed. Jolie, noticing his exhaustion, suggested they head back home. With what looked like a cheerful nod, Caleb followed her lead, joy and exuberance still evident in his tired eyes. A lightness she hadn't felt in years fueled each step. Gone was the gnawing emptiness that had been her constant companion, replaced by a joy that settled warmly in her chest.

CHAPTER TEN

The Follow Spot

Jolie sat at the edge of her bed. her fingers curled into tight fists against her thighs, the knuckles white. One by one, she mentally cataloged the items on her imaginary to-do list. The last item on the list wasn't a task, but a pit in her stomach. Detective O'Neil's words were a request that felt more like a demand. The steady rhythm of Caleb's breathing only served as a reminder of how much she dreaded facing the evening. The possibility of a succubus lurking in the club dominated her mind. Jolie had to figure out a plan, all while keeping her cool and not letting herself get carried away with Detective O'Neil.

The giant mound under her covers stirred. Caleb woke up and attempted to untangle himself from the blankets. After a few minutes of grunting, snorting, and blanket-flipping, his large head emerged from beneath the covers. "Geez, Caleb," Jolie chuckled, "I'm running out of room for you in here."

Caleb's transformation was astounding. There was almost no trace of his once delicate features. His square jaw and strong muzzle resembled that of a mastiff, except for his floppy ears which still partially obscured his eyes. As he yawned, his sharp teeth sparkled a pristine white. He emerged from the blankets and shook his body vigorously, causing the bed to tremble beneath him. He was now the size of a Great Dane, with a broad chest that showed no signs of his past malnourishment.

Jolie got up from the bed and opened the balcony door for him. However, Caleb didn't budge until she placed the remainder of last night's meal on the floor for him. As she finished packing her bag for the club, she found Caleb waiting by the door with his leash by his feet. She smiled at his eagerness, but she couldn't bring him with her. "Caleb, I'm sorry but I have to go to work. You can't come with me," she said apologetically.

Caleb seemed to understand her words. However, he still tried to protest by shoving his leash toward her with his foot. Jolie chuckled and shook her head. "I know you want to come, but it's not safe for you. I promise I'll bring you something new for dinner. How about Chinese food?" She suggested, hoping to appease him.

Caleb's ears perked up at the mention of food, but he still didn't agree with her plan. As Jolie put on her scarf and long coat, Caleb followed her to the door, his leash in his mouth. He positioned himself in front of the door, blocking her escape with a determined look in his eyes. She grabbed her bags and tried to squeeze past him, but he didn't budge. She knew she should have been aggravated by his behavior, but all she felt was a twinge of guilt. With a sigh, she leaned in and kissed him on the head. "Be good," she whispered. "I'll be home soon." She couldn't bring herself to look at him as she closed and locked the door.

When Jolie arrived at The Black Cat House, the atmosphere was quiet. The employees were just starting their preparations for the night, and the buzz of anticipation had yet to fill the theater. She dropped her things by her vanity and grabbed some makeup from her trunk. She then made her way out to the theater to begin sleuthing. She settled at one of the better-lit tables, keeping one eye on the employees and one eye on her mirror as she expertly applied her makeup. The security was tighter tonight. Boden had brought on three new guards. Currently they were all standing imposingly around the outer walls with their arms folded over their black T-shirts. Rori was also in attendance, her small stature contradicting her fierce presence as she directed the preparations and kept a keen eye on the waitresses.

Jolie's eyes snagged on Mikhail as he set out bottles for the evening. The muscles in his forearms flexed beneath his rolled-up sleeves. He caught her looking, and a slow, wicked grin spread across his face. A gleam shone from his icy blue eyes. He held her gaze for a beat before flashing a conspiratorial wink in her direction. Jolie felt a familiar heat prickle her cheeks. She bit back a sigh. "Honestly, Mikhail," she muttered under her breath and turned back to the intricate business of blending eyeshadow.

Wyn slid onto the worn leather booth beside Jolie. The clink of ice was a soft prelude to the amber liquid sloshing in her glass. A faint, increasingly familiar scent, a blend of cinnamon and something subtly floral wafted from her direction.

"I missed you, Jolie," Wyn said, a hint of longing in her voice. "I haven't had anyone to talk while I was sitting all alone in my apartment. It was so sad." Wyn wiggled closer, her hips pressed against Jolie's. Her scent was intoxicating, driving all sense of purpose from Jolie's brain.

Taking a sip of Wyn's bourbon to gather herself, Jolie asked, "So, anything exciting happening?"

Wyn's face lit up at the invitation to gossip. She slid her arm into Jolie's and leaned in conspiratorially. "Well, the first night after it happened, Rori was furious," she whispered. "I think she believes that Boden's security team fell asleep on the job."

Jolie nodded. It was no secret that Rori had little patience for lax employees. She could only imagine the earful that Boden had gotten.

Wyn grinned manically, clearly enjoying having an audience. "And get this, Falyn is taking a little break," she continued, pulling Jolie even closer. "Rori called her a shit-stirrer and told her to take a vacation."

Jolie's interest grew. She knew that Rori and Falyn had a rocky relationship, but she never would have guessed that it had reached this point. "Has Rori brought in another dancer?" she asked, her priorities shifting slightly. While the information wasn't directly related to her mission, it could still affect her standing in the lineup.

Wyn shrugged. "Not yet, but you know Rori. She always has something up her sleeve." Jolie nodded in agreement; despite her brief tenure, she knew how calculated Rori could be. It was not the news she was hoping for. Jolie felt a sense of urgency to figure things out. She now had a goddess, a detective, and a dog demanding she find answers.

Jolie turned back to Wyn, her mind spinning with questions. She needed more information, anything that could help her make sense of the chaos unfolding at the club. "Any other incidents?" she asked, her tone serious as she searched for any clues that could lead her to the truth.

Wyn's eyes widened at Jolie's question, and she let out a laugh, clearly amused. "Are you looking for something in particular?"

Jolie hesitated, her mind raced as she debated whether to confide in Wyn. "I don't know what to think anymore. I was asked to inform the police of anything weird happening at the club," Jolie finally admitted, her voice heavy with uncertainty.

Wyn's eyes widened in shock, her hand instinctively covering her mouth. "Wait, what? I thought it was just a drug overdose," she exclaimed, her voice muffled by her hand.

Jolie shook her head, her gaze fixed on her mirror as she explained, "There were no drugs in his system. Detective O'Neil thinks it's a homicide."

Wyn sat back in her seat, her jaw dropping open in disbelief. "Shut your mouth!" she exclaimed, punctuating her words with a sharp slap to Jolie's arm. "No way."

Jolie let out a sigh of relief, thankful to have someone to share her burden with. "I know, it's hard to believe. But please, don't tell anyone else. We can't risk spreading rumors or causing panic. Mostly, Rori can't find out."

Wyn clasped her hands to her chest, her eyes wide with excitement. "So, you're investigating? Who do you think it could be?" She leaned closer to Jolie.

Jolie felt a twinge of guilt for confiding in Wyn. "I have no idea. I highly doubt any of the staff could be capable of something like this," she said, mentally berating herself for her lack of tact.

Wyn scoffed, her eyes narrowing in disdain. "Seriously, have you ever talked to some of these girls? The only thing keeping them from pulling off something like this is their lack of intelligence," she said, her tone dripping with sarcasm.

Just then, Rori appeared behind the booth, her hands on her hips as she addressed them. "Shouldn't you girls be getting ready for the show? The house is opening in ten minutes," she reminded them, her tone firm.

Though the six-inch heels she wore only brought her to 5'9, she was not to be trifled with. Her two-tone red and black hair was styled into an elaborate pile of curls on top of her head, and her curves were amplified by her silver fringe dress. Her numerous tattoos were set off against her tan skin. One arm and both legs were covered in colorful designs. Many of them matched Boden's to signify their many years together. When the house opened, she would turn heads wherever she went, and Boden would keep a close watch on those heads.

"We're leaving, Rori. Sorry," Wyn declared as she and Jolie gathered their things from the table, both eager to escape Rori's menacing gaze. Before they could fully make their exit, Rori reached out and grabbed Jolie's arm, stopping her in her tracks. She held her in place until Wyn was out of earshot, her eyes serious.

"Be careful of that one," Rori warned, nodding toward Wyn's retreating figure. Jolie furrowed her brow in confusion. Sure, Wyn could be annoying, but it seemed odd for Rori to give such a warning.

"You mean Wyn?" Jolie asked.

"Just be careful," Rori repeated. "She's a wild one, and you seem much more..." Her words trailed off as she turned and disappeared into the crowd. Jolie made her way backstage, her mind still lingering on Rori's warning. She checked the set list posted inside the dressing room door and saw that she was scheduled to perform at the end of the first set and in the middle of the second. This would give her enough time to finish getting ready and ample opportunity to observe the crowd during the third act.

CHAPTER ELEVEN

Sequins After Midnight

Jolie's shoulders finally uncoiled as the booming music of the main theater shifted to a softer, more ambient hum. She slipped through the heavy velvet curtain that served as a barrier between the intensity of the stage and the bustling backstage. The scent of hairspray, sweat, and faint perfume from the dancers' gowns permeated the entire space.

From her vantage point in the shadowed wings, Jolie scanned the opulent theater. Rori was currently laughing with a group of patrons. Her arm looped casually around one of their shoulders, a glass of champagne poised near her lips. Even from this distance, Jolie could see the glint in Rori's eyes as she expertly steered the conversation.

Further out, a wall of dark T-shirts formed a silent, moving perimeter. Boden strode through the theater, stalking past tables like a predator. His eyes were sharp and unwavering as they swept across the mingling guests. He lingered for a fraction of a second on faces that seemed out of place or on hands that lingered a moment too long. His team mirrored his vigilance. Their eyes missed nothing.

The opulent theater felt like a fortress. Against this backdrop of controlled revelry and unwavering security, the possibility of dark intent seemed impossibly remote. Who, Jolie mused, would be foolish enough to strike amidst such a sea of watchful eyes?

This was her element, the moment she could truly blend in, invisible in plain sight. She took a breath. She could do this. She would find some bit of information to keep Detective O'Neil away from the club and out of her hair.

But as she unlatched the sturdy oak trunk that served as her portable dressing room, a cold knot tightened in her stomach. While her meticulously folded silks and satins were there, she had forgotten to pack a simple dress for her post-show recon.

She sank onto the velvet stool before her vanity. The mirror reflected a face drained of its usual composure. The glitter lipstick she had carefully applied, a streak of red sparkles across her mouth, now seemed garish. How could she possibly search for intrigue in worn sweats? The very thought sent a fresh wave of despair through her. The window of opportunity was closing.

The urge to admit defeat and retreat, to melt back into the anonymity of her apartment, rose within her. A voice cut through the rising panic.

"You're still here?" Wyn questioned, changing into her next outfit. "I thought you always left after your last act." Wyn braced herself as she pulled the ribbons on her black leather corset, her waist shrinking under the strain, amplifying her voluptuous hips even further.

Jolie let out a sigh as she sat in front of the mirror, her mood darkening with each hairpin she removed from her ornate hair. A small part of her had been looking forward to hunting down suspicious activity. With an aggravated groan, she turned to Wyn and muttered, "I wasn't going to leave, but I am now. I forgot to bring something to wear."

Wyn slapped Jolie's hand away from her hair and grinned. "Don't worry, I've got you covered. I always bring extra outfits."

A cold dread seeped into Jolie's chest as she surveyed Wyn's overflowing rack. Silk clung to impossibly thin straps, sequins shimmered on barely there bodices, and sheer panels hinted at more skin than fabric. Each garment screamed a personality Jolie didn't recognize. A wave of self-consciousness washed over her. She couldn't imagine herself in any of them, uncomfortable and exposed. "That's alright, I'll just go home," she said, trying to hide her disappointment. But Wyn was not one to give up easily.

"Don't be silly," Wyn insisted, tossing Jolie a long black dress with a daring slit up the side. "This will be perfect on you."

Jolie held up the dress and raised an eyebrow skeptically. It was unlike anything she had ever worn before, with an asymmetric top, a single strap, and sections cut out from the back and torso. But as she looked closer, she noticed the silver threads woven into the soft fabric, giving it a subtle shimmer in the soft light. "It's interesting," Jolie remarked hesitantly, unsure if she could pull off such a bold look.

"Oh, stop, it will look great on you," Wyn reassured her, her eyes sparkling with excitement. "Now hurry up and try it on, or I'll put it on you myself."

Reluctantly, Jolie wiggled into the dress and straightened out the skirt. To her surprise, it hugged and amplified her slim curves in all the right places. Jolie felt positively daring in it, and she was relieved that it wasn't as scandalous as she had initially feared. "It will work," she admitted with a small smile.

Wyn stood back and appraised Jolie with a critical eye. "It's perfect. You should wear your black glitter heels with it, or maybe the red stilettos?"

Jolie's face lit up with gratitude. "Thank you, Wyn. I really appreciate it." Gone was the hesitant stranger. In her place stood a woman radiating quiet power. The theater, with all its possible pitfalls, no longer seemed like a gauntlet to be run, but a stage awaiting her entrance.

"You can buy me a drink later," Wyn said with a playful wink before turning back to finish changing. It had been a while since Jolie had been close to anyone, and Wyn's relentless pursuit of fun and adventure was refreshing. Despite their differences, Jolie found herself starting to like Wyn. A weight settled in Jolie's chest. Friendship with Wyn was a bridge too far, a risk her ordered life couldn't withstand. It was better to keep her distance.

With a heavy heart, Jolie made her way out into the bustling theater. The noise and commotion of the crowd enveloped her, making her feel both exhilarated and on edge. She hugged the outside wall, trying to avoid the eager patrons. The theater was packed, every booth filled with smiling and laughing customers. Waitresses wove through the crowd, expertly balancing trays of drinks as they made their rounds. Jolie admired Rori's dedication to keeping the glasses full and the atmosphere lively.

She chose a stool near the far corner of the bar. It offered a vantage point from which to survey the room. Jolie slowly began to realize that she wasn't the only one people-watching. Many of the faces she had been fixating on were also scanning the room, searching for their next bit of excitement. It wasn't just the show that brought people to The Black Cat House anymore, Jolie realized. It was an entire experience: the atmosphere and the possibility of danger.

A faint pressure, a silken brush against her elbow, jolted Jolie from her contemplation. She spun around, the movement bringing her face-to-face with Mikhail. His smile was a slow unfurling. It revealed a flash of perfectly white teeth. "Hello, love," he murmured.

His dark hair, a contrast to his pale skin, was drawn back with almost severe elegance and secured at his neck. The brutal line of his high cheekbones and the sharp angles of his jaw were magnified by this simple act. It lent him an air of ancient lineage, of something carved from marble. He lounged against the polished bar. The fabric of his dark shirt stretched taut across the lean, powerful muscles of his shoulders and chest. In the dim light, his eyes held a dangerous glint, a flicker of something untamed that made Jolie lick her lips.

Jolie's own smile felt brittle, a fragile shield against the sudden onslaught of sensation. Her skin prickled. An unsettling response that warred with an undeniable, magnetic pull. "Hi, Mikhail," she managed. Her voice caught slightly and betrayed the emotions churning within her.

His hand, surprisingly warm and impossibly soft, brushed hers. The contact was fleeting, yet it sent a wave of heat cascading up her arm. It dissolved the tight knot of anxiety in her chest. The wolfish edge she had perceived just moments before seemed to melt away. It was replaced by breathtaking beauty, an almost otherworldly grace. Her own smile blossomed.

"How's the night been?" Her eyes met his. She leaned in, a subtle invitation in the curve of her back. Her fingers traced the condensation ring left by a forgotten glass.

Mikhail's gaze flickered over her. "Busy," he admitted. His voice vibrated against her senses. He shrugged, a casual gesture that somehow managed to highlight the taut muscles in his shoulders. "A lot of newcomers, you know? But definitely better now that you've graced me with your presence." The air around him filled with the comforting scent of cinnamon. The warm scent clung to him, mingling with the faint scent of his cologne. A soft, involuntary giggle escaped Jolie's lips.

Just then, Mikhail's eyes caught something. Annoyance crossed his features; there was a growing crowd of patrons at the far end of the bar. "Excuse me," he murmured. "Gotta run. Don't you go anywhere." He offered her a quick nod and a promise in his eyes.

Jolie watched him go. Her gaze lingered on the confident sway of his hips, the way his well-fitted pants stretched taut across his powerful glutes. Even as the sight held her captive, dread began to creep into the edges of her awareness. The fog began to recede. What had she been doing? Flirting with Mikhail, of all people. Her stomach turned. What had come over her?

"Hey." The brusque sound snagged Jolie's wandering thoughts and pulled her back to the amber-lit bar. She swiveled in her chair. Rori stood beside her and placed an almost apologetic hand on Jolie's shoulder. Rori frowned deeply as she watched Mikhail.

"Mikhail," Rori's voice, surprisingly robust for her size, cut through the din of conversation. Her demand echoed even over the clinking of glasses, "Whiskey."

Mikhail continued to arrange the drinks on the tray, flashing a charming smile at the waitress as she walked away. He turned to look at Rori, his eyes sparkling. "Only if you make it three glasses," he teased, his voice smooth and confident.

Rori's eyes rolled so far back, Jolie half-expected to see her pupils disappear completely. The clinking of ice against crystal echoed as Rori reached for a third glass. She leaned in, her voice a conspiratorial murmur that barely registered above the conversation around them. "I don't like him much," she whispered, a slight tremor in her voice betraying a depth of feeling beyond simple dislike.

"I think," Jolie began, her lips curving into a smile that felt both genuine and a little dangerous, "that I might just agree with you."

Rori poured three shots and handed them out, downing hers in one swift motion before grabbing the bottle and her glass. She gestured toward Mikhail with her bright red nail. "That's all you get until we close, and all you'll ever get on the house," she declared, her tone unwavering. "Come on, Jolie."

Jolie followed Rori, her eyes scanning the room as they walked. Boden was already seated at the table, munching on bruschetta and flatbread with hummus. The Black Cat House may have offered only a humble, small-plate menu, but it was enough to satisfy Boden's constant hunger. Jolie marveled at his ability to eat so much without gaining a single pound.

Rori slid into the booth next to Boden. She grabbed a piece of bruschetta and took a bite. "Shouldn't you be watching for trouble?" she asked jokingly, nudging Boden with her shoulder. Boden chuckled and wiped his hands on a napkin before tossing it at Rori.

"Woman, I have ten guys on tonight. Let me be," he replied, gesturing to the security scattered around the bar.

Rori pursed her lips, a movement that hid the amusement simmering beneath.

"Finish that, and I'll pour you another one," Rori chirped, a playful glint in her eyes as she watched Jolie cradle the almost empty glass of amber liquid. Rori's intention wasn't to pressure, but to offer a bridge.

"I shouldn't," Jolie murmured. The ice clinked softly against the glass as she lifted it to her lips.

"Yes, you should," Rori insisted, patting Jolie's hand. "I hate drinking alone." The corners of Jolie's mouth lifted, a genuine smile this time, not the polite curve she'd offered earlier. She'd almost forgotten the initial tension she'd felt when she had first arrived. Now, the flow of conversation and the shared laughter had eased that away. Boden was a picture of sober virtue. He sat stiffly, his hands clasped neatly in his lap, a glass of sparkling water untouched beside his plate.

Rori's bright eyes shimmered as she casually draped her arm over Boden's broad shoulders, a playful smile tugging at the corners of her lips. "So, Jolie is not a fan of Mikhail?" she taunted, raising an eyebrow in amusement.

Boden chuckled and lowered his head, propping it up with his hands on his forehead. "Really? I thought you were convinced she'd fall for his charms. Isn't that what all the ladies do?" he teased back.

Rori pretended to pout as she leaned in closer to Boden. "I guess even I can be wrong sometimes," she gave him a playful wink before planting a soft kiss on his cheek.

Jolie, who had been nursing her second shot of whiskey, finally spoke up. "I get the feeling you two are having a laugh at my expense," she grumbled, taking another sip.

Rori's bright eyes danced with amusement. "Not at all. You seem to be the only woman in this place who isn't swayed by his charms," she pointed out, gesturing toward the handsome bartender who was currently serving drinks to a group of giggling women.

Boden glanced sheepishly at Rori before turning back to Jolie. "I've been getting a lot of flak for hiring him. Rori's had to deal with all the fallout," he explained, regret creeping into his voice.

Rori leaned forward. "Every waitress wants to work on his shifts, and when they do, I get complaints that they neglect their tables and spend all their time at the bar," she revealed with exasperation.

"And of course, it's all my fault," Boden muttered, pausing his chewing to express his annoyance.

Rori nodded emphatically. "Yes, very much his fault," she agreed, taking a long sip.

Lina approached their table and placed a plate of fried mushrooms and French fries in front of Boden. He eagerly rubbed his hands together and dug in, much to Rori's amusement. She shook her head and smiled at him.

Lina cleared the empty plates from their table. "That's his second order of mushrooms already!" she exclaimed, amazed by Boden's insatiable appetite.

Rori stopped mid-pour, her eyes widening in shock. "Are you serious?" she asked incredulously.

Boden shrugged and struggled to speak with his mouth full of food. "Hey, I didn't have dinner tonight, and I'm starving. You fed the kids, but there wasn't enough left for me," he complained and gestured at nothing in particular.

Rori pointed the bottle of whiskey she had begun to pour at Boden. "That's because your kids eat just like you do," she teased before turning back to Lina. "Hey, can you bring some flatbread to table three? They've had a few too many drinks and not enough food. Tell them it's on the house," she instructed.

Lina nodded and walked away, shaking her head at Boden's bottomless stomach.

The emcee, a man whose laugh lines seemed permanently engraved by a thousand smoky dive bars, finally choked out the last of his raunchy jokes. A collective exhale rippled through the tightly packed tables.

It was in that sliver of quiet that Wyn materialized. She didn't just approach. She wove through the throng, a serpentine grace in her movements. Her sequined halter top caught the light. She eased herself onto the bench next to Jolie. The contact was immediate. A subtle pressure as she squeezed in, her hip pressing against Jolie's.

Boden, hunched over a plate of greasy mushrooms, gave a perfunctory nod in Wyn's direction, his focus already back on the flaky breading and dipping sauce.

Wyn leaned in, her voice a purr that vibrated under the soft music filling the theater. Her arm stretched across Jolie's thighs, fingers brushing the slit of Jolie's dress before settling, possessively, on Jolie's lap. "So," she breathed, her gaze sweeping across the faces, a sly smile playing on her lips, "what's the poison of choice tonight?"

"Whiskey," Rori replied, planting her arms on the table. "You missed the last break. Where were you?"

"Sorry, I got caught up," Wyn explained, reaching for a fry. However, her attempt at snatching one was met with a stern look from Boden as he quickly moved his plate out of her reach.

"By who?" Boden raised an eyebrow, finding ways to guard his food from Wyn's grabby fingers.

Wyn giggled, playfully mimicking a shy, demure girl. "Why would you say that?" She then proceeded to pour herself a generous amount of whiskey.

"Because we know you," Rori laughed, the ice clinking in her now-empty glass. She extended the cup toward Wyn, a silent request for a refill. Boden, his patience visibly thinning, didn't bother to look their way. With a sigh that seemed pointed at their frivolous chatter, he efficiently stacked the empty plates.

"Perhaps," he suggested, his voice laced with a carefully controlled edge, "a little less commentary and a little more appreciation for the performance?" The disapproving glances from surrounding tables, once subtle, had become a current of collective hostility. A heavy hush fell over their group.

The spotlight exploded across the stage, catching the dancer in a shimmering halo of gold. Jolie let out a barely audible breath. The tension finally eased as Wyn's hand, reluctantly, slid from her thigh. The memory of warmth remained, a brand seared into her skin. The implied offer still pulsed in Jolie's mind, a dangerous siren song offering a promise she was increasingly tempted to collect. Wyn's flirtations meant nothing, she told herself. Absolutely nothing, but the certainty felt thin, like a veil threatening to tear.

Jolie's attention moved between the two women. Rori possessed a stillness that pulsed with contained force. She was a queen surveying her domain. Her shoulders were squared, her jaw set, and her eyes seemed to bore directly into the heart of the dimly lit stage. You could feel the years in that gaze, each flicker of her pupils an understanding of the countless hours of discipline and the dedication that polished raw talent into something formidable.

Wyn was a study in perpetual motion; it was as if the idea of sitting still might physically hurt her. She shifted in her chair. Her hands flicked and gestured, her eyes darted to every shifting shadow, every sparkle of light. Jolie felt a dizzying sense of disorientation just watching her.

The sheer difference between them was a puzzle that begged to be solved. It was more than just their demeanor. When Rori moved, it was like the rustle of ancient leaves, a whisper of something untamed. A subtle power radiated from her, a primal energy that smelled of damp earth after a spring rain and the cool, silver glow of a moonlit forest. Boden, whenever he was near, amplified that sensation.

Wyn, on the other hand, was a sudden, exhilarating burst of spice. Her presence was a bright, insistent warmth, like a crackling fire on a cold night. Or the sharp, sweet tang of freshly ground cinnamon. Being near her was like inhaling a heady perfume, a dizzying blend of zest and playful mischief that left Jolie feeling a little breathless and entirely too curious.

The burlesque show unfolded before them, a brilliant display of flesh and fearless self-expression. In a world where women were often reduced to objects, these performers reclaimed their bodies. Using nudity not as submission, but as a defiant act of empowerment. It was a bold, breathtaking spectacle, drawing a diverse crowd. Rori and Boden had not only built successful careers as performers but parlayed their talents and ambition into a thriving club and a burgeoning real estate portfolio. Their success was a testament to their resilience.

As the opening chords of the music swelled, Jolie saw a flicker of movement heading toward them. A burly security guard, his face impassive beneath the harsh stage lighting, moved silently through the throng toward Boden. He leaned in close, a brief, almost imperceptible exchange of words passing between them. Boden's response was a curt nod; a flicker of something darkened his expression. Maybe urgency? Anxiety?

He lingered for a moment, a hand briefly resting on the edge of their booth, before bending and pressing a quick, almost perfunctory kiss to Rori's temple. Then, with a brisk, purposeful stride, he disappeared backstage. Leaving behind a trail of unanswered questions in his wake.

Jolie's curiosity flared into a full blaze. She turned to Rori, whose expression was now a mask of serene indifference, the kind practiced by someone who had mastered the art of hiding secrets. "Where's Boden going?" Jolie asked, her voice low, a challenge wrapped in a question. Rori's silence was answer enough. Jolie felt a twinge of anxiety as she pressed her luck, unable to stop herself from asking, "Is everything okay?"

Rori's face remained stoic, offering no clues to Jolie. "Just routine. Don't worry," she replied, her tone guarded. As the last dancer finished their dance and the house lights came up, Boden finally returned.

He looked at Jolie and Wyn with a tired expression. "Alright, girls, pack up and go home. I'm exhausted."

A hollow ache settled in Jolie's chest, a weight where excitement had resided just hours before. Tonight had yielded nothing but fatigue. The vibrant energy of the human world was a relentless current dragging her under, leaving her bone-tired and utterly drained. The thought of repeating this night after night made her stomach clench.

Backstage, the hushed quiet was a relief after the clamor she'd just left. A wave of petulance washed over her. Humans weren't the only creatures with needs, she thought, a faint, bitter smile twisting her lips. Her gnawing emptiness was as much a demand for sustenance as it was a cry for escape.

Wyn appeared behind Jolie, her makeup still intact. "We should get a drink," she suggested, leaning against Jolie's back and draping her arms over her shoulders.

"I've had more than enough to drink. I'm going home," Jolie replied, feeling the steady thump of Wyn's heart against her back. The closeness was almost unbearable, stirring up unfamiliar desires within her.

Wyn buried her head in Jolie's neck, her warm breath tickling her skin. "Then I'll come with you. We can drink at your place," she whispered. Her scent and warmth clouded Jolie's senses. She could almost taste Wyn on her teeth, the tang of blood and the rush of warmth. It was tempting, so tempting. Her lust threatened to overtake her rational thoughts. It had been so long since she felt the warmth of someone pressed against her.

Jolie stood up suddenly, almost knocking Wyn over. "No," she said firmly, trying to push away her desires and regain control. It was too risky. Jolie could feel the heat of her anger radiating off her as she spoke; her words dripped with a mix of need and aggression. "No, this is not a good idea," she said firmly, her jaw clenched, hands balled into fists.

Jolie grabbed her bag and stormed out the back door, not bothering to look back at Wyn's shocked expression. As she made her way home, anger at herself and the world burned bright within her, making her pace quick and determined. Her lack of control was inexcusable, but she knew she shouldn't have taken it out on Wyn.

The usually stoic mask she had meticulously constructed felt like a crumbling ruin. The memory of the easy laughter she shared with Mikhail, the way his gaze had lingered a beat too long, started a strange itching beneath her skin. Then there was Wyn, leaning in with that infuriatingly gentle smile, her hand brushing Jolie's lap. Even drinking with Rori felt like another tiny crack in her composure. And Detective O'Neil . . . he had ignited a different kind of fire, a raw need that felt both thrilling and terrifying.

It was as if a dam had broken with a thousand insidious leaks. Each interaction was a trickle, widening the fissures until the floodgates threatened to burst. Panic tightened her throat. Losing this control, this carefully curated detachment, felt like losing herself.

She couldn't go straight home; there was too much energy surging through her. Anxiety pressed into her skin, threatening to tear it. She wanted to scratch, to scream, to do anything to release the pressure. She ran past her apartment and toward the water. The street blurred under her feet; she launched herself onto a fire escape and then cartwheeled to the roof. She paused and scanned the city skyline, picking a direction. Then she ran again, leaping from roof to roof until she felt the pressure subside. She made her way more slowly back to her apartment.

Her run had done nothing to stop the churning in her gut; her knuckles were white where she gripped the doorframe, and she ground her teeth so tight she felt the muscles ache. Her anger quickly morphed into shock when she saw Caleb sitting in the middle of a pile of torn pillows. White fluff was scattered around him like snow, and he looked up at her with a pouty, angry expression on his face.

Caleb's leg rose, a defiant, slow arc against the remains of her couch. The sense of impending disaster engulfed her. "Don't you dare," she hissed, the words sharp in the tense silence. The command was more of a desperate plea than a genuine reprimand. "Bad dog!" she added, the phrase feeling pathetically inadequate in the face of Caleb's glare.

Panic clawed at her throat. The couch, already ravaged, was teetering on the brink of utter destruction. This was the last straw. She couldn't handle one more thing.

Her stern front crumbled. "I'm sorry, alright?" she whispered, her voice cracking. The words tumbled out, a torrent of guilt and exhaustion. "I shouldn't have locked you in all night. I forgot . . . I completely forgot to feed you. My poor, hungry boy." She swallowed. "I'll order pizza," she stammered, the offer growing increasingly extravagant in her desperation. "Two pizzas!" Her eyes, filled with remorse and the fear of another catastrophe, pleaded with the stubborn dog. "Please . . . please don't pee on the couch. I'm so sorry."

The harsh lines around Caleb's mouth relaxed. Slowly, he lowered his leg from the ripped cushions. Jolie could see that the genuine contrition in her voice hadn't been lost on him. A sound like a frustrated snort escaped him before he ambled toward the balcony door.

She opened it with a sigh of weary resignation. The cushions were destroyed. Long, jagged tears gaped along the seams and spilled forth a cascade of fluffy innards. Thankfully, the fabric itself seemed mostly intact, though it would require more than a quick stitch. She traced a finger along one of the gashes, a silent calculation in her eyes. Duct tape would hold it together for tonight. A proper repair would have to wait until after she had rested. Caleb watched her from his position leaning against the doorframe as she began the painstaking task of gathering the stuffing and patching the wounds with silver duct tape.

After Caleb's dinner, she sat on the edge of her bed. Her voice was soft, laced with a hesitant apology. "Come here, boy."

Caleb lumbered over, his massive frame a gentle earthquake on the wooden floor. He settled his head in her lap, a mountain of fur and muscle. His deep eyes gazed up at her with unsettling intelligence. She felt the weight of his disappointment. "I know, buddy," she whispered, her voice catching slightly. "Being cooped up all night isn't fair, I know. But I can't take you everywhere. It's just . . . not possible."

She pointed to the balcony door, its glass reflecting the moonlight. "Tomorrow, I'll leave this open for you. You can get some fresh air, feel the breeze. But you need to stay here, okay? Just . . . here." She pulled him closer, the scent of dog and home a bittersweet comfort in the quiet understanding that passed between them.

After a few moments of contemplation, he let out a deep sigh and licked her face before shaking his large head. Relieved that their little disagreement was finally over, Jolie hugged him tightly, feeling the warmth of his furry body against hers.

"You know, Caleb," she said, trying to lighten the mood, "if you had peed on those cushions, I would have had to eat you." But instead of finding her joke amusing, Caleb let out a low, soft growl.

Chapter Twelve

The Bloodstained Bustle

istress washed over her. Jolie had another night of performances ahead of her, and another night of spying on her colleagues. It was a task she had already grown weary of and had little to show for her efforts. Another night of pretending. It was exhausting, and she had yet to come up with something to tell Detective O'Neil. As she mulled over her options, she couldn't shake off the feeling that it was all for nothing.

Butterflies filled Jolie's stomach; the thought of her last encounter with Wyn crept into the corners of her mind. Wyn lived in a world of close contact. Her personal space was fluid, to put it mildly, but fluid didn't excuse the way her breath hitched in Jolie's ear as she whispered things far too suggestive.

She needed to talk to Wyn. To lay down some clear, firm boundaries. But how? The thought of confronting Wyn filled her with a peculiar mix of trepidation and steel. She pictured Wyn's wide, expressive eyes. The quick, almost childlike smile that could melt glaciers and the underlying intensity that lurked beneath. Wyn had a simmering power Jolie had yet to understand.

"I can't keep letting this happen," she said, her voice quiet but firm with resolve. With a sigh, she hugged Caleb, seeking comfort in his warmth. "I just want to stay home tonight," she mumbled, her voice muffled by the scruff of his neck. "What do you say I call in sick?" Caleb responded with a loud snort, sounding almost like a quacking duck.

Getting ready for work felt like scaling a mountain. Each muscle protested, a chorus of aches and weariness. She shuffled into the kitchen, the worn floorboards groaning. Jolie reached for the blood packets. She settled on two. A pathetically insufficient remedy for the hollowness gnawing at her.

The wig cabinet, a relic from a life she barely remembered, loomed in the corner. Twenty years. Twenty years since she'd last been so exhausted she needed to wear a wig. She ran a hand over the smooth, synthetic strands of a dark bob, its glossy sheen mocking the dullness of her own reflection. Even blood offered only a temporary reprieve. She should just run. The thought flooded her mind, unwanted but not entirely without merit.

A low groan rumbled from the bedroom. Caleb was still lost in slumber. Guilt pierced Jolie; the thought of abandoning him clawed at her conscience. But the alternative? To continue sneaking around, spying on her friends, and putting herself at risk. The weight of it all felt crushing.

"It's not sustainable, Caleb," she whispered to the empty room, her voice cracking with a mixture of defiance and despair. "This isn't a life. It's a . . . a bloody lie." The words hung heavy with her fears. The city, with its glittering lights and hidden shadows, suddenly felt suffocating. She needed to escape. But how long could she truly outrun her own past?

She looked around her meager apartment. The remnants of a solitary life. A tear traced a path down her cheek. She swiped at it, almost angrily, then sighed.

Jolie's brows knitted together tightly. She was a master of emotional detachment. Yet, after decades of building walls around herself, she couldn't help feeling an unfamiliar pang of something akin to love for these people. "Damn it all," she muttered. "Why does leaving feel like losing a part of myself?"

It was decided. She couldn't run. She'd figure out how to protect these people that she had unexpectedly grown so fond of. Determined, Jolie pulled her hair up in a bun and secured the wig in place.

The streets were alive with warm spring weather, and Jolie took her time walking to work, savoring the sights and scents of the city. She pulled her scarf tighter around her neck, relishing the feeling of the soft fabric against her skin. As she strolled, she eavesdropped on the conversations around her, listening in on the daily lives of the people she passed by. When she finally arrived at The Black Cat House, the bustling activity backstage was shocking after her peaceful walk there. Dancers were already getting ready, taking up every inch of space they could find. Jolie navigated her way through the bedlam, scolding herself for being later than usual.

Wyn's usual spot at the station was empty, signaling that she must have had the night off. Jolie let out a small sigh of relief. In Wyn's absence, Jolie no longer had to worry about keeping her resolve intact. She could relax, at least for the night. As she looked over the night's schedule, a sense of unease took over. She was listed for only one act. It was unusual for anyone to only have one act in a night. Her mind raced with worry, questioning if Rori was making permanent changes to the lineup. She was scheduled to be in the second set, which gave her enough time to find Rori and ample opportunity to observe the crowd during the third act.

Jolie scanned the buzzing atmosphere in search of Rori's signature red and black hair. She finally spotted her by the bar, looking like she was ready to camp there all night. Jolie assumed she must have been dealing with more issues with the waitresses and Mikhail. Carefully considering the best approach, Jolie slowly made her way to the bar. Mikhail was behind the counter, effortlessly preparing garnishes and flashing a greedy smile at the waitresses. The only thing keeping the chaos at bay was Rori's disapproving frown.

Rori was a study in controlled disdain. Her eyebrows were drawn together in a tight, disapproving line. Her gaze, sharp as a tack, darted between Mikhail and Boden, who sat stiffly, his face strained.

Her disapproval wasn't subtle. It radiated from her in painful waves. She'd caught snippets of their conversation when she approached, a clipped, icy tone from Rori, punctuated by Boden's increasingly apologetic murmurs.

Jolie felt a pang of sympathy for him. He wasn't blind to Mikhail's flaws, but the pressure to keep the club running was immense. Rori's simmering disapproval was a potent weapon, far more effective than outright confrontation.

Gathering her courage, Jolie subtly cleared her throat. Mikhail's gaze stayed steady on Rori, attempting playful banter to curb her obvious distaste. But Rori met his advances with a cold stare that slowly curdled into undeniable hostility.

With a sigh that was more performance than genuine defeat, Mikhail pivoted. His attention, now unmoored from the fortress that was Rori, landed on Jolie. A smile spread across his face. "And for you, my dear?" His voice was a low, disarming rumble. "What can I tempt you with tonight?"

Jolie instinctively drew her hands closer, tucking them primly into her lap. The memory of their last encounter left her feeling exposed and vulnerable. Whatever effortless charm Mikhail possessed could dismantle her walls, and she was utterly unprepared to face it again.

Rori's eyes snapped toward Jolie, her lips curling into a scowl. "She's not here for you. She's trying to find the right time to talk to me." Her words dripped with scorn, and Mikhail quickly backed away to the other side of the bar. Rori turned to face Jolie, her expression softening slightly. "I assume you want to discuss tonight's schedule." She leaned against the bar, her elbow supporting her weight as she jutted out her hip. She waited patiently for Jolie to speak, but when she remained silent, Rori rolled her hand to coax words from Jolie. "Out with it."

Jolie shifted nervously, her hands rubbing together. "I noticed I'm only scheduled to perform once tonight."

Rori nodded, a hint of frustration creeping into her voice. "Yes, we had to make some last-minute changes. We have too many girls and not enough time." Her eyes darted toward the preparations happening in the theater behind them.

"Rori," Jolie began, her voice almost swallowed by the ambient noise. She tried to appear calm, but her words trembled slightly. "I . . . I don't understand. Is something wrong? This job . . . it means everything to me. I love working here, I really do. I'd be devastated to lose it." The sincerity in her voice was laced with desperation that tugged at the edges.

Rori's hands shot up in a gesture of bewilderment. "What in the goddess's name are you talking about?" Her eyes were now wide and frantic. "What 'losing your job' nonsense is this? I haven't even thought about letting you go, Jolie! You're one of my best!"

Jolie's confession was barely audible. "I've never . . . I've never been dropped before," she said, her focus fixed on Rori. The softening of Rori's face was a slow, visible thaw, the initial shock giving way to concern.

"Charles didn't call?" Rori's red lips thinned to a disapproving line, her eyes narrowing with a confusion that bordered on anger. A low, guttural "God damn it, Charles," escaped her lips. She took a moment, her shoulders bunched before releasing in a visible sigh.

"I overbooked," she explained, her voice calmer now, but the tension still there. "Charles was supposed to give you a call to let you know you were bumped." Rori, sensing Jolie's stunned silence, fidgeted, her usually composed demeanor cracking. A blush unfurled across her cheeks. "So, um," she began, "I . . . I said yes to two out-of-towners. Completely forgot I'd already booked one last week." She wrung her hands; the movement betrayed her usual air of control. She paused, searching for the right words. "It means some people, you included, only get one slot tonight. But," she added, a hint of apology in her voice, "if you want, I can book you for another day."

Jolie felt the heat creep up her neck. The knot of anxiety in her stomach tightened. This wasn't like Rori. Rori, whose life ran on a Swiss-watch schedule, whose to-do lists were works of art, had double-booked.

The tension eased with a slow exhale. "Oh," she breathed, the words a soft release. "It's fine. I don't need another day."

Rori's eyes widened, a flicker of understanding, then relief, dawning in their depths. "You really thought I was . . . subtly trying to get rid of you?" she asked, a nervous laugh escaping. The question hung between them for a moment before Rori added, with a self-deprecating grin, "Never. Just a colossal screw-up. It's rare, but when it happens, Boden never lets me forget it."

Jolie's initial shock morphed into amusement. The image of Rori, normally the epitome of unflappable competence, being relentlessly teased by Boden was oddly endearing. The slight unease from the misunderstanding vanished, replaced by a warm feeling of camaraderie and admiration for Rori's honesty and self-awareness, even in the face of her rare and thoroughly human blunder.

Jolie's gaze dropped to the worn, scuffed toes of her shoes. "Surprises," she mumbled. "They're . . . not my thing."

Rori's hand settled gently on Jolie's shoulder. Her smile was soft, understanding, the kind that chased away shadows. "No, I suppose not," Rori agreed. "But you're family here. We've got your back."

The words wrapped around Jolie like a much-needed hug. The Black Cat House wasn't just a building. It was her sanctuary. Even Rori's exaggerated grimace at the sight of Jolie's disastrous wig, a tangled mass of synthetic strands, elicited a chuckle. The teasing felt less like criticism and more like a playful jab from a sister.

"I know, I know," Jolie conceded, fingers nervously picking at the rat's nest atop her head. "It'll be tamed before tonight's performance. I promise."

Jolie watched Rori walk away, the word "family" echoing in her mind. It had been so long since she had truly felt wanted.

Jolie leaned against the bar and contemplated her sudden change in demeanor. Most people seemed to recoil from her. To flinch away with distrust. Here, it was different. She was welcomed rather than repelled. She couldn't determine why. Before the answer could begin to form, a shadow fell across the polished bar.

"Ready for that drink?" Mikhail's voice broke through her thoughts. He didn't wait for an answer, already reaching for a shaker. He leaned in, his gaze surprisingly direct. There was quiet appraisal in his eyes, as if he were cataloging the unique contours of her features. His smile was somehow both irritating and strangely captivating. It was the kind of smile that promised mischief. "Gin?" His voice was honeyed, persuasive.

The warmth of her earlier thoughts, the fragile tendrils of a new, unexpected kinship she'd found within The Black Cat House, still clung to her. She found herself nodding. "Yes, please. A Clipper Ship tonight," she replied.

He reached for the gin and measured the liquid into a chilled shaker. He didn't break eye contact as he worked. She swallowed as his tongue, a flash of pink, slicked over his lower lip in a deliberate, slow movement.

"Clipper Ship it is," he murmured. The words seemed to coax her into relaxation. The scent of juniper and lime swirled in the air.

He slid the drink across the counter, the condensation beading on the glass. "What are you doing after the show?" he asked, his voice dropping an octave. He leaned forward. His elbows rested on the bar, and his eyes searched hers in a silent invitation. The clinking of glasses and the murmur of distant conversations faded into the background, leaving only the sharp, clear sound of his question.

She'd told herself she disliked him. His roving eyes and constant, almost calculated flirtation set her teeth on edge. Yet, as the potent sweetness of the cocktail unfurled on her tongue, she found herself smiling back at him.

The laughter spilled out of her, easy and unbidden. The cascade of bright notes surprised even her. Mikhail's eyes seemed to drink her in. He'd leaned closer, the scent of sandalwood and cinnamon clinging to him. "You look beautiful when you laugh."

Jolie shook her head. "I'm beautiful all the time." It was a dance, a delicate push and pull of words. She'd found herself caught up in its rhythm, forgetting for a moment the very real reasons she should be keeping her distance.

Then, his tactics shifted. It wasn't a loud declaration but a subtle lean-in, his voice dropping to a husky murmur. "You know," he said, his gaze locked on hers. "We should explore this further. Just us."

A cold prickle traced a path down her spine. The warmth that had flowered in her chest just moments before withered. It was replaced by a sudden awareness. Her smile, so readily offered before, evaporated.

"I don't think that's a good idea," she managed. Her voice came out devoid of any of the lightness it had possessed moments before.

Mikhail's hand covered hers where it rested on the wood. A jolt, not entirely unpleasant, shot up her arm, a ripple of warmth spreading through her veins. His grip was firm, thumb tracing slow, deliberate circles on the back of her hand. The strangely intimate gesture sent a tremor through her.

"Are you sure?" he countered. His voice was a low rumble that licked against her skin. He tilted his head, his eyes searching hers. "I think you and I could be remarkable together. We'd understand each other, wouldn't we?" The soft stroking of his thumb continued.

The icy fort she'd built around her heart began to splinter. Each shard of resistance dissolved like frost under a spring sun. A whisper coiled in the quiet space of her mind. *What if he finally sees you? What if this is what you've been craving all along?* It wasn't her thought, not really, but it became consuming.

The room tilted, and her vision blurred. Mikhail moved closer. His lean, pale chest, cool against her own. His weight pressed down on her. His breath tickled the tip of her nose before his lips finally, tentatively, met hers. It was a soft, uncertain brush, a question more than a claim.

The sharp, jarring sound of shattering glass ripped through the suspended moment. The spell shattered with a violent clatter; it yanked her back to the present. Mikhail's eyes were locked onto hers, and he was still rubbing the soft skin of her hand. A visceral recoil propelled her hand away as if burned. *I'm falling apart.* She'd promised herself that no one would ever get close to her again, but between Mikhail and Wyn, she couldn't resist the temptation.

Jolie's eyes narrowed and lingered on Mikhail's charming smile; she was finally coming to her senses. "Oh, that line? A classic, I'll bet," she said, her voice laced with playful sarcasm, though the playful part felt strained.

He didn't flinch. "Guilty as charged," he confessed, a grin playing on his lips. "But with you, it's different. Truly different."

Frantic wings fluttered in her stomach. The ice in her glass clinked as she lifted it. She took a long, slow sip, the icy liquid doing little to quench her inner fire. She was tempted, oh so tempted, but she wouldn't give in. "Thanks," she said, her voice carefully even. "But no, thanks." She met his eyes with a silent plea: *Please, don't make this harder than it already is.*

Mikhail's smile faltered for a moment, but he quickly recovered. "Well, the offer still stands if you ever change your mind," he said, flashing her a charismatic smile before walking away. She was flushed with relief as she watched him go.

Jolie hurried from the theater to the protection of backstage; each step was a small attempt to outrun the encounter with Mikhail. It wasn't just his words, though they had coiled around her with a disquieting intimacy. It was the way his eyes had seemed to peel back layers she hadn't even known existed. She ran a hand over her arm. The touch of his fingers still a prickle beneath her skin.

Jolie sat at her vanity, her reflection staring back. Her careful composure barely concealed the frantic flutter beneath her skin. Mikhail's words replayed in her head. She picked up a brush and began to tame the wig. It was a futile attempt to ground herself. Each stroke of mascara felt like a calculated act of defiance against the unsettling wave of emotion threatening to engulf her. Outwardly, she was ready. Inside, however, a storm raged.

CHAPTER THIRTEEN

The Shimmy

After the final curtain fell, Jolie scrubbed her face clean and prepared to exit the theater. Rori had been right. The wig was a monstrosity. A cheap, itchy synthetic atrocity sat atop her head like a plastic helmet. With a snap, Jolie unpinned the offending thing. She didn't bother to fold it. Instead, it sailed into the overflowing trash bin.

Stepping out into the cool night air, she shook her head. She let her own dark curls cascade around her shoulders. It wasn't just a change of hair. It felt like shedding her skin. She inhaled deeply. The scent of damp earth and distant exhaust mingled on her tongue.

The peace lasted only as long as it took two steps into the shadowy alley. Hunched in the inky darkness sat Caleb. His enormous head, crowned with soft, floppy ears, tilted inquisitively. A low growl rumbled in his chest, but his tail thumped a gentle rhythm against the grimy concrete. "You sly dog," she chuckled. "How did you get out?" The answer, of course, was obvious. She'd left the balcony door open as promised.

Caleb snorted. It was almost as if he were laughing at her forgetfulness. "Did anyone see you jumping off the balcony?" she asked. She was half-joking. Caleb snorted again. She took it as a sign that he had managed to escape unnoticed. With a sense of relief, she scratched behind his soft, floppy ears.

"Time to go home, my friend. Are you hungry?" She already knew the answer. Caleb eagerly rubbed his face against her hand. "There's some Chinese food on the way. We'll get you some," she promised as they walked off into the night.

Jolie took her time walking down the street. She carried the takeout bag from Caleb's new favorite restaurant. As she strolled, Caleb bounded around her. His tail wagged with excitement. It was a peaceful night. Just a few people were out and about. They all seemed to take notice of Caleb's size and the fact that he was without a leash. Some even moved to the other side of the street. It was hard to believe that just a few weeks ago, Caleb was a tiny, scrawny puppy. Jolie pondered how old Caleb really was. He acted like a puppy, but as a barghest, he could be older than the city itself.

When they reached her apartment, the scent hit Jolie first. A wave of cologne pricked her nose and made her tongue involuntarily twitch. O'Neil. Each step up the stairs seemed to amplify the scent. Reaching the top, she saw him. He leaned against the wall by her apartment door. The muted glow of his phone illuminated the sharp angles of his jaw and the way his tailored suit molded to the broad expanse of his shoulders. It tapered down to a leanness at his hips. She couldn't look away, but she didn't need this additional hassle tonight. Not with her defenses as low as they already were.

The air in the hallway crackled as Caleb let out an angry growl. He then positioned himself by the door. His frame was suddenly rigid; he resembled a granite sentinel. Detective O'Neil lifted his head from his phone. His expression remained a blank slate.

Jolie fumbled in her coat pocket. The metallic jingle of her keys was a small, almost frantic sound. Her fingers brushed against worn fabric, a crumpled receipt, then finally, the metal. She was suddenly filled with dread at him seeing the state of her apartment. The precariously balanced tower of unread books on her nightstand. The scattered shoes by the door that never quite made it into the closet. The thought struck her as odd. He had been here before, but suddenly what he thought of her mattered. She hated the realization and illogically blamed Mikhail and Wyn for cracking open her defenses.

"It's getting pretty late," Jolie murmured. Her voice was a little breathy. She turned to Danny. He stood a few feet away. His arms were crossed; a faint smile played on his lips.

The corners of her mouth, despite her best efforts, were already starting to lift. "Have you been out here long?" she managed.

"Not long," he replied. His voice was soft. "I tried waiting for you at the club after your set, but you left rather quickly." Danny chuckled; it sent shivers down Jolie's spine. "As for the late hour, hopefully I'm not bothering you. This case requires later hours than normal." He shifted his weight as he let his eyes linger on her. "Plus, I have a feeling you're a night owl."

Jolie laughed. She felt the tension in her shoulders ease. "I like to make a quick exit and avoid my adoring fans." She opened the door and gestured for Danny to follow her inside. She quickly made her way to the kitchen.

"I hate to tell you this, Detective, but there's nothing to report from the club," Jolie said. She pulled out a plate and filled it with chow mein for Caleb.

"Are you sure about that?" Danny leaned against the counter. His arms folded over his chest. Jolie took him in. She noted how good he looked in his fitted suit. The fabric hugged his muscles in all the right places.

A wave of exhaustion washed over Jolie as she set Caleb's plate on the floor. Lethargic, she leaned against the counter. She watched Caleb gobble his food with the ferocious hunger of a starved animal. Her mind, however, was far from the mundane task of feeding her pet. It churned with conflicting possibilities. Confiding in Danny, despite the growing connection she felt to him, felt impossible.

"Aside from Rori's almost obsessive attention to detail. She's practically micromanaging everything, and the added extra security. Yes, I'm sure," she replied. Her voice was tight.

Danny's face hardened. The ease of his demeanor was replaced by seriousness. "Maybe they're expecting more trouble," he said. His gaze was intense.

Jolie's eyebrow shot up. A flicker of intrigue filled her eyes. "What do you mean?" The cryptic warning drew her attention.

He shrugged. A noncommittal gesture offered no further explanation. The casual mention of "more trouble" sent a jolt of fear through her. She'd desperately hoped this case had no connection to Rori and Boden. She had finally begun to feel a sense of home at The Black Cat House. The idea that they were capable of such unspeakable acts was almost unbearable.

"I'll keep an eye on things at the club," she promised. She hoped her words would reassure Danny. "And I'll let you know if I find anything suspicious." Jolie turned to clean up Caleb's empty plate. "I can't help but wonder why you keep making house calls?"

Ignoring her question, Danny took a step closer to Jolie. His presence was almost overwhelming. "Do you mind if I have a glass of water?" he asked politely. His voice was low and smooth. Jolie took in his intoxicating scent and let it overwhelm her good sense. She could hear the steady thumping of his heartbeat. It was almost tempting enough to make her lose control; it had been too long since she had last eaten. Danny's proximity was making it increasingly difficult for her to resist the urge.

As Jolie filled a glass of water from the tap, Danny continued speaking. "I'm not exactly sure why I came by either. I was heading home and found myself here." His voice wavered slightly during his nonanswer. He took another step toward Jolie. "We've been checking employment records. But it seems that burlesque clubs aren't exactly known for their thorough record-keeping," he explained with a hint of frustration.

Jolie shook her head at his statement. "It's all part of the act. Keeping our day jobs separate from our 'naked jobs,'" she joked. Her smile widened. For a moment, she forgot about the danger that lurked outside and the weight of responsibility that rested on her shoulders. In that moment, it was just her and Danny.

Danny reached for the water glass. His fingers grazed the back of her hand. The touch was featherlight, but charged; it sent a surprising wave of heat prickling up her arm.

His presence consumed her. A subtle pressure built against her upper lip. A familiar ache that she fought to keep in check. Her gaze drifted. Her eyes traced the line of his jaw and the subtle rise and fall of his chest beneath the crisp fabric of his shirt. Images, vivid and unwelcome, flashed through her mind. She imagined the taut strength of his biceps beneath her touch. The smooth expanse of his skin that she could sink her teeth into. Her fingers tingled; they craved that forbidden contact.

She took an involuntary step closer. The world narrowed to his intoxicating proximity. A thick fog of raw desire blurred the edges of her composure. His voice was a sudden, sharp counterpoint to her own internal chaos.

"Jolie? Hey, you alright?"

The question ripped through the haze. She instinctively brought a hand to her mouth. Her fingertips pressed against the sensitive flesh. She was terrified by the possibility that her control had finally faltered. That the telltale points of her fangs had betrayed her craving.

"Yes, sorry. It's been a long few days," she replied. She tried to compose herself. Danny seemed oblivious to her moment of weakness.

"Let me take you to dinner tomorrow, as a thank you," he offered. He took another step closer to her.

Jolie's mind raced. She was torn between her primal desires and her moral code. "No, no, thank you. You don't have to do that," she said. She tried to resist the pull toward him.

"I want to," Danny insisted. His eyes fixed unwaveringly on hers. "Or we could order in. My treat." He boldly placed his hands on her hips. His gaze was intense and purposeful.

A strangled gasp escaped Jolie's lips; realization slammed into her like a physical blow. Her seductive glamour had ensnared Danny. She hadn't meant for this to happen. His eyes were now clouded with a possessiveness that chilled her to the bone. He advanced. His body was a warm, encroaching presence. His hands found purchase on her back. She could feel the heat radiating from him. The strength she'd sensed in him was now a tangible force pressing against her. The seductive pull nearly won. The thought of surrendering, of indulging in the intoxicating pleasure, flickered tantalizingly close. But she couldn't. With a surge of willpower, she pushed him away. A forceful shove sent him stumbling back. It was more than just a physical rejection. It was a mental wall she raised. A determined severance of the spell she'd unwittingly cast. She couldn't manipulate him. She was better than that. She had to be.

Jolie lowered her voice into a deep, gravelly tone. She channeled all her energy into her words. She locked eyes with Danny; her gaze was intense and commanding. "You're exhausted. It's time for you to go home and get some rest."

Danny stopped in his tracks. His hand fell away from her waist. A perplexed expression crept across his features. "I am tired," he repeated. His voice carried a hint of confusion.

"Yes, very tired. You need to go home and sleep," Jolie reaffirmed.

"I should go home," Danny muttered. His eyes darted around the kitchen as he stumbled backward. He placed a hand on his head. He looked as though he might collapse at any moment. "I don't feel too great."

Jolie placed a comforting hand on his shoulder as she guided him toward the door. "It's alright. There's nothing to worry about. You're just tired. Tomorrow, you'll wake up feeling better. Tonight will just be a distant memory." With a gentle push, she ushered him out the door. "Goodnight, Detective."

"Goodnight," Danny mumbled. His steps were slow and unsteady as he made his way down the hallway. Jolie waited until she could no longer hear his footsteps before closing the door and leaning against it.

"That was a close one, Caleb." Caleb stared at her and tilted his head. He let out a low snort. Jolie pouted at his reaction. "Don't laugh at me. That could have ended badly." Caleb seemed to shrug. Then he turned his attention to the leftover Chinese food on the counter. Jolie shot him an exasperated look. "Really, that's all you can think about? Food?"

The pre-dawn light, a pale wash on the horizon, did little to soothe Jolie's restless mind. Danny's image burned behind her eyelids. The sharp angles of his jaw. The muscles flexing beneath his shirt, the memory of their encounter. The electric jolt that had passed between them. It played on repeat. Had it been real, that undeniable spark? Or a figment of her wishful thinking?

As the sun edged closer, her dreams took a darker turn. They ventured into forbidden territory. She inhaled deeply. His scent filled her senses; she could almost taste the lingering hint of his sweat. The image of his hands became overwhelmingly vivid. She saw them tracing the curve of her shoulder. The delicate skin of her neck. The strands of her hair. She imagined the pressure of his lips. They were featherlight at first. They brushed along the bridge of her nose.

"Danny," she whispered. Her body throbbed with a yearning that transcended mere desire. His lips found hers, and a searing kiss ignited a fire. His hands began to explore her. They awakened a symphony of sensations. Her back arched involuntarily as his fingers danced across her stomach. They sent a wave of heat flooding through her. A low, guttural moan escaped her lips. His touch ignited every nerve ending. A rhythmic pulse built to an unbearable crescendo. She buried her face in the warm hollow of his neck. Her tongue finally tasted the subtle saltiness of his skin. She surrendered to the utterly intoxicating feeling.

Then, the instincts she had fought so hard to suppress surged to the surface. Her fangs elongated with terrifying swiftness. The overwhelming urge consumed her. She bit down. The sharp points pierced his skin. The warm rush of his blood flooded her senses, and the moment of ecstasy curdled into horror. She felt his heartbeat falter. She tried to pull away or to turn her head, but her body was locked in a gruesome embrace. Her vampire nature asserted itself with brutal efficiency. She was killing him. She drained the life out of his body. She couldn't stop. Panic clawed at her throat. Frantic attempts to push away met with her own immovable strength. The warmth under her lips faded; it was replaced by the chill of death. As the life leached from him, a terrifying realization washed over her. She had succumbed to her darkest impulses. Her lover now became the victim of her monstrous hunger.

Jolie bolted upright in bed. Her body trembled. She risked a glance at Caleb. His peaceful slumber was unbroken. Thank goddess she hadn't disturbed him with her terrifying dream. But even as she eased back onto the pillows, there was a chilling residue of guilt and fear.

Chapter Fourteen

Silk and Shadow

The rain beat a rhythm on the double doors leading to the balcony. Exhaustion clung to Jolie and left her irritable. She stared out the door. The sheets of water obscured the city beyond.

"Caleb," she whispered. Her voice was groggy with sleep as she splashed cold water onto her face. The image of pain still clung to the edges of her mind. The lingering memory of vivid, disturbing dreams remained.

Caleb grunted in acknowledgment as he devoured some leftover Chinese food. "I have a bad feeling about The Black Cat House," she said as he lifted his head between mouthfuls. She met Caleb's gaze and saw the worry in his soft amber eyes.

Each footfall on the pavement echoed in her ears. Even the cool night air, which usually brought calm, offered nothing. It did little to lessen the premonition of something dreadful looming like a storm cloud on the horizon. She was late, hopelessly late, yet her feet moved with leaden slowness.

When she finally reached the alley entrance, she was surprised to find it shut and locked. She banged on the door a few times, hoping someone would hear her and let her in. But no one came. Perturbed, she made her way around the block to the front of the building. She pushed through the small crowd gathered at the main entrance. To her surprise, The Black Cat House was almost empty. The theater felt cavernous and echoed with the faint hum of the ventilation system. Jolie turned to the group huddled at the bar. Lina had her arms draped possessively around two waitresses. Mikhail leaned close and whispered to them across the bar. The security guards stood like statues at strategic points around the perimeter. Their impassive faces betrayed nothing.

A prickle of unease crawled up Jolie's spine. Her attention was drawn to the muffled voices emanating from the back. It was coming from the dancers' dressing room. She tilted her head and strained to decipher the words, but only snatches of hushed tones reached her. She felt the dread growing. Each step toward the bar felt heavy.

"Jolie, where have you been?" Lina's voice was harsh and accusatory. It surprised Jolie. She and Lina had never been close, but her outright hostility caught Jolie off guard.

"I overslept," Jolie replied, feeling defensive. But before she could say anything else, Lina cut her off.

"Overslept? It's 6 p.m.!" Lina snapped. Her tone dripped with contempt.

Jolie's anxiety twisted into fear as she realized that something was wrong at The Black Cat House.

Mikhail poured shots for the group, a look of concern etched on his face. "There was an accident," he said. His voice was thick and heavy.

"Accident? Don't you mean murder?" Lina snarled as she tucked one of the other waitresses more tightly under her arm. Jolie struggled to remember the name of the waitress, but it finally came to her. Tam. She was only waitressing until she could get a slot on stage, but with her unique style, burgundy hair, and acrobatic ability, she would surely be a crowd favorite once Rori gave her a chance. Maddy sat off to the side of the bar, as far away from the others as she could get. She held a glass of whiskey tightly. The heat of her hands melted the ice into the liquor. She kept her eyes down. Her blonde hair was still in its curlers, waiting for her to set it into finger waves.

Jolie surveyed the other sobbing figure under Lina's other arm, Penelope. The Black Cat House's wannabe goth part-time waitress. Her tight, dark clothing and disheveled, short purple hair made her stand out. "Poor Penelope found her in the back bathroom." Tam's voice and hands were shaking as she spoke. Her drink sloshed all over the bar before she could even take a sip. Mikhail pushed a second glass toward her.

"Have another shot, Tam," he said.

Jolie's mind raced as she tried to figure out who Penelope had found in the bathroom. Could it be Wyn? Or worse, could it be Rori?

"Wait, found who?" Jolie asked. Her voice trembled.

Lina stepped in to fill in the details. "Penelope found Candice in the back bathroom. Just like the guy from last week," she said. Her voice was laced with sadness. Tam's hands were shaking so badly that she lost half of her drink to the bar. Mikhail quickly retrieved a pint glass and poured another shot, hoping the large glass would help the alcohol make it into her mouth instead of on the bar.

"She wasn't even supposed to work tonight. Why was she here?" Tam asked. Her voice cracked.

Lina let out a sigh. "She worked last night, so it must have happened then," she said, trying to make sense of the situation. Penelope lifted her head. Her eyes were red and bloodshot from crying. Her black makeup was smudged and streaked down her face. It settled into every fine line.

"You mean she was here all day like that? Alone?" she asked. Her voice trembled with shock and sadness.

Lina pulled Penelope closer, trying to comfort her. "It's okay, love. She didn't know she was alone," she said, her voice filled with compassion. The group stood in silence. Each lost in their own thoughts and emotions. The once bustling club now felt heavy and somber.

The tequila burned a fiery trail down Jolie's throat. The harshness was a welcome distraction from the tremor in her hand as she signaled Mikhail. She needed another shot.

Last night's events played on a loop behind her eyes. The unsettling feeling clung to her. She pushed a stray strand of hair behind her ear. Her gaze swept over the huddled knot of faces at the bar. "Anyone see Candice after closing last night?" she asked. Her voice was tight. "Was she with . . . anyone unusual?"

Mikhail simply shrugged. "I didn't see her with anyone at all."

Lina raised an eyebrow and kept her arms tightly wrapped around the girls. "You were one of the first to leave. How would you know?"

Mikhail's shrug was nonchalant, but Jolie could sense there was more to his answer. "She wasn't spending much time with anyone that I saw, is all I meant." Jolie let her eyes wander over his face, searching for any hint of what was putting her on edge. He was leaving something out. She was sure of it. Unfortunately, she didn't know what.

Jolie lost track of the conversation as Rori and Boden walked out from the back. They flanked Detective O'Neil. Trailing behind them was Charles, who had a deep frown pulling at his features. It was obvious how mad he was, but he stayed silent as the others talked. The murmur of their approach faded as Jolie struggled to decipher Boden's words. Mikhail and

Lina's argument was anything but muted. It pulled her attention from Boden's conversation with a rising crescendo of harsh words and sharp intakes of breath. Each syllable was an agonizing shard of glass against her eardrums. Lingering frustration gnawed at her. The subtle nuances of vampire control, so effortlessly mastered by her Maker, still eluded her.

She pivoted, catching the tail end of Mikhail's words. His voice was low and laced with chilling amusement. "Naive. She should have been more careful about whom she trusted." Mikhail's shrug was infuriating. "After one murder already, no one should have been here alone. You can't deny that."

Jolie felt a surge of anger rise within her. She couldn't believe Mikhail was trying to shift the blame onto the victim of a brutal murder. But before she could say anything, Detective O'Neil's voice cut through the tension. "I understand your concerns, but we need to focus on finding the killer," he said. His tone was firm and commanding. "We can't afford to waste time pointing fingers. Now, does anyone have any information that could help us?"

Jolie tried to replay every detail of the previous night in search of a missed clue, but her focus kept drifting toward Danny. He moved among the others, asking questions in low tones, but never once did his eyes meet hers. It wasn't by chance. He was deliberately avoiding her. A flicker of irritation stirred in Jolie as she looked for an opening to draw his attention. But before she could make a move, he hastily concluded his conversation and turned to leave.

Boden's hand rested lightly on Detective O'Neil's shoulder as he guided him toward the exit, a picture of polite dismissal. Jolie yearned for a single backward glance, a flicker of recognition in his eyes. However, Danny didn't turn to look at her. The sting of his indifference cut so deep she expected to start bleeding. Had he remembered? How much of last night's mishap had he retained? Guilt, sharp and bitter, pricked at her conscience.

Jolie followed Danny's retreating figure. Boden closed the heavy oak door behind him. The metallic sound of the deadbolt sliding home echoed in the quiet. She turned and found Mikhail leaning against the bar. A knowing half-grin stretched his lips. Jolie could practically feel him dissecting her, his silent assessment more potent than any spoken word. Mikhail's grin widened with a subtle tilt of his head.

"About time you got here. We already sent the rest of the dancers home," Rori's voice, sharp as a stiletto, pulled Jolie from her thoughts.

Jolie plastered on a grimace. "Overslept," she mumbled.

Rori's skeptical gaze lingered. "Overslept, huh? Wouldn't that have something to do with a certain . . . detective?" Rori's words were almost as pointed as her glare. There was a warning in her tone. "You need to be more careful."

Jolie looked between Rori and Mikhail. He was drinking in every word. Heat flooded her cheeks. She looked down, focusing intently on the swirling patterns on the bar top. A sigh escaped her lips, a silent plea for a change of subject. "What happened last night?" she asked.

Rori whipped her long, dark hair over her shoulder as she turned back to Jolie. "Just give me a minute, and I'll fill you in." Rori had caught sight of Boden approaching with two of his security guards in tow. "Make sure Tam and Penelope get home safely," she instructed the guards.

The door slammed shut behind the retreating waitresses. Rori's hand snaked behind the bar. Her fingers closed around a whiskey bottle. "Mikhail, you're free to go." Her voice was clipped. The dismissal was sharp enough to cut the air. Mikhail's scowl deepened as he gathered his black leather jacket. He brushed past Jolie on his way out. When his eyes met hers, the warmth was gone. Instead, there was a darkness that sent warning bells ringing.

Only Boden, Rori, Jolie, and Lina remained. They exchanged glances, a silent understanding passing between them. They moved to a small table tucked away in a shadowy corner. Their movements were slow and quiet, each waiting for the final sound of Mikhail leaving before relaxing.

Rori rubbed her temples. A long, shuddering sigh escaped her lips, the sound heavy with frustration. Her voice, when it finally came, was tight with barely contained fury. "That . . . man," she spat the word out, "he's useless, Boden. Do you have any idea what he was saying about Candice? I need him gone. For good."

Boden's jaw tightened with irritation. "I can't just kick him to the curb for being a jerk, Rori," he said. His voice was low as he draped a reassuring arm around her shoulders. "But don't worry. I'll put out feelers for some fresh bartenders. We'll get this sorted."

Rori nodded. "Thank you," she said, leaning into Boden's embrace.

Lina pushed a dark curl behind her ear and turned the conversation back to Candice. "We weren't even five minutes into prep when Penelope found her," she said. Her voice was filled with sadness.

Rori let out another sigh. "I had sent her back to clean up the area for the dancers, and then we heard her scream," she explained. Her tone was heavy with guilt. "Candice was in the same state as the guy from last week. No wounds, no struggle, but very dead. And that blue, silvery white color . . ." The four of them fell into silence, each lost in their own thoughts and emotions.

The energy around them felt brittle and cold. Jolie's throat tightened. "Last night?" she finally managed.

Boden's gaze was bleak. His shoulders slumped with a weariness that mirrored her own. He didn't meet her eyes. His stare was fixed on some unseen point beyond her shoulder. "Had to be," he murmured. His voice was rough. "No reason for her to be here today. She must have worked late."

The image of Candice, alone in the empty bar, sent a chill wrapping around Jolie's spine. Why? The question gnawed at her. She couldn't picture Candice staying late voluntarily. Who would have asked her? Her eyes darted around the room, trying to conjure the faces of those who had been there the night before. But they were indistinct, offering no answers.

The confusion settled deep in her bones. She looked from Boden to Rori. Their faces were blank, offering no comfort, no clue. The silence stretched. Rori finally spoke up. Her voice dripped with disdain. "You need to be more careful about who you hire."

Boden bristled at the accusation. "You're too judgmental. We can't discriminate."

Rori's eyes narrowed. "Maybe so, but I wouldn't have hired him. He is too dangerous."

Boden glared at his wife. "Oh, and Wyn isn't?"

Jolie's confusion only grew. She could understand why Mikhail was dangerous. He had a way of creating drama. But Wyn was different. Flirtatious, yes; dangerous, no. She turned to Lina, hoping for some insight. Lina slumped in her chair, her eyes cast down.

Jolie's brow furrowed. A deep crease etched itself between her eyes. The air was filled with unspoken things. Her instincts warred within her. She could trust them. She could feel that in her bones, but they were hiding things from her. The scent of night winds and deep forests rolled off Boden and Rori, but it was tainted with fear. She could smell it on their skin. Lina's heartbeat raced in her chest, fluttering like a panicked bird. The scent of her fear almost drowned out the hints of fresh grass and sunlit meadows. Jolie found no answers there.

Boden's sigh was heavy. He slammed his empty water bottle onto the table. The plastic crushed underneath his hand. He turned to Rori. "You have to tell her," he said. His voice was firm.

Rori's response was indifferent, a flick of her wrist that dismissed not only Boden, but Jolie as well. Boden pushed himself up, and a groan escaped his lips as he stretched. The tautness of his muscles was visible beneath his shirt. "Fine," he said. The words were laced with weary resignation. He started for the door. His shoulders slumped in defeat. The tension in the room crackled with the unspoken failures of the night. "Let's go," he muttered, more to himself than to Rori. "I'm starving, and that kitchen's closed."

Rori let out a tired yawn. Her eyes drooped with exhaustion. "You're thinking about food now?" she said, shaking her head in disbelief. "We just had a traumatic event happen, and all you can think about is your stomach?"

Boden's exasperation was evident as he turned to face Rori. "I didn't even get to eat!" he exclaimed, throwing his hands up in the air. Boden turned toward Jolie. "We're staying closed tomorrow, so you have the day off. Just one day, though," he added with a pointed look.

Lina, who had been quietly observing the exchange, stood up and stretched her arms above her head. "Do you still want me to come in tomorrow?" she asked.

Rori let out another yawn. "Please, if you can. I could use the help," she replied. Her eyes pleaded. "Let me know when you're ready, and I'll come let you in."

The three women stood on the sidewalk as Boden locked the doors. Rori and Lina made plans to meet the next day, but Jolie barely listened. Her mind was consumed with thoughts of Candice. She had never paid much attention to her, or any waitresses at the club, for that matter. But now she questioned whether she could have done something to prevent this tragedy. Lost in her thoughts, Jolie barely registered Boden's voice calling her name.

"Jolie," he said again, this time with more urgency. "Are you going to be okay? Do you need a ride?"

Jolie snapped out of her daze. Her eyes met Boden's concerned gaze.

"No, I'll be fine," she replied, forcing a smile. "I'll just walk home."

Lina linked her arm with Jolie's. "My car is in your direction. I'll walk with you," she offered. She gave Jolie a reassuring smile. "She'll protect me," she added, tilting her head toward Jolie. As they walked toward Lina's car, she couldn't shake off the feeling of guilt and helplessness that consumed her.

Once they were around the corner, Lina dropped her arm from Jolie's and silently increased the space between them. Her movements were graceful as she glided away, taking the scent of clover with her. Jolie had always admired her, despite the coldness she felt from Lina. This was more like the Lina she had known these past few months. She was always nonchalant and distant, never letting anyone get too close.

"What are you working on for Rori tomorrow?" Jolie began, leaning closer. She watched Lina meticulously brush a nonexistent crumb with a fingertip. Her eyes were glued to the sleeve of her jacket.

Lina mumbled, "Just tidying up." The words were flat, devoid of any inflection.

An opportunity. She could offer to help, blend in, investigate. She brushed a casual hand against Lina's arm, light but insistent.

"Let me give you a hand," Jolie offered. Her smile was carefully controlled and innocent. "Wouldn't want you to be stuck there all day."

Lina let out a cold laugh. Her contempt was evident in her normally bell-like voice. "No, you can't help," she said, sarcasm wrapping around every word.

Jolie stopped walking and turned to face Lina. The moonlight reflected off her dark skin, giving her an ethereal glow. Her piercing gray eyes seemed to crackle with electricity.

"Why not?" Jolie's voice snapped the air between them.

Lina's laughter, a light chime only moments before, now deepened. Jolie could almost taste the bitterness of exclusion.

"Wow, Rori was right. You really don't know," she said, shaking her head. She let out a sigh and twisted her mouth before speaking again. "I get that you mean well, but you can't help. You just can't."

Jolie's jaw tightened, the muscles bunching visibly beneath her skin. "What are you not telling me?" Simmering resentment rose in Jolie's throat, as sour as bile.

Lina's hand gestured vaguely toward a beat-up Honda Civic. Its paint was chipped and faded. "My car's over there. See you in a few days," she said. Her voice was tight, and she avoided looking at Jolie.

Jolie watched Lina retreat. A knot tightened in her stomach. "Lina, wait!" she called. Her voice was sharper than she intended. "Stop hinting at things. I deserve an explanation!"

Lina halted. Her shoulders slumped. She rubbed a hand across her eyes. The gesture revealed a weariness that went beyond simple fatigue. "Look, I'm sorry," she mumbled. "I'm doing a spiritual cleansing, and your energy is just . . . too much. It'd completely mess it up."

Jolie stared. Her annoyance morphed into bewildered confusion. A spiritual cleansing? Her energy? The words felt alien, a language she didn't understand. Before she could formulate a question, Lina climbed into the Civic and locked the door.

The engine sputtered to life, then roared. The sound was swallowed by distance as Lina sped away. Jolie remained there with her arms crossed tightly against her chest. Her irritation warred with unease. A thousand unanswered questions swirled in her mind. She needed answers, and soon. But for now, she was left alone with the lingering scent of exhaust fumes and the unsettling silence of unanswered questions.

Chapter Fifteen

After Last Call

Jolie trudged along the dimly lit streets. Her hands were buried deep in her coat pockets, her lips pressed into a tight line. She could not shake the feeling that something was off. Everyone around her seemed to know something she did not. But what that something was, she could not quite put her finger on. A rock skipped across the pavement. The sound barely registered in Jolie's preoccupied mind. Then another rock, closer this time. Every hair on her arms prickled. The scent of damp concrete and nearby dumpsters sharpened. The subtle shift in air pressure was a warning. Her hunter senses flared; she was ready.

The footsteps were heavy. They matched her own pace perfectly. She could hear the faint sound of a knife being rolled over in someone's hand and the quickening of their breath. Jolie's muscles tensed. She slowed her pace. The man still followed her. She could easily outrun him, but something inside her yearned for confrontation. She turned into the next alley. Her eyes flashed with determination as she faced her pursuer. He turned the corner. His knife glinted in the moonlight. Jolie's eyes narrowed as she focused on her prey. He was young, and his sandy-blond hair was disheveled. His brown eyes filled with dangerous determination. She could sense the excitement radiating from him, the thrill of the hunt. But she was not afraid.

"Oy!" he called out. His voice was rough and menacing. "Give me your bag."

Jolie's lips curled into a sly smile. "No," she replied confidently. Her voice was laced with defiance. He took a few steps closer. His sneer grew more pronounced.

"Listen, bitch," he spat. "I ain't playing. Hand it over!" She could see the hunger in his eyes. But she felt no sympathy for him. He knew what he was doing, and he deserved whatever was coming to him. Without hesitation, Jolie sprang toward him. In a flash, she had him pinned against the cold brick wall of the alley. The knife clattered to the ground as she pressed her forearm against his neck, cutting off his air supply. He struggled against her. Anger and fear were evident in his movements.

"Let go, bitch!" he choked out as she continued to press firmly into his neck. His hands clawed uselessly at her arm.

Jolie did not yield. She could feel his pulse racing beneath her grip. She reveled in the power she held over him. She leaned in closer. Her face was only inches from his. She could smell the familiar scent of fear rising from him. Her Maker had taught her that fear made the blood sweeter. In that moment, as she held her prey in her grasp, Jolie knew that she was about to feast on the most delicious blood she had ever tasted.

Her lips curled into a smirk. They revealed the sharp, menacing fangs hidden behind her smile. The moonlight lit her face, casting the hollows into deeper shadow. She extended her fangs and watched his horror as they glinted in the light. She felt his body begin to shake as she leaned in. She was transfixed by the pulsing artery in his neck. She snarled and then her teeth pierced his skin. He gasped in pain. His body struggled against her hold. She held on tight. The sweetness of his agony flowed into her mouth and intoxicated her senses. She could feel his heartbeat pounding against her lips. She lost herself in the moment and forgot everything else around her.

Harsh barking and growling pierced through the air, interrupting Jolie's blissful trance. She turned. Her fangs were still bared. She hissed a warning at the source of the disturbance. It was Caleb. He lowered his head and bared his own teeth. A low growl rumbled in his chest as he mirrored her warning. Jolie was pulled back into the present by the saddened look in his eyes. She could see his disappointment, and she felt her own bubbling up inside her. She had lost control. Now she was paying the price for it. She slowly retracted her fangs and turned back to the trembling boy in her arms. Caleb sat down. He kept a watchful eye on the situation. The boy did not deserve death for his mistakes. She felt disgusted with herself and let out a heavy sigh.

Jolie looked into the boy's eyes. She tried to summon the strength of her glamour. "Relax," she said softly. "Everything is going to be okay." As she spoke, she felt his body relax and his pulse slow down. She leaned in and gently licked the wound on his neck. She used her healing powers to speed up the process. Then she met his gaze again. "You're tired," she whispered. "Very tired. You're going to go home and fall asleep. When you wake up tomorrow, you'll realize it was all just a horrible dream. One that will make you want to turn your life around. You'll get a real job and dedicate your free time to charity."

Caleb snorted behind her. He was clearly amused by her suggestion. But the boy in her arms smiled lovingly at her, his eyes filled with gratitude. "I'll get a job," he promised. His voice was filled with determination. Jolie nodded. She released the boy and watched as he stumbled away. Jolie emerged from the alley with her shoulders slumped; disgust turned the taste of blood on her tongue to ash. She glanced back at Caleb. His usually proud posture wilted. His tail, usually held high, was tucked shamefully between his legs.

She wiped her mouth with the back of her hand. The gesture was clumsy. "So," she began. Her voice was a low rasp. "You thought the charity part was a bit much?"

Caleb tilted his head. His amber eyes were clouded with a deep, unsettling concern. He did not meet her gaze. Instead, he began to walk away. Each step was slow and deliberate. His powerful frame radiated hurt.

A sharp pang of regret, raw and visceral, pierced Jolie. "Caleb!" she called. Her voice cracked. "Wait." An apology felt inadequate. It was a pathetic attempt to stem the bleeding wound she had inflicted on their fragile trust.

She hurried after him. "I know, I know it was wrong," she confessed, her voice full of genuine remorse. "But he tried to mug me!" She gestured wildly. Her explanation was clumsy and unconvincing, even to her own ears. "I . . . I just . . . reacted. I'm glad you were there. Truly. You stopped me from . . . from doing something terrible."

Caleb stopped and trotted back to her. He nuzzled his head against her leg and licked her hand. It was a silent forgiveness for her impulsive behavior. Jolie beamed at the gesture.

Caleb's eyes seemed to say that this was her only second chance. A warning to be more careful in the future. Jolie knelt and wrapped her arms around the big dog's neck. "Thank you," she whispered. Her voice was filled with gratitude. "Can I tell you about my day now?" she asked.

Caleb seemed to nod in understanding. Jolie continued to talk to him as they made their way back to her apartment. She shared all the details of the second murder at the club, as well as the secrets she felt everyone was keeping from her. Once they reached her apartment, Jolie could not wait to soak in a hot bath and relax her tense muscles. She poured in some lavender-scented bubbles and sank into the tub. She closed her eyes and let the warm water soothe her.

"I wasn't sure I believed the whole succubus thing," she admitted. Her voice was low and uncertain. "Which is silly. I mean, I know vampires are real, and I guess you're real too."

Caleb froze mid-bite. Half a slice of pizza hung from his large jaw. He let out a low, rumbling growl.

"Sorry," she mumbled. "You know what I mean."

The sigh that escaped her lips was heavy. She pulled the stopper from the drain with a tug of her toe. The swirling vortex was a visual representation of her internal struggle. "I know I'm clueless," she admitted as she stepped from the steaming water. "But it's always been them and us. Humans and vampires. Now it's everything. It's just . . . overwhelming."

She reached for her towel. It was a thick, marshmallow-soft cloud of fluffy white. She began to rub it vigorously against her skin. The movement was almost frantic, a desperate attempt to rub away the confusion clinging to her like lingering steam. "Maybe we should visit our friend Seb tomorrow," she suggested, looking for a welcome distraction.

Caleb's tail gave an approving thump against the floor as he watched Jolie slip into her sweats and T-shirt. "I hope you remember the way there because I sure don't," she joked. Caleb playfully nipped at her hand as Jolie followed him out of the bathroom. She prepared herself to explore a world she never knew existed.

CHAPTER SIXTEEN

Intermission

With only a few hours of daylight left, Jolie and Caleb ventured toward Seb's store. The late hour allowed Jolie to abandon the protective scarf that she usually wrapped around her face and neck. Caleb, in his usual dog-like manner, could not contain his excitement. He sniffed every tree and building along the way. He then proudly marked his territory by peeing on anything he deemed worthy of his ownership. Jolie, on the other hand, remained more cautious and aware of her surroundings. Even with the fresh blood she had consumed the night before, her energy had started to wane. She longed to reach Seb's store and take refuge in the musty stacks of books.

The bell above the door jingled as Jolie pushed inside. The familiar scent of aged paper and leather cooled her frayed nerves. Her fingers itched to trace the spines of the towering bookshelves and to dive into the pages. She pictured herself lost amongst them, the weight of the world fading as she succumbed to the stories. But Seb's voice echoed in her mind. "No browsing." She stood rigidly. Her hands clasped tightly. The promise of untold adventures was just out of reach.

Seb's warm smile greeted them as he entered the room. "Ah, if it isn't my wayward vampire and her trusty spirit dog. Please, come and have a seat." He led them to the same sitting room as before. Only this time it was immaculate. The dust had been wiped away. The furniture had been repaired. The tables had been polished, but the faint scent of burning herbs still lingered in the air.

Seb gracefully entered the room, balancing a tray of steaming tea and a mug of warm blood. All were accompanied by a delectable ring of coffee cake that made Caleb's tail wag like an eager puppy. Seb softly tittered at the sight of Caleb eagerly awaiting his treat. "Your barghest still has quite an appetite, doesn't he?" Seb chuckled. His eyes twinkled with fondness.

Jolie laughed in agreement. She stroked Caleb's sleek fur. "Yes, he does. I'm starting to worry about him getting too chubby."

"Well, he'll slow down once he's done filling out," Seb reassured her. He cut a generous slice of cake and placed it on the floor for Caleb to enjoy.

As Jolie took in the cozy scene, she was amazed by the quick transformation of the room. "The place looks incredible. Did you hire someone?"

Seb looked up with a puzzled expression. "Hire someone? To do what?"

Jolie's cheeks flushed with embarrassment. She worried that she might have come across as rude. "To clean. The place looks spotless."

"Oh, that," Seb chuckled. He waved her concerns away. "No, it's just the pixies."

Jolie could not stifle the laughter that bubbled up at the sheer absurdity of Seb's words. "Pixies? You're joking, right?"

The clink of Seb's spoon against his teacup punctuated the silence. "Did you read any of the books I gave you?" he asked.

He waited. The steam from his Earl Grey curled around his face as Jolie fidgeted. Guilt twisted in her stomach. Her gaze darted away from him. "I . . . uh . . . skimmed the vampire one and read a bit of the encyclopedia," she admitted, her voice low.

Seb's sigh was a long, drawn-out exhalation heavy with unspoken disappointment. He steepled his fingers. "The encyclopedia, Jolie. The important one is the encyclopedia."

Her cheeks burned. She felt as though he could see the unread pages mocking her from across the city. A mumbled apology barely escaped her lips.

He took another slow sip; the liquid was amber in the dim light. Leaning back in his chair, he began to weave a story of the strange world of pixies. Seb's explanation was as captivating as it was bizarre. Creatures so shy they were almost myth, yet somehow capable of ingraining themselves into the very fabric of a house, if only coaxed by simple tributes of milk, honey, and bread. In return, they would maintain the household. Their magic ensured that not a speck of dust remained. It was an oddly whimsical contrast to the darker, blood-soaked reality Jolie had lived in.

She marveled at the thought. When she was still human, tidiness had never been her strength. Her mother's sharp words about her cluttered room still echoed faintly in her memory. If only she had known then about pixies, how different things might have been. A wry smile tugged at the corner of her lips as she imagined the little creatures sweeping through her chaotic life.

"That's incredible," she said. A hint of longing filled her voice.

His voice dropped; it became a conspiratorial murmur that drew her in. He described faerie courts hidden in moonlit glades. Their ancient rivalries were as complex and deadly as any human war. Sprites, he said, flitted between worlds, their wings barely visible. Brownies were the shadowy guardians of the forest; they lived in quiet harmony with the ancient trees.

The sheer complexity of it all made her head spin. She listened and tried to process the convoluted web of alliances and enemies until, finally, she threw up her hands in disbelief.

"Oh my god, you've got to be kidding me!" she blurted. Her voice was breathless with astonishment.

Seb's frown deepened at her interruption. "Once again, you should have read the encyclopedia. May I continue?" he asked.

Jolie nodded eagerly and guiltily lifted her cup to her lips. The drink, though warm, lacked the vibrant satisfaction of her recent feeding. She refocused and forced herself to pay attention to Seb's words.

Each species possessed a complex social structure. A government of its own, often at odds with its neighbors. Their personalities were as unpredictable and passionate as any human's.

Seb took a bite of his cake. He glanced over at Caleb and tossed him a playful wink as he took another bite of cake. "So, what have you discovered about your murder?" he asked.

Jolie frowned, her brow furrowed in thought. "Well, there was another murder at the club. But as for your succubus theory, I have no idea how to even begin figuring out if anyone at the club is a succubus."

Seb sighed and rubbed his temples. He opened his mouth to speak, but was quickly interrupted by Jolie. "I know! I should have read the encyclopedia," she blurted out.

Seb could not resist casting an exasperated glance skyward. "If you knew that, then why didn't you just read it?" he asked. He turned to Caleb. "Is she always this difficult?"

Jolie sank back into the worn chair. A frustrated sigh escaped her lips; her fingers traced the rim of a half-empty mug. The guilt was a heavier burden than any physical hunger. The ancient vampires possessed self-control she could only dream of. Stoic, disciplined creatures rooted in their ancestral lairs. They were statues while she was a storm, messy and unpredictable. But maybe that could be her strength. The key to a different kind of power.

Seb's voice, though gentle, barely reached her over the discord of her own thoughts. His bushy eyebrows twitched in dismay as he prodded for more information. Jolie could sense his impatience. She knew she needed to give him something. Something that helped her stand out. Something that would help her discover the murderer. She hesitated before answering. "I am very strong."

"No, too human." Seb shook his head. He was clearly not satisfied with Jolie's initial answer. "What else can you do?"

Jolie took a moment to gather her thoughts before responding. "I have heightened senses," she admitted reluctantly. "But I'm not very good at using them. I can sometimes hear conversations, but not as well as I should be able to."

Seb's expression softened. He understood Jolie's struggle to relearn all the gifts she possessed. "That's a start," he said encouragingly. "What about smell? Can you use that to your advantage?"

Jolie paused. She considered Seb's question. She had never really thought about it before. She closed her eyes and focused on Seb. She took a deep breath to let his scent wash over her senses. "You smell like moss and freshly turned earth," Jolie said. She opened her eyes and looked at Seb with amazement. "There's also the hardness of granite in your scent. It's unlike anything I have encountered before."

Seb chuckled, clearly pleased with Jolie's progress. "Very good," he said with a smile. "So, do all humans smell different, or do they only smell different because they're not human?"

Jolie had never thought about it before. Fundamentally, all humans should smell the same to her, like a delicious meal waiting to be devoured.

"I suppose they should smell the same, but often they smell different," Jolie said. Her mind whirled with this new information.

Seb flipped his hand in the air. He encouraged her to continue with her current train of thought. Jolie searched through her experiences. "Humans always smell like food." Saying it out loud caused her to grimace, but it was true. "The blood is the strongest smell, but there is also a saltiness. They cover it with perfumes and scented soaps." Jolie's mouth twisted in understanding. "Outside of the perfume, they should all smell relatively the same."

Seb nodded, but he was not fully satisfied with her answer. "There are many fae among us at all times . . ." he said, his tone serious. Slowly, further realization dawned. Her eyes widened as the truth took shape. Seb gave a knowing nod. A glimmer of amusement danced in his gaze as he watched the light of understanding settle in hers. The subtle differences in scent she had noticed meant they were not human at all. Seb's lips curled into a sly smile; it was as if he had heard her very thoughts.

"But remember, just because you bump into a succubus doesn't mean they're the killer," Seb said. His voice was low and carried a warning laced with amusement. Then, with a sudden, playful jab of his finger, he added, "But don't let that stop you from keeping a close watch on any fae acting . . . shifty." A smirk tugged at the corners of his mouth.

Jolie smiled softly, but a prickle of concern sneaked through her. There were countless fae she must have brushed shoulders with, their true nature hidden from her. Jolie's mind began to sift through the people at the club. The other dancers, Rori and Boden, and even the patrons. There had been so many smells. Were there that many fae around her always? Her gaze drifted to Caleb. His silhouette stretched and relaxed against the warmth of the fire. A stray strand of her dark hair fell across her cheek. She tucked it behind her ear.

Turning back to Seb, she asked, "How does a succubus kill?"

Seb's smile faded. His brow furrowed in thought as he leaned back in his chair. The dim light from the fireplace cast flickering patterns across the worn wooden shelves lined with books.

He took his time and weighed the gravity of what he was about to say. "Most succubi don't kill," he began. His voice was low. "But there are always those on the fringes. Fae that see humans as little more than cattle, mere playthings. They take lives without a second thought."

Jolie's stomach twisted with guilt. Memories rushed back of the days when she had walked that very path. When she had been one of those fae, she too had been indifferent to the human lives she drained. Her eyes darkened as shame surged within her. The weight of her past was a heavy burden she carried. One that felt even more suffocating now.

"But how do they kill without leaving a mark?" she managed to ask. The thought haunted her. The idea that death could be so effortless, so clean, and yet so final.

Seb gestured to the towering shelves of ancient texts surrounding them. "I don't need to remind you that all the answers you seek are in those books," he said. His voice was gentle but firm; it urged her to seek the knowledge for herself. Jolie's gaze lingered on the towering shelves. Her heart sank at the daunting task that awaited her. The sheer volume was overwhelming. Her smile faltered at the thought.

Seb noticed the flicker of doubt cross her face. With a more serious tone, he continued, "Succubi feed off life itself, the energy that flows through every living cell. Their touch sparks a reaction. It releases that energy while simultaneously destroying the cells. They absorb that energy through . . . intimate contact, often a kiss. The longer the contact, the more damage is done. Prolonged exposure weakens the system. It makes the victim susceptible to sickness, or worse . . ."

"Death," she whispered, her voice barely carrying over the crackling flames. Her gaze remained fixed on the fire, its light reflected in her eyes as she processed the reality of the situation.

Seb's tone turned slightly annoyed. "As I said, not usually. In fact, we haven't had a death by succubus in Seattle in fifty years."

"Why do you keep emphasizing that?" Jolie asked. She looked back up at Seb.

"Because it's important for you to understand that being a fae or even a vampire doesn't automatically make someone evil," Seb explained. He got up from his chair and stretched his arms above his head. "Now, it's getting late, and I'm not much of a night owl. I should probably turn in. But before you go, I am sending you off with another book." He moved to the shelf in the back of the room and selected another volume. "Here, take this." He handed her *Thornwick's Exhaustive Encyclopedia of the Fae Folk*. "It will have more detail than the last encyclopedia I gave you. It'll be helpful, but only if you read it." His eyes sparked as Jolie snatched the book from his hands. She scoffed and feigned insult.

Jolie turned to leave. But before she could go, another question needed asking. "One more thing, Seb. Why didn't my Maker ever tell me any of this?"

Seb's expression turned serious again. "That's a conversation for another time. I have a feeling you already have your own theories. Come and see me again on your next evening off, and we can talk more."

As Jolie made her way out of the shop, she heard Seb's final words calling after her. "And don't forget to read the books." Then she heard the clicking of the bolt as Seb locked up for the night.

CHAPTER SEVENTEEN

Behind the Feathers

Jolie strolled through the deserted streets. Her mind was consumed by her conversation with Seb. She could not shake the feeling that her Maker keeping her in the dark had been one more factor of manipulation. He had always been obsessed with control. He was convinced of his superiority over all living beings; admitting that there was more to their world would have been a blow to his ego. He would never have risked any of his children becoming curious about life outside of him.

Preoccupied, she navigated the familiar streets on autopilot. Rounding the corner onto her street, a sudden stillness descended. The city noise seemed to melt away. She unclipped Caleb's leash, the clack of metal against metal, the sound of freedom released. Caleb exploded into motion. A joyous blur of tan fur, he launched himself forward. His long legs were a piston-driven engine; he devoured the ground with effortless strides. Jolie smiled. The tension eased from her shoulders as she watched him go. She was about to set the food she had ordered for him down and join his exuberant run when a sweet voice cut through the night. "Jolie."

The sound of her name pulled her from the fleeting joy. Jolie froze mid-step. Her senses were on high alert as she tried to pick up anything beyond the sharp, acrid stench of urine that clung to the alley. The faint rustle of movement behind her was followed by a familiar voice in the damp air. "Hey, Jolie."

A wave of irritation washed over her before she even turned around. Of course, she thought. It had to be her. With a resigned sigh, Jolie slowly spun to face Wyn. Her muscles tensed as she braced for the inevitable; she forced a smile that felt more like a pout.

"Wyn, hi," she managed. The words were clipped and far from genuine.

Wyn's lips curled into a slippery smile; her darkly painted eyes gleamed as she sauntered forward. "I thought that was you," she purred. Her tone dripped with sweetness.

Jolie's gaze flicked over Wyn's outfit. She took in the tight black dress that hugged her curves with brutal precision. The silver zipper that ran down the front strained over her hips. Her combat boots were scuffed but deliberate; they added a rough edge to the ensemble. Wyn's vibrant red hair was usually worn cropped into a sharp bob. Tonight, it was slicked back with a false ponytail spilling down her back.

It was a look that could have been laughable, cheap, almost garish. Yet somehow, Wyn made it work; she exuded a strange allure that left Jolie feeling begrudgingly intrigued.

Jolie swallowed her annoyance and worked to keep her composure. She did not have the energy for this. Wyn had a knack for appearing at the worst times. She forced Jolie into uncomfortable exchanges that she desperately wanted to avoid.

"I've been busy with work," Jolie replied. She kept her tone clipped. She hoped to end the conversation before it could drag on.

"Oh, yes, work," Wyn echoed. Her voice oozed sarcasm. "Funny, I haven't seen you there much lately. Or anyone since it's been shut down."

Jolie shifted, as discomfort crept over her. Wyn's words cut through the pretense with ease. She was not wrong. Jolie was working fewer hours with the closures.

"I've . . . had a lot weighing on me," she admitted. Her voice wavered with hesitation. The truth felt like a fragile thing; it barely held together under the weight of Wyn's scrutiny.

Before Wyn could push further, Caleb appeared. His hulking frame bounded up beside Jolie and buried his snout into the bag of chicken she carried.

Wyn's eyes widened as she took in the sight of the massive dog. "Whoa, some dog!" she said.

"Yeah, he's special," Jolie replied. A smile tugged at her lips as she ruffled Caleb's fur. She grounded herself in his familiar warmth. "I was just heading home to feed him."

Wyn's eyes lingered on Caleb. Her brow arched as she assessed his sheer size. "What do you feed him? Whole cows?" she asked. She tilted her head, the teasing note in her voice barely masking her curiosity.

Jolie chuckled softly. "Something like that," she said as she patted Caleb's side.

Jolie used the pause to try to make her escape. "I should be going." She turned to continue her walk. She hoped Wyn would take the hint and leave her to her evening routine, but Wyn seemed determined to stick around. She slipped her arm into Jolie's and began to walk with her down the street. "Where do you live?"

"Just up here." Jolie pointed in the direction of her apartment. She hoped to send Wyn on her way quickly.

Wyn was undeterred. "Oh, I'll walk with you. I'm headed that way, anyway." She held up her bag with bottles clinking inside. "I was on my way to this party, and they told me to grab some booze. Now I'm late, and I bet all the fun has already started."

Wyn's laughter, a bright, tinkling sound, was impossible to ignore.

Jolie found herself unconsciously mirroring a small smile. A crack formed in her wall of aloofness, fascination breaking through her resistance. "What kind of party?" she asked. The sharpness of the question betrayed her own surprise at its utterance. The ease with which Wyn had pulled her into the conversation was unsettling.

"A play party," Wyn replied with a mischievous glint in her eye. "Is this your building?" she added as they approached Jolie's apartment building.

"Yes," Jolie answered. She was a bit confused. "What's a play party?"

"Let's go inside. I'll pour a drink for us and tell you," Wyn suggested. "Your dog looks ravenous, anyway." With that, she slipped her arm out of Jolie's and headed toward the entrance. Jolie hesitated and glanced down at Caleb. He barely registered Wyn's presence while he scratched at the door and whined, demanding to be let in. With a sigh, Jolie followed Wyn inside. She made a mental note to keep a close eye on her.

Jolie lingered near the door. She watched with a mix of irritation and amusement as Wyn wandered freely through her kitchen. Though the intrusion gnawed at her, she kept her thoughts guarded. Wyn's casual question about glasses jolted Jolie from her musing. Wordlessly, she reached into a creaky cupboard and retrieved the only two she owned. She handed them over. As Wyn inspected the mismatched pair, Jolie felt a flush of embarrassment at how little energy she put into blending in with humans.

Wyn quipped about not hosting much company. It prompted a soft, self-deprecating chuckle from Jolie. "I prefer solitude," she said. But Wyn, either oblivious or indifferent, ignored the hint. With a grin, she pulled a bottle of bourbon from her bag as though it were a treasure.

Jolie accepted the glass she was offered and took a slow sip. She let the fiery liquid burn its way down her throat as Wyn floated a suggestion. "You should come with me to the party. They'd love you."

Jolie's brow furrowed. "Parties don't hold much appeal for me," she replied coolly. She shook her head. "I'll pass."

Wyn shrugged. "Yeah, I know. Brooding in darkness is more your style." Wyn sauntered into the living room. Her hips swayed with each step. A flicker of envy stirred in Jolie as she watched Wyn's effortless confidence. She followed Wyn to the living room and settled into her old recliner. Wyn made herself comfortable on the couch.

"Okay, better idea. Host a party here," Wyn suggested.

Jolie's lips curled into a derisive snort. She drained half of her glass in one long swallow. The burn did little to cool the simmering irritation in her chest. Jolie wanted to disappear. She wanted to melt into the plush fabric of her armchair. Wyn, bless her oblivious heart, continued. Jolie tried to subtly suggest she give up and go home. However, subtlety was a language Wyn did not understand.

Wyn laughed, her voice ringing through the apartment. "You'd love it," she said. "Everyone is really welcoming. You'd fit right in."

Jolie raised an eyebrow. Jolie had a hunch about the kind of party Wyn was alluding to. Flashes of her past swept through her mind. There had been a time when she thrived at parties like these. She remembered the firm, possessive pressure of Viktor's arm entwined with hers.

He'd steer her through the throng. Each turn was a calculated flourish devised to draw all eyes. Then he'd leave her on her own to hunt. Well, not exactly hunt. She was no more than a lure, a treat perfectly dangled to catch his next meal. The memory of tangled limbs, a symphony of gasps, and wet, tearing sounds made Jolie shudder. She took another sip of her drink.

"That's quite the reaction. Does it mean you're interested?" Wyn sauntered over with a bottle to refill their glasses. A flutter stirred in Jolie's stomach at the sight of Wyn's charming smile. But she quickly pushed it aside. There was no way she'd slip back into old habits. Taking a deep breath, she downed a generous gulp of bourbon. She hoped to drown the memories that lurked at the edges of her mind.

Wyn perched on the arm of Jolie's chair and leaned in close. "So, where are you from?" Genuine curiosity lit up her eyes.

Jolie let out a soft sigh. "Everywhere and nowhere," she replied cryptically. It was the truth. Her life had been a series of fleeting locations. She never settled long enough to call any place home. It was the only way she knew to survive.

Wyn chuckled. "Well, aren't you a mystery wrapped in an enigma?"

Jolie smirked at the comment. She was used to being viewed as someone who kept people at a distance; it was a necessary shield.

"Okay, so we won't delve into your past . . . Or the murders. Too heavy," Wyn said. She attempted to steer the conversation in a lighter direction. "What should we talk about instead?"

From her seat, Jolie glanced over at Caleb. He was now nestled in the tangled sheets of her bed in the far corner of the room. He was completely uninterested in both the conversation and Wyn. His large form sprawled across the pillows. It made it clear that he had no intention of offering any support. A pang of disappointment tugged at her. She had half-hoped for a bit more loyalty. Maybe a growl or even a playful nip to chase Wyn out of her apartment. But Caleb remained blissfully unhelpful.

Jolie stretched out her legs and stifled a yawn. She felt the weariness creeping in. "Why don't you tell me about yourself?" she asked. She shifted the focus away from the uncomfortable scrutiny aimed at her.

Wyn shrugged. Her fingers lazily swirled the ice in her nearly empty glass. "I'm boring," she replied casually. Her tone was dismissive. "Born and raised here. Nothing special."

Jolie raised an eyebrow at Wyn's response. Her self-proclaimed modesty seemed far from the truth. There was something about Wyn that hinted at a deeper story. A hidden complexity she was not ready to share. But before Jolie could probe any further, Wyn's lips curled into a wicked smile. She changed the subject.

"So," Wyn began. Her voice carried an undercurrent of mischief. "Detective O'Neil was asking about you the other day at the club." She paused, savoring the moment. "He seemed more interested in where you were than in poor Candice."

Jolie's hand froze mid-sip. The memory of her heated last encounter with Danny flashed in her mind. She had not spoken to him since, and yet, despite the danger, she had felt something during their brief interaction. There was an unexpected connection that left her feeling both intrigued and vulnerable.

She swallowed and pushed those thoughts aside. She forced herself to respond with indifference. "I doubt that," she said. Her voice was steady, but lacked conviction. "He's just doing his job."

The thought of Danny's inquiry lingered. Could it be? Had he actually asked about her? Her carefully constructed veneer of nonchalance crumbled. She remembered that night. The unspoken longing in his eyes. She wanted it to be real, but he was a detective, a man of logic and procedure. She was a world away from his structured reality. One misstep, one wrong word, and it would all come crashing down.

Wyn flashed a charming smile and leaned in closer. Her eyes sparkled with mischief. "Well, maybe not more interested in you than Candice," she teased. Jolie's stomach churned with disappointment. But before she could dwell on her fleeting hopes, Wyn continued. Her voice was covert. "But he does ask about you every time he comes in. I think you have an admirer, my dear."

Jolie let out a nervous laugh at Wyn's words. "Oh, please, he's not an admirer. He's just a cop hell-bent on cracking this case. He thinks it's linked to other murders," she said as she eased herself away from Wyn's encroaching presence.

Wyn's eyes widened in surprise. "He told you that? When?" she asked. She leaned in with eager curiosity. Before Jolie could respond, Wyn's face lit up with a manic excitement that was almost unsettling. "Oh my god! He was here!" Wyn exclaimed. Her jaw dropped in awe. "What happened? Spill everything! He's so incredibly handsome," she gushed. Wyn slid off the arm of the chair and pressed the curve of her hip into Jolie's side. In this position, she was only a breath away from sitting in Jolie's lap.

The unexpected proximity sent a blush creeping up Jolie's neck; warmth bloomed in her chest. The way the light danced in Wyn's red hair. The subtle curve of her smile as she leaned in to refill their glasses. It all felt intensely, intoxicatingly real. "Careful," Wyn purred. Her voice was a low murmur. "Mixing business with pleasure could land you in some serious trouble."

Jolie shook her head. Her grin widened. "Oh, he's not mixing anything. He's just asking lots of questions," she replied. Her tone was as flat as she could make it. A shiver ran through Jolie at the thought of the handsome detective asking about her. She was growing increasingly annoyed with herself. "What did he ask about me?" she asked. She was unable to contain her curiosity.

Wyn leaned in. Her gaze was piercing as she locked eyes with Jolie. "Nothing really, but it's not what he asked. More like how he asked it," she whispered with a devilish grin. Jolie's cheeks blazed. She let Wyn twist her into knots. Of course he had not asked about her, and now she just felt foolish. Yet there was still a delicious tremor at the thought of him.

"Wyn, stop. You're being ridiculous," Jolie protested. She took a sip of her bourbon. A hint of disappointment swirled within her over Danny's lack of initiative. She was treading into dangerous territory. Wyn was only making it harder to resist.

Wyn rested her chin on Jolie's shoulder. Her warm breath tickled her neck. "Too bad, huh?" she replied. Jolie felt heat creep through her core as Wyn's body pressed against hers, her breasts firm against Jolie's arm. With each exhale, Wyn's words seemed to leave a trail of fire on Jolie's skin. "You're always so cold," Wyn whispered. Her lips were dangerously close to Jolie's ear. "Let me warm you up." She draped her leg over Jolie's and wrapped her arms around her. She stroked her shoulder.

Wildfire spread low and fast. Wyn's presence was a heady perfume. It was intoxicating and utterly disorienting. Reason whispered warnings, but it was a losing battle. The glass in her hand suddenly felt heavy. With a sigh that was half surrender, half defiance, Jolie set it down. The space between them shrank. Her fingers, light as feathers, grazed Wyn's cheek. Then they trailed down the delicate curve of her neck and found the frantic rhythm of her pulse. Jolie swallowed as her lips brushed Wyn's. It was a tentative exploration that quickly blossomed into a deeper, more urgent demand. Her tongue searched for the sweetness of Wyn's response. Wyn's arms encircled her and pulled Jolie in until there was no space left between them. Only the breathless press of skin against skin remained.

Jolie gasped as Wyn's fingers traced the delicate curve of her spine. The warmth of Wyn's hands ignited a burning fervor. A shiver ripped down her body as Wyn's touch drifted lower. She cupped the fullness of her breasts, and a low moan escaped Jolie's lips.

Wyn shifted. The weight of her body settled onto Jolie's legs. Wyn's hands rested on Jolie's hips. They guided her closer and molded their bodies together. Jolie's fingers tangled in Wyn's hair. She pulled Wyn down into a deeper, more frantic kiss. The taste of Wyn's lips was intoxicating. A heady mix of bourbon and something fierce. The world narrowed. It faded to the urgent rhythm of their breaths and the pounding of Wyn's heart. Her resistance crumbled. There was only Wyn, and the exquisite surrender that followed.

Wyn's laughter warmed the air as she whipped up her skirt. A flash of creamy skin appeared. The moonlight caught the delicate sheen of her thighs and revealed intricate garters woven with lace as fine as spider silk. Jolie's fingers trembled as she traced the delicate pattern. The scent of Wyn's perfume was spicy and intoxicating. It filled Jolie's senses. She could feel the sharp points of her fangs pressing against her lip. Each caress of the garter was a test of her willpower. It was a dance on the precipice of yielding to the irresistible pull. The risk was clear. But for now, the exquisite torment of restraint was almost as sweet.

Wyn's lips met Jolie's again. She shivered. Jolie leaned back and let her head fall in ecstasy as Wyn's skillful tongue worked its magic down her neck. It had been far too long since she had felt the touch of a human. The waves of pleasure rolling through her body felt almost foreign. She could not resist the urge to explore further. Her hand slid between Wyn's legs. She relished the tremors that ran through Wyn's body. Pressing her lips to Wyn's, Jolie kissed her with fervor. Her fingers moved in rhythm to Wyn's ragged breaths. She was completely lost in the moment. Consumed by the taste of cinnamon and cloves on Wyn's lips and the spicy, musky scent that enveloped her. The taste of Wyn was intoxicating, a heady blend of something wild and unfamiliar. Yet, beneath the pleasure, a discordant note sounded. There was a persistent hum of warning in the back of her mind. She pulled away. Wyn's scent clung to her like a second skin. She buried her face in the crook of Wyn's neck. She inhaled deeply. The kiss was now forgotten. Jolie's focus narrowed to the scent that dominated her senses. Cinnamon. Not the warm spice of a bakery, but something darker, sharper, almost acrid. A cinnamon twisted with a strange, underlying sweetness that prickled across her senses. The truth slammed into her, brutal and undeniable. The heat of Wyn's skin and the overwhelming scent of cinnamon. None of it belonged to a human being.

Jolie's grip on Wyn's arms was tight. She forced them to her sides. Meeting Wyn's frightened eyes, Jolie stood up, flipped Wyn around, and pinned her to the floor. Wyn let out a squeak of surprise and fear as Jolie's knee pressed into her back. It made it difficult for her to breathe.

"What the fuck, Jolie!" Wyn gasped. Her voice trembled with a mix of shock and pain.

Jolie's face contorted. Her fangs bared as she growled at Wyn. "What are you?" she demanded. Her tone was low and menacing.

Wyn let out a small sob. Her heart was a frantic drum against her ribs. "What? I don't . . . what the hell are you doing to me?" Wyn stammered. Her voice trembled with fear and confusion. Her eyes were wide with terror.

Jolie's grip tightened around Wyn's throat. Her fingers dug in with controlled but threatening pressure. Her eyes narrowed dangerously as her fangs glinted beneath her lips. "I will snap your neck," she hissed. Her voice was low and lethal. "What are you?"

Wyn's face paled. Her breath came in shallow gasps as she clawed at Jolie's hand. Panic consumed her. The question remained unanswered. Wyn's desperate attempts to speak turned into strained gasps.

Before Jolie could press further, a massive force barreled into her from behind. It knocked her off balance. She stumbled and released her hold on Wyn. Jolie spun around. Her fangs were bared and ready to fight. Her snarl froze as she came face-to-face with Caleb. His massive form towered over Wyn. She lay on the floor, coughing and gasping for air.

"Move, Caleb!" Jolie growled. Her voice a sharp command. Her eyes were locked on his, fierce and unwavering. "She isn't human."

But Caleb did not move. He stood firm. He stared down at Jolie with an unimpressed expression. His deep, amber eyes seemed to roll in disbelief. They silently conveyed a message that cut through the tension in the room: *No shit, Sherlock.*

The weight of Caleb's defiance deflated Jolie's aggression. She let out an annoyed sigh. Her fangs retracted as she sank to the floor. The intensity of the moment began to fade. "Caleb, we need better communication," she muttered. Her voice was laced with disappointment and a hint of regret. "If she's not human and harmless, I need to know ahead of time."

Her eyes moved to Wyn; she was still catching her breath. She trembled as she pushed herself up. A sharp twist gripped Jolie's stomach. But she shoved it aside. Instead, she focused on Caleb. He stood calm and composed. He had always known the situation was under control.

Jolie sighed again. She raked a hand through her hair. "This could've gone smoother," she admitted. Her tone was softer now. Though the disappointment still lingered in her voice.

Caleb gave her a slow, knowing look. His eyes said, "No kidding."

Wyn's coughing had subsided. She pulled down her skirt. Her face flushed with embarrassment. "How did you miss the fact that I wasn't human?" she asked. Her voice shook slightly.

Jolie's shoulders slumped. The weight of her actions drained her. Shame burned in her cheeks. Wyn's quiet presence beside her felt like an accusation. A contrast to the frantic energy that had fueled her moments ago. A choked sob escaped her lips. "I'm so sorry, Wyn," she whispered. Her voice was soft; her eyes finally met Wyn's. Remorse sculpted into her features. She fumbled for words. The inadequacy of her apology was a fresh wave of humiliation. "I . . . I've never encountered . . . anything like you before," she stammered. Her voice caught. "I didn't even know fae existed until recently." The admission was a fragile confession. It laid bare her ignorance and the depth of her blunder. Bitter self-loathing coiled in her stomach.

Wyn let out a heavy sigh and slowly climbed onto the couch. She worked to keep her distance from Jolie. "Maybe I should just leave. I'm going to be covered in bruises tomorrow. Fuck, Jolie," she muttered. She hugged her legs to her chest and rocked back and forth. Tears streamed down her face. Her carefully applied eyeliner was now ruined.

Caleb climbed up next to Wyn and leaned his body against hers. Jolie felt a pang of jealousy at how easily Caleb was able to provide comfort to Wyn. She knew she had to make things right. "I'm sorry, Wyn. Really, I am. Let me make you some tea, and I'll try to explain everything," Jolie offered.

Wyn wiped her tears away and managed to smile. "I'll stay, but only if you add more wood to the fire. It's freezing in here," she said. Her voice was still trembling. Wyn wrapped her arms around Caleb, finding some warmth in his honey-colored fur. Relief washed over Jolie's face, and there was a visible softening of the lines around her mouth.

CHAPTER EIGHTEEN

Pin and Tuck

The firelight painted Wyn's face with shifting colors of orange and amber. But the warmth did little to ease the coldness that had seeped into Jolie's core. Wyn sank deeper into the cushions of Jolie's sofa. She wrapped the soft wool blanket around her shoulders. Steam curled from her mug. The chamomile tea's delicate scent mingled with the wood smoke from the fire. Across the room, Jolie's fingers traced gentle patterns across Caleb's fur as he slept peacefully in her lap. The flames crackled. Their light chased shadows across the walls. Jolie's voice was low and hesitant as she spoke of her life both before and after her transformation. Her words sketched a life Wyn had never imagined. Wyn took a deep breath. Her nerves finally calmed as curiosity flickered in her eyes. "So, what exactly is Caleb?" she asked.

Jolie silently wished the conversation could veer back toward Wyn. But she was relieved that Wyn seemed relaxed enough to engage. "Caleb is a barghest," she replied.

Wyn's brow furrowed. Her gaze darted between Jolie and the hulking figure of Caleb. "I thought they were just a legend," she remarked. Disbelief laced her words.

Caleb lifted his head and let out a low, rumbling snort. It was as if he were personally offended by Wyn's ignorance. Jolie chuckled softly. Her hand ran affectionately through his fur. "He despises it when people say that." A small smile tugged at her lips.

Wyn, now fully settled and relaxed, raised an eyebrow. "No offense, Jolie, but why is he with you? From what I know, barghests aren't exactly known for choosing vampires as companions."

Jolie's hand never left Caleb's head. "He believes I'm special," she said. Her voice carried a mix of pride and uncertainty. "Though he could be mistaken," she added with a self-deprecating smile.

Wyn could not resist a sharp retort. Her lips curled into a playful smirk. "Or maybe he thinks you're in dire need of help. After all, you did mistake me for a human."

Jolie sighed. She rolled her eyes at the jab. But a reluctant smile spread across her face. "Touché."

"Well, I guess we both have some surprises up our sleeves," Jolie said. She nudged Caleb playfully with her foot. She tried to keep the mood light. Though a pang of remorse still lingered from her earlier actions. "I must admit, there's a lot I don't know about the world outside my narrow view. My Maker only ever taught us about humans and vampires."

Wyn's curiosity pushed her to probe further. "Where is your Maker now?"

Jolie's expression darkened. "I have no idea," she said. Her voice was tight with repressed emotion. "I escaped from him. It was a perilous decision. But I couldn't endure the abuse and control any longer. I was fortunate to find a powerful witch who helped me break free."

Wyn's eyes widened. A mixture of shock and admiration was evident in her gaze. "Wow, that's impressive. Defying the rules of the vampire world takes a lot of guts."

Jolie exhaled a wistful sigh. The weight of her past settled heavily on her shoulders. "I know. But now I'm alone and exposed. I must stay hidden to avoid being found and punished, or worse."

"But you're not truly alone, you know that, right?" Wyn said earnestly.

"I'm beginning to realize that. And of course I have Caleb," Jolie said. Her voice softened as she looked at the massive dog. As if on cue, Caleb rolled over. He exposed his belly for a rub. When Jolie obliged, he wagged his tail in contentment.

Jolie's brow furrowed slightly. Her gaze shifted between Caleb and Wyn. "Caleb protected you. So you must not be a threat. But I still don't know what you are."

Wyn met her gaze with a calm but inscrutable look. Jolie heard Wyn's heart race as she debated whether to reveal her true nature. "I am a succubus," she admitted. She braced herself for Jolie's reaction.

"What?" Wyn's confession took Jolie by surprise.

"I'm a succubus," Wyn repeated slowly.

Jolie's mind raced with questions. Did Wyn know that the killer at the club was a succubus? Was she in danger? "The same kind of fae that's been killing people at the club," she said cautiously. Her eyes locked with Wyn's.

Wyn's expression shifted. Her face became a mask of grim seriousness. "I know. I knew the moment we entered the bathroom that night, but it wasn't me," she insisted. "I am not a killer."

A wave of relief washed over Jolie. The tension in her shoulders eased as she realized that Wyn was telling the truth. Caleb trusted her, so she must have been. The tangle of worry in her chest began to unravel, but her concern for the broader situation remained. The dark reality of the murders loomed large. Wyn could be a crucial piece in unraveling the mystery.

Jolie's eyes searched Wyn's face. Her brow furrowed in anxiety. "Do you have any idea who it could be?" she asked. The dim lighting of the room cast long shadows on the walls, accentuating the worry etched into Jolie's features.

Wyn's gaze dropped momentarily. Her fingers absently traced the edge of her mug as she considered the question. Her eyes grew somber. "There are whispers of others on the fringes of the community. The ones who always seem a bit off." The air between them seemed to grow colder. Wyn stared past Jolie at the flickering fire as she spoke. "But even with the rumors, I have no idea who it could be." Wyn sat up straight. Her hands trembled. "Killing a human goes against everything we were taught. We have a strict code. Plus, succubi that kill get weird."

"What do you mean, weird?" Jolie struggled to reconcile Wyn's lack of leads with the severity of the situation. She needed information that only Wyn had.

Wyn shrugged. "I don't know. They go crazy over time. They get reckless. There is something about killing humans that makes us go almost feral. There was a story about one, many decades ago. She stopped showering and just hung out on a hiking trail, attacking people. Really weird stuff like that."

"How does that happen?" Now Jolie was intrigued. She knew some vampires who acted like that.

"No idea." Wyn took another sip of her tea and clutched the mug to her chest.

Jolie's exasperation bubbled just beneath the surface. She forced herself to take a deep breath and try a different subject. "How many succubi usually frequent the club?"

Wyn sighed deeply. She ran her fingers through her vibrant red hair. "It varies," she said. Her voice carried an undertone of sadness. "On any given night, there could be anywhere from one to a dozen. But I assure you, no ordinary succubus could be behind these deaths."

The revelation hit Jolie like a cold wave. The notion that fae were mingling around her. That they could be concealed within the ordinary fabric of her world left her feeling both astonished and uneasy. The club was a hidden realm of the supernatural.

"What about the other employees?" Jolie pressed. Her voice was edged with determination as she sought any possible lead.

Wyn's lips curled into a knowing smile. "You truly have no idea, do you?" she asked. She shook her head with a faint, rueful smile. "I'm afraid I can't divulge that information. The fae code is strict about revealing such details."

The room seemed to grow darker around them. The flickering shadows emphasized the walls of secrecy that barred Jolie from the answers she sought. Jolie rubbed her temples in irritation. "People are dying, and you won't tell me who's responsible?" she exclaimed. She was unable to contain her exasperation.

Wyn's expression softened as she reached out to place a comforting hand on Jolie's shoulder. "Jolie, I don't know who is behind this," she said. Her voice was gentle. "I also can't tell you who is fae and who isn't. Those are not my secrets to disclose. Imagine if someone found out you were a vampire and shared it with anyone they pleased. We have strict rules for a reason." Wyn leaned back and shrugged. "Plus, no one working at the club would do this."

Jolie could not argue with Wyn's logic. But it was still challenging to know that there were people out there responsible for these deaths, and she could not do anything about it. "Don't your people want to take action against this?" Jolie asked.

For the first time in an hour, Wyn let out a laugh. "Your people?" she repeated. "That's such an archaic turn of phrase." She relaxed back onto the couch. She let out a yawn. "I can tell you this much. Our elders are actively investigating the situation. Unfortunately, we haven't been able to pinpoint the culprit."

As Jolie stretched, trying to relieve some of the tension in her body, she remarked, "Well, it seems we have that in common."

Wyn's smile broadened. Her earlier tension melted away as she made a lighthearted request. "Would it be possible for me to borrow some pajamas? I plan on staying here tonight, or today. I've lost track of time."

Jolie chuckled at the sudden shift in Wyn's demeanor. Wyn was quietly returning to her familiar, carefree self, despite all that had transpired between them. Jolie retrieved a pair of her rarely worn silk pajamas from the closet, hoping Wyn would appreciate the touch of luxury.

Wyn changed and settled into Jolie's bed with Caleb curled up beside her. Jolie watched with a bemused smile as the two settled into a cozy slumber. The sight of them, Wyn comfortably nestled in the softness of the silk and Caleb sprawled contentedly, was oddly endearing.

Jolie shook her head with a soft laugh. She felt an unexpected sense of displacement as she observed the scene. The sun was still hours away from rising. With nothing left to do, she curled up on the couch. The gentle crackle of the fire soothed her. As the flames slowly dimmed to embers, Jolie's eyes grew heavy. With a hopeful thought for the clarity that the next day might bring, she drifted off to sleep.

CHAPTER NINETEEN

The Feather Boa

Jolie's spine groaned. A thick, syrupy haze clung to her thoughts. Her limbs were heavy as unworked clay. The apartment pulsed with Caleb's frantic energy; his nails struck the worn linoleum of her kitchen as he danced through the room. A savory cloud of sizzling bacon drifted its way through her apartment.

"Morning, sleepyhead!" Wyn's voice, a bright chirp, cut through the haze.

Jolie dragged herself to the bathroom to splash some cold water on her face. The mirror reflected a worn-out vampire. Her once youthful features were now gaunt and sunken. She saw the weight of nearly two hundred years in the hollows of her face. A pang of hunger reminded her of the rejuvenating power of a good meal. With a heavy sigh, Jolie wiped her face and resigned herself to wearing a wig again tonight at work. She made her way to the kitchen. Her steps were slow and lethargic. Jolie figured Rori would disapprove of this wig as well, but she did not have the energy to care.

"You look like you've been through hell," remarked Wyn as she pulled two blood packs from the fridge and began emptying them into a cup. "When was the last time you ate?"

Jolie rubbed the back of her neck. She tried to recall. "I'm not sure. Maybe yesterday? Where did you get bacon from?"

Wyn smirked and winked at Caleb. "I made a trade with one of your neighbors." Before Wyn could continue, Jolie let out a dramatic groan. Wyn's eyes fluttered to the ceiling. "Relax, I'm not talking about my body. It's the booze in my bag that I'm referring to." Wyn shook her head and went back to filling Jolie's glass. "Man, you really need to eat more often. Your mood is terrible when you're hungry."

Jolie let out a sigh and slumped her head onto the table. She closed her eyes. "I know. It's just this situation, this city. I feel like my life is getting out of control."

Wyn's fingers clawed through the empty depths of Jolie's kitchen drawers. She searched until finally a triumphant, sharp intake of breath announced her success. She slid into the only other chair that Jolie owned with a glass, blood packets, and a steak knife. Her movements were deliberate as she emptied the blood packets into the glass. Her gaze focused on a precise mix. "Why do you think your life is out of control?"

Jolie's eyes settled on Wyn. She waved her hand around Wyn's aura to make her point. "You, the detective, everyone. It's like everybody is making me do things I wouldn't normally do."

"People," Wyn murmured, "they don't yank the reins from your hands. You still have choices. Maybe we are just giving you fresh choices you never knew you needed."

"I don't think we qualify as people," Jolie mumbled.

Wyn let out a chuckle and shook her head. "Oh, come on. I've heard vampires were melodramatic, but you take the brass ring. Look, you need to get over it. We may not be like humans, but we're still people. And interesting ones at that," she said with a wink.

Jolie ignored Wyn and reached out for the glass eagerly, but Wyn pulled it away with a cagey smile. "Not quite ready yet," she said teasingly. Jolie groaned in disappointment. "You'll be much better off once you accept what you are and what you can offer the world," Wyn declared, conviction in every word.

Wyn picked up the knife, and before Jolie could protest, she winced as the sharp blade cut into her pale skin. "This would be easier if you actually had a sharp knife, but fae blood packs a punch, and you need one," she explained. Her brow furrowed in concentration.

Jolie stared, her mouth agape. Wyn's arm looked even paler against the crimson that was steadily dripping into the glass. Each drop fell with an imagined heavy thud. The guilt, sharp and sudden, clawed at Jolie's throat. It was not just blood. It was the utter selflessness of the act. Wyn, with her quiet strength, was offering a piece of herself without hesitation. The sting of her stubborn refusal to truly embrace Wyn burned with a fresh intensity.

Perhaps Wyn was right. Perhaps, buried beneath Jolie's own self-doubt, was something worth sharing. Something worth giving. The world might want what she had to offer.

Wyn was still talking; her voice broke through Jolie's thoughts. "A bit of my blood and you'll feel good as new," she said confidently. "Of course, I'll have to feed before tonight, but that can be managed."

Jolie felt a tinge of fear at the thought of Wyn feeding on someone, but she could not deny that she needed her help. "How do you know this will work?" she asked. Her voice was barely above a whisper.

Wyn simply shrugged. Her nonchalant demeanor never wavered. "I dated a vamp once," she said matter-of-factly.

Jolie's eyes widened in shock. "Seriously? How?" she blurted out.

Wyn burst into a fit of laughter at Jolie's bewildered expression. She squeezed her arm to increase the blood flow. The wound began to close on its own. "What do you mean, how?" she chuckled. "I met him, he was hot, we dated."

"Yeah, but was he allowed to socialize outside his family?" Jolie's voice cracked with incredulity. Her elbows dug into the table as she leaned in.

Wyn's jaw tightened. She pulled her arm away from the glass. The wound had already healed. "Yeah. They kept to themselves. We made it work for a short time, though." She nudged the untouched cup toward Jolie.

Jolie's fingers wrapped around the glass. Her first sip was hesitant. The first taste hinted at something vaguely bitter. Caleb, a whirlwind of fur and frantic energy, darted beneath the table. His nose creeping up to the plate of bacon, his whines pointed.

Wyn laughed and began to feed him small pieces of bacon between her own bites. "I'm starting to get the impression that your Maker was a bit of a dictator," Wyn said. "But not all vampires are like that. I mean, sure, you guys can be cliquey and needy, but at least most get out of the house sometimes."

Wyn tossed the rest of the bacon to Caleb and got up from the table. "Well, I'm going to go visit a friend. I'll see you at work tonight." She leaned over to kiss Jolie on the top of her head. "And when you're done being all melodramatic and freaky, I'll show you just how good a vampire and a succubus can be together." She paused at the door, an impish grin plastered on her face. "Oh, and you should totally invite that hot cop friend of yours. I bet he'd be into it." Wyn chuckled as she closed the door behind her.

Jolie listened to the sound of Wyn's retreating steps fading down the hallway, then lifted her glass and downed the remaining blood in one gulp. The rich, viscous fluid coated her tongue. A pulsing warmth began to grow within her. It spread like spilled ink. It chased away the ache that had settled in her bones. Her thoughts cleared. A clean, sharp clarity bloomed. Time to face the day.

CHAPTER TWENTY

The Alter Ego

As she drew closer to The Black Cat House, the more Jolie wondered if she had finally lost her mind. She looked down at Caleb. He happily tugged on his leash and chased shadows. He was so full of joy, and she could not resist including him in her night. "So, remind me again how you convinced me to do this?"

Caleb simply ignored her and continued to frolic down the street. But as they neared the back door of the club, Jolie's nerves started to kick in. Rori and Boden were not going to be happy about having a dog in their club.

"Caleb, I don't think this is a good idea. Rori and Boden are going to kill me if they find you," she said, trying to reason with the excited pup, but Caleb just snorted. Whether in agreement or annoyance, Jolie could not tell. She pushed open the back door and was immediately hit with the familiar clutter of backstage.

Rori must have pulled out all the stops for the reopening. There were a few more performers than usual. Jolie's heart sank as she recognized one of them as Falyn Fatale. Jolie could not believe Rori had given her a second chance after her last outburst, but it was like Rori to give a resident performer another shot. There were also two new traveling dancers: D'vil Sin Claire and a hula hoop performer she knew from the circuit. Jolie made it to her spot between Cherry Stems and Wyn. They were both in various stages of makeup and undress. Caleb immediately curled up beside her dressing table. The other dancers' eyes darted between Caleb and Jolie, their faces reflecting a mixture of curiosity and thinly veiled disapproval. One girl subtly wrinkled her nose; another let out a barely suppressed giggle. Jolie pretended not to notice. She unpacked her bag to the rhythmic thump of Caleb's tail against the wooden floor. His massive frame, a mountain of muscle and fur, filled a surprising amount of space in the cramped dressing room. Yet he remained utterly still. A silent, comforting presence.

One pair of eyes in the room was not focused on Caleb. D'vil's striking brown eyes were instead fixed on a spot over Jolie's shoulder. Even without turning around, Jolie could sense Wyn's presence as she moved closer. Wyn took her time rolling up her stockings and securing her garters. Wyn relished every second of being watched by D'vil. Jolie's knuckles whitened, a phantom heat bloomed in her core, an ache tightened her chest. She swallowed. She could almost picture it. Wyn's fingertips tracing D'vil's jawline. Wyn's breath sliding across D'vil's skin. The thought sent a jolt through Jolie; it made her stomach clench.

Wyn's laughter was bright and undeniably alluring, as it danced in the room. Jolie watched as Wyn leaned in. She placed a hand possessively on D'vil's arm. A bitter tang rose in Jolie's throat. She turned back to her vanity and took a deep breath. She counted to ten before opening her eyes, envy and jealousy would not consume her. Wyn approached and draped her arms over Jolie's shoulders, her warm breath brushed against Jolie's ear. Wyn's voice, a silken murmur in her head, purred, "Don't be jealous, darling. I always save a little something special for you."

Jolie's muscles tightened. She turned to face Wyn with a sharp glare. "Why are you in my head?" she hissed through gritted teeth.

Wyn's eyes twinkled as she replied, "Lover, you're in my head. Remember, you drank my blood." Wyn was deeply amused by the look of horror that flashed through Jolie's eyes. "Yup, you and me, we're connected now."

Jolie rubbed her temples in irritation and let out a sharp exhale. "Not for long, I hope."

Wyn's laughter died down. She grew serious. "Probably just a few hours. You never know, you might just enjoy it." With that, Wyn wandered away. Jolie watched as she sauntered over to D'vil and seductively draped herself across her vanity. Wyn's words and her hands struck up two conversations simultaneously. Jolie felt jealousy return once again.

She turned her attention back to Caleb. He was attempting to make himself invisible. She sighed, it was time to introduce him to Rori. Jolie led him toward the theater.

"Caleb, just try your best to remain quiet and inconspicuous. We need to lay low and avoid drawing any unwanted attention." Jolie's eyes scanned the crowded bar until she spotted Rori.

Rori held a commanding line under the warm glow spilling from the ornate chandelier. She crossed her arms; her voice sliced through the clatter of preparations. "No liberal pours tonight, Mikhail. Our inventory spreadsheet is practically weeping red ink."

A choked laugh spat from Mikhail's direction. "Perhaps you're the one draining the reserves."

A guttural growl vibrated in Rori's chest. A sound seemed to snag in the air and Jolie felt the hair on the back of her neck rise. There was something in that growl that triggered a primal urge to flee. Angus, a staggering shadow in a crisp uniform, materialized beside Rori. His cloth was a blur as he wiped down an already shining counter. His usual stoic presence seemed strained. Angus was usually security. What was he doing behind the bar? Knowing Boden, this was likely his idea. A human shield between Mikhail and Rori.

Rori's focus swiveled. Angus visibly shrank under the intensity of her stare. "A sidecar, Angus. Now."

A fresh wave of snickers erupted from behind Angus. Rori's eyes snapped back. Her gaze was a silent inferno directed at Mikhail. Apprehension tightened Jolie's stomach; turning back seemed like the sensible option. A swift retreat from the brewing storm. But her feet, as if possessed by a different will, propelled her forward.

She slid onto a stool beside Rori. Caleb nestled against her leg, a warm, furry anchor in the swirling tension.

Angus began to sweat as he fumbled with the liquor bottles. The scent of woods, moss, and moonlit nights swirled between Rori and Angus. Something pricked at the edges of Jolie's mind.

A shadow fell over the bar as Rori's narrowed eyes locked onto Angus. Her lips thinned. Behind him, a low, mocking chuckle rumbled. Mikhail. Angus flinched, his shoulders hunched as brandy sloshed. It painted a golden stripe across the dark wood. Rori's face was a mask of cool disdain. "Shut it, Mikhail," she barked. "Go be useful."

Rori's posture softened, a subtle shift as she leaned forward. Her hand landed with surprising softness on Angus's shoulder. He visibly sagged. The tension drained from his frame like water from a sieve. "You'll do great," Rori murmured.

With renewed, if shaky, resolve, Angus poured the amber liquid. His hand was steadier now. He slid the drink across the bar. Rori raised it to her lips. A pucker crossed her mouth before she quickly hid it. "Perfect," she declared. Her voice was as smooth as the liquor. "You're gonna do great." A bashful grin, boyish and out of place, flashed across Angus's face. He turned and moved down the bar to adjust the cocktail shakers.

Rori pivoted to Jolie. "He'll do fine, right?"

"Of course," Jolie replied. She pitched her voice lower. "Angus will do just fine. Lina and Tam are on tonight. They'll steer him right." She hesitated. The question bubbled up. "But why is he behind the bar?"

Rori sank onto a stool. Her body uncoiled. "To keep an eye on Mikhail."

Jolie's brow furrowed. Keep an eye on Mikhail? Was this about the disappearing inventory, or Rori's simmering distrust?

The sharp tang of pine needles in the air thinned as the tension dissipated. Her brow furrowed as she tried to discern where the scent had gone. Jolie was so distracted that she missed Caleb inching closer until his tongue swept across the back of Rori's hand. Rori jumped slightly and stared down at Caleb. Her mouth hung open.

Before Rori could say anything, Jolie jumped in. "With everything that's been going on, I thought it might be a good idea to have some extra protection," she said. Her words trailed off as she realized the absurdity of her decision. It had to be Wyn's blood that led her to such reckless decision-making.

Thankfully, Rori saved her from having to explain further. "A guard dog, huh?" she said. She stood up from her stool and knelt to meet Caleb's eyes. She stroked his ears and held his gaze for a few moments before smiling. "Miss Jolie Mason, you never cease to amaze me. Hopefully, the health inspectors don't show up, and we can keep him backstage."

Rori's unexpected acceptance was a small miracle. Caleb, sensing Jolie's relief, thumped his tail against the sticky floor. Jolie released a silent plea to the goddess of mischief. *Lyssa, please let this go smoothly.* She led Caleb back to her vanity and gently released him. She reminded him to behave and stay backstage.

Jolie began styling her hair. She carefully pinned it up high in the back and let it fall gracefully over one eye. As she finished with the hairspray, she noticed Caleb sneezing on the floor. "Sorry, but I can't risk my hair falling down on stage," Jolie said with a chuckle. "You'll get used to it if you stick around long enough."

Wyn's laughter announced her arrival. Her violet robe, embroidered with silver thread, gaped open. It revealed the smooth expanse of her skin for all to see. Lina swept into the room behind her. She carried a tray heavy with drinks.

"I heard someone was a hungry boy," Lina trilled.

Caleb's tail began a furious drumming. A steaming plate, piled high with golden-brown chicken fingers, landed before him. He did not pause. He tore into the crispy crust of the first piece.

Wyn's movements were as fluid as warm honey. She set a tumbler of amber liquid on Jolie's vanity, the condensation immediately forming a ring on the old wood. She then glided through the space and passed out more glasses. Jolie watched as Wyn's hand lingered a beat too long on D'vil. She leaned forward and let her robe fall open as she offered D'vil a particularly plump olive.

Jolie's fingers tightened around her glass. She swallowed and turned her attention to the lustrous fabric of her costume laid out before her. Each sequin danced with an inner light, a promise of the brilliance she was about to unleash.

"Alright, ladies, let's get our act together. The theater is filling up, and we only have twenty minutes until curtain call." Charles's jaw was set. A granite-hard line pressed against the glare of the bare bulb overhead. His eyes swept across the room.

"Falyn, you're up first. Wyn, be ready to follow." The words were clipped and precise. They cut through the rustle of crinoline. He did not wait for an answer before turning and exiting the room.

Jolie took a slow sip of her bourbon. She moved on to her makeup routine, a ritual she had perfected over the years. Same liner, same highlights, same lips. But maybe tonight she would add a little twist. She rummaged through her makeup case and found her collection of glitter. With a mischievous smile, she decided to play up the green in her eyes with a swipe of purple glitter on her lids. "Ten minutes, ladies!" Charles's voice echoed through the dressing room.

"Thank you, ten," the dancers replied in unison. Jolie stood up and started to put on her costume. Her amplified hearing picked up the dull buzz from the theater. Tonight seemed emptier than usual. The patrons who were already seated spoke in hushed tones; their energy was subdued. Jolie worried about the impact it would have on the show. The Black Cat House relied on its dancers to entertain and distract the audience from their worries, but with all the negative energy in the air, Jolie feared for the club's longevity.

As Falyn's music began to play, the crowd fell silent. Jolie quickly grabbed her final costume pieces and headed to her spot in the hall. Wyn was already preparing for her entrance. "No stage kittens tonight," Wyn whispered to Jolie, referring to the role of stage cleanup. "Seems they were too scared to come in, so we have the goon squad instead."

Wyn tilted her head toward two of Boden's security guards. They were dressed in all black and standing by the door, waiting to clear the stage between acts. "I'm not sure how I feel about you all picking up my unmentionables," she teased. "I might not get them all back."

The larger security guard, whom Jolie suspected was Abernathy, Angus's brother, did not budge from his spot. Like all of Boden's team, he was covered in tattoos, and his head was shaved bald. It made it difficult for Jolie to distinguish between them.

Jolie focused her mind on her upcoming act. She began mentally rehearsing her movements and steps. She was just about to make her first big reveal when D'vil entered the hallway. Jolie sighed with relief. Wyn had limited time to flirt with Falyn's act about to end.

Falyn, a blur of silk and motion, nearly bowled Wyn over as she brushed past them in the tight hallway. The sting of the near collision ignited a flash of fury in Wyn that was strong enough for Jolie to feel. A barbed retort formed on Wyn's lips, but instead of unleashing her anger, she let out a barely observable snort. Her eyes lingered on Falyn's retreating form before a playful, mocking sneer danced across her face. She then turned and took her place in the wings, waiting for her cue.

The opening notes of Wyn's acrobatic piece washed over Jolie. She closed her eyes. The melody, a vibrant current, flowed through her. It silenced the chatter in her mind. The roar of the crowd shuddered through the worn wooden planks of the stage. A visceral tide washed over Jolie with each cheer. From the corner of her eye, she watched D'vil. Her movements were as subtle and elegant as a willow branch swaying in a gentle breeze. Jolie noted the delicate curve of her jawline. The almost ethereal quality of her features were framed by a cascade of dark hair. She could see why Wyn was drawn to D'vil. She had a classic beauty that reminded Jolie of her own past.

As Wyn's music continued, Jolie pushed aside the thoughts that threatened to consume her. She could not afford to be distracted. Not now, when she was about to perform. She forced herself to focus on her routine, but it was a constant struggle.

Memories of her first burlesque job flooded her mind. They took her back to when she was just a naive twenty-year-old working as a stage kitten in a burlesque house. None of the dancers ever stayed for long. They were in constant motion. Traveling from city to city, performing in different shows. As a stage kitten, Jolie's job was to pick up discarded costumes and pack them into bags before the dancers rushed off to their next destination. It was a fast-paced and competitive environment. Everyone vied for the best tips and the most attention from the audience, but amidst the chaos and constant movement, a few dancers began to stay on for longer periods of time. One of them was Ginger Sherry. A seasoned performer who took a liking to Jolie. Ginger saw potential in the young stage kitten and took her under her wing. Jolie could still remember the feeling of Ginger's warm smile and the sound of her infectious laughter echoing through the dressing room.

"Jolie, are you ready?" Abernathy's voice snapped her back to reality. Jolie let out a string of curses under her breath as she hurried past him and through the stage door. She could feel the adrenaline coursing through her veins as she stepped into the bright spotlight. She transformed into her stage persona. Her posture exuded seduction. Her smile promised more than just a tease. Her eyes smoldered with desire.

The sultry beat of her song pulsed through her body as she set up the first reveal. The audience's eager anticipation fueled her movements. But even as she danced, Jolie could not shake the nagging presence of Wyn in the back of her mind. Consuming Wyn's blood kept her in two worlds. She was fully aware of Wyn's feelings and actions, even as she tried to focus on her own moment.

Jolie could feel Wyn trying to coax D'vil away from prying eyes. With a deep breath, Jolie removed her first glove and tossed it aside. She sensed Wyn and D'vil entering the bathroom and locking the door behind them. Jolie placed the middle finger of her second glove between her teeth. The fabric clung to her skin as she slowly pulled it off. She felt the heat rising in her belly. It cascaded down her legs and up to her breasts. The intense pleasure that Wyn was experiencing leaked through their psychic connection. It made Jolie's movements more primal and intense. Despite her best efforts to maintain control, Jolie could feel her resolve slipping with each passing moment. She removed her skirt with a slow, deliberate spin. Her back arched, and her head fell back as she let the fabric fall to the floor. The sensations coursing through her body, fueled by Wyn's escapades, were too overwhelming to ignore. She trailed her hands over her skin. Her nails left red marks in their wake. She found herself lost in the pure pleasure of dancing for herself. In that moment, Jolie was no longer performing for an audience. She was lost in the sensations, the connection with Wyn, and the feel of her own body. It was a moment of pure liberation.

As her song came to an end, she snapped out of her trance and realized she had missed her cue for her final reveal. She could feel the eyes of the audience on her. They were eagerly waiting for the dramatic finale. Jolie locked eyes with the crowd. Her gaze was hungry and intense. She began to imagine how easy it would be to choose any one of them to fulfill her desires. And then she saw him. Detective O'Neil. He was sitting at the back of the theater, and his eyes were fixed on her. A wicked smile spread across her face as she confidently removed her red sequined bra. She let it fall carelessly to the ground. She stood there for a moment. Her posture dared the detective to look at her. And with a beguiling grin, she turned and strutted off the stage.

It wasn't until she stepped into the hallway that Jolie became aware of the roaring crowd. The theater was not close to being packed, but the cheers and whistles were deafening. As she made her way back to her vanity, she could feel Caleb's curious gaze on her. She slumped into her seat. She was still trying to process what had just happened. The realization of how she had just behaved hit her like a skillfully thrown brick. She could feel her face flushing with embarrassment. Every fiber of her being wanted to disappear.

Avoiding any chance of meeting her own reflection, Jolie hastily wiped the glitter from her face. Her hands trembled as she began to reapply her more subdued makeup. She had sworn to herself that she would look for clues between her two performances. But now, the mere thought of facing the theater felt unbearable. The sting of her performance still echoed in her mind, a humiliation too fresh to shake.

This was Wyn's doing. Her endless torrent of emotions had pulled Jolie under. Wyn had clouded her senses and muddled her thoughts until she could hardly think straight. Every pulse of Wyn's energy had pushed Jolie to the edge. The idea of stepping out into the crowd felt impossible.

As if summoned by some unspoken force, Wyn sauntered over. Her robe was lazily draped open. "Come now, Jolie," she said with a smile. Though a flicker of unease shadowed her gaze. "The audience is eagerly awaiting your return. You wouldn't want to keep them waiting, would you?"

Anger flew from Jolie like arrows. Wyn bit her lip and gently placed a hand on Jolie's shoulder. "I'm sorry. I didn't realize it would be so strong."

Jolie sucked air through her teeth. No matter how hard she tried to keep her distance, Wyn had somehow managed to slip past her defenses and become her friend. Not just any friend, but one who knew the truth about Jolie and accepted her as she was. Her flaws, secrets, and all. That kind of friendship was rare and worth enduring a few disappointments for. With it came inevitable moments of exasperation. Wyn, with her boundless energy and impulsive behavior, would often test her patience.

Jolie took a breath. "It's fine, Wyn," she sighed as she pushed down the last vestiges of her anger. "You were just trying to help."

But Wyn, ever perceptive, saw through the thin mask Jolie wore. Wyn sat beside Jolie and leaned into her. She rested her head on Jolie's shoulder. "I can feel it. You're upset. And I get it. You feel humiliated."

Jolie scoffed. A sharp edge filled her voice. "I doubt you can even begin to understand. Humiliation isn't something you're familiar with, is it?"

Wyn's smile faltered for a heartbeat, but she quickly bounced back. "You're being ridiculous. They adored you out there. You had them practically spellbound."

A small smile crept across Jolie's face at Wyn's unbridled enthusiasm. She let out a soft breath. She rested her head against the surface of the vanity. She let the chilled wood soothe her heated thoughts. "Alright, fine. Can you just pass me my green dress?"

Wyn offered an exaggerated roll of her eyes. "You are so melodramatic, Jolie. But yes, I'll fetch it."

Jolie couldn't help but smile as she dressed and steeled herself to face the adoring crowd once more. Wyn's lingering presence offered welcome comfort despite its impact on Jolie's life.

CHAPTER TWENTY-ONE

The Smoke and the Tease

Wyn and Jolie made their way through the crowded room toward the bar. Angus was hard at work behind it. His hands shook as he poured drinks and served customers. Lina stood off to the side, watching Angus and occasionally pointing him toward the correct bottle.

Mikhail leaned with one elbow propped against the bar. He buffed a wine glass until it gleamed like a captured moonbeam. His eyes drifted lazily toward the frantic energy unfolding on the other side, offering Angus no help with the crowd.

Angus's face dripped sweat from his desperate concentration. He fumbled with a sprig of rosemary; the herb escaped his grasp and landed in the soapy water of the sink. Mikhail's lips curved into a slow, gloating smirk before he smoothly turned back to his task.

Jolie flashed a warm smile at Angus. Despite his gruff appearance, he was surprisingly shy and quiet. "We'll go easy on you tonight. Two bourbons, neat," she said, trying to encourage him.

Wyn shook her head with a devilish glint in her eye. "We'll take two martinis, darling."

Jolie offered a tightly pursed smile that didn't quite reach her eyes, a silent reprimand. Wyn laughed and gave Jolie's arm a playful slap. "Don't worry. He's got it."

Angus reached for a shaker. He measured the gin with shaking hands. He slid two glasses across the polished bar. The liquid sloshed and traced wet streaks across the wood. "You owned that stage tonight." He kept his shy eyes focused on the bar. Jolie smiled; the words felt like a warm tide washing over the cool, crisp gin.

Jolie sipped the drink. It wasn't right, but she wouldn't tell Angus that. "Thank you, but I felt like a mess up there."

"It was the mess that made it great," Angus replied. "You looked like you were meant to be on that stage, like there was nowhere else you'd rather be. You should let go more often."

Mikhail's expensive loafers scraped against the sticky floor as he sauntered over. He stopped beside Angus, his posture a study in confidence. He leaned in, and his voice became an oily caress. "Let me pour you new ones. I suspect you'd prefer a drink from a real craftsman."

Wyn lifted her martini glass to her lips. "Shove off."

Mikhail's hand shot out, aiming for her slender fingers. Wyn's arm snapped back in a lightning-fast evasion.

His gaze swiveled and settled on Jolie. An unsettling smile stretched across his face. "And you," he said. His eyes locked with hers. "You don't want me to shove off, do you?"

Jolie's vision narrowed. A crimson tide surged behind her eyes. A fierce, untamed instinct clawed at her throat: the burning desire to launch herself across the bar and feel the satisfying crunch of bone beneath her hands. The sharp, damp scent of a forest floor after rain flooded her senses. It battled a deep, intoxicating wave of cinnamon. The spice was so potent it threatened to unravel her control and coax her into dangerous surrender.

"This is perfect, Angus," Jolie said. Her voice remained carefully controlled. "Thank you."

Angus offered a curt nod as he moved to the opposite side of the bar. As he left, so did the scent of wild, open spaces. Only the suffocating cinnamon remained.

Mikhail seized the opportunity. "Come on," he scoffed. His tone dripped with condescension. "You can't possibly believe he did a good job."

Jolie tilted her head. Her drink became a silent shield. She lifted the glass. The cool liquid welcoming against her lips, she gave no response.

Mikhail's impatience pricked. "What? You're not talking to me now?"

Jolie set her glass down on the bar. "I will not engage in a battle of wits with an unarmed opponent."

The sharp bite of gin escaped Wyn's flared nostrils. The fine spray misted across the bar as her snort turned into a giggle. Her hand flew to her mouth. She wiped away the residue and stifled her growing laughter.

Mikhail's pupils bled into ink. His face became a contorted mask of fury. "Really." The word dripped with venom. "I imagine your detective friend can hold a better conversation."

Before Jolie could respond, Mikhail steamrolled on. "You're a hollow echo, you know. If he ever glimpsed the truth of you, he'd bolt, or worse."

Jolie's cheeks drained of color as Wyn hurled the dregs of her drink. The meager droplets landed on Mikhail's sleeve. "Leave her be."

Mikhail's gaze was daggers as he turned to Wyn. "Or what?"

"Enough!" a voice boomed from behind them.

Mikhail stepped away from the bar. His eyes narrowed into razor slits. Jolie and Wyn swiveled. Rori's sharp jab to Boden's ribs earned a clearing of his throat. "Mikhail, pack it in. Your shift's over."

Mikhail bared his teeth as a guttural curse escaped his lips. The grimy rag hit the floor with a defeated thud. He pivoted, a storm cloud personified, his shoulder slamming into Angus's side as he blustered past.

Boden moved along the bar until he had Angus's attention. He hooked a finger and drew Angus into his orbit. Rori let out a soft, almost inaudible sigh. She motioned to Lina, a silent command to take the reins behind the bar. "I'll cover your tables."

Lina nodded. Her expression was sharp and focused. She grabbed a shaker and began to fill orders.

Wyn's fingers snagged Rori's sleeve. Her grip tightened, and sudden anxiety filled her eyes. "Angus isn't in trouble, is he?"

Rori's hand covered Wyn's and gave a gentle squeeze. "He'll be fine. He should have shut Mikhail down sooner, but Angus has a soft heart. Putting people in their place isn't his way."

Jolie, her face still pale, announced, "I'm going to blend in." The venom in Mikhail's words had lodged itself deep. A seed of dread bloomed in her chest. Did he know her true nature?

Wyn's hand shot out. Her fingers closed around Jolie's arm and stopped her mid-stride. "Don't pay any attention to what he said."

Jolie's nod was quick. Her eyes fixed ahead as she melted into the throng of the theater. She retreated to a dark corner near the stage and nursed her drink. She watched her fellow dancers laughing and flirting with the audience. A twinge of envy stirred as she watched Wyn bask in the crowd's adoration. She could still sense Wyn's excitement, though it was not as strong as before. Even that small amount was enough to make her crave the feeling of being adored by an audience.

Lost in her thoughts, Jolie was caught off guard when a familiar voice spoke behind her.

"Can I buy you a drink?" Detective O'Neil said. His hand rested lightly on her lower back.

Jolie took a sharp inhale. A rush of excitement came at his touch. "Detective O'Neil," she said, trying to keep her voice steady. "It's been quite some time."

"Has it really been that long?" Danny's eyes sparkled as he spoke.

Jolie felt an uncomfortable flutter in her stomach. Her shoulders straightened. The tremor in her hands subtly disappeared as she smoothed down her skirt. "You've been so focused on catching your killer," she said, trying to deflect the attention. "I had expected to see you more often."

"I might have been a bit too eager. Plus, it was wrong to involve you," Danny said with a coy smile. He gestured toward his table. It was impossible to ignore his well-defined muscles, with the way his sleeves were rolled up. "Shall we sit?"

The rough texture of Danny's hand was a landscape of calluses earned from years of hard work. *Maybe carpentry?* she wondered. The thought sparked a fleeting image of him shaping wood, the grain yielding under his powerful grip. It sent a surprising jolt of warmth up her arm as his fingers laced through hers. She inhaled sharply. His scent was subtly masculine and clean, with a hint of salt. It was undeniably human. The reassurance, though unnecessary, settled a fear deep within her. Her perception of the world was shifting. Edges blurred. Colors intensified. It was like finally seeing the world in high definition after a lifetime of watching a grainy black-and-white film.

Danny sat beside her. His shoulder brushed hers as he turned to the waitress. His voice vibrated through the plush velvet of the theater booth. "Another bourbon, please. Make it a double for the lady." His intense stare held a flicker of something she couldn't quite decipher. His glass sat untouched, a dark amber pool reflecting the stage lights. His profile was mesmerizing. The muscles in his jaw worked subtly as he spoke. His smile started as a slow, uneven bloom at the corner of his right lip before gradually lighting up his left. She found herself utterly captivated.

The urge to touch him, to feel the warmth of his skin against hers, was overwhelming. She felt a wild, reckless desire to press her cold hand against the side of his neck, to feel the pulse beneath his skin, to breathe in the salty tang of his sweat. It rose inside her, fierce and demanding.

His eyes, however, flickered away from the stage for a split second. They darted toward a shadowed corner of the theater. He was scanning the room, almost unconsciously searching. As the haunting melody of the second act swelled, Danny edged closer to Jolie. "Are you certain you're safe working here?"

There was a pause before she answered. She sensed an odd tension in his question. His tone carried a thread of concern, but his eyes remained cold and detached. Jolie measured her words carefully. Her instincts were on high alert. "Nothing is certain," she replied softly, "but Caleb and Boden's elite security detail are watching over me."

Danny's face was shadowed and hid deeper emotions. His arm was casually draped behind her. The intoxicating scent of his skin stirred something deep inside her, a distraction she couldn't afford. She fought to steady herself. Her growing attraction to Danny only made things more complicated.

The dancer twirled across the stage, her music rising to a crescendo. Jolie exhaled. It was her cue to slip away and prepare for her own performance. Her fingers lingered against Danny's sleeve, a fleeting goodbye before she veered toward the shadowed wings. Her thoughts were a chaotic swirl of Mikhail's sharp words and Danny's halfhearted smile. A sigh escaped her lips. It carried with it the certainty of Seb's withering disappointment. She had yet to find a single other fae in her midst, although she could sense them all around her.

Chapter Twenty-Two
The Ghost Light

The velvet curtain fell. Waves of applause vibrated through the the-ater. Jolie hurried backstage. She scrubbed at her makeup; defiant residues of glitter clung to her skin. She motioned to Caleb. He bounded along beside her; he was just as anxious as she was to be out of the stifling theater and into the coolness of the night.

The backstage door groaned open. It revealed a sliver of night. Darkness swallowed them as they stepped out into the alley. A shadow detached itself from the brickwork. Before a word escaped, she registered his presence. His scent tickled her senses.

"Figured I'd escort you home," Danny's voice slithered from the dark-ness. He stepped into the glare of a streetlight. "Though I guess you already got your bodyguard."

Jolie's lips curved into a reluctant smile. The corners crinkled just enough to betray the amusement battling her wariness. "Very funny." Her voice was a carefully modulated low hum. The playfulness in her tone was a thin veneer; it barely concealed the underlying tension. She allowed herself a fleeting glimpse of the genuine mirth in his eyes. It was a brief respite before the walls went back up.

As they started walking toward Jolie's apartment, Danny took the leash from Jolie's hand. "I'm surprised Mr. Rudel didn't have a problem with a dog in his club," Danny said.

"I don't think I've ever called him Mr. Rudel," Jolie replied. "And Rori is the one in charge, and surprisingly, she didn't have a problem with Caleb being here."

Danny chuckled. "It's obvious that Rori is in charge. But I don't think she's as tough as she seems. I've seen her and Boden when they think no one is looking. He may be the muscle, but she's the heart."

Jolie was slightly taken aback by how observant Danny was. "How did you figure all that out so quickly?"

Danny smiled. "I'm a detective. It's my job to notice things when no one else does." Jolie laughed. Guilt settled in her chest. He walked so casually beside her, but he was oblivious to the darkness within her. The comforting weight of his hand rested lightly on Jolie's shoulder.

The absurdity of it hit her. A human was shepherding a vampire and a creature straight out of a fairytale back to their lair. The image made her want to laugh and cry simultaneously. A soft sound, half-chuckle, half-sigh, escaped her lips; it held behind it the weight of a century of secrets.

She slipped her arm through his. The contact sent a spark of fear, desperation, and exhilarating need through her.

"What's so funny?" Danny asked. He pulled Jolie a little closer. His breath was warm against her ear as they walked through the dimly lit street.

"Nothing, really," she replied. Her voice was light with amusement. "I'm just amazed sometimes by how the world works."

Danny studied her face. "How long have you been in Seattle?"

"A few months," Jolie answered. She tried to sound vague. She was thankful for the change of subject. "It's my favorite city to live in so far."

"Where else have you lived?" he pressed. His tone was casual, though the questions felt more probing.

Jolie hesitated. She glanced at Caleb trotting ahead of them. "Oh, all over the place," she said quickly. She waved off the question as if it were inconsequential. She wasn't about to dive into her past. Not with him. "What about you?"

"I've been here all my life." Danny's response was smooth. Without missing a beat, he asked, "Where were you before Seattle?"

The smokescreen of casual conversation crumbled. This was not a conversation at all. It was a meticulously orchestrated interrogation. Each seemingly innocuous question was a carefully placed landmine. She had fallen for his charm, his easy laughter, and the way his eyes crinkled at the corners when he smiled. Now those same eyes held danger. The smile felt far less genuine.

She chewed on her lip. The taste of bitter regret was thick on her tongue. She had been so eager to believe him. Her attraction had left her blind to his subtle manipulations.

Caleb, sensing the shift in her, moved with purpose. The leash, barely taut a moment before, tightened subtly in Danny's hand. Caleb didn't glance back, but Jolie saw the quiet shift in his body. It was not a forceful pull; it was a more strategic repositioning. Caleb had created a few crucial feet of distance between Danny and her.

By the time they reached her door, the tension between them was thick in the night air. Jolie fumbled with her keys. Caleb stood protectively between them. He ensured that Danny kept his distance. His eyes remained fixed on the detective.

Jolie turned, stealing a glance at Danny. He was leaning against the wall opposite her door. His posture was casual. But his eyes were sharp; they watched her intently. His hands were tucked into his jacket pockets. Something about the way he held himself made her wary.

His stare was piercing, though his face remained unreadable. There was a flicker of something in his expression. A shadow passed too quickly for her to grasp. He stepped forward. It was as if he were compelled to close the distance between them. But he hesitated and leaned back again with a sigh.

The moment stretched. Jolie's mind raced. She knew she needed to break whatever strange tension had settled between them. She opened her mouth to say goodnight, eager to end the encounter. But Danny beat her to it.

"I should be going," he said abruptly. He stepped away from her door and into the shadows. His tone was flat but edged with something darker.

Relief washed over her. She nodded. "Goodnight, Detective."

Without waiting for him to respond, Jolie slipped inside. She pushed the door open just enough for her and Caleb to pass through. She closed it quickly. The lock clicked into place like a shield, pressing her back against the door. She exhaled. The tension finally released from her body. For the first time since meeting Danny, her attraction was overshadowed by a creeping sense of wariness. Something had shifted. She no longer wanted to see him again.

Jolie tracked his progress by the diminishing echo of his steps down the hallway. He halted on the stairs. She heard the thin, reedy trill of his cell phone. Her focus sharpened. She strained to catch fragments of his whispered words.

"No . . . not yet. I know," a sliver of his voice touched her ears. It dissolved into the ambient hum of the city.

A frustrated breath escaped Jolie's lips. *Years of neglect,* she cursed inwardly. The very senses she craved now were elusive and untamed. She should have been training. She wrestled her attention back. She slammed a mental fist down on the intrusive roar of the highway. "The dog is . . . I know . . . It's different." His words were cryptic.

Was he talking about Caleb? She pushed, but only the final, fading sound of Danny's footsteps answered.

CHAPTER TWENTY-THREE

The Green Room

Iron pricked Jolie's nose as she twisted the cap off the chilled blood packet. Its viscous contents oozed into her mug. She popped it into the microwave and set the timer. The balcony door was open. The sounds of late afternoon in the city streamed into her apartment. Murmured voices, laughter, and the rush of traffic overwhelmed her already tired senses. She had barely registered the ding of the microwave when a frantic drumming erupted at the front door.

Jolie's shoulders tightened, and she cursed silently. Caleb nudged her calf with his wet nose. "Alright." The words were rough against her dry throat. The insistent thudding continued. The air in the kitchen seemed to throb with her annoyance.

She padded across her apartment. The rhythmic pounding was a relentless drumbeat against her skull. Her mug felt rough beneath her fingers as she lifted it. The warm, faintly tart liquid did little to chase away the lingering haze. As she reached the door, she was overcome with unease. There was something vital. Something forgotten. It was slipping through her grasp. "Who in their right mind . . ." she began. The question dissolved into a low growl as her hand reached for the doorknob.

"Jolie! For crying out loud, open up! We're burning daylight!" Wyn's voice was strained with urgency.

Jolie's shoulders sagged. A slow exhale escaped her lips. Caleb surged past her legs. His tail banged against the doorframe. It was a joyous greeting to the storm that had just arrived. Wyn, barely waiting for the door to swing inward, bulldozed into the apartment. "Get dressed. Now. We're on the clock." Her words were clipped. Her eyes were narrowed, focused on some unseen deadline.

Jolie remained anchored in the doorway. She tilted her head and appraised Wyn. Wyn's usual explosion of color was gone; denim hugged her legs, ending in sensible boots. Her blazer was a muted gray, and she paired the bland ensemble with a plain white tee. Her signature fiery hair, usually a wild halo, was tamed and slicked back. Her face was scrubbed bare and missing its usual flamboyant makeup.

"Why are you so covered up?" Jolie asked.

Wyn's gaze sharpened. A silent accusation came in the flick of her wrist as she gestured toward the heavy front door. "You have the meeting with the elders today, remember?" Wyn's voice was sharp as a splinter. "A fact I impressed upon you just last night."

Jolie's fingers instinctively tightened around her mug. A wave of heat, unwelcome and prickly, crept up her neck. "The elders?" she mumbled. A sudden, vivid image of Danny's laughter flashed behind her eyes. She dragged a hand over her brow. "My head . . . It's a bit fuzzy."

Jolie took a drink from her mug. "I don't remember," she admitted meekly. "I must have been too caught up in the moment."

Wyn let out an exasperated sigh. "Well, you need to get ready now. We can't afford to be late for this meeting."

Jolie dug through the laundry basket. The scent of stale fabric did nothing to calm her frayed nerves. She snagged a faded T-shirt, a dark gray sweater that smelled somewhat clean, and a pair of jeans that still held the fading scent of fabric softener.

"Ready?" Wyn's voice boomed from the doorway.

Caleb scrambled into the back seat of Wyn's ancient VW Bug. Its faded blue paint peeled in places; the cracked leather of the car's interior snagged on Jolie's sweater as she slid into her seat.

Wyn turned the key. The engine sputtered and slowly came to life. As they drove, Jolie began to fill Wyn in on the strange encounter she had with Danny the night before. The car lurched forward onto the narrow road. The interior creaked with every turn. The cramped space made it hard to get comfortable, but Wyn seemed unfazed. Her focus was fixed on the road ahead.

Wyn's brow furrowed as Jolie described the unsettling tension between her and Detective O'Neil. Wyn's hands gripped the wheel tightly. She navigated through the congested streets with an intensity that mirrored her thoughts. She wove between cars and cut around slower drivers with calculated turns. Each swerve made Jolie's stomach flip. Her mind raced to keep up with the chaotic drive and the memory of Danny's uncomfortable stare.

When Jolie finished, Wyn finally spoke. She slowed the car to a crawl as they approached a narrow curve. "That does sound strange," she said. Her voice was low and thoughtful. "I don't like it, Jolie. You should probably steer clear of him." She shot a quick glance at her from the corner of her eye. A look of concern deepened the lines on her face.

Realizing she had let her focus slip, Wyn hit the gas hard. She jolted the car forward with an unexpected surge of speed. The tires screeched as the Bug darted into the next lane. It narrowly avoided a delivery truck.

Jolie's stomach leaped into her throat. Her fingers dug into the door handle. The world outside blurred as they sped down the highway. The tiny car felt far too fragile for Wyn's aggressive maneuvers. Jolie swallowed her rising panic. She tried to steady herself as she heard Caleb's pulse quicken from the backseat.

"Could you, maybe, not decapitate us before I avoid him?" Jolie muttered. She was only half-joking. Her eyes were wide with genuine concern.

Wyn glanced at her, smirking slightly, but she eased off the gas just a touch. "Relax, we're fine," she said. Her tone was playful despite the recklessness of her driving. "But seriously, Jolie. Stay away from him. Something's off, and I don't want to see you get hurt."

Jolie nodded. Her grip on the door loosened slightly as she forced herself to relax. In the back seat, Caleb scrambled as Wyn took another sharp turn. It caused the dog to slide helplessly across the cracked leather seat. His claws scratched against the surface as he desperately tried to find something to brace himself against. Jolie grimaced as she heard the thud of him hitting the side of the car.

"Jesus, Wyn!" she yelled. Her voice was filled with genuine fear. "Where did you learn to drive?"

Wyn shrugged. She was completely unfazed by the commotion she was creating on the road. "Oh, you know. Around," she said with a nonchalant wave of her hand, as if narrowly avoiding a collision was just part of the thrill. "This is my sister's car, anyway. I don't have a license. I can't pass the test." Her words were delivered so casually that Jolie almost missed the terrifying admission.

Before Jolie could even respond, Wyn whipped the car around another corner. She narrowly avoided a woman struggling to parallel park. The woman's startled face flashed by the window. Her expression quickly turned to fury as she flipped them off, her hand shaking angrily in the air.

Jolie could feel Caleb's heart pounding within her own chest. Her mind flooded with horrifying images of their car crashing into a lamppost or careening off the road. She glanced back at Caleb. He had managed to steady himself for a moment. His wide, worried eyes met hers.

She turned back toward the front. Her voice was barely a whisper as she muttered, "I would've never guessed." Her knuckles were still white against the door handle; her stomach was twisted in knots.

Wyn glanced at her with a wicked grin. She clearly enjoyed the wild ride. "Relax, Jolie. We're not gonna crash. Probably."

Jolie swallowed hard, trying to calm herself. But Caleb's frantic attempts to stay upright were enough to keep her nerves on edge. Every swerve of the car sent him sliding across the back seat. His claws scraped the leather as he desperately tried to find footing.

"Probably," Jolie muttered under her breath. Her eyes darted back to Caleb once more. She was no longer sure whether her intense dread was from the reckless drive or Wyn's carefree attitude masking something deeper. Either way, she could not shake the feeling that this ride, and everything that followed, was going to lead them somewhere dangerous.

Wyn navigated the car onto a quiet residential street, ignoring the speed limit. "Oh, so now the stick-in-the-mud is funny," she quipped. A hint of nervousness filled her tone. "Relax, we're almost there." Jolie glanced out the window. Her eyes were wide with surprise as she took in the unfamiliar surroundings. This part of the city was unlike anything she had seen before. It had beautiful tree-lined streets and sprawling houses.

"Where are we, exactly?" Jolie asked.

Wyn shrugged as she made a sharp turn. "I think it's called Lake Sammamish." A note of uncertainty filled her voice. As they drove down a long driveway toward the water, Jolie's eyes were drawn to the main house in front of them. It was a grand, three-story structure. The wood was painted a deep slate blue. It had dark red doors and shutters. It reminded Jolie of old New England; it was clear that the owner had an eye for the past. The brick steps leading up to the front door were lined with large planters.

As they got out of the car, Jolie noticed several other buildings surrounding the main house. All were designed in the same colonial style. She could not imagine what it must have been like to live on such a luxurious estate.

Wyn ran her fingers through her hair. She tried to smooth out the wild strands as she straightened her outfit. The nervous energy rolling off her was palpable, and her normally confident demeanor seemed frayed around the edges. "Okay, just remember to be on your best behavior," she said. She cast a sharp glance at both Jolie and Caleb. "Both of you." Wyn's finger jabbed at Caleb's nose. Caleb did not flinch. Instead, he let out a low, deliberate growl. Jolie smiled at the absurdity of the situation. "Isn't this your family?" she asked. Her voice was filled with teasing curiosity. "Why are you so nervous?"

Wyn sighed. The exasperation was clear in her tone as she shot Jolie a pained look. "Sometimes, you can be so dense, Jolie."

Jolie raised an eyebrow, surprised by Wyn's sharpness. Her friend was often blunt with her, but not mean. "What did I say?" she asked. The air around them felt heavier by the second.

Wyn ran a hand down her face. "I'm sorry," she muttered. Her voice was a touch softer now. "I'm just . . . stressed. I'm not actually related to any of the elders. Well, not by blood. It's all through marriage." Her eyes moved nervously around the estate, and anxiety crept into her voice. "They don't think much of my family. It's always a struggle to maintain our reputation here. To prove we belong."

Jolie's amusement faded. She had always assumed that all succubi were like Wyn, flamboyant and powerful. Wyn always seemed so confident in her place in the world. But now it seemed there was far more to Wyn's story than she realized.

As the three of them neared the grand front doors of the estate, the atmosphere seemed to shift. The massive doors stood like wardens. Jolie picked up the faint scent of something spicy and earthly. It made the hair on the back of her neck stand on end.

Extravagant carvings were chiseled into the stones lining the walkway. Each depicted scenes of ethereal beings: some were twisted and dark; others were eerie and graceful. Standing before these doors, she realized how little she knew about the inner workings of Wyn's world.

Caleb trotted beside them. He was now unnervingly quiet; his usually playful demeanor was replaced with a newfound alertness, as if expecting danger to emerge from the shadows. He too seemed to sense the weight of the place.

"Is there anything I should know before we go in?" Jolie asked quietly. As if speaking too loudly might disturb the ancient spirits lingering around them.

Wyn gave her a tight-lipped smile. But there was no humor in her eyes. "Just stay close," she replied. Her tone was forced. "And remember, we don't belong here. Don't do anything to make them regret meeting with us."

Jolie nodded. Her curiosity mingled with apprehension as they approached the grand double doors. Whatever lay beyond was an invisible force; it was ancient and powerful, and it waited just on the other side. Caleb walked beside them. He tried his best to exude an air of regality and aloofness. Compared to Jolie and Wyn, he seemed to fit in much better.

As they reached the brick porch, the double doors opened. A young woman dressed in a dark suit with a crisp white blouse stood and welcomed them in. Her hair was pulled back in a severe bun, and without a word, she motioned for them to follow her into the foyer. She pointed to a set of chairs against the wall and then disappeared down the hallway. Her heels clicked along the marble and wood floors.

Jolie leaned over to whisper in Wyn's ear. "Do you know who she is?"

Wyn nodded. "She's one of the elders' grandchildren. It seems like she's being groomed to take over. Most likely through a vow of silence to sharpen her other forms of communication." As they heard the footsteps stop and a door close, she added, "It's all part of the Kafkaesque hierarchy."

Jolie's eyes widened in surprise. "Wait, you're all telepathic too?"

Wyn shook her head. "Not quite. But with practice, we can plant thoughts in your mind from a distance. It's quite useful."

Jolie took in the opulent surroundings. The walls were adorned with royal blue wallpaper. It was accented with intricate gold filigree and sconces that lit the way. There were no overhead lights. But the soft glow from the lamps on the walls reflected off the white marble floor.

The whisper of silk announced her approach before Jolie and Wyn even saw her. Each footfall was deliberate and slow, the sound swallowed by the ornate, high-ceilinged space.

The woman seemed to float rather than walk. A languid, almost hesitant progress. Her light silk dress was muted pink and blue; it swirled gently around her ankles. The fabric clung in places, revealing the delicate curve of her hip; elsewhere, it billowed. Her hair cascaded down her back in loose waves. Bare feet barely made a sound on the polished floor. A single, delicate gold anklet shimmered at her ankle with each slight movement.

A smile stretched across her face. It revealed teeth too perfect to be entirely natural. It was the kind offered by a hostess to an unwelcome guest. "I apologize for the wait." Her voice was soft, almost melodious. A carefully cultivated lilt grated on Jolie's ears. The words were laced with a subtle, almost imperceptible sweetness that felt more like poison than honey. Jolie noted the faint tremor in her voice. The woman gestured for them to follow her. "The elders are ready to see you now. Please come with me." She began to lead them down the long hallway. Jolie and Wyn followed closely behind.

Jolie whispered to Wyn. "I never expected succubi to be so different from one another."

Wyn grabbed her hand. Her grip was rough and urgent. "Shhh, your bigotry is showing," she scolded. "Besides, that one is human. Probably someone's pet."

Jolie's brow furrowed. The implications tore at the edges of her consciousness, but before she could probe further, they were at the threshold of a room that reeked of old money and something unsettling. It was not just the opulence. Not just the polished wood flaring under the light of colossal chandeliers, or the thick, plush carpets swallowing sound. Not even the drapes of heavy silk hung in sea-foam green and midnight blue. It was the stillness. A suffocating, expectant stillness prickled her skin.

The windows offered a breathtaking view of the lake. But Jolie barely registered it. She was riveted on the three figures within. They sat gathered around a small, inlaid card table. Their attention was completely absorbed in a game she did not recognize. Something involving hand-painted cards and oddly shaped, weighted tokens.

Two women and a man. Their clothes, though clearly expensive, spoke of a time long gone. A woman in a jade-green gown, its silk shimmering faintly, held a gilded teacup. Her rings, numerous and gaudy, sparkled as she adjusted her playing cards. Beside her, a man in a maroon velvet smoking jacket, his cravat slightly askew, leaned back. His eyes were narrowed in concentration. A faint smell of pipe tobacco clung to him. The third, a woman in a severe black dress, her hair pulled back harshly, tapped a long fingernail against the table. Her expression was unreadable.

Wyn, her posture rigid, stood before them. Jolie mirrored her stillness. Her own apprehension was a lead weight in her chest. The three figures at the table remained oblivious. Their world seemingly contained within the confines of the game. Finally, the woman in green glanced up. Her eyes lingered on Wyn before shifting to Jolie with a soft frown. Her lips, painted a startling pink, barely moved as she uttered a single word, her tone curt. "Well?"

The woman in the flowing dress gracefully circled behind the woman in green and cleared her throat. "I would like to formally introduce our esteemed guests," she announced. "First, we have Abelina, daughter of Alexander." Jolie felt a jolt of shock at the name. It was clear that "Wyn" was not her real name, but the new one seemed to fit her even less. Wyn gave Jolie a warning look, silently urging her to keep quiet. The woman continued. "Accompanying her, we have Jolie Mason, the vampire, and Caleb, the barghest."

The woman in black spoke first. Her voice was soft and raspy. "We typically do not entertain the undead," she said. She eyed Jolie with suspicion. "However, the presence of the barghest speaks for the vampire. Please take him to the kitchen and find him something to eat."

A young man in a fitted gray suit emerged from the shadows of an alcove. His eyes immediately locked onto Caleb's leash. The dog's body tensed. A low, guttural growl escaped between his bared teeth. He refused to be led away like some common pet. The three elders turned to face the commotion.

Jolie knelt and stroked Caleb's head reassuringly. "It's okay, Caleb. I'll call for you if I need you." Reluctantly, Caleb allowed himself to be led away.

The three elders returned to their game. The woman in the flowing floral dress said, "The elders are ready to hear from you." She gestured toward the trio. Wyn approached the woman in black, who eyed her warily.

"Elder Camille," Wyn greeted with a respectful nod. The woman sat up straight. Her sharp features were heightened by the pull of her white hair away from her face. Camille's presence commanded attention without effort.

Wyn then turned her gaze to the woman in green, Giselle. Her eyes sparkled with impish curiosity behind her delicate wire-rimmed glasses. They sat perched on her nose. The deep green of her dress perfectly matched the emerald stones embedded in her jewelry. Giselle dealt the deck of cards she had been shuffling absentmindedly, though her interest was clearly piqued as she looked up at Wyn.

Lastly, Wyn addressed the male elder, Aluin. His round face was framed by a graying beard that gave him an air of gentleness. His eyes, however, were hard beneath his bushy brows. He watched Jolie intently as if weighing her every movement.

Elder Giselle placed her cards gently on the table and adjusted her glasses. The thin chain around her neck caught the light with each movement. "You wanted to speak to us about something?" she asked. Her voice lilted with curiosity as she tilted her head to one side. Her eyes sparkled as though she already knew something interesting was coming.

Jolie stepped forward and joined Wyn. Her hands twisted nervously in front of her as she summoned the courage to speak. Her throat felt dry. She could feel the weight of the elders' stares pressing down on her. Especially Camille's cold, disdainful gaze. "Yes, well . . . it's about the murders at The Black Cat House, actually," she managed. Her voice trembled slightly as the words tumbled out.

At the mention of murder, Elder Camille's lips curled into a dismissive sneer. She crossed her arms. Her expression hardened as she scoffed. "Murder?" she repeated. Her tone dripped with contempt. "We don't trouble ourselves with the sordid affairs of The Black Cat House and its riffraff. Those people are beneath us," she added. Her voice was cold.

Elder Aluin placed his cards down on the table with a satisfied smile. He took a long sip of his drink. "A murderous succubus will always be our problem. What Camille means to say is we will handle it as we see fit." His tone was stern, yet tinged with a hint of amusement.

Jolie could not contain her eagerness and blurted out, "So you have an idea of who it is?" She leaned forward. Her eyes were wide with hope.

Elder Aluin's gaze shifted toward Jolie. His expression was unreadable. "I didn't say that," he replied cryptically. "But this matter must be handled within our own ranks."

Jolie felt her irritation bubbling up inside her. People were dying, and the elders seemed more concerned with their own laws and traditions than with doing anything to stop it. "You can't just cover this up!" she exclaimed. Her voice was laced with annoyance. "I need to know how to put an end to this."

Elder Giselle spoke up. "They are humans, dear," she said with a sigh. "We are not the same." She brushed a strand of hair from her face. Her expression softened for a moment before returning to her usual sternness. "But that does not mean we are heartless. The succubus responsible for these killings is obviously unaligned. They do not respect our ways. When we find them, we will deal with them according to our laws." She motioned for the woman in the flowing dress, who had been standing silently behind the elders, to lead Jolie and Wyn back to the front door.

Jolie knew the conversation was over. The subtle shift in Elder Giselle's posture was a silent dismissal more potent than any spoken word. Giselle's hands, gnarled and veined like ancient roots, adjusted a playing card. Jolie's own hands clenched into fists. She could not let it go.

"Wait." Jolie's voice, though strained, held a tremor of desperate hope. She planted her feet firmly. "When? When will you deal with them?" Her gaze, unwavering, locked with Giselle's. It was a challenge. A silent plea for understanding, for action.

Giselle did not flinch. Her eyes held a chilling stillness. They were old eyes. Eyes that had seen countless hopeful pleas meet a grim reality. A faint smile played on her lips. It was not kind. It was not cruel, exactly. It was simply knowing.

"When the time is right," Giselle answered. Each syllable was a tiny blow against Jolie's hopes. She did not look away from the cards. "And you, child," Giselle added. Her voice was low, with a hint of warning. "Must learn patience. Some battles are won not by rushing in, but by waiting for the opportune moment."

The woman in the flowing dress guided Jolie toward the heavy oak door. Her hand was light as a feather. Each step the woman took was deliberate and measured. She silently closed the door and left Jolie and Wyn standing alone in the hallway.

Jolie's nails dug into her palms. Her frustration finally came to a boiling point. "I can't believe it. They don't care," she burst out. Her voice was tight with unshed tears. She did not look at Wyn. Instead, she fixed her eyes on a section of the hallway's molding. The weight of disappointment visibly crushed her.

"They care, Jolie. They just have a very different way of showing it. They're a bunch of old prigs, stuck in their ways." Wyn sighed. "I'm sorry this was useless. I have no idea why they agreed to meet with us."

Just then, the door to a side room opened. The same woman emerged. She led a content-looking Caleb. The woman paused before handing Caleb's leash to Jolie. "You know, being invisible to them has its advantages. I hear all sorts of things." Her voice was soft, almost conspiratorial.

Jolie met her gaze and smiled. "What's your name?"

"Elder Giselle named me Allure. She isn't as bad as she came across." Allure's posture was withdrawn. "I've been with her most of my life."

Jolie shrugged and rubbed the back of her neck. "I guess I'll take your word for it."

Allure's soft demeanor vanished. Her face grew serious as she leaned in closer to Jolie. Her voice dropped to a hushed tone. It was barely above a whisper. "They care more than they let on," she said. Her eyes flicked toward the shadows of the room as if wary of unseen ears. "The elders are worried. Even if they pretend that they're not."

Jolie felt a chill crawl down her spine at Allure's words. There was something dangerous simmering beneath the surface of the succubi world. Allure continued, her words quick and urgent, "There's a new group of succubi. Young, reckless, and angry. They're not just talking about overthrowing the elders. They want to wreak havoc in the human world. They think it's time for a shift in power. They don't care who gets caught in the crossfire."

Wyn's breath caught in her throat. The idea of rogue succubi disrupting the fragile balance between their kind and humans was terrifying. The elders were powerful, but if there was any truth to what Allure was saying, the succubi were on the brink of war. Not only with their own kind but with unsuspecting humans who had no idea of the dangers lurking among them.

Allure lowered her voice even further. "They also really wanted to meet you. I'm not sure why."

Confusion twisted across Jolie's features. "Me?" The idea felt absurd.

With a glance back toward the hallway, Allure's urgency increased. She swiftly handed Caleb's leash to Jolie. Her hand brushed against Jolie's for a moment. "Stay sharp. There's more going on than you know," she said. Her voice was low and intense. Then, without waiting for a response, Allure turned on her heel and disappeared down the long corridor. She left them standing in silence.

Chapter Twenty-Four

The Tassel Spin

As they drove down the highway, Jolie could not shake the uneasy feeling that had been gnawing at her since they left the elders. She turned to Wyn, but she was abruptly cut off before she could even speak.

"I have no idea who is involved in this underground," Wyn admitted. Her voice was laced with disappointment. "And I have no idea how to find out."

Jolie frowned. She sensed that there was more to the story. "Are you sure? Is there something you're not telling me?"

Wyn hesitated. Her eyes were glued to the road ahead. "There are some things I can't tell you without jeopardizing my family's standing even further."

Jolie's eyes widened in disbelief. Her voice rose, laced with urgency. "Wait, what do you mean? Either you truly don't know what's going on, or you're deliberately keeping things from me."

Wyn remained silent. Her lips pressed into a tight line. Her knuckles were white as they gripped the steering wheel. She didn't turn to look at Jolie; she refused to acknowledge Jolie's accusations.

The car felt smaller. It was suffocating as tension wrapped itself around them. Jolie slumped back into her seat. A mix of irritation and disappointment weighed on her. She stared at Wyn, waiting for an explanation, for some sign of understanding. Wyn's silence spoke louder than any words. The tightness in her jaw, the refusal to look at her, only deepened Jolie's sense of betrayal.

"People are dying, Wyn," Jolie said. Her voice was softer now, but full of desperation. "We can't afford to keep secrets. Not now."

Wyn's expression did not falter. Her eyes were unblinking as the road stretched out before them. The only sound in the car was the rumble of the engine. She remained silent; her body was rigid. She offered neither explanation nor comfort.

Anger flared hot in Jolie's chest. She crossed her arms over her body. She was just beginning to trust Wyn. But now, the silence between them felt too wide to cross.

Jolie turned her head toward the window. She watched the city blur past them. Her thoughts swirled. What was Wyn hiding, and why? The silence stretched on. It was broken only by the occasional sound of tires rolling over asphalt. Jolie knew there was more to this, more than Wyn was letting on. If her friend would not talk, then Jolie would have to find the answers on her own.

By the time Wyn pulled the car to a stop outside Jolie's apartment, the tension had solidified into a wall between them. Jolie did not wait for Wyn to say anything. She unbuckled her seatbelt and swung the door open. She stepped out into the cool air. Caleb jumped down beside her, his leash trailing behind.

Jolie turned back to Wyn. She still had not moved; her hands gripped the wheel tightly. "If you change your mind," Jolie said. Her voice was cold and distant. "You know where to find me."

Wyn's voice cracked. "Jolie," she called. Her hand instinctively reached out, then retracted. "Wait. There's someone. Someone who might know something. But don't get your hopes up. It's a long shot."

Jolie stopped, her back turned to Wyn. The stiff lines of her shoulders betrayed her inner turmoil. She could hear the tremor in Wyn's voice, the hesitant pauses.

Jolie swallowed. The lump in her throat was surprisingly heavy. "I understand," she managed. Her voice was rougher than she had intended. "A long shot is better than nothing. Thank you." The words were sincere. The relief washed over her in a wave.

Wyn had come through. In that moment, the fragile hope felt like a lifeline. As Jolie looked into Wyn's troubled eyes, she could see the inner conflict playing out behind them. Wyn's usual confident, defiant demeanor was gone. It was replaced by a vulnerability that softened Jolie's anger. Wyn wanted to help, but it was twisting her up inside. Jolie was putting her in an impossible position. She was forcing her to choose between loyalty to her family and doing what was right.

Jolie swallowed hard. Guilt began to creep into her chest. She had not meant to push Wyn so far. To lean on her so heavily, but desperation had clouded her judgment. Wyn was caught in the middle of something bigger than either of them. Jolie knew that asking her to take sides was unfair.

Jolie softened her gaze. Her voice was gentler now. "I'm sorry," she murmured. Her words were muffled by regret. "I didn't mean to put this all on you. I know it's not easy . . . with your family and everything."

Wyn looked away. Her lips pressed into a thin line as she stared at her lap. "It's not that I don't want to help," she whispered. Her voice was barely audible. "It's just . . . I don't know how far I can go without losing everything."

Jolie nodded slowly. She understood the depth of Wyn's struggle more than ever. She reached out and rested a hand on Wyn's arm. "I know. And I don't want to make things harder for you. But I can't do this alone. I need you, Wyn. We'll figure it out together, okay?"

Wyn glanced up with glassy eyes. She gave a small nod. The weight of the moment pressed down on them. Wyn let out a ragged sigh before continuing. "I don't know what's going on exactly. But I do know someone who might know about the underground; she knows everyone. Or everyone wants to know her."

Jolie gazed at Wyn with a mix of gratitude and confusion. She could not understand why she had been so kind to her. Jolie leaned in and kissed Wyn on the cheek. "You've done so much for me. I don't know how to thank you," she whispered before pulling away.

The corners of Wyn's mouth tugged upward. "So, about making amends," she drawled. Her tone was light but pointed. "How about you grace us with your presence at the party tomorrow?"

Jolie offered a silent, sardonic roll of her eyes. The very thought of the party sent a shiver of revulsion down her spine. Before she could voice her utter lack of interest, a furry blur ran past her and lunged through the car window. Caleb planted wet kisses on Wyn's face. His tail thumped against the side of the car. Giggles erupted from Wyn. They were full of genuine joy. Caleb was excellent at breaking the tension.

"Come on, Caleb. Let's go," Jolie called as she walked away. Her heels clicked sharply on the pavement as she strode away. Each step was a determined rejection. "I'll . . . consider it," she mumbled over her shoulder. Her voice was barely noticeable above Caleb's joyful barks.

As Jolie closed the door behind them, she let out a sigh of relief. All she wanted to do was crawl into bed and sleep for a few more hours. After a moment of contemplation, Caleb tilted his head to the side. "I know," Jolie said. "Let's order some pizza, read some books, and go to bed early." Caleb's tail thumped in agreement. But he tilted his head again, as if to suggest something else. "Oh, you want to go for a run too?" Jolie laughed. "Okay, let's make a plan. We'll take a nap first and then go for a run when the sun is finally down."

With that settled, Jolie pulled the covers up to her chin. Her eyelids fluttered shut. But sleep did not bring peace. Instead, the stale, musty scent of the old theater filled her nostrils. It was a phantom smell that clung to the edges of her dreams. She was back there, in that first theater. The echoing silence of the theater where everything changed.

Viktor's voice vibrated not just in her ears, but deep within her chest. "I will be your guide," he whispered. "I will protect you."

The hunger was a gnawing ache in her belly. It clawed at her. It was a constant reminder of what he had not warned her about. Hesitantly, her feet traced the familiar route through the darkness. Each step brought a flood of memories. The chilling touch of his hand. The taste of blood. The agonizing transformation. A ragged sob bubbled up in her throat as the weight of her changed life pressed down on her. Tears streamed down her cheeks. They blurred the already dim surroundings. But her feet moved. They were compelled. They retraced the path of that fateful night. An invisible thread pulled her forward.

"No, please stop." The whisper was lost in the frantic rustling of Jolie's sheets. Sweat beaded on her forehead. It plastered stray strands of hair to her skin. Her eyes darted back and forth beneath closed lids. In her dream, she sleepwalked toward the dressing room. A marionette pulled by invisible strings.

Jolie's fangs elongated and pierced the fullness of her lip. A shudder racked her frame as she fought against the tide of instinct. Her fingernails dug into her palms.

The dressing room door creaked open under her involuntary push. It revealed Ginger. She was bathed in the soft glow of a single vanity bulb. Ginger's smile was almost too bright. "You were fantastic, kid," Ginger purred. "I have no idea what changed, but wow, you were amazing."

The air shimmered. Then it fractured. The vanity and the walls around her shimmered in dripping crimson. The metallic smell of blood flooded her senses. Viktor stood amidst the carnage. His face was partially obscured by shadow. A chilling, gleeful smile stretched across his lips as he licked Ginger's blood from his fingers. Jolie looked down. Blood dripped from her chin and soaked her dress.

Jolie's scream tore through the quiet room. Caleb, roused from sleep, was at her side. His eyes filled with fear that matched, and perhaps even surpassed, her own. She bolted upright. The lie, "It was just a bad dream," caught in her throat.

Instead of a gentle splash, Jolie plunged her face into the icy water. A desperate attempt to shatter the lingering images. She did not just avoid the mirror; she recoiled from it. The click of Caleb's claws across the floor was a lifeline. "I need air, Caleb," she choked out.

Caleb nudged her legs in agreement. Jolie quickly changed into her sneakers and leather coat. They made their way to the balcony of her apartment. Without hesitation, they leaped into the night and landed silently on the street below. They ran through the quiet city. Their feet barely made a sound as they navigated the streets and jumped onto balconies to avoid pedestrians. When they finally reached the rooftops, they played a game of tag. They chased each other over the buildings. With each leap, Jolie could feel her past slipping away. The darkness within subsided for now. Soon she felt like herself again. The dream and its haunting images pushed to the back of her mind.

Jolie stopped on a rooftop. She took in the breathtaking view of the city skyline. Caleb continued to run in circles around her. His tail wagged happily. She smiled at his carefree spirit. He relished his freedom from the confines of their apartment and cramped car rides. "Are you ready for some food, buddy?" Jolie asked. She knew the answer already. Caleb barked in excitement, his tongue lolling out of his mouth.

They returned to their apartment building. Caleb's dinner in hand, they entered through the front door and climbed the stairs. As they approached, Jolie's eyes immediately caught sight of a beautiful bouquet resting just outside her door. It stood out, its beauty odd against the neglected hallway, a striking arrangement of long-stemmed red roses.

Setting down the pizza boxes absentmindedly, Jolie stepped toward the flowers. Who would send her roses? She carefully plucked the card from between the blossoms. She squinted at the hurried, almost illegible scrawl on the tiny note.

"Sorry I missed you. Danny."

Jolie froze. The card slipped slightly in her fingers. Danny. The memory of his unsettling energy from the night before flashed in her mind. Part of her wanted to smile, to think that maybe this gesture was a sign he was starting to see her in a different light. But beneath the surface, dread twisted in her gut. Wyn's warning echoed in her head. It was a reminder that Danny was not as simple as he seemed. There was something . . . off.

She sighed and tried to push the conflicting emotions aside as she buried her face in the roses. Their sweet, intoxicating scent filled her senses. It momentarily soothed the tension coiling inside her. It had been so long since anyone had sent her flowers. Jolie allowed herself a fleeting moment of contentment. She let the romance of the gesture wash over her, but her instincts screamed at her to be cautious.

Caleb padded over to her. His large, comforting presence was always there when she needed it most. He rested his head on her shoulder. His warm breath tickled her neck. Jolie smiled faintly and placed a hand on his fur, but her heart felt heavy. She could feel the weight of his silent concern, a reminder that things were not right.

"I know," Jolie whispered. She frowned as she looked down at the roses. She stroked Caleb's head. Her mind raced with the contradictions swirling around Danny. The flowers were a sweet gesture, yes. But they did not erase the wariness that had been growing inside her. The odd bits of the phone conversation that she had overheard still lingered in her mind. No matter how beautiful the roses were, they could not distract her from the truth. She could not trust him.

With a sharp breath, Jolie straightened; determination surged through her. It did not matter what Danny's intentions were or how he saw her now. She could not let herself be swayed by empty gestures, not when something darker lurked beneath the surface.

Jolie ripped the card in half, then in half again. The small pieces fluttered to the floor like confetti. They landed softly on the rose petals. She stared at them for a moment. The once-beautiful bouquet was now tainted by suspicion and uncertainty. Jolie stepped over the discarded flowers. Her heart was heavy, but her resolve was clear. As she entered her apartment, she closed the door firmly behind her.

Once safely inside, she changed into comfortable sweats and settled on the couch. She grabbed the books that Seb had lent her. She had yet to look at *Charms and Chants for Warding and Protection*. She decided to start there. A prickle of excitement ran down Jolie's spine as her finger traced the curves of the warding runes. The book, its aged paper crackling softly beneath her touch, felt imbued with power.

Her impatient fingers brushed aside a stack of books from her coffee table, sending them tumbling with a soft thud. Then she found it: a sharpie. A thrill coursed through her.

"Caleb!" she called. Her brow slightly furrowed in concentration as she knelt beside the door. The ancient script held close. Caleb's eyelids, heavy with slumber, did not even flutter. His sigh, a puff of air, spoke of his skepticism.

Her movements were not hurried. Each rune was drawn with deliberate precision. A deep breath came before each stroke. The sharpie's point glided across the wood. She wrote the runes above the door, below it, and flanking the frame. The runes pulsed with faint energy. Then, a sudden wave of heat radiated from them—a bright glow, like captured sunlight, flared briefly before melting back into the wood.

Jolie's jaw dropped, her eyes wide and unblinking. There was a tangible shift in the air, a deep feeling of safety and protection. The silence in the room felt different now, richer, somehow more secure. "Wow," she breathed. She ran a hand over the now-invisible runes. "I think . . . I think it worked."

Feeling emboldened, she repeated the process on all her windows and balcony doors, each time with the same result. A warmth bloomed in Jolie's chest. She had not seen anything happen, not really, but the air felt different, lighter somehow. Caleb continued to snore. He was completely unmoved by what she had accomplished. A satisfied smile tugged at the corners of Jolie's mouth. With a soft thump, the book and sharpie landed on the coffee table. Her fingers traced the embossed title of the volume Seb had given her: *Thornwick's Exhaustive Encyclopedia of the Fae Folk.*

Jolie crawled into bed with Caleb and snuggled under the covers. She opened her book to the page on succubi. She hoped to find some useful information that could help her in her hunt for the murderer. However, instead of their weaknesses, the page displayed a meticulously drawn chart. A spiderweb of familial connections, each branch adorned with symbols representing titles and estates.

Only one section offered anything of genuine interest. A small annotation reiterated their aversion to iron. Not lethal, the note clarified, but incapacitating. She traced the next passage. The text spoke of their accelerated healing. Impressive, yes. But the carefully measured phrasing hinted at vulnerability. Faster than humans, slower than her own. The final sentence was blunt: decapitation. The only true method of death.

"Well, that's not exactly groundbreaking news. It's a well-known fact that decapitation is an effective method of killing." Jolie's voice held a hint of sarcasm as she glanced down at the Caleb-shaped lump under the blankets. She nudged him with her knee. She hoped to get some sort of response from her sleeping companion. "Sometimes I envy humans for their rich mythology," Jolie mused. "In their stories, every monster has a fancy weakness. It would have been nice if some of those weaknesses were actually true." She nudged Caleb again, but he only let out a muffled grunt in response.

"Looks like I'm just talking to myself," she sighed in resignation. Jolie's eager thumb flipped toward the Vs. Her eyes raked across the dense text. "Vampirism . . . a viral exchange in blood droplets. If, when dying, a human ingests vampire blood, it ignites a parasitic occupancy, their husks reanimating." Jolie's brow furrowed with the new information.

"Weakened by solar radiation but not overtly harmed," the book droned. Its words were dry. "Blood their sole sustenance, yet they can mimic the ingestion of human food." Jolie swallowed. She was aware of all this.

She turned the page. "Superhuman speed and extreme strength. A devolution toward savagery with the passage of centuries." Jolie shook as a chill ran through her. She made a silent plea that no such darkness would stain her own soul. "Considered pariahs amongst the elder fae, their presence denounced among the ruling courts."

Jolie snorted. "Rude."

The paper whispered as Jolie turned another page. "Vampire hunters." She closed her eyes and then willed herself to read on. "New recruits trained by masters," she murmured. "Usually, only one to two recruits per master. They are trained to hunt and track their prey until they find them in a weakened state." Her knuckles tightened on the book's cover. "The first attack is usually a stake through the heart. Which will incapacitate the vampire but not kill them, then decapitation."

A cold dread seeped into her bones. She pictured the sharp, brutal efficiency. The paper crackled once more as she slammed the book shut.

"Always decapitation," Jolie breathed. The words caught in her throat. "Good to know a stake through the heart won't actually kill me," she added. A brittle, humorless laugh escaped her lips. "Just makes me a sitting duck."

Jolie's fingers brushed against the soft fur of Caleb's scalp. His breath remained steady. The solid warmth beneath her hand anchored her despite the ever-growing list of dangers she'd have to face.

CHAPTER TWENTY-FIVE

The Strut

Jolie's boots clicked along the alley as she made her way to The Black Cat House. A grin tugged at the corner of her mouth. Back at her apartment, she had opened her trunk of old vinyl records, looking for inspiration from her past. Each record represented routines honed to a polished sheen and applause long since faded. Reminiscing had given her an idea: she would resurrect the costume, the dance, the sinuous hip movements, but infuse them with the pulsing beat of a modern track. It had been ages since she had created something new, and while this wasn't as fresh as she had hoped, it was comforting to feel her creativity return.

Jolie slipped through the back entrance. She tossed her things toward her dressing table before making her way to the bandstand. Caleb curled up on her discarded coat, keeping a watchful eye on the dancers backstage. Jolie approached the bandleader with determination. Her vision caught like a brush fire, and within moments, the musicians began weaving her song into a fresh melody. Everything was falling perfectly into place.

After thanking the bandleader, Jolie slipped through the performer's door and onto the stage, where her gaze immediately fell on Danny, Rori, and Boden huddled together in animated conversation. Their laughter filled the air, and the ease with which they stood together made Jolie frown. Danny was striking as ever, dressed in a fitted black coat over a crisp white shirt, his presence exuding a quiet danger. Jolie's mind flashed to the flowers from last night, and her frown deepened.

Danny's face lit up as she approached. "Miss Jolie, always a pleasure to see you," he greeted. His voice was low and laced with warmth. A smile lit up his features.

Rori raised an eyebrow and cast a glance between them. She placed a hand on Danny's shoulder, her expression unreadable. "Come, Detective, let's find you something to eat," she said smoothly, guiding him away to a booth and directing a waitress to the table. Jolie watched them depart as she sorted through her feelings. Seeing him here unnerved her.

When Rori returned, Jolie greeted her with a false smile. "I'm debuting a new act tonight," she announced, her excitement returning like tiny bubbles.

Rori's expression softened, but her tone remained firm. "About time," she replied. Her eyes sparkled with an undercurrent of warning as she continued. "You know getting involved with that detective is a dangerous game."

Jolie's eyes widened in surprise, momentarily thrown off by Rori's sharp insight. The knowing smirk that played on Rori's lips only deepened, making her amusement clear. "Oh, don't look so stunned, darling," Rori teased. "We all saw you two tucked away at that table the other night."

Heat crept up Jolie's cheeks, a soft laugh escaping her despite the embarrassment. She had been so foolish as to think no one had noticed. "That was a mistake I won't be making again," she admitted.

Rori nodded, her expression more serious now, though a hint of understanding flickered in her eyes. "Good," she replied. "There's danger in entangling yourself with men like him. You've got too much at stake to be reckless."

Jolie was again caught by surprise. There was something hanging in the air between them, an unspoken truth that Jolie had yet to discover. "Is everything okay, Rori?"

Rori let out a sigh. Her eyes scanned the room before she answered. "Nothing is going on tonight, but that doesn't change the damage that the last couple of weeks have done." She looked at Jolie, her eyes pleading for an answer that would make this all go away.

Jolie's heart sank. The Black Cat House was beginning to struggle. The competition was already fierce, and now the audience was dwindling. One death was a novelty; two were dangerous. Rumors were beginning to swirl. One wrong move, one more bad rumor, and they could lose everything.

"It seems everyone is off their game tonight," Jolie said, gesturing toward the nearby waitress who had placed lamps meant for the center tables on the side tables. Rori quickly rushed over to correct the mistake, leaving Jolie alone with her thoughts.

Jolie took a detour before heading backstage; the theater lights began to dim as Jolie veered toward the bar. She waved to Lina. "Kitchen kicking yet?"

Lina's nod was quick, a slight tilt of her head as she wiped down the counter. "Sure is. Bring your shadow again tonight?"

Jolie laughed. "He does have a penchant for the breaded."

"Tonight, I'll even make it a double," Lina winked and turned to write down Caleb's order.

The kitchen door creaked as it opened and closed. Mikhail's aura preceded him, a shadow detaching itself from the periphery. His motorcycle jacket was still creased from the ride. He dropped his duffel bag with a dull thud and cut a direct line toward Jolie. She pivoted, trying to retreat into the backstage chaos, but he materialized before her, a human roadblock.

"Wait." His hands shot up, palms outward, a gesture of surrender. "Just give me a minute."

Jolie planted her hands on her hips, a silent challenge. The air around them crackled with unspoken tension.

"I'm sorry I was such a prick the other day." Mikhail's voice was low as he closed the gap between them. "Things just get intense in here." His gaze moved around the room in silent acknowledgment of the frantic energy of the venue.

A sliver of understanding pricked at Jolie's defenses. Was it genuine, or another well-rehearsed evasion? The edges of her resolve softened. She let her shoulders drop, a small smile touching her lips. "Yeah, it's been a whirlwind."

As the words escaped, a prickling sensation crawled up her spine. Eyes. She turned, and there he was. Danny's gaze was accusatory and fixed on them. The muscles in his jaw bunched and released. Jolie felt a rush of surprise. Mikhail let out a low, dismissive scoff, and Jolie's attention snapped back to him. She had been caught, her gaze lingering too long on Danny's silent interrogation.

"So, what's the story with you two?" Mikhail's voice held a possessive edge, his body shifting subtly to eclipse her view of Danny.

A cool fire ignited in Jolie's core. "That's none of your damn business."

Mikhail's laughter was a jagged sound that made Jolie's teeth ache. She pressed her fingertips to her throbbing temple. These men. Their endless assertions. Their territorial jabs. They were exhausting.

"Not that it matters," she began, her voice a low, tight wire. "But there's nothing happening there."

Mikhail's shadow engulfed her as he advanced. His body radiated a prickly heat as he brushed against her, an unwelcome invasion of her personal space. "Good." The single word was a pronouncement. "He's nothing but trouble."

Jolie recoiled. "You're overstepping. Back up."

His eyes narrowed into sharp shards of contempt. "You actually think he likes you?" Another laugh erupted, this one a cruel, mocking echo. "This is going to be so much fun."

He spun on his heel and strode away. A retreating force of pure, unadulterated disdain. Jolie's throat tightened. A frustrated sigh bubbled up in a desperate urge to lob a verbal grenade after him. But the words caught in her throat. Defeated, she turned toward the dressing room. A low, guttural grumble escaped her lips, a sound of pure, unadulterated annoyance. "Stupid Mikhail," she muttered. "What a fucking jerk."

"What was that, Jolie?" Lina stood framed in the doorway, an oasis of calm amidst the backstage chaos. She monitored the other dancers as she absorbed their quiet requests.

Jolie flinched, her shoulders hunching. "Nothing, sorry." She brushed past Lina, her movements jerky and agitated.

"I'll get you a bourbon," Lina called after her.

As if by the combined will of all involved, the night passed uneventfully. The audience left quickly after the final curtain. Jolie watched the other dancers as she packed up her things, noticing how most hurriedly threw their unfolded costumes into their trunks before making a quick escape through the back door in pairs. Jolie could feel their fear, even without her heightened senses. It was not fear of murder, but of something almost as devastating. A diminishing audience meant a loss of revenue, and ultimately, the loss of their jobs. The Black Cat House was their livelihood.

Jolie carefully locked her trunk and made her way through the almost empty theater. Caleb trotted silently behind her. She was looking for someone who could help alleviate her fears. She needed a reassuring smile from Rori or Boden's honest assessment of the club's future. Even Abernathy's imposing frown would help, but no one was in sight, so she reluctantly left through the front door. With a sigh, Jolie turned to Caleb and said, "Well, I guess it's just you and me tonight. Let's head home."

Caleb shot out into the street as they exited the club. His nose searched the air. Jolie followed close behind. "Caleb, stay close. I'm not in the mood for a run tonight."

Lost in her own thoughts, Jolie rounded the corner and almost didn't notice Danny before she heard his voice. "I was waiting to see you mingle in the theater, but you stayed backstage," he said with a smile, reaching down to scratch behind Caleb's ears. Caleb gave Danny a few halfhearted tail thumps before backing up to Jolie's side.

Jolie could not bring herself to return his smile. "Yeah, slow night. We should be going."

"Ah." Danny looked down at his shoes and then fell in step beside Jolie. "Did you get my flowers?"

Jolie paused and decided to lie. "No."

Danny slid his hands into his coat pockets as they walked down the damp street. The glow of distant streetlights reflected off the rain-slicked pavement. "No leash for Caleb tonight?"

Jolie's gaze remained fixed on the shimmering asphalt. Her arms folded tight across her chest, a deliberate shield against his proximity. "He doesn't need one anymore." The truth was that Caleb had never needed to be leashed, and she was done contorting herself to pretend he did.

Danny slowed his pace, subtly positioning himself just behind Jolie, fingers brushing against something hidden in his pocket. "I've got a lead," he started, his voice low. "Hoping it pans out . . ."

Before he could finish, Jolie raised her hand abruptly, stopping him in his tracks. "Shhh. Do you hear that?"

Danny tensed. He shoved his hands back into his pockets, hiding what he was holding. "No," he whispered. "What is it?"

"Shhh," Jolie hushed him again, her body going rigid. She could hear it, faint but unmistakable: footsteps. They were moving slowly but deliberately toward them from further down the street. Too quiet for any casual passerby.

Danny's eyes darted to the shadows, but the darkness beyond the alley's entrance gave nothing away. Jolie squinted into the night, trying to catch sight of whoever, or whatever, was approaching, but the figure remained hidden.

Caleb lifted his head, nose twitching as he scented the air. His hackles rose as a deep, rumbling growl escaped his throat. His senses picked up what they could not see. Jolie's body tensed. Caleb's reaction was all the confirmation she needed; whatever was coming toward them was not human. The air around them thickened with unnatural energy, something dark and menacing drawing near, just beyond the veil of the night.

Danny wasted no time pulling his gun from his holster. "I don't hear anything, but it's obvious Caleb does," he said, his eyes scanning their surroundings. "Stay here."

Jolie knew that they were being watched, but could not track the location. Sending Danny alone down the dark alley was stupid. She motioned for Caleb to follow. She didn't trust Danny, but if he got hurt, it would be worse for everyone. Her tension grew as she kept her eyes on Danny and Caleb. She trailed slowly behind, watching their every move for any sign of danger. Danny disappeared into the darkness, following Caleb's lead. Jolie strained her ears to listen for any clue of what was happening.

The silence was deafening, broken only by the sound of Danny's nervous breaths echoing in her ears as she strained to hear more. When she lost sight of Danny as he turned a corner, her anxiety peaked. She reached the bend in the alley and prepared herself for the worst. But when she turned the corner, everything appeared fine.

Danny stood at ease, his gun now safely back in its holster. He turned to face her, a small smile on his lips. "It's nothing," he reassured her. "Just an animal or the wind."

Jolie tilted her head. "Yeah, I guess we're all just a little jumpy," she replied, though the calm in her voice was an act. They were still being watched, she could feel it—a dark presence lurking just beyond reach. But she was not about to share that with Danny. Not yet. She needed space to poke around the shadows alone, and for that, the detective had to be out of her way.

"You should head home now," she said, her tone firm. "It's not safe to be out here alone."

Danny hesitated, a flicker of suspicion crossing his face, unsure how to respond. But Jolie's eyes locked onto his. "Go now," she repeated, this time pushing her will into his mind. He blinked, then nodded, turning mechanically toward his car.

As soon as he was out of sight, Jolie crouched down to Caleb. His eyes glowed in the dim alley light, ever watchful. "Whatever that was, it was not human. I need you to follow him home, make sure he's safe. But stay hidden; I don't want you to be seen."

Caleb gave a low growl of understanding before darting off into the shadows, his large frame moving swiftly and silently after Danny. Jolie watched him disappear into the night, her body still teeming with unease.

With a final glance toward the street, Jolie slipped deeper into the alley, her senses on high alert as she scanned for any trace of what had been stalking them. The further she ventured, the darker the world became, the city's lights fading behind her. Then she heard it: a laugh, soft but sinister, curling through the still air. It was not the strung-out cackle of a blitzer, but something far more calculated. Coldness clung to it.

Jolie froze, trying to pinpoint the source. But the presence vanished as quickly as it had come, leaving only the echo of its chilling amusement behind. She had no chance to glimpse what it was, but she could feel its malice lingering, retreating into the night.

She forced herself to remain calm as she made her way back to her apartment. Even once inside, she could not shake the cold sense of unease in her gut. Fear was a luxury she could not afford, not now. She needed to stay sharp.

A shiver pricked Jolie's arms as she stepped onto the balcony. Unanswered questions gnawed at her; the Seattle air, heavy with rain, stuck to her skin. Unsettling images replayed in her mind: a fleeting shadow and the unsettling feeling of being watched. She could not relax, not until Caleb returned. She saw him then, a dark figure moving silently across the rooftops. Only when he reached the balcony did the tension finally seep from her shoulders.

CHAPTER TWENTY-SIX

The Dressing Room Gospel

Jolie jabbed a finger at the worn spines of Seb's books. Their titles mocked her ignorance. Each rereading had only deepened the knot of frustration in her stomach. Hours bled into one another. Finally, with a groan that echoed the protest of her weary bones, she stood. Bare feet hit the cold floorboards. She paced, the worn rug beneath her feet offering no solace. "Caleb," she whispered, her voice barely rising in the quiet room. The lump in the bed remained motionless. "Caleb," she tried again, this time with a hint of urgency.

The lump grunted, and Caleb poked his head out from under the blankets, his one visible eye squinting at her. "I'm worried," she confessed, her voice trembling slightly. "I feel like there's something important that I'm missing." Caleb's eye fluttered closed again, and soon she was watching his chest rise and fall with each snore.

Jolie huffed in irritation before yanking the covers off the bed, startling him awake. "Caleb, get up," she commanded, her voice sharp with insistence. "We're going to see Seb."

She dressed quickly, pulling on a thick coat and wrapping a scarf around her neck to ward off the spotty sunlight. Her worn brown boots were scuffed from countless outings, but she slipped them on without a second thought. Caleb groaned as he reluctantly sat up, his large frame sluggish. Jolie, however, was too focused on the task ahead to give him more than a glance. There were answers to be found, and Seb was the only one who might have them.

Grabbing a scrap of leftover food for Caleb and a blood pack for herself, she paused briefly in the kitchen. She leaned against the counter as she drank her meal through a straw. The tang of blood hit her tongue, but it did little to quell the exhaustion clouding her mind. The pieces of information she had collected over the past few days felt jumbled, disconnected. Nothing made sense, and the lack of clarity gnawed at her.

With a frustrated sigh, she tossed the empty pack into the trash and pushed herself away from the counter. She needed to focus. Seb had a knack for seeing through chaos, but she needed to ask the right questions. The problem was that she did not even know what those were.

Jolie shoved open the door and stepped into the gray morning, Caleb trotting reluctantly at her side. She felt lost, weighed down by a growing sense of helplessness, but she could not afford to let it paralyze her. Seb would have answers, or at the very least, a direction to follow. The thought of facing him without a clear plan left a bitter taste in her mouth; he would be annoyed by her lack of progress.

As they wound through the narrow streets, Jolie's thoughts were a tangled mess of indecision and melancholy. She hoped the brisk walk would clear her mind, but the weight of uncertainty clung to her. Caleb, however, was in his element. His tail wagged furiously as he drank in the sights and smells of the city, pausing to sniff every corner and greet the occasional passerby with a friendly nuzzle. His enthusiasm was impossible to ignore, and despite her brooding thoughts, Jolie found herself smiling at his antics. Caleb's joy was contagious, pulling her out of the fog that clouded her mind.

As they neared Seb's store, the familiar sight of its weathered windows brought a spark of anticipation. Her mood began to lift, buoyed by Caleb's exuberance and the hope that Seb might finally offer some clarity. They paused a few buildings down, Caleb taking his sweet time selecting the perfect bush to claim as his own. Jolie let out a soft laugh and glanced around, her gaze wandering over the quiet street. The rhythm of the city had a calming effect, its pulse steady and constant.

That was when she saw her.

Lina slipped down a narrow set of stairs leading to a basement-level shop. Curiosity sparked within Jolie, and she found herself scanning the building, searching for any sign of what had drawn Lina. Her eyes finally landed on a small, faded plaque near the bottom of the stairwell. The lettering was worn and dark, almost invisible in the shadows. But as Jolie squinted, she made out the words, "Custos Mysteriorum," scrawled in cramped, gold cursive.

Jolie frowned in thought. What was Lina doing in a magic store? She was curious to see what the little shop had to offer, but Lina's coolness toward her made her hesitant to approach uninvited. Before she could contemplate her next move, Caleb tugged on his leash, eager to continue their walk.

The brass bell above the door jangled as Jolie pushed it open. She froze, a breath catching in her throat. Before her, the cramped space of Seb's shop erupted with chattering voices and snapping camera shutters. Seb looked as if he might spontaneously combust.

A woman with a sunflower hat the size of a satellite dish bellowed into her phone, oblivious to the surrounding chaos. A child, his face sticky, bounced a bright pink stress ball against a display of antique books. Each shelf trembled precariously. A sea of hands reached for books, flipped through their pages, and then returned them to different spots along the shelves. One woman, a storm of paisley and determined sniffing, held a rare old book aloft, examining it with a magnifying glass as if searching for a hidden flaw.

Sweat beaded on Seb's forehead. The blush creeping up his neck was visible even on his already flushed skin. He gritted his teeth. With a muttered apology, he extricated himself from the throng. He steered Jolie toward a shadowed doorway. "Just a minute, Jolie," he whispered, his voice tight with strain. He nudged her into the quiet sitting room, the door clicking shut behind them like a sigh of relief. Seb's voice carried through the door, "That's it. Everyone out."

A grateful smile settled on Jolie's face as she sank into the worn armchair. The fire crackled merrily, throwing dancing shadows that chased the gloom from the corners of the room. Caleb, his head resting against the worn carpet, snored softly. The scent of rosemary and thyme floated from the flames, a gentle anesthetic to the sensory overload of the shop, relaxing Jolie's senses, and she closed her eyes for a moment. The exhaustion of the past weeks finally caught up with her, and she drifted off into a peaceful slumber.

Jolie's eyes snapped open to a voice right by her ear. She jerked back in her seat. Seb's face was mere inches from hers; his bushy eyebrows furrowed in concern. He continued to squint and stare at her. She ran a hand through her tangled hair, trying to smooth it out before Seb could see how disheveled she looked.

"What's wrong?" Seb asked, tilting his head and reaching out to grab Jolie's chin in his right hand. He lifted her face into the warm glow of the fire, his piercing gaze examining her features. "You look gaunt. When did you last eat?"

Jolie shrugged off his hand, feeling slightly annoyed at his intrusion. "This morning, I'm fine," she replied, trying to brush off his concern. Seb let out a heavy sigh and handed her a mug of warm blood.

"I meant something fresh, not these blood packets," he clarified.

"I don't eat fresh," Jolie replied, feeling defensive.

"Well, you need to," Seb insisted, his voice taking on a more serious tone. "Going out in the sun, running around all night, trying to keep up with a barghest . . . You need to take better care of yourself."

Jolie looked down at the warm mug clasped in her hands. She swirled the cup, the tang of iron from the blood rising to meet the faint, earthy scent of damp rock rolling off Seb. "I'll try," she murmured. She set the mug down. "Why do you have blood packs, anyway?"

Seb shrugged, pouring himself a cup of tea from his chipped pot. "Eh, I get all types in here. What brings you by today?"

Jolie watched as Seb sliced a few thick slices of pound cake and tossed one to Caleb.

"Well, I met some succubi," Jolie said with a confident smile, her cheeks flushed with embarrassment as she remembered how she had realized that Wyn was not human.

Seb let out a snort, his lips curling into a smirk. "Just met or finally realized what they were?" he asked, his tone teasing.

Jolie laughed, shaking her head. "Both, but probably more the latter," she admitted. Seb leaned back in his chair, eager to hear more. She enthusiastically obliged, only leaving out the parts that made her blush. She provided him with all the details of meeting the elders. "I get the feeling they don't really care about what's happening," she concluded, defeat curling around her words.

Seb shrugged nonchalantly as he munched on a slice of cake. "They probably don't care beyond finding out who has that much contempt for their authority," he said, bitterness in his voice. "It's just part of who they are. Their priorities are elsewhere."

Jolie's brows furrowed. She drained her mug and placed it between them on the worn little table, her mind still reeling from her encounter with the powerful succubi. "They were rather ridiculous if you ask me," she said with a hint of disdain, remembering the elders' extravagant jewelry and outdated clothing.

Seb shot her a disapproving look as he scooped up her mug and made his way to the kitchen. "You shouldn't judge," he chided gently, his voice fading as he disappeared down the hallway. "You'll never know how you'll look when you reach a few thousand years old."

Jolie's gaze drifted to Caleb, stretched out next to the crackling fire, his chest rising and falling in a steady rhythm as he slept. Her frown deepened at the thought of living for another thousand years or so, the world evolving around her. Would she still be living and working the same way? Or would she adapt to the ever-changing world?

The thought made her uneasy, knowing that as an immortal, she would have to constantly adapt to the changing world around her. Burlesque had already changed so much since she first became involved. She had managed to survive the legal crackdowns of the 1920s and 30s thanks to her Maker's protection. But since then, she had tried everything from comedy to vulgarity to stay relevant. If burlesque fell out of fashion again, she would be out of a job with no other skills to fall back on.

Seb returned from the kitchen with another full mug for Jolie, placing it gently in her hands. "So, what's your next move?" he asked.

Jolie sighed, taking a sip from her mug. She let the hot liquid sting the back of her throat. The zesty iron was mellowed by a generous shot of bourbon. "I don't have one," she admitted. "Detective work isn't exactly my forte."

Seb leaned back in his chair, studying Jolie closely. "You have a whole network of people you can turn to and rely on," he reminded her. "My suggestion is that you spend some time getting closer to them."

Jolie hesitated, uncertain if she was ready to let others in. "I'm not sure that's the best idea," she said softly.

"I think you underestimate the world around you," Seb replied, a hint of amusement in his voice.

Jolie's thoughts drifted to Lina and the quaint little shop. "Seb, do you happen to know a shop called Curios of Mystery?" she asked.

Seb took a moment to chew thoughtfully on his cake before responding. "You mean Custos Mysteriorum?" he asked, a smile tugging at the corners of his lips.

Jolie nodded eagerly. "That's the one. It's just down the street."

Seb wiped the last few crumbs from his vest, letting out a contented sigh as he settled back into his favorite armchair. He interlaced his fingers on his chest, his mind drifting over Jolie's question. "What makes you ask about that shop?"

Jolie shrugged, pausing to take a sip of her tea. "I saw a coworker go in there on my way over here. I was just curious."

Seb pondered her words, his eyes twinkling. "You could always just ask your coworker about it."

Jolie let out a small sigh, sipping the last of the blood from her mug. "Yeah, probably not. She's not exactly my biggest fan."

Seb raised an eyebrow, a hint of concern in his expression. "Why do you think that?"

Jolie sighed again. She tucked her legs underneath her and let the soft, worn upholstery envelop her. "I don't know. She's always polite to me, but I can tell she doesn't really like me."

"You should find out why."

Jolie shook her head, a small frown forming on her face. "There's no need, Seb."

"Jolie, you can't keep hiding from people. That's why you haven't learned anything," Seb scolded. "You'll be better off if you just open up and let people surprise you."

Seb always had a way of cutting through her defenses and getting to the heart of the matter. She stretched her arms above her head; the tension in her muscles released. "As always, it's been less than enlightening being around you, Seb. But I should probably head home and get Caleb some food." At the mention of food, Caleb's ears perked up, and he opened one eye, his tail thumping softly against the carpet.

"Nonsense," Seb said, getting up from his chair. "I've already closed the shop for the day, and I have a stew cooking. You'll stay for dinner." Before Jolie could protest, Seb was already bustling around the room, clearing away the tea tray and wiping crumbs from the coffee table to the floor. Jolie felt guilt creep in as she looked at the extra work that would create for Seb's pixies.

"Here, let me help," she offered, taking the tray from Seb and gesturing for Caleb to follow. Together, they made their way to the small, makeshift kitchen behind the sitting room. Jolie placed the tray on the counter next to the small sink and two-burner stove, taking in the limited space and supplies. She could not imagine how Seb managed to make anything in this tiny kitchen.

Seb noticed her curious expression and chuckled. "You're probably wondering how I managed to cook a stew in here."

Jolie nodded. Seb moved to a cabinet and pulled aside black curtains so worn that they looked gray. He opened the door hidden behind them, revealing a narrow flight of stairs. "Come on, this way."

Jolie and Caleb followed Seb down the stairs. The smell of damp, musky earth filled her senses. The walls were made of the same old wood as the rest of the shop, and the lights above were bare bulbs; there was nothing plush about this stairwell. As they reached the bottom, Seb opened another door and led them down a short hallway.

The hallway was a step up in frills, a contrast to the bare stairs behind them. Soft lights lined the walls, casting a warm glow from the bulbs delicately covered in antique shades. The faded and mismatched wallpaper seemed to suggest that multiple hallways had been joined together to create this unique space. She caught glimpses of carvings in the wooden baseboards. Seb led them to the second door on the right, and as they entered, Jolie was immediately greeted by the warmth and brightness of the kitchen. The worn and cracked tiles on the floor were covered in soft rugs. The appliances were relics from a much older time, with an ice chest and wood-burning stove taking center stage in the corner. Jolie took a seat at the butcher-block table in the center of the room.

"Seb, how far below ground level are we?" Jolie asked, still in awe of the hidden world they had entered.

Seb's smile widened, his eyes lighting up with pride. "You like it? We're in the old Seattle underground. After the great fire, they just built on top of the remains, leaving plenty of space to dig in and create a cozy home. Many of the things you see here, I found and refurbished myself. It's a bit of a dwarf thing." He shrugged. The glint of lamplight on a chipped enamel teapot caught Jolie's eye. Seb gleefully noticed and began to explain. "Found this buried under a collapsed privy. It took me three weeks to coax the grime off." He chuckled, the sound warm and slightly gravelly. His eyes shone with pride as he demonstrated the perfectly functional spout. The aroma of woodsmoke and simmering herbs hung in the air.

Seb ladled the steaming soup into deep, rustic bowls. He uncorked a bottle of pinot noir, the ruby liquid catching the firelight, its aroma a heady blend of dark fruit and earth. The setting, humble yet deeply comforting, mirrored the warmth of Seb himself. His grin was a genuine, heartfelt expression of contentment. Caleb's rhythmic slurping sounds a quiet soundtrack to their shared meal.

"Thank you for inviting us, Seb. Caleb really needed something nutritious." Jolie sipped her mug of warm blood. Caleb did not lift his head but agreed with a hearty tail thump.

Jolie sank a fork into a yielding chunk of potato. Its slick surface was surrounded by a deep, brown broth. She lifted the bite and brought it to her lips. Thyme and the subtle prickle of rosemary danced across her tongue. Her brow lifted. Seb heavily seasoned his stew, so much so that she could taste a whisper of what it was like to be human again. "Not bad, Seb."

He chuckled. "High praise indeed," he replied, "from a vampire."

CHAPTER TWENTY-SEVEN
Corsets and Coffins

The evening with Seb was life-altering. For the first time in years, she felt like she was more than just a brooding creature of the night. Jolie let out a heavy sigh. "I really don't want to go to work today," she muttered to Caleb, who seemed entirely unbothered by her distress. She slowly packed her bag, trying to delay the inevitable. When she could no longer put it off, Jolie wrapped her hair in a scarf and slipped on her heavy wool coat. She couldn't risk getting sick from sun exposure; she was tired enough. "Are you coming with me tonight, Caleb?" He had crawled back into bed and made himself comfortable under the covers.

He lifted his head and seemed to contemplate her question. "I'll throw in some chicken strips if you come," Jolie added, hoping to entice him. She felt safer with her faithful barghest by her side, watching out for her. Caleb finally rose from his spot and stretched his four legs, as if making a statement before trotting to Jolie's side. "I'd rather stay home, too, so thank you for coming with me," she said.

They arrived at The Black Cat House in record time, settling in long before any of the other dancers arrived. Right away, Lina brought out a double order of chicken strips for Caleb. A question sat poised on Jolie's tongue about Lina's trip to the magic shop, but a prickle of nerves tightened her lips.

Jolie felt the weight of the club's hardships. The backstage crew was short-staffed, with Boden's security team stepping in to help when needed. Even the female vocalist of the band was taking some time off. Jolie knew that the waitstaff had been with Rori and Boden for a long time, and they were loyal, but with the lack of business, their tips were suffering, and some might have to leave if things didn't improve.

Jolie could hear Rori's voice through the walls, directing the hostesses to seat people at the center tables and not to open the side tables until they were full. Her tone lacked optimism, and Jolie knew that the audience would most likely be light. Feeling a sense of dread, Jolie avoided going out into the theater and facing Rori's worried gaze. Instead, she busied herself with completing her hair and makeup, trying to distract herself from the harsh reality of their struggling club.

Despite the difficult situation, Rori and Boden were determined to maintain the quality of performance. They had not yet cut the number of dancers, and Jolie admired their resolve. Wyn arrived on time, which was unlike her usual tardiness. Jolie noticed the excitement in her friend's eyes as she quickly made her way over to Jolie's side.

"Hey, I've been digging around," she said, her voice low. "I have someone who's willing to talk with you. Let's chat after work."

Jolie scanned Wyn's face for any clues. "Of course," she replied. "Is everything okay?"

Wyn's breathless tone and gleaming eyes told Jolie that this was something big, and she couldn't wait to find out more. "Yes, of course." Wyn placed a quick kiss on the top of Jolie's head. "I gotta get a drink."

Wyn rushed to the bar, her footsteps pounding on the floor. Jolie watched Caleb as he nestled deep within the folds of her thick wool coat. He looked serene, but Jolie saw the subtle tremor in his nose and the almost imperceptible jerk of his head as a nearby trunk unlocked. The faintest prickle of static electricity crackled in the air around him. Caleb was on high alert.

Lina approached and placed the overloaded tray, groaning under the weight of glasses and bottles, onto the vanity's surface. The scent of bourbon and the floral hint of gin filled the air. Jolie turned her attention from Caleb and decided to use this chance to attempt a conversation. "How's the crowd tonight?" she asked.

Lina tried to hide her disappointment. "It's better than the last few nights, but nowhere near the level it used to be. Rori's drink specials seem to be bringing in a rowdier crowd, which should give our show a boost at least."

Jolie winced at the mention of drink specials. It was a clear sign that the bar was in dire need of some extra cash.

Jolie stayed backstage throughout the entire show, keeping a watchful eye on Caleb. The dog was starting to pace back and forth, sniffing the air with anxious urgency. She knelt to stroke Caleb's fur, trying to comfort him. "What's wrong, Caleb? I wish you could tell me what you need." She suggested some food options, hoping to ease his restlessness. Caleb shook his head, uninterested in eating. He continued his pacing, his nose high in the air as he searched for something.

Feeling a growing sense of annoyance, Jolie made her way to the back door. "Do you need to go out?" she asked Caleb, unlocking the door and pushing it open.

Instead of darting outside, Caleb stood unmoving, staring at her with an unreadable expression. Jolie sighed. "Fine, I'll leave you be," she muttered. A flash of resentment flickered through her. What good was a mythical dog that could not talk?

"I think he's shocked you'd open the alley door with no one here to protect you," came a voice, flat and unexpected.

Jolie jumped. Instinctively, her hands rose in a defensive stance. She spun around to see Danny standing in the shadows. Caleb, without missing a beat, stretched lazily but deliberately between them, his large body acting as a silent barrier.

"He's just anxious," Jolie said, nodding toward Caleb, though she was not entirely sure of that herself. "I can't figure out what he wants." Caleb's nose twitched as he sniffed the air, ears sharply attuned to every sound, his posture alert.

"He probably just smells all the food," Danny quipped, taking a few steps closer.

Caleb let out a low, warning growl that froze Danny in his tracks. He took a step back, hands raised in mock surrender. "Wow, I guess we're not friends anymore."

"Why, Detective, I didn't realize you were in the middle of an interrogation," came Wyn's playful voice from the theater door. A sordid grin played on her lips as she strode toward them. "I think I could find my way to being cooperative."

Jolie pressed her lips together to stifle the laugh that bubbled up, shaking her whole body in her relief to see Wyn. The tight knot in her stomach loosened, the weight of Danny's presence visibly lifting. The detective's smile at Wyn was carefully constructed. His lips stretched thin over teeth, the corners not quite reaching his eyes, a polite mask barely concealing the suspicion simmering beneath. "Good to see you again," he said, though there was unmistakable apprehension in his tone.

Wyn obviously made him uncomfortable with her brazen flirtation, and today was no exception. Her fingers absentmindedly toyed with the neckline of her dress, and she licked her lips before she replied, "Not as good as it could be, Danny."

Her eyes lingered on him with a teasing look that made his smile falter. He glanced at Jolie, shaking his head with a sigh. "I'll leave you to it," he muttered before turning on his heel and heading for the door.

Once he was gone, Jolie braced herself, knowing that Wyn was not about to let this moment slip by without her usual teasing. But Wyn's expression shifted into something more serious than Jolie expected. "I don't like that guy," Wyn said, her voice low and sharp. "Always hanging around but doing nothing to solve the case. Does he know?"

Jolie's heart skipped a beat, knowing exactly what Wyn was hinting at, but she tried to play it off, her voice steady. "Know what?"

Wyn's smile grew sly as she leaned in closer. "What you are," she whispered.

Jolie froze. "No. Of course not," she said, though the words tasted bitter in her mouth.

Wyn shook her head, her voice edged with warning. "I think he's starting to put the pieces together."

Chapter Twenty-Eight

Blood on the Stage

Security struggled to disperse the lingering crowds. Laughter, raw and unrestrained, bounced off the walls, Rori's drink specials making it far too easy to overindulge. Boden's security did their best to usher them out; their faces were tight with strain as they nudged and gestured at the eddying mass of bodies.

Jolie, now a shadow in her simple sweats and worn T-shirt, slid into a vacant booth. Wyn held court with a cluster of men. Their voices were a low rumble of insistent offers. One thrust a half-empty whiskey glass toward her, his grin wide and unyielding. Another leaned in. His words were lost in the boisterous din, but his intent was clear in the eager tilt of his head. Wyn laughed and offered him a playful slap.

Caleb, ever watchful, lay hidden beneath the table at Jolie's feet. His eyes locked on her as he subtly kept guard. Jolie let out a long, slow breath when she heard the lock click into place behind the last patrons to shuffle out. Rori, her face scored with the fatigue of a long night, barked curt instructions to the departing waitstaff. Most scurried away, relieved to be heading home. They left behind only those closest to Boden and Rori.

Wyn finally sauntered over to Jolie, balancing four drinks with surprising grace. She slid into the seat beside her, all smiles. "Who are those for?" Jolie asked, eyeing the drinks warily.

"For you and me, sweetie," Wyn replied with a sly grin.

Jolie narrowed her eyes, her patience growing thin. "How about we skip the drinks and you just tell me your news?"

Wyn pouted playfully. "Why be such a stick-in-the-mud? Lighten up for once," she teased. She took a long sip and licked her lips provocatively. Jolie's frown deepened. Wyn shifted uncomfortably, sensing she had pushed too far. "Sorry," she mumbled. "I'm just starving, and it's making me cranky."

"Hungry?" Jolie raised an eyebrow. "But I saw you eating earlier."

Wyn rolled her eyes. "Human food doesn't cut it. I haven't fed in days, and I'm missing vital nutrients." She sighed. "The elders are on edge, so most of us are lying low. All this pent-up energy in the club is making things worse."

Jolie chuckled softly. "And making you say some really dumb stuff."

Wyn laughed along with her. "Yeah, it really is."

Grinning, Jolie took one of the drinks in front of her and downed it, enjoying the burn of alcohol warming her from the inside out. "So, what's this news you've been dangling in front of me?"

Wyn's face grew serious. She drained her glass and reached for another. "I found someone who's willing to talk. You can meet her tomorrow night. If there is something to know, she'll know it."

Jolie's mood brightened instantly. "That's amazing! Is she coming here?"

Wyn hesitated, avoiding eye contact. "No . . . we'll have to go to her."

Jolie narrowed her eyes. "Where?"

"Don't freak out," Wyn said, placing a calming hand on her arm. Jolie felt a pulse of magic radiating from her, an attempt to soothe. "It's at her party."

Jolie's eyes widened. "Her party? No. Absolutely not."

"I know, I know," Wyn rushed to explain. "But that's the only way she'll agree to meet." Jolie groaned, rubbing her temples. "Fine. If that's what it takes."

Wyn's excitement returned instantly, her grin wide. "Great! Just make sure you wear something nice."

Jolie smirked. "I'll wear sweatpants."

Wyn shrugged. "That could work."

Before they could continue, Abernathy's booming voice echoed through the room. "Alright, ladies, time to pack it in! And make sure to leave together." He began ushering out the last of the staff.

Jolie and Wyn gathered their things in haste, exchanging a quick farewell with Rori as they slipped out of the theater. They wove past the dressing rooms, giving a quick wave to Charles as they went. Maddy stood to the side, letting them pass. She held her things tightly to her chest before darting back out into the theater and out the front door. It was shocking to see Maddy back at work; she was the only stage kitten to return, and Jolie was sure she had a stronger preservation instinct than that.

Caleb trailed behind, nose to the ground, as he sniffed intently at every corner. They passed Boden and his security team, finishing their final sweep of the rooms. Boden nodded at them, giving a short wave. "Stay safe tonight," he called.

Jolie opened the back door, letting Wyn step through first. She paused when she heard Wyn let out an exasperated sigh. Throwing her hands up, Wyn groaned. "Seriously? Am I the only one not getting lucky tonight?"

Jolie barely registered the comment; her attention immediately moved to the far end of the alley. There, silhouetted by the dim streetlight, stood a couple deeply entwined. The woman hung limply in the man's arms. Her body was unnaturally still. Something was wrong.

Squinting against the shadows, Jolie focused. Her heart sank when she recognized them. "Mikhail!" Jolie's voice cut through the stillness like a blade.

He spun around, startled, his grip tightening around the woman.

"I found her like this," he said, his voice too smooth for the tension in the air. "I was going to get help."

Jolie's eyes narrowed, suspicion gnawing at her. This did not feel right. Wyn glanced at Jolie, her flirtatious mood evaporating, replaced with sharp wariness. "And exactly where were you planning to take her, Mikhail?" Wyn asked, her voice dripping with suspicion.

Mikhail stiffened, his eyes darting between them. "I was heading to the back entrance. I thought someone inside might know what to do."

Jolie stepped forward, her pulse quickening. "Let her go. Now."

Mikhail hesitated, but under Jolie's piercing gaze, he slowly lowered the woman to the ground and stepped away. Jolie approached slowly, her eyes on Mikhail. "Stay where you are."

It was at this moment that Caleb chose to burst through the doorway, a blur of muscle and fur, growling and barking fiercely. He knocked Wyn and Jolie aside as he barreled into the alley, heading straight for Mikhail.

"Caleb, no!" Jolie shouted. She reached out in vain to restrain him, but the dog was already halfway to his target. Caleb planted himself between Jolie and Mikhail. His stance was low and menacing, teeth bared, muscles coiled like a spring ready to snap.

Jolie took a breath and cautiously approached. She placed a calming hand on Caleb's back. Her eyes darted to Mikhail, who looked poised to flee. His body was taut with tension, eyes shifting nervously between the two women and Caleb.

Wyn scrambled to her feet, confusion written across her face as she looked between them. "Mikhail, what the hell is going on?" Her voice trembled, though she tried to mask her fear. Jolie watched him closely; there was an odd blue glow to his eyes that she had never seen before.

Wyn took in a sharp breath just as the pieces clicked into place all at once.

"Oh my god!" Wyn gasped, her hand flying to her mouth. "Jolie, it's him! He's the one! Look at his eyes!"

The realization hit Jolie like a wave, but before she could react, Mikhail lunged at her, his face twisting into something monstrous. Jolie barely had time to register the attack before Caleb moved. He launched himself into the air, colliding with Mikhail and slamming him hard against the brick wall.

Jolie's instincts screamed at her to protect the unconscious woman. She darted forward and positioned herself over the woman's limp body, her eyes fixed on the struggle between Caleb and Mikhail. "Caleb, keep him away from her!" she ordered.

Caleb immediately shifted his position. He placed himself like a guardian between Mikhail and the woman. His growl deepened and echoed in the narrow alley. Mikhail snarled, his unearthly nature fully emerging. His eyes glowed faintly, and his mouth twisted into a sneer larger than humanly possible. He hissed at Caleb, but the dog did not budge.

Wyn's voice shattered the tension. "Rori! Boden! It's him! It's Mikhail!" she screamed into the night, terror vibrating in every syllable.

The alley buzzed with tension and the hum of magic stirring beneath the surface. Mikhail's eyes flicked to the shadows, searching for a way out, but with Caleb blocking his path and Wyn's cries alerting the others, his options were running out. Jolie took a few steps forward, determined not to let Mikhail escape, quickly realizing she had no weapon. Cursing under her breath, she vowed to be better prepared in the future. The rapid sound of footsteps echoed behind her and drew her attention to the club door.

Boden and Abernathy burst through first, followed by Rori and two other security guards. In that moment, Jolie's focus wavered, which was all Mikhail needed. Caleb's sharp bark was the only warning she got before Mikhail's fist slammed into her jaw. The impact sent her stumbling back, pain flaring through her face.

Jolie hissed and bared her fangs in fury. Before she could react, Mikhail had already vanished. He sprinted down the alley with supernatural speed. Caleb wasted no time. His growl carried through the air as he launched himself after Mikhail and disappeared into the night in pursuit.

Wyn rushed to Jolie's side, her face pale with concern. "You okay?" she asked, her voice shaky.

Jolie wiped the blood from her lip, her jaw throbbing. "I will be," she muttered, eyes narrowing in the direction Mikhail had fled. "But I swear, next time, I'll be ready."

With Mikhail and Caleb now out of sight, Jolie redirected her attention to the woman lying unconscious in the alley. She could hear the faint beat of the woman's heart. It was weak but steady. "How is she?" Jolie asked as she knelt beside Rori, who was already tending to her.

"She'll survive," Rori replied, her voice calm but focused. "But we need to watch her. If she's not stabilized soon, she could slip into a coma." Rori gently cradled the woman's head in her lap. Wyn hurried off to fetch Lina, leaving Jolie with the rest of the group.

Boden's hand rested on Rori's shoulder. She lifted her head to meet his eyes, and for an instant her irises blazed with a vivid, impossible yellow. Jolie's question died on her lips as Rori's eyes narrowed. "Go on." Rori nodded to Boden. "Pack justice should be served on Mikhail. We'll handle things here."

The damp brick of the alley bit into Jolie's palms as she braced herself. A low thrumming vibrated the very earth beneath her feet, a tremor that resonated deep in Jolie's bones. Her throat constricted as Boden peeled off his shirt. His chest was a canvas of midnight ink that coiled and writhed like trapped serpents across his chest and shoulders.

There was a symphony of rustling fabric and snapping leather as the alley transformed. The stale city smell bled away, replaced by the sharp, clean bite of moonlight and the damp, primal musk of ancient forest floor. Jolie instinctively drew her hands closer. She could imagine the feeling of the cool, yielding embrace of moss and brittle fallen leaves beneath her fingers. Four forms blurred, their human shells dissolving in a dizzying cascade of discarded clothing. Muscles bunched and stretched into a rippling fusion of raw power. Limbs elongated, and bodies contorted with an impossible, bone-popping grace. The air crackled, charged with an energy that made the fine hair on Jolie's arms stand on end. Where men had stood moments before, there were now four hulking shapes of smoke-gray fur. Their eyes burned gold as they surveyed their surroundings. Jolie's vision swam as the impossible solidified before her.

"Werewolves," she whispered, her voice finally breaking free. "All of you . . . The scent of the wild forest . . . Well, that tracks."

One of the wolves, larger than the others, with a striking white patch on its chest, turned toward her. Its eyes gleamed. She could see amusement crackling in them. Jolie tilted her head. "Boden?"

The wolf threw its head back and let out a resounding howl. The sound echoed through the alley, primal and fierce. Jolie's body shook in response.

Another howl answered from the distance. Caleb.

Without thinking, Jolie broke into a run. The wolves joined her. Their paws hit the ground with deadly precision. Boden, in his wolf form, raced ahead. His powerful body cut through the darkness like a shadow. He howled again, and somewhere in the distance, Caleb answered, playing their eerie game of Marco Polo through the night.

The wolves led her through winding streets, weaving past alleyways and silent buildings until they came upon an abandoned warehouse on the south edge of the city. Caleb stood outside, waiting. His ears perked, and his amber eyes locked on Jolie. He was calm but alert, ready for whatever came next.

Jolie placed her hand on Caleb's back. His body was tense under her fingers. "He's still in there, isn't he?" she asked, turning to meet Boden's glowing eyes. "Let's go."

The splintered door groaned open, its hinges rusted. Once inside, the pack scattered. The shadows swallowed them into the vastness.

The wolves inhaled the stale atmosphere, nostrils flared, searching. Caleb followed suit, his nose sweeping through the vast space. His breath rumbled low in his throat. Jolie remained still. Her eyes darted, her ears strained against the oppressive silence. The only sounds that dared to pierce the gloom were the frantic skittering of unseen things in the walls and the steady, metronomic drip of water somewhere in the blackness. She closed her eyes, picturing the layout. Mikhail was a phantom here.

The broken windows allowed slivers of moonlight to filter in. Debris from old construction and discarded shelves littered the space. It created a labyrinth of hiding spots and shadows. Jolie made her way up the creaky staircase to the upper level. It was only partially floored with flimsy railings meant to prevent falls. Her eyes scanned the jagged silhouette of the warehouse. She needed a higher vantage for a chance to find him.

A sound sliced through the silence. Mikhail's laughter. Not a booming guffaw, but a low, cold rumble. It coiled around her, echoing off the skeletal steel girders and decaying concrete. Jolie pressed herself against a crumbling brick wall. "Mikhail?" she rasped. The cackling ceased, but the echo of its mirth lingered, a promise and a challenge. He was here. Somewhere, he was waiting.

Mikhail laughed again, taunting her. "I've wanted to share this with you for so long."

"What are you talking about?" Jolie scanned the room, searching for any change in the shadows that could reveal his position.

"The ecstasy of the kill. As a vampire, you understand, don't you?" His voice floated like smoke, taunting and seductive.

"I don't kill anymore," Jolie asserted.

"Because you're weak. I could teach you so much," Mikhail sneered, his words dripping with arrogance.

Just what she needed: another delusional man trying to dictate her actions and drive her toward madness. "I hate to burst your bubble, but I've already been down that road, and it's not my cup of tea," she retorted, feeling him shift slightly to her right. She bared her fangs and slowly circled him, waiting for the opportune moment to strike.

"You're itching to go back to that life. I can see it in your eyes. You're hiding from everyone, afraid of your true self." His voice grew more forceful, excitement evident in his tone.

"I'm done hiding," she snarled, hearing him shuffle in the shadows once again.

"That bar was too easy. The humans were practically begging to be fed on. Pathetic creatures," Mikhail laughed. "And the owners. They'll believe any flimsy denial. They could stand to be a little less supportive of their community."

The erratic crackle of Mikhail's voice painted a picture in Jolie's mind. Each breathless gasp between phrases revealed a subtle Doppler effect. She traced the subtle changes, a faint smile on her lips as she pinpointed his location. With a growl, Jolie lunged into the shadows, but Mikhail managed to dodge her attack. She quickly swiveled midair and caught his shoulder. Her attempt sent them both tumbling to the ground and rolling toward the railing.

Jolie's eyes tracked his movement only as a blur of motion. A dark, swift shape that mirrored her own reflexes. One instant, he was there, a coiled spring. The next, searing pain exploded across her cheekbone, and blood flowed into her mouth. The world tilted violently as his fists, hard as granite, drove her backward. She stumbled, a strangled gasp escaping her lips. Her body landed with a sickening thud against the wall, the impact jarring every bone in her body. She slid to the floor, her vision swimming with white stars. In a split second, he was on top of her, pinning her down.

"I've always been curious about vampires," he taunted.

His face was mere inches from hers; his smile twisted into a devilish grin. He savored her fear. The unsettling curve of his lips seemed to mock her. His face twisted into a contorted expression that suggested a deranged pleasure in the torment he unleashed.

Jolie could feel the magic in his touch. It slithered out from his fingertips and wrapped itself around her arms, tugging at the edges of her consciousness. A sweet whisper meant to calm her and pull her to his will. A soft caress that was almost impossible to ignore.

Jolie closed her mind to him. She needed to break contact before he pushed past her defenses. She turned her head and sank her fangs into his shoulder, causing him to scream and pull away. "That won't work on me," she boasted. Jolie launched herself at him again. Her knee connected with his chest, and he doubled over. With a snarl, she grabbed his hair and flipped him over her leg. He landed on his back. In one swift move, she was on top of him, pinning his arms with her shins and gripping his neck in her hand.

Jolie could hear the wolves coming up the stairs, driven by Caleb's worried baying. She raised an arm. "It's okay. I'm okay . . ."

As Jolie tried to finish her sentence, she suddenly felt her weight shift. Mikhail pressed against her legs, prying his arms loose. She gasped and instinctively threw her arms up to protect herself, but it was too late. Mikhail had already freed one arm and was reaching for the discarded metal pipes on the floor. Panic surged through her as she realized she was defenseless against his attack. She braced herself for impact, but it came sooner than expected. The metal pipe came down with brutal force, and she felt her right arm snap. She cried out in pain as she fell back, trying to scramble away from Mikhail's swinging pipe.

The wolves closed in, their glowing eyes reflecting the hunger of the hunt. Jolie's breath quickened as she backed away, her injured arm hanging limp and useless at her side. Mikhail stood before her, makeshift weapon in hand and a cold, triumphant gleam in his eyes. She knew she was no match for him now, but the wolves might be.

A flash of movement caught her eye. A young wolf, smaller than the others, circled behind Mikhail. In an instant, he lunged with his teeth bared. But Mikhail was quick. He pivoted, swinging the metal pipe. It connected with a revolting crunch. The young wolf yelped in pain as he tumbled to the ground, his body skidding across the floor.

Seizing the moment, Mikhail darted for the edge of the balcony. Before anyone could react, he leaped over the railing and vanished into the gloom.

Jolie stumbled to the railing, her head pounding from her injuries. She leaned over, cradling her broken arm. She scanned the shadowy depths below, searching for any sign of him. Mikhail was gone. She cursed under her breath, gripping the railing tighter as her vision blurred. Caleb's whimper brought her back. She turned and saw the worry in his eyes. She gave him a soft smile. "I'm okay, or at least I will be."

Jolie turned to see Boden tending to the young, injured wolf. A low rumble emanated from Boden. "Lay still, Jared."

Boden's calloused fingertips probed the swollen purple bloom on the young wolf's forearm. He carefully traced the sharp ridges of his ribs. Each touch was an intentional, measured pressure. "That arm's splintered clean through," Boden murmured against the sharp intake of Jared's breath. "And those ribs . . . They'll knit, boy. They'll knit."

Jared groaned as he sat up. Jolie tried, and sometimes failed, to keep her eyes focused on their faces and not their naked bodies. Boden watched her with a chuckle. He brushed off her discomfort with a wave of his hand. "Yeah, that happens. We're used to it." Nevertheless, she was not. There was something terribly unnerving about how casual they all were, and she had no idea where she was supposed to avert her eyes.

Boden then turned to Jolie as she found a spot on the ceiling to look at. "How's your arm?" he asked. He took a step toward her.

Jolie recoiled. The faint scent of blood, both hers and Jared's, clung to the damp night air. Unease prickled up her spine. It was not that she did not trust Boden, but her blindness to the world around her would take some time to process.

"I'll mend fast," she managed.

Boden patted her good shoulder. His smile grew, a sudden, unexpected warmth that eased the tension knotting in her shoulders. A silent promise that they would be there when she was ready.

Jared let out a string of curses under his breath. "I can't believe I missed that damn maggot," he growled. He tossed a rock with his good hand.

Jolie's head whipped around, her eyes connecting with his. In a blink, her pupils snapped back to the ceiling, as if burned by an unseen fire.

Charles knelt next to Jared and patted him on the shoulder. "You did well, kid. Don't beat yourself up."

Shadows pooled in Jared's eyes, a flicker of something raw and heavy that no bravado could mask. He was all lean muscle, a warrior's frame honed by countless drills. Yet he held an innocence she could not quite place. His fair hair stood out against the shaved heads of the men around him. His arms had a surprising absence of the dark markings that adorned the skin of most of Boden's lieutenants.

Boden reached out a hand to help Jared up. "Charles is right, kid," he reassured him with a pat on the back. "Don't beat yourself up. We need to get back."

Jared nodded and clenched his jaw in determination. "Yeah, I know. Can't let that bastard get away with what he did." His hand instinctively went to his wounded arm.

Boden turned to the rest of the group. "Let's move quickly. Caleb, Jolie, you two as well. We need to get back to the club before anyone spots us." He glanced at Jared with concern etched on his face. "Can you still shift with your injury?"

Jared nodded, gritting his teeth against the pain. "Yeah, but I'll have to go a bit slower on three legs." Without another word, Boden's group shifted into their wolf forms and took off into the night. Jolie tried her best to keep up, but her body was exhausted, and her arm throbbed with every step. She soon fell behind the pack, struggling to keep up. Caleb stayed by her side, matching his pace to hers.

CHAPTER TWENTY-NINE

The Rhinestone Shroud

When Jolie and Caleb reached The Black Cat House, Abernathy and Charles were already there, waiting by the back door. Relief washed over her when she saw him fully dressed.

"Has Boden made it back yet?" Jolie asked, her voice trembling slightly.

Abernathy shook his head. "Not yet, Jared had to go slow, but I'll stay here until he does. If we don't see them soon, I'll head out."

Jolie gave a tight nod and followed Caleb inside, grateful for his steady presence beside her. The adrenaline from the night's events still surged through her, making her limbs shaky. She leaned against the wall, trying to steady herself.

"Any cops around?" she asked, scanning the room for any sign of law enforcement.

Abernathy shook his head again. "No, Rori said they took statements and headed to the hospital with the woman. They know it was Mikhail, though."

Jolie let out a bitter laugh. "Like that'll help."

Before she could dwell on the hopelessness of it all, the theater door creaked open. Wyn peeked through, her eyes widening at the sight of Jolie and Caleb.

"Shit, Jolie, you look awful." Wyn rushed over. She hooked Jolie's good arm over her shoulder while Charles lifted her other side; they helped her inside to where the pack was gathering. Jolie collapsed into a booth, her gaze sweeping over the group. Rori bustled in the kitchen, while Lina served food to the returning wolves. The warmth of the room and the soft chatter of the people around her were soothing, despite everything.

"Lina, help me out," Wyn called, gesturing to Jolie's swollen arm. "It's really bad."

Lina approached. Her hand glowed faintly as she touched Jolie's injured limb. Jolie felt a tingle of magic course up her arm. Hope sparked that Lina could heal her, but Lina frowned, shaking her head apologetically. "I can't fix this one. Sorry, Jolie."

Jolie sighed, the pain and irritation coiling tighter inside her. Before she could spiral, Wyn piped up again, sounding exasperated. "Aren't you, like, a super powerful sorceress or something?"

Lina gave a casual shrug. "Nope. Earth mage. My magic draws from life energy . . . And vampires cancel that out."

The room was beginning to spin around Jolie as Lina's words sank in. Jolie blinked in disbelief. "Werewolves and mages, oh my," she muttered, unable to stop a nervous laugh. Wyn's look of defeat sobered her quickly.

Wyn crossed her arms. "You're losing it."

"I'm not delusional," Jolie said, leaning against Lina for support. "I'm just trying to process the fact that there's a whole world out there I didn't know existed. At least now I get why you don't like me." Jolie's voice softened.

Lina sighed, helping ease Jolie back against the booth. "It's not about liking you or not. Being near you makes me feel sick. Your . . . energy clashes with mine. It's like having the flu."

Jolie winced as the heavy theater door creaked inward again. Boden filled the doorway, his face grim as he half-carried Jared inside. Each breath Jared took seemed to take monumental effort. Lina instantly rushed to his side, her face etched with worry. Her hands, hovering inches above Jared's arm and then his ribs, shimmered with a soft light. The faintest lavender glow pulsed in time with the almost inaudible whisper of her incantation. Boden, looking weary but relieved, took a flask from Angus and offered it to Jared. "Drink up. You've earned it."

Rori emerged from the kitchen, wiping her hands on a towel. "Wyn, fetch some more food for our warriors."

"I'll be right back," Wyn said, patting Jolie's leg before darting to the kitchen.

Boden sat beside Jared, his gaze softening as he watched Rori approach. She buried herself in his arms, trembling slightly. "I was so worried," she murmured.

"We're alright," Boden reassured her, pressing a gentle kiss to her forehead. "We'll get through this."

Jolie glanced down at Caleb. He leaned his weary body against her, his head resting on her legs. Rori smiled as she handed out plates, making sure Caleb had his own portion of steak and chicken under the table. But Caleb stayed put, not moving to eat.

Wyn crouched down, giving Caleb a soft nudge. "Go on, boy. We've got her covered."

Jolie stroked Caleb's head. "It's okay, Caleb. Eat. I'll be fine."

Boden's firm and commanding voice filled the quiet space. "Someone fill us in on what happened while we were gone."

Wyn immediately shot her hand up with a grin. "Oh, let me! But first—" She started unbuttoning her shirt. "Someone needs to feed Jolie."

"Wyn, no!" Rori exclaimed, waving her hands. "You'll just cause more trouble. I'll do it."

Jolie's fingers clenched. A wave of heat washed over her at the thought of them feeding her like some kind of infant. Shame flooded her system. Would seeing her drink disgust them? There was also the growing sense of anger which began to overwhelm her; each one of them had deceived her.

"You all knew," Jolie whispered. "You didn't say anything. About you . . . about me." She could feel their gazes. They pinned her like a specimen under glass. The deep scent of the forest in the air suddenly seemed stronger. It was a sinister reminder of the truth that had been deliberately kept from her. "No one's feeding me anything. I can't believe you all lied to me."

Rori sighed, rolling her eyes. "We knew when we hired you. Most of our employees are fae. Wyn's a succubus," she said matter-of-factly, gesturing at her. "And Lina's a mage."

Jolie waved her good arm. Her expression was tense, her voice edged with irritation. "Right, and you're all werewolves. But I'm not feeding on any of you." She clenched her fist, exasperation simmering just beneath the surface as the absurdity of the situation hit her all at once. She let out a sharp breath as she turned away from the group. She tried to mask the swirl of emotions that churned within her. "I'm not some charity case," she muttered under her breath, bitterness creeping into her tone.

It wasn't just about refusing to drink their blood. It was about the feeling of being cornered by her own circumstances. She was once again forced into a reality where she had no control. The sulking wasn't just anger; it was the exhaustion of always being on edge, of constantly battling what she was, who she was supposed to be, and the gnawing fear that maybe she couldn't outrun either.

Rori approached cautiously. Her footsteps were light as she placed a gentle hand on Jolie's tense shoulder. "We didn't tell you because we figured you needed your space. It was obvious you were hiding, and we wanted to respect your boundaries," she said softly, her tone warm.

Jolie tensed at the touch, but Rori's words began to thaw the icy barrier she'd built around herself. The weight of her stubbornness lifting as her pain and confusion ebbed. Despite the embarrassment still lingering in her chest, Jolie could feel genuine concern radiating from them. They weren't trying to push her or force her hand. They had simply wanted to help. And truthfully, she was too exhausted to keep fighting.

Jolie nodded in reluctant surrender. "Fine," she muttered. A trace of her earlier irritation still clung to her voice. "If you put blood in a glass, I'll drink it, but not from a vein."

Rori's lips curled into a small, understanding smile as she nodded, squeezing Jolie's shoulder before stepping back. "Of course," she said. Her voice was steady, as though this was the most natural request in the world.

With a reassuring pat on Jolie's back, Rori glanced at Charles. He immediately understood, retrieving a knife from the sheath at his belt with a quiet hiss. His movements were unhurried, deliberate, as though this was routine.

Rori returned with a glass, setting it down on the table between them. "You're safe here, Jolie," she said softly, watching as Charles made a small, precise cut along the inside of his wrist. He held his arm over the glass, and crimson liquid began to pool at the bottom.

Jolie stared at the glass, her stomach twisting as the familiar scent of blood filled the air. She swallowed hard, knowing this was what she needed, but still grappling with the discomfort of it all. The offer and the vulnerability it required were difficult to accept.

Jolie sipped cautiously from her glass. The rich taste of blood was both soothing and strange on her tongue. She watched Lina lean back from her work on Jared, wiping the sweat from her brow. The healer's face was lined with exhaustion, but there was a flicker of satisfaction in her tired eyes. She surveyed her patient one last time before straightening, the tension in her posture easing slightly.

"I've done what I can," Lina announced. "There'll be some stiffness, but you should heal fully in a few days." Her fingers flexed, remnants of the magic she'd woven still tingling in the air.

Jolie leaned back against the plush booth, her own exhaustion a dull weight in her bones. She was still getting used to the depth of the world around her, but for the first time in as long as she could remember, she felt a rare sense of calm.

She glanced around the room, the murmur of voices filling the space as the others began to relax. Jared stretched cautiously, testing his newly healed arm, while Rori and Boden traded quiet smiles. Jolie realized with sudden clarity that these people weren't just coworkers. They were something more. Something she'd been searching for without even knowing.

Family.

The thought struck her unexpectedly, a warmth spreading through her despite the chaos and danger still swirling around their lives. The pack shared stories, laughter bubbling up as they recounted old memories and inside jokes. They had already accepted her, despite the secrets she had kept, despite her resistance to the life they'd opened to her.

For once, she wasn't the outsider looking in. Jolie took another sip from her glass, feeling the weight inside her lift, just a little. She was part of this now, scars and all. And no matter what came next, she knew she had finally found her place.

Lina's voice cut through the warm haze of Jolie's thoughts, the easy camaraderie shifting. "So, how did you explain the woman's injuries to the authorities?" she asked.

Rori stretched out her legs with a tired yawn, her exhaustion seeping into her words. "I didn't. Figured that's their job."

Wyn, sitting cross-legged on the floor, looked up with a furrowed brow. Concern etched across her delicate features, though her tone carried its usual lightness. "But what if he comes back for revenge? I mean, I'm not much of a fighter. More of a lover, really."

Jolie could see the tension in Wyn's posture, though she tried to play it off. Lina, leaning on a booth, nodded in agreement. "Rori and I have been talking about that. It'd be a good idea to ward all the doors, just in case. If he comes back, we can't leave anything to chance."

Wyn's fingers drummed nervously on the edge of the table, her usual calm demeanor starting to crack. "Then why haven't you done it yet?"

Lina shifted uncomfortably. "I've been trying to find a book," she admitted, her voice lowering. "It has the proper warding techniques, but it's old and very rare. I can't seem to track it down anywhere."

Jolie chimed in. "Have you tried asking Seb?"

Lina's brow furrowed in confusion. "Who's Seb?"

Before Jolie could answer, Boden, who had been quietly observing the conversation, leaned forward. "Seb Rockvein. He runs a bookshop down in the market. He's a dwarf, if I recall correctly."

She looked at her friends' faces, confused by their shocked expressions. "He's actually given me a few books already. Why do you all look so surprised?" she asked.

Jared, who had been focused on his meal, paused, wiping his mouth before speaking. "Rockvein? The grumpy, stubborn little twit who runs that dusty shop?"

Boden chuckled softly, nudging Jared with his elbow. "Respect your elders, lad."

Turning to Jolie, Boden's expression softened. "We've had . . . let's say, some memorable encounters with him in the past. He can be a bit particular about who he helps."

Jolie shrugged, entirely unbothered. "I've never had any issues with him. In fact, we're sort of friends. I can go ask him for the book you need."

Lina's face lit up, a glimmer of hope replacing her earlier disappointment. "That would be incredible, Jolie. The book's called *Charms and Chants for Warding and Protection*. I've been looking for it everywhere."

Jolie chuckled. "Oh, that's an easy one. I have that book in my collection," she revealed, earning several surprised looks.

"No way! I've been looking everywhere for that book!" Lina exclaimed, her disbelief unmistakable in her tone.

Jolie wanted to laugh at Lina's reaction, but they were just getting along, and she didn't want to ruin it.

"Yeah, I actually used it to ward my apartment against magical elements." Her tone was nonchalant, but she half-hoped it would impress Lina.

Lina's eyebrows shot up in surprise. "Wait, it actually worked?"

Jolie nodded, a hint of pride in her voice. "Yep, it was a piece of cake. Just write the runes, they glow, and you're done."

"That's impossible! That type of magic is the exact opposite of your life force," Lina argued.

Rori raised her hands in a peaceful gesture. "Come on, guys. We all know that Jolie isn't your average vampire. I have a feeling we're just scratching the surface with her abilities." She winked in Jolie's direction. She stretched her arms over her head and yawned, signaling that it was time to call it a night. "Let's wrap things up here. Jolie, can you bring that book with you tomorrow?"

Jolie nodded, rising from her seat along with her friends. They made their way to the front door, with Abernathy helping Jared out of his seat while Caleb stayed glued to Jolie's side. Boden locked the door behind them as they exited. He paused and watched as Lina drove away in her car. "Jolie, are you sure you don't want to stay with us tonight? The pack provides protection."

"I'll be fine. My apartment is warded, and Caleb is with me," Jolie reassured him with a small smile.

The rumble of SUV engines faded into the night as the werewolves disappeared down the street. Boden's last words were barely audible above the engine's growl. "Be careful. Get home safe." Jolie watched them go, their taillights swallowed by the inky blackness. A wave of gratitude, warm and fierce, washed over her. Caleb's presence was a solid comfort at her back. They took off running, his strides matching her own frantic pace.

Reaching her apartment building, she glanced around. A large wolf stood silhouetted against the streetlight, its broad frame a reassuring presence even from a distance. Boden had left nothing to chance.

Chapter Thirty

Stage Fright is a Mortal Luxury

Caleb's ample frame unfurled and stretched as he ambled toward the balcony doors. A gust of air, sharp with the scent of damp earth and the city's exhaust, rolled in through the open door. It bit at the edges of her consciousness. The potent fae blood from last night still coursed through her veins. It had mended the broken bones, but the gnawing hunger remained. She found herself clinging to the hope that Wyn would forget all about tonight's mission.

Reaching for her phone, Jolie scrolled through her messages, but there was still no word from Wyn. She turned to Caleb, a plan forming in her mind.

"I have no idea when Wyn is coming to get me tonight, so I'm going to order a few pizzas," she told him with a grin.

Caleb's eyes lit up with excitement, his tail wagging furiously. Jolie made the order, choosing all of Caleb's favorite toppings, and then turned to the kitchen to make herself a mug of warm blood. As she waited for the pizzas to arrive, Jolie settled on the couch with a book, the fire crackling in the fireplace beside her.

Caleb curled up beside her and quickly began snoring again. She laughed and scratched behind his ears. "You made quite an impression on the wolves," she whispered, her hand still stroking his head. "I'm proud of you." Caleb's tail thumped happily.

The sound of a loud knock on the front door startled Caleb out of his peaceful slumber. With a piercing bark, he jumped up from his comfortable spot on the couch and scampered toward the door. His tail wagged uncontrollably behind him. As Jolie opened the door, Caleb's excitement reached a fever pitch. He jumped and yipped around the entrance, trying to get a glimpse of the food.

The delivery person offered Jolie two steaming cardboard boxes. A faint grease stain smudged the top of one. With a grateful smile, she deposited one box onto the floor. Caleb, already circling like a hungry shark, whined a happy greeting. The other box disappeared into the refrigerator. Jolie watched Caleb, his cheeks puffed with pizza, a single strand of cheese clinging to his chin. A giggle escaped her lips as she turned her attention to her own relaxation.

Nestled in the fragrant steam of her bath, the tension eased from her shoulders, inch by slow inch. The warm water enveloped her, softening last night's anxieties. She ran her hand over her damp skin. Tonight, she would need to dress much differently from her stage persona. She needed to be bland, unremarkable. Plain clothes, a ponytail, no makeup. However, as her bath cooled, Jolie still had not heard from Wyn. Jolie dared to dream: a crackling fire, the pages of her book turning slowly, a quiet contentment settling over her like a warm blanket. That was heaven. The thought had soothed the dull ache of obligation that the party represented.

Jolie frowned at the insistent buzz of her phone: Wyn. Jolie's frown deepened as she read the text. "Fifteen minutes."

Jolie sighed. Heaven, it seemed, would have to wait. The leisurely soak became a frantic scrub. She scrambled from the tub, water clinging to her. She dried herself with a towel in a hasty, inefficient swipe. Wiping the steam from the mirror, she took in her reflection. Her hair remained a cascade of damp waves. Her face bore the telltale signs of annoyance and frantic preparation.

When Wyn arrived, Jolie felt envy creep into her cheeks as she took in her friend's amazing outfit. Tight black pants and a red halter top showed off Wyn's hourglass figure. Jolie looked down at her own outfit: a pair of jeans, boots, and a plain gray sweater. She immediately felt like the frumpy older cousin next to Wyn's glamorous appearance.

"Hold on," Jolie said and disappeared into her bedroom. She rummaged through her closet, trying to find something that would make her blend in with the crowd at the party. She finally settled on a black tank top and a leather jacket. It was not as flashy as Wyn's outfit, but it would do. She quickly changed and joined Wyn, feeling a bit more confident in her appearance. "Okay, let's go."

Jolie made sure to grab her copy of *Charms and Chants for Warding and Protection*. She had promised Lina and Rori that she would drop it at the club. As a final addition, she grabbed a kitchen knife from the counter and tucked it into her bag. She was determined never to be caught empty-handed again. Before leaving, Jolie left the balcony door open so that Caleb could come and go as he pleased, reminding him to avoid being seen and not to go searching for Mikhail on his own.

Jolie followed Wyn down the stairs. "So, do you want to tell me what I'm in for?" Excitement and nerves in every word.

Wyn giggled. "Not really. I think it'll be more fun if you figure it out on your own."

Jolie rolled her eyes at her friend's cryptic response. Wyn liked to keep things interesting.

Chapter Thirty-One

The House Headliner

The chill of the deserted street seeped through their thin coats. The streetlights cast long, wavering shadows that swayed with their unease. "So," Wyn started, her voice a little too bright, trying to cut through the prickling silence. "We're doing this. Together."

Jolie kept her eyes focused on the bus stop ahead. "Yup, and I have a clear goal: get in, get information, and get out before I lose you to temptation."

Wyn nudged Jolie's arm. "Right, right. But you know, before we dive into the questions. Maybe a little preamble? You can't just waltz in and start interrogating people. We need to be approachable, friendly."

Jolie's lips thinned. "Friendly is dangerous, especially for you." She rubbed her hands on her pants. "The sooner we get this done, the better."

"But what if they shut down immediately?" Wyn countered, her brow furrowed. "What if they clam up because you're giving off . . . I'd rather be anywhere but here vibes?"

Jolie visibly recoiled at the implication. "My vibes are irrelevant, and I would rather be doing anything else."

"Your strategy involves you looking like you've just swallowed a lemon," Wyn muttered, earning a sharp glance. "Look, just one drink. A casual hello, maybe a comment about the weather . . . Then we can deploy the charm offensive. Or, you know, your brand of intense questioning."

Jolie exhaled, a puff of mist disappearing into the darkness. "One drink," she conceded, her voice flat. "And then we get the information we need."

Wyn's shoulders relaxed slightly. "One drink, then the intel. Deal?"

Jolie gave a curt nod. "Deal."

Wyn shook her head. "I feel like I've just negotiated with a computer."

A guttural groan escaped Jolie's lips as she rolled her eyes skyward. Her boots slapped a furious rhythm against the sidewalk. Each stride was an aggressive declaration that left Wyn trailing in her dust. The bus lumbered to a halt, and Jolie yanked herself up the steps. Wyn was a shadow that clung to her heels. Fluorescent lights wavered overhead as Jolie sank into the seat and turned to Wyn. Her usually composed friend was now nervously adjusting and readjusting her top. Jolie raised an eyebrow, sensing that something was off. "Are you nervous?"

Wyn let out a deep breath and looked up at Jolie with worry in her eyes. "What if he's there?" she whispered, her voice shaking.

Mikhail. Murderer. And the possible leader of the group they were trying to track down. She had not even considered the possibility of running into him, but now that Wyn had brought it up, the thought sent shivers down her spine.

"I highly doubt it," Jolie replied, trying to reassure both herself and Wyn. "Too many people are aware of what he is now. I doubt he would risk exposing himself in public."

"But he has friends out there, people who share his beliefs," Wyn argued, her voice panicked.

Jolie knew Wyn had a point. If Mikhail had allies, they could easily sabotage their mission and put them in danger, but she refused to let fear dictate their actions. "Then we stick together," she declared. She grabbed Wyn's hand and gave it a reassuring squeeze. "We're in this together, remember?"

Wyn managed a strained smile and nodded. As the bus pulled up to their stop, Wyn's hands were still trembling. Jolie stepped off the bus, pulling Wyn with her.

Darkness pressed down, swallowing the faint streetlights. Each rustle of leaves sounded like laughter. Wyn's frozen breath plumed white as they trudged onward.

They turned down a dark street, and the house stood before them. It wasn't just large. It was an immense white behemoth that seemed to absorb the little light that remained. The windows were sealed tight, dark rectangles like vacant eyes staring out at the world. Inside Jolie saw fleeting movement, a shadow detaching itself from the drapes and an almost imperceptible shimmer behind the lace of a drawn curtain. The house pulsed with unseen life.

A tall stone fence formed a barrier around the property, obscuring the backyard completely. The faintest sounds carried through the night air. A muffled murmur of voices rose and fell like a tide, sounds both oddly cheerful and intensely unsettling.

As they approached the imposing front door, Jolie felt a prickling sensation on her skin, a heightened awareness of magic that hummed beneath her skin. The heavy oak door seemed to absorb the sound of their knuckles as they rapped. Inside the jumble of voices was a raucous blend of laughter and urgency, all punctuated by the clink of glasses. She strained her senses to isolate individual sounds, to decipher the intentions hidden within the swirling words. The air itself vibrated with a restless energy that felt both exhilarating and terrifying.

Jolie could detect a mix of humans and succubi, but there was also an unfamiliar presence. The door swung open, interrupting her thoughts. A man's grin stretched wide, revealing teeth a shade too white against his deeply tanned skin. He'd spent far too much time in a tanning booth. *Did they still have those?* Jolie mused. His dark hair was pulled back in a haphazard ponytail. The tie barely contained unruly curls that escaped to frame his full face. His eyes, though, were the real problem. Dark, intense, and smoldering with heat.

The man was shirtless, with a roadmap of faded tattoos on his chest. Once vibrant splashes of color, now muted and blurred like old photographs. His demeanor hinted at a life lived hard and carelessly. The sheer arrogance of his posture, the way his chest puffed slightly as if expecting admiration, grated on her. But it was not the vanity, or the faded ink, or even the intensity of his gaze that truly unsettled her. It was the way his eyes lingered on Wyn. There was a hunger in their depths that sent icy fear through Jolie. Her hand instinctively went to the small knife tucked into her purse.

His smile did not falter. It seemed to intensify, sharpening the already unsettling angles of his face. "Hey, doll. We weren't sure if you were coming," he said, his tone filled with eagerness as he looked at Wyn. Jolie felt the muscles in her back tighten as a wave of protectiveness toward her friend washed over her, but she masked her discomfort with a polite smile. She had a feeling that this night was only going to get more complicated.

Wyn flashed a sweet smile and introduced Jolie, placing a gentle, reassuring hand on the man's chest. "Jolie, this is Kevin."

Kevin stepped aside, allowing them to enter the main living room. The space was bustling with elegantly dressed guests sipping cocktails and enjoying decadent food. Jolie felt a wave of relief wash over her; it seemed much more relaxed than she had feared. Maybe this party would not be as bad as she had anticipated.

Kevin subtly shifted his position until his hand found Jolie's. He did not just take it. He claimed it. His fingers interlaced with hers with a possessive squeeze that made her want to yank her hand away. She didn't, and his lips grazed her knuckles. It lasted a fraction too long, a calculated tease. Jolie's initial response was a silent scream inside her head. She could feel the heat rising in her cheeks; her blush hid the simmering anger that threatened to boil over. The corner of his mouth twitched. A smug, almost triumphant grin that made her want to retaliate with something more forceful than a mere eye roll. The urge to wipe that expression off his face was almost overwhelming.

Kevin, clearly undeterred, made his way to a plush sofa. He gestured for them to join him on either side. Wyn slid into her seat effortlessly, but Jolie remained standing. Her instincts urged her not to get too comfortable in this unfamiliar space. Kevin, ever persistent, draped his arm over Wyn's shoulder. His fingers rubbed her arm. Jolie could feel her patience fray as she watched his antics.

Before Jolie could snap, Wyn intervened. "We're looking for Paige. She wanted to meet Jolie," she said, sending Jolie a look that urged her to calm her temper.

Kevin's expression turned to one of disappointment as he removed his arm from Wyn's shoulder. "I don't doubt she does. She's in the back. I'll see if she's available." He got up and disappeared behind a set of curtains that separated the front room from the rest of the house.

Jolie took a seat next to Wyn, letting out a small sigh. "Ew, he's gross," she muttered, making a face.

Wyn chuckled and got up to start mixing cocktails at the bar. "Be nice, he's our host," she reminded Jolie, giving her a playful nudge.

Jolie grinned. Despite the awkward encounter with Kevin, she was starting to relax and enjoy herself. "I thought this Paige person was our host," she said, taking a sip of her cocktail.

Wyn laughed. "Well, she is the one throwing the party, but Kevin is the one who owns this beautiful house and graciously offered to host it for her," she explained as she gestured around the room.

Jolie's head dipped into a nod. She drank in the scene. Muted lamplight glinted off the polished wood. A crystal decanter sat beside a silver ice bucket frosted with condensation. Velvet drapes, the color of a twilight sky, hung heavy and still, muffling the faint murmur of conversation from the other side of the room. The scent of expensive perfume and lilies from a lavish arrangement on a nearby table lingered around them. A low fire crackled merrily in the hearth; the light cast dancing shadows that stretched and shrank across the Persian rug beneath her feet. This was a home meant to flaunt its excesses and wealth. Jolie's lip curled in annoyance.

Wyn practically vibrated with excitement. She steered Jolie through the throng of fashionably dressed guests, her arm a possessive curve around Jolie's. Each introduction was punctuated by a delighted pointing of her finger. A dazzling smile illuminated her face as she proudly displayed Jolie.

Jolie, however, felt the weight of those eyes. The murmur of conversations seemed to hush slightly as Wyn propelled them forward. Words replaced by the distinct prickle of observation. The collective weight of their scrutiny settled on Jolie's shoulders, the scent of expensive perfume suddenly cloying. "You're right," Jolie whispered. "They're definitely . . . taking me in."

"Well, you are the new girl," Wyn replied nonchalantly, taking a sip of her drink. "The new girls are always the most popular, especially when they look like you." Her voice trailed off, and her eyes drifted toward the back room, a gleeful sparkle in them. "We'll have to move back there soon," she added with a suggestive smirk.

Jolie pinched her thigh, trying to bring her back to reality. "Focus, we're not here for hanky-panky," she scolded playfully.

"Hanky-panky? What are you, like seventy?" Wyn giggled, taking another sip of her Manhattan.

"Actually, closer to one hundred and fifty," Jolie replied with a smirk. "But seriously, who is this Paige that we're supposed to meet?"

Wyn's smile faltered for a moment as she thought. "Paige is . . ." Her voice trailed off as she stared at a young man across the room.

Jolie shook her head and pinched her friend's leg again, this time harder. "Ow, what the hell? Okay, okay. Paige is a major player in the party scene. Everyone knows her or wants to know her. I've met her a few times, and she has a thing for succubi. She'll know Mikhail. I'm sure of it," Wyn finally answered, snapping back to reality.

Jolie let out a sigh and shook her head. "Let's just get this over with." They made their way toward the back, passing through the heavy velvet curtains and into a room entirely different from the front of the house. Jolie snorted at the sight before her, quickly covering her mouth as Wyn shot her a look.

The dress code was revealing and seductive. Everywhere Jolie looked, she saw pasties and thongs paired with garters or thigh-highs and sky-high heels. The men, though slightly more covered, still placed themselves on display. Some couples chose to escape to a more private area, indulging in their desires away from prying eyes, but for others, the thrill of putting their activities on display was too tempting to resist.

They soon spotted Kevin standing in the doorway of another room, a smug grin on his face as he motioned for them to follow. Jolie and Wyn exchanged a glance, then trailed behind him. As they entered, their eyes fell upon Paige.

She lounged casually on a blue chaise, draped in a silk robe and stockings, but little else. The robe was left wide open, a deliberate display of her body. Paige's confidence was obvious. She dared everyone in the room to stare. She relished their attention. Her black garters cut sharp lines against her porcelain skin. Dark waves of hair framed a face that echoed the glamour of the 1920s, sultry and bold. Her bright red lips curved into a huntress's smile, a silent challenge to anyone who approached. As people greeted her, she welcomed them with a kiss, as if collecting their adoration.

Jolie frowned. Her discomfort deepened when Kevin sat beside Paige and began stroking her thigh as she rested her legs across his lap. "Can we wait until Kevin's off doing something else?" Jolie muttered, her unease clear.

Wyn gave her hand a playful kiss. "Come on, let's just get this over with. My focus is slipping fast."

With a resigned sigh, Jolie followed Wyn. She prepared herself for whatever encounter lay ahead with the bold and unapologetic Paige.

Chapter Thirty-Two

Velvet Underground

Wyn made the introductions. Her voice faded away as Paige focused on Jolie. Paige's hand, long and pale as bone china, stretched toward her. Jolie could feel the pull, the need to reach out and take Paige's hand.

Paige radiated a dangerous warmth, like embers clinging to smoldering logs. A soft smile touched Paige's lips as Jolie's palm closed around hers. Jolie's mind went blank, and she acted on instinct, leaning in and pressing her mouth to Paige's knuckles. The air thickened; the scent of jasmine enveloped her.

Her mind screamed caution. But the allure of the unknown drowned it out. "It's a pleasure to finally meet you." Paige's voice was a low alto. It was smooth as river stone and carried with it a hint of wild vanilla.

Jolie's eyes landed on the subtle curve of Paige's jaw. "The pleasure is all mine," she replied, her voice huskier than intended. She swallowed.

Paige's smile widened, revealing a set of teeth that were unnaturally sharp. "Kevin, dear," she purred, her voice dripping with charm. "I'd love some alone time with these lovely ladies. Would it be possible for me to use the blue room?"

Kevin's initial reaction seemed to be one of protest, but he quickly thought better of it. "Of course. Whatever your heart desires," he replied, gesturing toward the room. The three women made their way to the back of the house, leaving Kevin alone on the divan.

Wyn closed the door behind them. Paige wasted no time making herself comfortable, wrapping her silky robe around her body and settling onto the makeshift bed.

Jolie's knuckles tightened as she lowered herself onto the cushions beside Paige. A subtle chirr vibrated in the air, mirroring the electric current that jolted Jolie's limbs. Jolie caught the almost imperceptible tilt of Wyn's head and the way her breath hitched just so. It was a silent echo of Jolie's own bewilderment.

Jolie cleared her throat. "So, Paige," she ventured, the words a fragile thread. "Kevin."

Paige's laughter rippled through the room. It was a low, smoky sound that seemed to caress their skin. Her eyes sparkled. "Kevin, yes," Paige hummed. "We have history, you could say."

Jolie watched Paige, the effortless way she held herself, the magnetism that seemed to radiate from her like heat from a fire. Envy grew in her chest, a yearning for that same effortless command, the ability to weave spells with mere words and a glance.

"I must say, I was quite taken with you as soon as I saw you," Paige continued, running a finger along the edge of her robe. "There's something about you that's . . . different. Special."

A sudden heat prickled Jolie's skin as Paige spoke. Her words, rich and warm like aged whiskey, wrapped around her. Jolie's fingers, as if with a will of their own, twisted the fringe of the pillow beside her.

"I couldn't agree more," Wyn chimed in, breaking the spell. "Jolie is truly one of a kind." Paige's gaze shifted toward Wyn. As her intense eyes moved from Jolie, so did the mysterious hold she had.

The room, once a large storage closet, had become a shrine to stolen moments. A touch of peony permeated the room from the decanter in the corner. Dim lamps bled a soft light, and pillows, plump and inviting, overflowed a narrow bench. Blue velvet swallowed the walls, the fabric muffling the outside world. Every fold, every carefully placed cushion, screamed of a labor of love, or perhaps, desperation. Her attention drifted back to Paige. A subtle tremor ran through Paige's shoulders as she chewed her lip.

The once flirty and seductive woman now retreated with her arms crossed over her chest, her eyes cold and hardened. Something had passed between Paige and Wyn that Jolie had missed, and it was clear that she was not in the mood for any more idle chitchat.

Paige spoke, her words sharp and clipped. "I don't want anyone to know that I've been talking about Mikhail." Her warning was clear. "We dated briefly, but he's not right. He has dangerous ideas."

With a confident smile, Jolie responded, "Where can I find him?"

Paige let out a sigh and rubbed her temples, her demeanor softening slightly. "Wow, you really get right down to business, don't you?" she remarked, almost in disbelief. "I don't really know where he is. When I found out he was with the agitators, I left him. We were only together for three weeks."

Jolie could sense the subtle shift in Paige's posture, the way she tightened her jaw and straightened her back in annoyance. Jolie reached out and placed a comforting hand on Paige's arm, gently urging her to calm down. "Paige, anything you can tell us would be helpful," Jolie said, her voice soothing and understanding. "Do you know what happened last night?"

Paige nodded, her confident smirk slowly returning. "Yeah, Mikhail got into a bit of a scuffle with a vamp and some shifters. The rumor mill is saying he came out on top." There was a devilish glint in her eyes, her words perfectly chosen to poke at Jolie.

Wyn winced at Paige's words and quickly interjected between the two women. "I wouldn't say he bested them," she corrected.

A muscle twitched near Jolie's temple. "This," she said, each syllable clipped and precise, "is utterly pointless." She stamped her foot as she stood and moved to the door. She immediately felt childish, but the simmering heat that was Paige's enigmatic energy was leaving her untethered. Even as Jolie's hand tightened around the doorknob, a flicker of something that felt oddly like longing trailed across her mind. It was a strange contrast to the resolute anger bubbling beneath the surface.

Paige held up her hands in surrender. "Wait, I don't want anyone to think I'm anything like them. I overheard him talking about their hideaway in the basement of a club they frequent, some closed metal bar south of the stadiums. I think it was called The Slag & Bone. Mikhail might be there," she revealed, her voice tinged with a hint of concern. "That's all I know."

Wyn sighed in relief, the tension leaving her body. "See? That's helpful," she said, wrapping an arm around Jolie and gently guiding her out the door.

Paige got up from her seat and let her robe fall open, once again flaunting her body.

"Be careful getting the vamp out of here," she warned with a scheming grin. "She's like candy to them." Paige squeezed past them and sauntered down the hallway, seamlessly blending back into the party.

Wyn and Jolie finally made it back to the waiting area by the door, which was now empty as everyone had migrated to the back of the house.

Wyn let out a sigh, disappointment dripping off her. "Do you think we could stay for a little while?" she asked.

"Not a chance," Jolie said as she closed the front door behind them.

Wyn pouted and stamped her feet. A low grumble started in her chest and exited her mouth in a petulant whine. "Ugh, you're so boring."

Jolie's eyes glinted in the darkness. A slow, almost imperceptible curl tugged at the corner of her mouth. "Boring, you say?" Jolie's voice carried a playful challenge. "Perhaps you're just looking in the wrong corners, Wyn."

Wyn dragged herself down the street. "Seriously, you're the worst," she huffed, the words escaping her lips like a gust of cold air. "I pictured having a vampire friend to be different. More sparkle, less . . . this."

Jolie swayed her hips. A tiny skip in her step evident as she relished Wyn's theatrical pout. "My dear." Jolie fell in step next to Wyn. "I'm . . . shall we say . . . vintage. Not exactly the fun demographic anymore."

Wyn halted abruptly, spinning to face Jolie. The streetlamp caught the frustrated set of her jaw. "You're not wrong," she conceded, a reluctant smile softening her annoyance. Then, with a sudden, surprising lightness, she wrapped an arm through Jolie's. "But I suppose you're not that bad."

Wyn pulled Jolie closer. "Should we hail a cab or wait for the bus?" Wyn's teeth chattered faintly against the chill of the night air. Unfazed by the cold, Jolie reached into her pocket and pulled out her phone to call Rori. She quickly relayed all they had learned from the evening, especially the part about The Slag & Bone.

"We're headed to Rori and Boden's." Jolie pulled Wyn along at a faster pace. "A car's coming. Rori arranged it. We just need to reach the main road first."

"Yeah, that's probably a smart move," Wyn agreed, her voice trembling slightly from the cold.

The street beneath Jolie's boots clicked in rhythm against Wyn's effervescent stream of tales. Laughter tumbled from her lips as she shared stories of the people Jolie had met at the party. She painted vivid portraits of a man who juggled flaming torches and a woman whose hat sported a miniature, live parrot. Each anecdote offered a welcome distraction. Yet Jolie's thoughts were a relentless tide pulling her back to Paige.

"So," Jolie began. She tilted her head, feigning casual observation as if merely admiring the skeletal silhouettes of oak trees against the dark sky. "What's the deal with Paige?"

"I'm not sure what you mean," Wyn replied, her tone guarded. "She's a major player. I told you that."

Jolie sighed and glanced over her shoulder. "You know what I'm getting at. What is she? She smells different."

Wyn stopped in her tracks, her expression pained. "Jesus, Jolie, you know I hate doing this." She looked around warily before matching pace with Jolie again. "She's not a succubus. She's an Aos Sí and of the Seelie Court. Old, like hella old, and all royal and shit."

Jolie's eyes grew wide. The Aos Sí had been in the encyclopedia. A race from forgotten eras, extremely powerful. Her throat tightened, a knot of disbelief and burgeoning awe. "Wow," she choked out.

"Yeah, and she's not someone you want to mess with," Wyn warned, her voice serious. "She's got connections and influence all over town, and she doesn't take kindly to people who cross her."

"Do you think she's like a princess or something?" Jolie asked. Her focus was pulled toward the shadows, her senses tingling as if they were being followed. She shook her head. Maybe she was just being paranoid.

Wyn chuckled, shaking her head. "More like a queen of the universe. She's a big deal, Jolie."

Jolie's brow furrowed with concern. "Is she evil?"

Wyn shrugged, pushing her hands into her pockets. "There's no such thing as good or evil in the world of fae. The Aos Sí only look out for their own kind. Humans, well, they're kinda just here for their entertainment."

As they made their way toward the lights of the main street, Jolie couldn't shake off the feeling of being watched. She grabbed Wyn's arm to slow their pace, trying to catch a glance of their pursuers. She could smell them in the air, their human scent mingling with the night. Jolie's body tensed. They were close, very close.

Their pursuers stepped out of the shadows. The taller one, with shaggy blond hair, smirked at them. "Hey Wyn, where are you off to so early?" He was accompanied by a shorter, stockier version of himself. Both looked barely twenty-one.

Wyn's eyes narrowed as she recognized the men. "Oliver?" Wyn said to the taller one. "Why are you following us?"

"We saw you leave and didn't get a chance to talk to you. Who's your friend?" Oliver's friend answered for him as he took a step forward, his gaze fixed on Jolie.

Wyn looped her arm through Jolie's, pulling her close. "We work together."

Oliver's friend moved closer, reaching out to touch Jolie. A wide grin spread across his face. "I've seen you dance. You're Jolie Mason!"

A rough hand clamped onto Jolie's shoulder. The touch burned through the fabric of her jacket. Before the boy could even register the shift, Jolie's body coiled. A guttural snarl ripped from her chest. Her hand shot out in a blur of motion and snatched his arm. Bones crunched under her viselike grip as she wrenched it behind his back. She forced him to his knees with a choked gasp. The sharp points of her canines glinted in the scant light.

"Yes, I am," she hissed, her voice dropping lower. "And I don't like to be touched."

Wyn's voice rang out in warning. "Jolie, calm down."

Oliver's mask of calm shattered. Panic washed over him. "Shit, man, what the fuck," he cursed, his voice trembling with fear. He instinctively turned to run, but before he could take a step, Wyn was on him. She tackled him to the ground, her strong arms holding him down. Oliver struggled against her.

Wyn struggled to hold the panicking Oliver in place. She stroked his face and hair gently, speaking to him in a soft, soothing voice. "It's okay, Oliver. We're going to be okay. Just breathe," she whispered, her touch bringing a sense of peace to his frantic mind.

Once Oliver was subdued, Wyn turned her attention to Jolie, who was still holding the other boy by his arm and the back of his neck. "Jesus, Jolie. Human, HUMAN! Let him go," she scolded, her eyes wide with concern.

Jolie's fingers uncoiled from his arm. But she kept her hands clamped to the nape of his neck.

Even as the sound left her lips, the words rang hollow. "They were stalking us. Maybe someone sent them," she offered, but her voice lacked conviction. The boy in Jolie's grip shook with fear. Tears spilled from his eyes.

Oliver reached up and wrapped his arms around Wyn, seeking comfort and protection. "I love you," he said, his voice muffled against her stomach.

Wyn's expression softened at Oliver's words, but she quickly regained her composure. "Yeah, whatever. Why are you following us?" she demanded, pushing him back down to the ground.

"You're beautiful, and I love you," he said with a lecherous tone, causing Wyn to roll her eyes. Oliver began to shake with sobs. "I wish you'd just love me."

Frustration and anger bubbled up inside Wyn as she looked down at the boy drooling on her pants. "See, they weren't going to hurt us," she snapped at Jolie. "Mother Lilith, this is bad."

Jolie, still trying to maintain her sense of righteousness, spoke up. "Well, they shouldn't be stalking us in the dark. Was I really supposed to think they had good intentions?" she reasoned. Her grip on the boy loosened slightly. The boy's sobs were intermixed with soft words begging for mercy.

Wyn locked eyes with Jolie, her expression stern. "You caused this problem, you fix it," she commanded.

Jolie reluctantly retracted her fangs and spun the boy to face her. She intensified her gaze, pushing her will onto him. "You're going to go back to the party and enjoy yourself. You never saw us leave," she commanded.

The boy's eyes glazed over as he nodded in agreement. "Yeah, I never saw you," he repeated in a dazed tone.

Wyn cleared her throat, interrupting their interaction. "That's not going to work because of Oliver." Wyn pointed to the boy still crying in her lap.

Jolie cursed herself for overreacting and bit her lip. "Alright." She paused, steadying her breath. She refocused on Oliver, catching his gaze. "This didn't happen. You never saw us leave."

His tear-streaked face softened, the panic fading from his eyes.

"Now go."

Oliver stumbled to his feet, and the boys bolted down the street.

Wyn shot Jolie a knowing grin. "Well, that could've been worse."

Jolie shook her head, guilt tugging at her. "Don't get too smug. I might've scrambled their brains. Nice touch with the love spell, by the way."

Wyn leaned against her as they resumed walking. "Thanks, your memory-wiping thing isn't half bad either."

A smirk tugged at Jolie's lips. "We do make a hell of a team."

Wyn laughed, and despite the mess they'd just been through, Jolie found herself chuckling too, the tension easing just as a sleek black SUV rolled up to whisk them away.

CHAPTER THIRTY-THREE

The Part of the Act No One Sees Coming

The car slowed and then stopped in front of a tall building that nearly reached up to the night sky. Its outer walls were a shimmering curtain of black, reflecting city lights. It was utterly unlike anything Jolie had ever associated with werewolves. She had pictured crumbling stone, moss-covered roofs, maybe a ramshackle cabin nestled deep in the woods. This was a modern marvel. Her jaw dropped, a silent gasp escaping her as the driver opened the car door.

The building entrance was meticulously landscaped with polished granite and topiaries pruned to geometric perfection. A man, broad-shouldered and thick-necked, stood guard. His face was a roadmap of weathered lines carved by the sun. The air thickened around him with musky scents of forest floors and spring growth. Unmistakably werewolf, but refined, like expensive cologne masking a wild heart. He was not the hairy beast of folklore; he had clearly mastered the art of blending in.

The doorman opened the heavy glass door; his eyes assessed them with cool indifference. Inside the lobby was an exercise in minimalist luxury: polished chrome, dark wood, and quiet efficiency. Behind a black desk sat a young woman with hair teased into a gravity-defying cloud of platinum blonde, her dark roots peeking out like a rebellious secret. Her fingers, adorned with long, hot pink talons, drummed a restless rhythm on the polished surface. Tattoos snaked up her neck and peeked out from beneath the sleeves of her tailored black jacket. She watched Jolie and Wyn, her eyes traveling from head to toe. Her gaze held none of the warmth of welcome, only a cool appraisal.

"We're here to see Mr. and Mrs. Rudel." Wyn smiled brightly. There was a subtle shift in the woman's demeanor that betrayed something akin to surprise beneath her indifference. The woman's features tightened further as she asked for their names.

"Wyn and Jolie," they answered in unison. She raised a skeptical eyebrow before asking them to wait while she checked with the Rudels. Jolie could feel the woman's irritation; they probably were not the typical visitors.

Jolie scanned the lobby as they waited. Her eyes fell on the sleek but comfortable dark furniture and the art decorating the walls. "They don't pay," Wyn said, answering Jolie's unspoken question. "They own it."

Jolie's jaw dropped. "They own the entire building?"

"You're in werewolf central," Wyn replied with an excited smile. "This is where the whole pack lives."

Jolie's eyes widened. "So, their pack members are all neighbors?"

Wyn nodded. "Yup, and there are even a few human renters. This place is huge."

Jolie was stunned. She had recently learned that werewolves tended to live in close-knit communities, but she never imagined it being on this scale.

The young woman beckoned them with a wave over to the bank of elevators, her bright fingernails illuminating the way. "You can go up now, thirty-sixth floor," she said.

Jolie leaned out of the elevator just as the doors began to close. "What's their apartment number?" she asked, unsure of how many apartments she would have to sort through on just one floor.

The young woman's smug grin grew wider. "Thirty-sixth floor," she repeated, as if it were some sort of secret code.

As the elevator doors opened at their destination, Jolie quickly realized what the young woman meant. They stepped out directly into Rori and Boden's apartment, the open floor plan stretching around them. The living room, kitchen, and dining room were flooded with the night sky from the floor-to-ceiling windows that overlooked the city; the views were stunning from this height. Behind the elevator, there were doors leading to the bedrooms and bathrooms, the only closed-off sections of the apartment. Beyond the living room, through sliding glass doors, was a large balcony covered in potted plants and patio furniture. Jolie's eyes widened in surprise as she took in the sight of Rori standing in front of the grill, expertly flipping burgers. And beside her, she could see what she assumed were Rori's kids playing soccer in the open space.

Jared emerged from the kitchen, balancing a tray filled with buns and burger toppings. His face lit up with a broad smile when he saw them, and he nodded his head, gesturing for them to follow. "Come on out to the deck," he said. "Boden and the others should be back soon."

Jolie leaned into Wyn and whispered, "Isn't it a bit late for dinner?"

Jared chuckled, lowering his voice in jest. "We're werewolves . . . kinda nocturnal and stuff."

Rori looked up at the sound of their voices and waved in greeting. Jolie followed Jared and Wyn out onto the balcony, taking a seat at the table.

She had never expected something so domestic from Rori, and it felt even stranger now that she knew she was a werewolf. But in this moment, surrounded by the warm glow of the city lights and the laughter of her friends, Jolie began to feel at home.

"How's your arm?" Wyn asked, genuine concern in her voice as she slid onto the seat next to Jared, subtly inching closer. Jolie shook her head. Wyn's gaze lingered on Jared longer than needed, admiration clear in her eyes. She did not blame her; Jared was easy to admire.

His lips twisted into a small grimace as he shrugged with his uninjured shoulder. "Still a bit sore, but functional. So, I'm stuck on guard duty," he said, irritation seeping into his tone. "I feel useless. Rori doesn't need me hovering."

Jolie felt a pang of sympathy. She could only imagine what it must have felt like to be sidelined by Boden. Without a word, she reached out, resting her hand on Jared's arm and giving it a gentle, reassuring squeeze. "I'm sure you're still a valuable asset to the team, even if you can't fight at the moment," she offered.

Jared gave her a small smile. But his attention was quickly diverted as Rori approached the table, a warm smile on her face. "You may be stuck with me, but you do get first dibs on food," she said. "Who's hungry?"

As if on cue, the children bolted from the far end of the terrace, shoving each other in their rush to the table. Jolie stiffened, slightly overwhelmed by their wild energy.

"Good lord, they eat like their father," Rori said with a laugh, shaking her head. "Enough! Sit calmly, please. We have guests."

As they waited, Rori gestured toward the children. "Kids, these are Wyn and Jolie. That's Aiden, Brea, and our eldest, Tobin." The children waved briefly before returning to their food with ravenous enthusiasm.

Jolie took a closer look at them. All three had their father's tall, lean build and sharp features. Tobin, who was around twelve, had a serious demeanor that made him seem older than he was. Brea, who looked to be around nine years old, watched Jolie as intently as Jolie watched her. She stood out with her dark hair and eyes, traits inherited from Rori. Aiden, the youngest at seven, had a contagious smile that lit up his entire face.

Rori's laughter, bright and bubbly, chased away Jolie's lingering anxiety. Rori and Wyn exchanged easy smiles, their conversation creating a backdrop for the evening. As Jolie watched them, a surprising sense of belonging settled deep in her chest. The clink of glass against the table startled her. Jared set a glass of ruby-red wine before her. "Sorry," he murmured, a teasing lilt to his voice, "no blood."

Heat flooded Jolie's cheeks. The reminder of her nature, her peculiarity, prickled at her. But before she could dwell on it, Rori's hand, warm and firm, covered hers, a silent reassurance. "Don't worry," Rori said gently. "They know. Probably more than you do." She laughed and sat down next to Aiden, who was still nibbling on his vegetables.

"Yeah, you're a vampire, but a nice one," Brea chimed in, her mouth smeared with ketchup. "Mom said you're okay."

Tobin, now on his second burger, shot his sister an annoyed glance. "Quit it, Brea. We're not supposed to talk about another fae." He quickly turned the conversation to himself. "I get to go on my first run soon."

"First run?" Jolie had never heard the term before.

Rori handed Brea a napkin, nodding. "Werewolf cubs don't shift until they're thirteen. It happens on the first full moon after their thirteenth birthday. It's a pretty big deal. The whole pack comes to welcome the new wolf. We're already planning Tobin's."

Tobin's eyes gleamed with excitement. "I'm gonna hunt a deer!"

Aiden, horrified, spoke up for the first time. "Mom said no killing!"

Jolie noticed Aiden's plate held only vegetables and chips, his face twisted in disgust at his brother's comment.

Rori quickly intervened. "Don't joke with Aiden like that, Tobin," she scolded, then turned to Aiden. "I've got veggie burgers for you right here, baby. They didn't touch any meat."

Aiden wrinkled his nose. "Eww, Mom! I think they did."

Rori sighed but kept her tone firm. "No, they didn't. Now eat."

Turning back to Jolie, Rori smiled. "He's a vegetarian. From the moment Aiden could talk, he was telling me how mean we were to other animals. He's a very modern wolf."

Jared suddenly stood, his relaxed expression fading into concern. His eyes darted toward the front door as he reached for his phone. "I'm going to check on Boden. They've been gone too long."

Rori waved him off with a soft chuckle, though there was a hint of worry in her gaze. "Go ahead, but don't fret. They've got everything handled."

Jared crossed the deck and vanished into the apartment. Tension hung in the air. Jolie felt Rori's stillness across the table. A rigid calm barely masking the tremor in her hands as she smiled thinly at the children. The city's usual soundtrack of horns, the far-off wail of a siren, all seemed to sharpen.

Minutes stretched. Then Boden strolled onto the deck with Angus and Abernathy flanking him like silent guards. Caleb, a tempest of puppy energy, followed and immediately launched into a dizzying circuit on the deck. Jared emerged behind them. The lines of tension eased from his face. Rori's shoulders, previously hunched tight, visibly unknotted. A breath escaped her lips.

The children's squeals filled the air as they raced to greet Caleb, their small hands grabbing for his fur as they chased him around the deck, laughing loudly. Caleb let them tug and play, his tail wagging excitedly.

Jolie sat at the far end of the deck, watching the scene with a smile. When Caleb bounded toward her, she wrapped her arms around him and sank her hands into the soft, coarse fur around his neck. "Where did you come from, big guy?" she asked with a light laugh, ruffling his ears.

Boden tossed Caleb a leftover burger from the grill. "He was waiting outside the club you sent us to. Damn good tracker, this one," he said, admiration in his tone as Caleb caught the burger midair.

But Jolie's smile faded as her attention shifted to Boden. His usual easygoing demeanor was absent, replaced by a tension in his jaw and a quiet heaviness in his expression. He took his time, greeting his family and grabbing a plate of food, but Jolie sensed the weight of what was to come. Her stomach twisted with unease.

Finally, Boden met her eyes. His head tilted as he walked over to her, regret in his features. "Jolie," he said softly. "I'm sorry. We didn't find anything."

Jolie frowned, her mind racing through the possibilities. She had been holding onto the hope that Boden's trip would yield some clues, some lead on where to go next. But it seemed that hope had evaporated into thin air. Plan A had failed, and now they were stranded in uncertainty.

"Looks like we're moving on to Plan B then," she murmured. Whatever Plan B was, they would figure it out, because giving up was not an option.

After Boden finished his meal, he sent the kids off to their rooms, where the promise of video games before bedtime had them eagerly rushing to the far side of the apartment. The apartment quieted as the adults settled into the living room. Boden lit the fire in the stone hearth before sinking into the dark leather couch, the orange glow casting shadows across his features.

"Well, that was a bust," Boden said. His voice was heavy with defeat as he ran a hand down his face. The crackling of the fire filled the silence, but even the warmth could not soften the disappointment in his tone. "No one was there. Not a single clue to follow." His mouth twisted slightly as he leaned back, the weight of failure evident.

"Oh man, she totally lied to us," Wyn growled, fists clenched at her sides. The irritation in her voice matched the tension in her posture. Her eyes flashed with anger.

Boden, sitting back in his chair, chuckled softly at Wyn's fiery reaction. "I don't think she lied to us," he replied calmly, his eyes betraying his exhaustion.

Abernathy, who had been pacing near the fireplace, stopped and crossed his arms. "But she's right to be pissed," he muttered. "We could smell them everywhere. They'd been there, just not when we showed up. The run-in we had last night probably spooked them."

Rori snuggled up next to Boden on the couch, and he instinctively wrapped his arm around her. The warmth between them was a moment of comfort amidst the chaos. "I sent the other boys home," Boden continued, his voice low and thoughtful. "We stuck around, hoping someone would show up, but nothing. Not a trace."

Jolie shifted in her seat, scooting closer to Caleb. The large dog rested his head on her lap, his presence grounding her. She sighed and ran a hand through his fur. "So, we're back to square one?"

Abernathy, leaning against the kitchen doorframe, finished off his beer with a shrug. "Looks that way," he muttered before disappearing into the kitchen for another drink.

Jolie jumped up from her seat and rummaged through her shoulder bag. "Oh! I almost forgot!" she exclaimed, pulling out the weathered copy of *Charms and Chants for Warding and Protection*. "This is for Lina."

Rori's eyes widened as she took the book, reverence clear in her expression. She flipped through the pages. "I can't believe you actually have this. It's insane."

Wyn, still bristling from earlier, crossed her arms and refused to let go of her annoyance. "Paige should've told us he was on the move. She's been sitting on this information for too long."

Rori set the book down, her patience slipping as she turned to face Wyn. "Look, just because Paige is ancient doesn't mean she knows everything. She didn't lie to us. We were just too late."

Rori pecked Boden on the cheek. "I'm going to go make sure your pups are actually getting ready for bed," she said with a soft smile before standing up and heading down the hall.

The last embers of the fire cast long, dancing shadows. Mikhail's disappearance had woven a thread of frantic energy through their earlier laughter, leaving behind only a frayed, anxious silence. Jared paced in front of the dying flames, his jaw clenched tight. His restless energy contrasted with the slumped postures of Angus and Abernathy.

With heavy sighs, they slowly dispersed, the remaining pack heading to their own apartments. Jolie approached Caleb. He lay sprawled before the dying fire, a furry mountain of canine contentment. His deep chest rose and fell with slow, even breaths. She gently nudged his shoulder. He barely stirred, a low growl vibrating from his chest.

Wyn presented a different challenge. She was slumped against the couch cushions, a rumpled heap of limbs and discarded clothing. Jolie knelt and gently shook her shoulder, but Wyn remained stubbornly unresponsive, a picture of absolute, peaceful oblivion.

Jolie sighed, glancing at Rori, unsure of what to do. "She's not moving," she said.

Rori waved it off with a smile. "Don't worry about her," she reassured. "Wyn can sleep here; we've got plenty of room. There's a spare bedroom for you and Caleb, too. There's no need to head out now."

A tremor of doubt ran through Jolie. The warmth of Rori and Boden's hospitality felt like a fragile thing she had not yet earned. Rori's words cut through her hesitation. "The sun is coming up, Jolie. You shouldn't be out alone." Reluctantly, Jolie nodded.

CHAPTER THIRTY-FOUR

A Hunter in the Front Row

The frigid water jolted Jolie awake as it slapped against her skin. She raked her fingers through the wild tangle of her hair, each strand resisting her efforts to smooth it into submission. She stepped out of the bathroom and was met with the clatter of four feet on polished hardwood.

She followed the sound into the main living space. It intermingled with the vibrant chaos of childhood. Jared sat with his shoulders hunched in concentration, wrestling a tire back onto a bright red fire truck. The air buzzed with the high-pitched squeals of laughter. The young woman from the front desk, her blonde hair a sun-bleached halo, knelt beside him. She held a cracker and a wedge of cheese in her hand; she watched Rori's children, giggling along with her antics. Nearby, Caleb crouched low, his nose twitching, he crept toward the cheese, preparing to pounce while the woman was not paying attention.

"Hey, Jolie, how'd you sleep?" Jared greeted her with a warm smile, causing the blonde to scowl. "Have you met Shona yet?"

Jolie nodded. "Yeah, when we got here last night. How are you?"

"Fine," Shona breathed, the word a sandpaper rasp. She didn't look away from the playing children, defiance in her fixed stare.

Jared's fingers settled on Shona's shoulder. His eyes darted between the two women. Jolie pushed a stray hair from her forehead, the gesture deliberately casual. "Where did everyone scatter to?" Her voice was light as a sea breeze.

"Rori and Boden headed to the club, and Wyn . . . I think she went home," Jared replied, visibly relieved.

Jolie nodded. "I'll swing by the club before heading home. Not even sure if I'm on the schedule today." She gave him a small smile and signaled Caleb to follow as she started toward the door. Caleb huffed as he moved to follow Jolie, his eyes still lingering on the cheese in Shona's hand.

"Nice seeing you again, Jolie," Jared called out after her, his voice warm. "What?" A low growl vibrated from Jared. Jolie's lips quirked as she pushed the door closed. She would leave Jared to whatever trouble he was about to get into.

When they hit the street, Caleb bounded past her. A joyous, guttural yip escaped his throat. He skidded to a halt, spinning in a tight circle, nose twitching as he lunged at the phantom movement of a napkin in the wind. His tail swung through the air in a rapid swish. Jolie laughed at his unrestrained joy.

He bounded up to her and placed two large paws on her shoulders before licking her face. Jolie groaned. "You really love spending time with the wolves, don't you?" Caleb pushed off her and began to run ahead, forcing Jolie to sprint to keep up.

The Black Cat House's back door groaned in protest as Jolie pushed it inward. The air hung thick and heavy, a strange mix of smoke and incense. Lina knelt before a doorframe. She traced the frame with a reverence bordering on obsession. Jolie's book lay beside her, its pages open and marked with notes and symbols. A low, rhythmic drone escaped Lina's lips, a chant that seemed to vibrate the air. Jolie could feel it in her chest, resonating with powerful energy. Behind her, Angus moved like a seasoned ritualist. He swirled the burning bundles, their fragrant smoke weaving a swirling, purifying curtain through the room.

Rori and Boden sat in a booth, keeping their distance and giving Lina a chance to work. Several figures, their faces obscured by shadow but clearly members of their security detail, remained rigidly at the periphery, their eyes watchful. The scene was unsettling, hypnotic, and utterly unlike anything Jolie had ever witnessed.

"Hey there, sleeping beauty," Rori called out. She approached, her tone lighthearted. For a moment, Jolie thought the comment was directed at her, but then she noticed Caleb bounding up to Rori's side. The big dog wagged his tail eagerly, earning himself a fond scratch behind the ears.

"Sorry, Caleb. Kitchen's closed for now. No chicken yet," Rori teased. Her fingers affectionately rubbed his fur. Caleb's tail continued to thump the floor with pure joy, unaffected by the lack of food.

"You're going to spoil him," Jolie quipped. She folded her arms and watched the two with a grin. Despite her teasing, it warmed her to see Caleb so content in Rori's care.

Shifting her focus, Jolie added, "I figured I'd come by to check on my work schedule. It looks like Lina's been busy." Her eyes drifted to the symbols Lina had painted, a soft glow still lingering from the ritual.

"Protection wards from your book," Lina responded without looking up, her voice calm but focused. "We're fortifying the place, just in case."

Rori nodded, glancing over at Lina's progress. "Yeah, she's almost done. I'd like to see Mikhail try to get in here again. Or anyone else who means to do harm."

Jolie's face hardened at the mention of Mikhail. "I can't believe he would have the audacity to come back here," she muttered under her breath.

Rori noticed Jolie's uneasy expression and placed a comforting hand on her shoulder. "I hadn't put you on the schedule yet; I wasn't sure if you'd be up to it."

But before Rori could finish her sentence, Jolie cut her off, determined to take back control of her life. "I'd like to work," she declared, her voice determined. "It would make me feel normal."

Rori put an arm around Jolie. "Of course. Go home and get your stuff. I'll put your first routine in the second act."

"Thanks. Can Caleb wait here? He seems quite content."

Caleb, who had climbed up into a nearby booth, had his head resting on Boden's lap. Boden absentmindedly stroked his head while reviewing inventory and making product orders. Rori looked over at them and chuckled. "Yeah, let's not interrupt that. See you soon."

Jolie rushed home in a sprint, relishing the freedom and the release of her pent-up energy. Each footfall landed with a soft thud, her speed helping her to glide across the pavement. Street signs blurred into streaks of color. The anonymity of the deepening twilight was comforting; it shielded her from the prying eyes of the day. The urge to keep running, to extend this exhilarating freedom, clawed at her, but responsibility won out.

Reaching her apartment building, she paused on the bottom step. The night air was filled with the scent of exhaust fumes, but it also carried something else. Her nose twitched as she took the steps two at a time. The scent was familiar: cinnamon and clove. Mikhail. She stood frozen, her senses straining in the dim light, searching the darkness for any sign of him.

A shiver clawed at Jolie's skin. The scent had begun its slow fade; Jolie estimated it had been at least six hours since Mikhail had been there. Still, each step she took was a calculated gamble. He could have planted a thousand traps. She ran her hand along the plaster of the corridor wall. Her ears attuned to the sounds of the old building. The dry whisper of mouse feet in the walls. The deep groan of timbers shifting their weight. Each sound registered and banished. Her gaze remained a hunter's, dissecting the light and shadow.

As she approached her door, dread sank in her stomach. A knife, its blade shining wickedly despite the shadows, pierced the wood. Impaled on the blade was a single, crisply folded letter.

Jolie took a sharp breath as she read the words written in Mikhail's refined handwriting.

I would have waited for you, but I couldn't get past your wards. You certainly are full of surprises. I have something for you, but you must come quickly, or it will spoil. Meet me at The Slag & Bone. Detective O'Neil would love to see you.

Jolie's fist clenched around the letter as the weight of the situation hit her. Mikhail was using Danny as leverage. Her knuckles went white, nails digging into her own flesh. Mikhail's sneering laugh replayed in her ears.

A curse escaped Jolie's lips. She saw it now: the pattern of Mikhail's barbed words. Each one leading to this moment. If only she'd paid attention, she could have shielded Danny. She should have warned him the moment she learned about Mikhail. He'd seen Danny as a pawn, perfectly positioned for his cruel game. If Danny died, it would be entirely her fault.

Fear and frustration surged through her as she paced the narrow hallway, her boots echoing on the floor. Her mind raced through options. She knew Mikhail's game; walking into a trap was exactly what he expected her to do, but she couldn't waste time either. If she waited too long, it could cost Danny his life. She needed a plan, and she needed backup. Fast.

Jolie stopped her pacing. She spun on her heel and pushed open the exit door, the cool night air hitting her face as she stormed down the stairwell. The urgency in her chest was like a fire, but she fought to keep it from clouding her judgment.

As she reached the street, she fumbled for her phone, her fingers trembling as she scrolled through her contacts. She found Rori's name and pressed the call button. Her impatience grew as she let it ring.

The moment Rori picked up, Jolie didn't waste time. "Rori, Mikhail has Danny. He's trying to use him against me. I need help."

"Wait, how do you know? Where are you?" Rori's voice became frantic.

"He was here at my apartment. He left a note. He has Danny at that old metal bar, The Slag & Bone." Jolie's voice cracked, her throat closing up in panic. She was wasting time. Without another word, she hung up the phone and quickened her pace. She needed to get to Mikhail and get Danny back before it was too late. She couldn't let Mikhail win this time. She couldn't let him hurt Danny.

Chapter Thirty-Five
Rouge and Ritual

Jolie vaulted a rusty fire escape, the metal groaning beneath her weight. She scrambled across rooftops, the gritty texture of the tar scratching at her palms. The city sprawled beneath her, a concrete labyrinth shimmering under the streetlights. She risked a glimpse down. A fleeting image of a patrol car's blue and red flash momentarily distracted her. She had to keep moving. Hunger gnawed at her, a hollow ache that tore at her stomach, but one she would have to ignore for now.

The Slag & Bone loomed ahead, a dark shadow even in the night. It looked deserted. Its peeling paint and shattered windows suggested emptiness and decay, but Jolie knew better than to trust appearances. She slowed, her senses flaring; the faintest whisper of spice and a barely perceptible shift in the air betrayed the presence of something supernatural. A succubus lurked just beyond the threshold of the club, her aura a cloud of malice. Jolie's senses couldn't reach beyond the front room, but there had to be more.

A bitter curse escaped her lips, the words swallowed by the city's nocturnal clamor. Decades of neglect had left her once razor-sharp instincts dulled, blunted by years of complacency, but there was no time for self-pity. The succubus beyond the door was growing restless. It shifted its weight, pacing. Her mind whirred, calculating, strategizing. Before anything else, before the fight, there was a more pressing need. She needed strength; she needed to feed.

Jolie's eyes darkened with hunger, her fangs lengthening in anticipation. Without hesitation, she burst through the front door. Her movements were a blur of speed and ferocity. The succubus pacing behind the door, a wiry woman, barely had time to register her presence before she was on her.

In one fluid motion, Jolie clamped her hand over her mouth and sank her fangs deep into her neck. The succubus's eyes went wide with shock. Before she could fight back, Jolie used her momentum to slam her against the far wall with a bone-rattling thud.

The succubus's blood flooded into her, warm and powerful. Jolie's senses sharpened, and her muscles coiled with newfound energy. She drank until the succubus's struggles ceased. As her lifeless body went slack in her arms, she let it crumple to the ground in a heap.

Wiping the blood from her lips, Jolie straightened. Her eyes scanned the hallway ahead. The first obstacle was down, but more were to come. There was no room for hesitation or second-guessing; she had to be ready for whatever lay beyond the next door.

Jolie's senses flared, and her eyes snapped to an approaching target. A second succubus appeared across the room, a mocking sneer curling her lips. The light from a shattered neon sign painted the scene in shades of violet and crimson. The succubus drew a wooden stake from her belt, its menacing point evident even in the dim light. Jolie felt anger surge within her.

In a flash, she propelled herself toward the far wall, using her momentum to bounce off it. She surprised her opponent as she spun gracefully in midair, landing behind the unsuspecting succubus and seizing her arm. The succubus, quick as a shadow, reacted and aimed for Jolie's heart.

Jolie ducked and weaved, dancing away from the thrusts, always staying just a breath ahead. The tension in the air crackled as the succubus pivoted, now slashing wildly with the stake. Each strike was fueled by her desperate rage. Jolie sidestepped a vicious jab and countered with a sharp block. She then unleashed a powerful kick to the succubus's chest. The force of it sent the succubus crashing against the bar, splintering wood and scattering old bottles like glass flowers.

Without pausing, Jolie leaped over the wreckage. She landed on top of the fallen succubus, her weight pinning her down. The stake clattered to the floor, out of reach. Gripping the succubus's head, Jolie twisted violently. A nauseating crack echoed as she broke the creature's neck.

"Not so tough after all," Jolie smirked, brushing dust off her hands as she stood.

She focused her heightened senses and searched for Danny. Relief washed over her as she sensed his life force burning a few floors below her. It was fading, but he was still alive against all odds. Her relief was short-lived. Circling his energy were two more succubi, their dark auras pulsing. There were more scattered throughout the building; she could sense nearly two dozen in the back of the building, biding their time, ready to strike.

With a deep breath, Jolie opened the door to the basement and descended, preparing herself for whatever lay ahead. She did not know if she could take on Mikhail, but she had to try.

Jolie's senses were on high alert as she moved slowly and silently, allowing her eyes to adjust to the darkness that enveloped her. The old steps groaned under her weight, making her cringe at every footfall. As she descended, she ran her hand along the cold, damp bricks of the wall. She could feel the dust from the stairs kicking up around her, creating a cloud that resembled an oncoming storm.

The basement was a large, open room with a dirt floor. Old bar furniture lined the walls, the remnants of a forgotten past. The buzzing lights overhead were weak, casting shadows in every corner and leaving the space in a perpetual state of gloom. The scent of old wood and earth assaulted her heightened sense of smell. At the bottom of the stairs, she turned and saw Danny lying unconscious, his head resting in the lap of a female succubus. Her long blonde hair fell over his face and shielded him from Jolie's view. The succubus was pale and gaunt, dressed only in a torn pastel nightgown. She was barefoot and dirty, and when she raised her head, Jolie could see the distinct glint of madness behind her eyes. Jolie recognized a glimpse of herself in the woman. She had been on the verge of this madness when she ran from her Maker. Being cooped up with limited access to the outside world changed you in terrible ways.

Danny's shirt was open, and the succubus gently stroked his chest. Jolie could see his chest rising and falling with shallow breaths. At least he was still alive, although by the color of his skin, she was not sure for how much longer. Fury began to boil within Jolie as she watched his life slowly slip away.

Jolie took a step toward Danny and then paused. A soft laugh floated from the darkness behind her. Jolie turned to see Mikhail, his eyes glowing with delight.

"Have you forgotten about me already?" he asked, his voice dripping with sarcasm.

Jolie cursed under her breath. She had been far too focused on Danny. Mikhail peeled himself away from the gloom. His lean frame was swallowed by faded denim and a stretched cotton shirt that strained over the hard planes of his chest. His hair was a tangle of midnight; it framed a face carved from sharp angles.

His eyes were twin pools of darkness. They locked onto hers. Each tiny hair on her arms prickled in protest. He did not move, not an inch, yet the air around him seemed to thrum with a poised, silent tension.

"Lost in thought, Jolie?" His voice scraped against the edges of the room, drawing the attention of the female succubus in the corner. "Danny has a way of doing that, doesn't he?"

Jolie growled and lunged. Mikhail sidestepped. Her dive met only air. His hand shot out, fingers tangled in her hair. He yanked her head back with a sharp crack. The rough, packed earth met her spine with a suffocating slam. A raw gasp tore from her throat; the impact vibrated through bone and sinew. Agony seared across her back, but the fire in her belly refused to be quenched. With a guttural grunt, she shoveled herself upward. Her eyes locked on Mikhail, a predator now stalking her prey.

"You're slower today, Jolie." Mikhail's voice was full of amusement. He paced, his movements fluid as oil, each step deliberate. "Or perhaps." He circled, his gaze sharp as broken glass. "You're just afraid of getting dirty."

Jolie studied Mikhail's stance. He squared his shoulders and set his feet. Confidence radiated from him. He had planned this. She could not afford to underestimate him, not now when every moment pulsed with the promise of violence. This was a battle for survival, and she was hell-bent on emerging victorious.

Jolie roared, a raw sound that tore through the dust-choked air of the abandoned bar. She launched herself at Mikhail. The atmosphere seemed to crackle and compress around her as the gap between them evaporated, every sinew screaming with the anticipation of impact.

Mikhail was a viper, not a stone. He did not wait. He erupted forward, his fist slamming into her face like a hammer blow. A blinding white starburst bloomed behind her eyes. It was followed by a searing inferno that ignited her cheekbones and the delicate bridge of her nose. The coppery tang of blood flooded her mouth. Her vision swam. The scattered debris dissolved into a nauseating swirl. An awful crack echoed in her skull, the sound of bone surrendering to his relentless assault. She fought in desperation to wrench herself free from the suffocating fog of agony.

"You thought that would be enough?" Mikhail's amused words cut deeper than any blow.

Her response was a choked gasp. A desperate attempt to clear the blood from her throat. She tasted grit from the floor. "I'm not done," she spat, her words defiant. The pain was a white-hot forge, but beneath it, a different fire began to flicker. The stubborn ember of her will.

Jolie catapulted her body into a whip of muscle and bone. This time, finding her target. A startled grunt tore from Mikhail as his weight crashed onto the packed earth.

Jolie uncoiled and landed on her knees with a sharp gasp. She wiped the crimson from her lips with a rough swipe of her forearm. She lifted her eyes to Mikhail as he slowly found his feet. Ravenous hunger flashed in his eyes.

Mikhail circled her. "We could have had fun, but the Vidar cannot survive." He came at her, preparing to connect a steel-toed boot with her ribs. Yet, this time, it was Jolie's turn to strike. Using her strength and his momentum, she propelled his body into the cement wall. Jolie heard the satisfying crunch of his shoulder snapping. She grabbed him and slammed his head backward into the wall, once, then twice. She was so focused on ending him that she didn't sense the female succubus behind her until the dagger was in her back. Her body shuddered in agony as the silver dagger plunged into her repeatedly.

Jolie fell back against the floor, barely hearing the woman's screams. "Fucking bitch! Mikhail, Mikhail, are you okay?"

Mikhail sputtered, spat blood, and coughed out, "I'll be fine, love. Just a headache."

"Let me finish her for you." The woman cradled Mikhail in her arms, cooing softly.

"No, not yet." Mikhail's soft laugh echoed in the basement. "Kill the human first and make her watch." Mikhail stood, untangling himself from the female succubus, and reached for Jolie. He grabbed her by the hair and turned her to face Danny. His breath was hot on her cheek as he held her close.

The woman swayed as she made her way leisurely back to Danny. She leaned over him, her fingers gliding over his face in a gentle caress. His skin responded with a soft, pale blue glow. "Wake up, lover. I have a present for you," she whispered, her voice a sultry melody that danced through the air.

Danny stirred, his eyelids fluttering as the shadows of sleep clung to him.

Across the room, Jolie fought fiercely against Mikhail's grip, but her body was sluggish and unresponsive, weary from the battle. Each movement sent fresh pain dancing through her wounds, sapping her strength. "Let him go!" she shouted, desperation fueling her voice.

Mikhail smirked, his eyes flaring with cruel delight. "Now, now, don't make me hurt you," he taunted. His grip tightened like a vise as he yanked her hair back, exposing her throat in a cruel twist. She gasped. The shock of the pain forced a sob from her throat, the reality of their predicament crashing over her like a wave. "You'll miss the best part," he added. The sinister satisfaction in his tone twisted her stomach.

Panic surged through Jolie as she turned to look at Danny. His eyes were glazed and distant. The urgency of the moment ignited a spark of defiance within her, drowning out the fear that threatened to consume her. With a sudden, furious movement, she twisted her body in a desperate bid to break free from Mikhail's grasp. He grunted in surprise, yet tightened his hold, forcing her neck into an unnatural arch that sent another jolt of pain shooting through her.

"Stop struggling," he hissed, his voice laced with cold menace.

Jolie's resolve began to harden like forged steel. She would not let them take Danny without a fight. She felt a rush fill her battered body, the fire of determination burning brighter than the agony. Summoning every ounce of strength, she delivered a sharp elbow to his ribs. He staggered back, surprise flickering across his face like a dying flame. Jolie seized the moment without a second thought.

With a fierce cry, she lunged forward, desperate to position herself between Danny and whatever darkness awaited him. Each second felt like an eternity. Mikhail recovered too quickly. His hand shot out and grabbed her wrist, hauling her backward. The sudden, violent tug wrenched a gasp from her. His arms clamped around her like iron bands. He crushed her against his chest, stealing the air from her lungs. Her fingers clawed for purchase but found only the fabric of his shirt.

"Let go," she choked out. The sound of her voice seemed impossibly small in the echoing space. He did not respond; his grip tightened. Jolie was completely and utterly alone.

CHAPTER THIRTY-SIX

Last Girl Standing

Mikhail's lips curled into a sinister smile as he licked Jolie's face and whispered in her ear, "That's right, my girl. You're no match for me."

Jolie's eyes squeezed shut, her body shaking with rage. She desperately tried to harness the growing resolve within her. Then she heard it. Wolves howled in the distance.

Mikhail's head snapped up at the sound, his grip on Jolie's hair tightening as he hissed, "Hurry up!"

Jolie's mind raced, searching for a way to capitalize on Mikhail's distraction. Lunging forward, she used her weight to throw Mikhail off balance. He stumbled. Jolie used the opening to twist his injured shoulder, causing him to cry out in pain. The female succubus, still trying to rouse Danny, turned in surprise at the commotion. With a screech, she launched herself at Jolie.

This time, Jolie was quicker. She grabbed the succubus by the shoulders and threw her to the ground. Jolie grabbed her hair and yanked with all her might, tearing her head from her shoulders, at last silencing her screams. She tossed the head aside and turned to face Mikhail.

The crunch of gravel echoed under his retreating boots. But Jolie wouldn't let him get away this time. This would end here now. Then, a ragged rasp pulled her focus.

"Jolie . . . is that you?"

Jolie's head whipped around. Danny's eyes were wide and clouded with pain. He blinked sluggishly; his skin was drained to a waxy pallor.

Jolie abandoned Mikhail's fleeing form, sprinting toward Danny. She said a silent prayer that the pack would find their quarry before Mikhail slipped back into the shadows. "I'm here, Danny!" Jolie exclaimed, heart racing as she rushed to his side. He was bloodied and bruised. His breaths came in shallow gasps. "We need to get out of here."

With a pained grunt, Danny struggled to his feet, relying heavily on Jolie for support. The scent of sweat and blood mingled with the acrid stench of decay from the remnants of the club. As they made their way toward the stairs, Danny's legs trembled beneath him. His movements grew more unsteady with each step. Before they reached the top of the battered staircase, he stumbled, collapsing against a splintered pile of wood that had once formed part of the club's decor.

Jolie's heart ached as she knelt beside him, concern in every line of her face. She scanned the extent of his injuries. A gash on his forehead oozed, while a bruise blossomed across his side. She inwardly cursed the chaos that had led them here.

"Danny, please," she urged, her voice soft yet firm.

He propped himself up against the debris, eyes shimmering with pain and anger.

Her attention was drawn to the scene unfolding at the top of the broken stairs. Mikhail and his remaining allies were locked in a fierce battle against a pack of snarling wolves and the dark figure of Caleb. She wanted to join the fray and defend her friends, but she couldn't leave Danny behind—not like this.

Just as she deliberated her next move, a jabbing pain pulled her focus back to the detective. She glanced down, shocked and tense. Danny was holding a jagged piece of wood, the sharp tip pressing into the skin right above her heart. His gaze was penetrating, his strength barely hanging on as he fought to stay conscious.

"Danny, I am not your enemy. We have to keep moving," Jolie implored, her voice steady as confusion wound its way around her mind. She met Danny's intense stare with her own. How did he know about using the pointy end of a stake against her? Did he know what she was, or was this just the first weapon he had found?

Danny shook his head. His voice came out hoarse and strained. "I'm not going anywhere with you. This is all your fault. I should have ended this sooner."

Jolie swallowed. He knew; he had to. He had known all along that she was a vampire. All this time, he had been hunting her. The full weight of her naivety bore down on her.

Jolie watched Danny's hands tremble as he gripped the splintered wood. A wave of relief flooded her as she realized she was in no real danger from him, not for now, at least. The fight for survival around them raged on, but in this moment, his uncertainty was all she could see. A frown creased her brow as she tried to reach him through the haze of confusion clouding his thoughts.

"I didn't do this." Her voice was urgent as she gestured toward the chaos engulfing them. She was desperate for him to understand, desperate to make him see that the true threat lay beyond them, not within their fractured alliance. "Look!"

For a few agonizing seconds, she feared he wouldn't listen. But then he slowly turned his head, eyes glistening as they scanned the wild battle happening around them. The chaotic sounds of growls and shouts filled the air. Wood splintered and glass shattered. He blinked as reality unfolded around him.

She watched his expression shift. The tension in his shoulders slackened as the weight of comprehension settled in. The makeshift weapon fell from his fingers, clattering to the ground and landing in the debris that littered the floor.

"I've been drugged," he whispered, the words barely more than a breath. He looked at her. His eyes widened, reflecting both vulnerability and a flicker of trust that hadn't been there moments before.

Jolie leaned closer. She had to get him moving. "Danny, I'm here to help you. I promise," she said. Her voice was steady as she brushed a hand against his arm, grounding him in this moment of clarity amidst the havoc around them. "Let's go."

She helped him to his feet and up the remaining stairs. The fight still raged around them. At the top of the stairs, Danny froze, his breath catching in his throat. In front of them were four large werewolves, snarling and baring their teeth. Caleb was locked in a fierce battle with Mikhail. Danny paused, paralyzed by fear and shock. Jolie began to pull him forward. "Come on, we have to go," she pleaded.

Danny tore his eyes away from the battle and locked onto Jolie, his voice shaky. "He's the one who took me. He came to me, saying he had important information." He gestured toward Mikhail. "He told me to meet him here. That he'd tell me the whole story and then turn himself in. I just had to come alone."

Jolie's jaw clenched, eyes narrowing as she watched the unfolding scene. "I know. He used you to get to me," she replied, anger in her voice.

Mikhail grabbed a wolf mid-lunge and hurled it through the air. The beast crashed near them but quickly scrambled to its feet, undeterred, and charged back at him.

Danny's eyes widened in disbelief. "Did you see that? He just threw a wolf like it was nothing!" he gasped, his voice wavering.

Danny's panic quickly overwhelmed him. He slumped to the floor and backed away from Jolie. His trembling form pressed against the corner of the room. His gaze was fixed on something behind her.

Jolie whipped around, her breath catching in her throat as the brutal fight between Mikhail and the wolves reached its grim conclusion. One of the larger wolves, fur bristling and teeth bared, had managed to overpower Mikhail. Its jaws locked around his neck in a deadly grip. There was a crunch, and with that, the fight was over.

The wolves stepped back, their eyes glinting in the dim light as they released Mikhail's lifeless body. A somber howl echoed into the night. It carried with it the message that the rest of the pack had dispatched Mikhail's group. The battle was finished.

Jolie stood frozen as the air around the wolves shimmered, warping reality. The beasts transformed, their fur receding as their forms twisted. In a flash, naked men stood in their place. Human once more.

Abernathy limped toward her, a deep gash torn in his leg. "Are you alright, kid?" he asked, his voice rough but concerned.

Jolie nodded weakly, feeling her own wounds slowly knitting back together. She leaned heavily against the wall, her strength failing. The violence of the night had left her shaken and vulnerable, yet somehow she had made it through.

Danny's heart was racing. Jolie could hear it echoing around her. His breath came in short, panicked bursts as he stared in shock at Boden. "Holy shit, I'm on drugs," he repeated. "None of this is real."

Boden, naked and utterly indifferent, approached Danny. His calm demeanor did nothing to soothe the rising panic in Danny's chest. Danny's eyes darted around the room as he crawled backward, pressing his body as far into the corner as he could.

Jolie slowly pushed herself off the wall. "Boden, this is new to him. He obviously only knew about me," she said, gesturing toward Danny. "And you're naked. You might want to give him some space."

Boden stopped in his tracks and raised his hands in surrender. "Good point," he said, finally acknowledging the awkwardness of the situation. "But we really need to go. Rori should be here soon with the cars."

Jolie approached Danny with cautious, measured steps. His breath was shallow, eyes wide with disbelief, as if the world had spun wildly out of his control. She crouched beside him, her voice steady but soft, trying to cut through the fog of panic.

"Danny, we need to leave," she said. "Yes, I'm a vampire, and they're werewolves, but we're the good guys. I promise. Please trust me. We don't have time."

But before the weight of her words could even register, Danny's body gave out. His eyes rolled back, and with a soft smack, he slumped against the stone wall, unconscious.

Jolie exhaled sharply. "Damn it," she muttered under her breath as she crouched beside his motionless form. She brushed a hand through her hair as she glanced up at Boden, who stood nearby, still bearing the raw energy of the transformation.

"We need to hurry," she said, urgency crackling in her voice. "If he wakes up and sees us, he's just gonna faint again, and I'm not about to let him die here."

Boden gave her a grim nod. "We'll move fast," he replied. He glanced around the room as if sensing danger on the horizon. "But you're right, his mind's cracking under the weight of all this."

Jolie's gaze shifted back to Danny, her heart tightening. His face was pale, a bead of sweat clinging to his brow. She could feel the fragile balance of his psyche hanging by a thread. The night's events had shattered his sense of reality, and they didn't have time to mend it.

She bent down, carefully lifting Danny's limp body into her arms. "Let's get out of here," she said. She stood and carried Danny through the broken glass and dust-covered floors.

CHAPTER THIRTY-SEVEN

Tips on the Stage

Rori and Lina pulled up to the apartment complex in their sleek, black SUVs. The air overflowed with tension as they quickly ushered everyone out of the vehicles and into the relative safety of Rori and Boden's apartment. Thankfully, Rori had arranged for her children to stay with a friend, granting them the quiet space they needed for Lina to work her healing magic and for everyone to recover.

Jolie lay trembling on the floor, her body ravaged by the night's events. Shadows clung to her skin. The residual energy of battle still lingered in her bones. Caleb, nearly untouched by the night's violence, stood vigilant beside her. His eyes bright, muscles coiled, ready to defend her from any lingering threat.

Lina moved with quiet focus, her hands glowing faintly with healing magic as she worked on Abernathy's torn leg. Blood stained the floor beneath him, but under Lina's touch, the jagged flesh began knitting together. Her magic pulled together muscle and skin like weaving a rug.

Nearby, Danny rested in one of the guest bedrooms, peacefully asleep after Lina's care had soothed his wounds and mind.

Jared arrived moments after Rori and Lina. He knelt beside Jolie. His presence was solid, reassuring. He extended his arm toward her, offering support.

"You should rest and eat," Jared said gently, concern threading his voice.

"No," Jolie mumbled. She was exhausted, but she tried to push herself upright. Pain coursed through her limbs, and her skin still tingled with the unnatural energy of the night. "I don't need it."

But her body betrayed her deception. A tremor rippled through her as she collapsed back against the floor. The battle. The blood loss. The final surrender of her adrenaline—it had drained her. Yet she fought against the vulnerability gnawing at her. She wouldn't allow herself to be weak.

"Jolie," Jared whispered. "You've been through enough. Let me help."

Jolie's resistance faltered as she looked around the room at her friends. Caleb's unwavering protection, Jared's steady presence, and Lina's magic wove through the air with the soft buzz of life. Jolie's eyelids fluttered, the weight of bone-deep fatigue finally winning. A shaky breath escaped her lips. "Alright."

Her hand, trembling slightly, reached out. She grasped Jared's arm like a lifeline. He responded instantly, his strong hand closing around hers, drawing her closer with a gentle but firm pull. His warmth radiated through her.

She leaned heavily against him, her head resting momentarily on his shoulder. She pulled his arm to her mouth and began to feed. His blood coursed through her; the warmth pooled in her stomach and spread out through her limbs. It revitalized her, but it was the nearness of Jared, the feeling of his solid strength supporting her, that truly replenished her. A current of shared energy, quiet and potent, flowed between them. It twisted through the space separating their bodies. The draining emptiness that had threatened to consume her began to recede, replaced by a slow, welcome surge of renewed strength. The faint scent of his aftershave settled like a comforting blanket around her.

When she was done, Jared gently lifted her head and placed a featherlight kiss on the crown of her head. The touch, brief but profound, anchored her to the present. It grounded her amidst the maelstrom of the last few hours.

Feeling steadier, Jolie rose to her feet. Her senses sharpened as she left the warmth of the room. She stepped out onto the patio where Rori and Boden stood beneath the pale glow of the moon. The crisp night air filled her lungs, clearing the haze that had clouded her mind. The distant echo of city life reverberated around them, but for a moment, she found respite.

Rori greeted Jolie with a warm smile. "Boden was just telling me the details of Mikhail's final moments. Angus will be rewarded for delivering the death blow."

A slow, grateful smile stretched across Jolie's face. She sank onto a chair beside them. "Angus," she murmured. The image of the large, dark wolf flashed in her mind. A blur of fur and teeth in the pandemonium.

Boden chuckled. "Don't you worry," he said, his voice a low drawl. "You'll be able to tell the difference between us in wolf form soon enough. You'll learn to recognize the subtle differences in gait, scent, even the way our eyes gleam." He gestured with a hand, the movement careful because of his wounds.

The still-healing wounds across Boden's arms and chest were bright and angry. Seeing them muted her own triumphant feeling. The surge of pride at facing down Mikhail and his group ebbed. She was far from invincible. The adrenaline-fueled mess illuminated more than ever that there was a desperate need for more training.

Rori's hand rested on Jolie's arm for a moment, a small, comforting weight against the turmoil inside. The touch grounded her, a tangible connection to the reality of her survival. "Oh, and just so you know, Lina managed to have a quick word with Detective O'Neil before he drifted off. Seems he'd been hunting you for some time. Apparently, you're quite the elusive target."

Jolie's stomach plummeted, and a sudden chill swept through her. Embarrassment flared hotly in her chest. She hadn't known, at least not until the harrowing moment when he had threatened to kill her. A bitter scoff escaped her lips. She shook her head in disbelief. Her eyes narrowed as the memory flashed before her. O'Neil's determined expression, the point of the stake pressed against her chest.

"I am such a fool," she muttered. Her voice wobbled as she leaned back against her chair. Her arms crossed tightly over her chest as if to shield herself from the weight of her own mistakes. The heaviness of it all—Mikhail, O'Neil, and the battle that had ensued—pressed down on her like a binding shroud.

How had I missed that? Her mind raced with questions that twisted like a knife in her gut. *How had I been so stupid?* Frustration gushed as she wondered how she could have overlooked such a critical detail in a world already fraught with danger.

There was a sudden shift in the energy around her. Jolie looked up and followed Rori's and Boden's gaze. She turned and looked toward the door to the balcony. Danny stood there, his expression conflicted; he shifted awkwardly from foot to foot.

Jolie's heart clenched painfully at the sight of him. She had hoped for a moment to gather her thoughts, to find the right words before facing him. But now, with him standing there, the tension building between them, she wasn't sure what to say. Fear and anticipation warred within her.

Boden steered Rori toward the open door and back into the living room. Danny backed away as they approached. Boden pulled Rori close to him as they passed Danny, his arm creating a protective cocoon around his wife. Behind them, Jolie followed. The air inside was charged with a tension that pricked her skin. Jolie tightened her fists; she could feel the tremor start in her knees, nervous, threatening to spill over.

Boden spoke first, his voice calm and reassuring. "Are you doing okay?" he asked, placing a hand on Danny's shoulder.

Danny pulled away from Boden and shook his head. "Physically, I'm fine. Mentally, I don't know if I can face the world after this," he admitted, his voice trembling.

Rori stepped forward. "Let me get you something to eat and drink. A beer, maybe?" she offered.

But Danny shook his head again, his eyes downcast. "No, I'm not staying. I just have a few questions." He took a step back as if to distance himself from the group. "What was Mikhail? Like, for real? A succubus?" he asked, his voice filled with disbelief.

Boden shrugged, a small smirk playing at the corners of his lips. "I know it's hard to believe, but doesn't it make sense? No human could have killed like that."

Danny locked eyes with Boden, accusation flashing across his face. "What about you? Shapeshifter? Werewolf?" His eyes swept up and down Boden's frame, as if searching for any trace of the monster lurking beneath his human exterior.

Charles slowly stood from his spot on the couch. Jolie watched him out of the corner of her eye. He was preparing to close the gap, just in case Danny made any aggressive moves toward Rori and Boden.

Danny turned his ire on Jolie, his voice filled with disdain. "And you, a vampire who saves humans and fights with wolves? Monsters, all of you," he spat, rage and bitterness making the words sharp. "Monsters out of a storybook."

Rori let out a heavy sigh, her patience clearly wearing thin. "I get it," she said firmly, crossing her arms. "It's hard to wrap your head around, especially as a vampire hunter. But we're not monsters, Danny. We don't kill. We own businesses, pay our taxes. We're just like you, living in this world."

Her reasoning didn't soften Danny's hard stare. His expression remained a mask of distrust and confusion. Without another word, he grabbed his coat and stalked toward the elevator, jabbing the down button with more force than necessary.

"Just like us," he muttered under his breath, loathing dripping from every word.

Boden stepped forward, placing a hand on the wall beside the elevator, leaning slightly toward Danny. "Don't you have anything to say to Jolie?" he asked gently. "She saved your life tonight."

Danny shook his head, refusing to even glance in Jolie's direction. His jaw clenched tight; spite simmered beneath his words. "I can't handle this right now."

Jolie's heart sank. The walls between them had grown too thick to break through. She realized with a sickening certainty that there was no going back. In his rejection, she knew she wouldn't be safe anymore. Not from him.

But Boden wasn't finished. His tone turned serious as he locked eyes with Danny. "You realize you can't tell anyone about this, right?"

The elevator dinged, and Danny stepped inside, his expression dark and unreadable. "No one would believe me anyway," he muttered, his voice barely a whisper as the doors began to close.

Before they could shut completely, Boden blocked them with his arm. He stared at Danny, cold and unflinching. "You need to leave us alone. Especially Jolie. It's not a request," he said, voice low and dangerous. "Nothing is gonna happen to me or mine."

He stepped back, letting the doors slide shut. Danny's glare was the last thing Jolie saw before the elevator descended, his animosity lingering in the air like a shield.

As the quiet settled around them, Jolie's mind raced. She hoped desperately that this was the last she would see of Danny O'Neil. But deep down, she wasn't so sure. Something told her she'd have to keep looking over her shoulder, waiting for the inevitable.

Chapter Thirty-Eight

Centuries of Reinvention

Jolie let out a weary sigh as she unlocked her apartment door. The weight of the night pressed down on her; every muscle in her body ached. Rori had insisted Jolie stay with them, but she had politely declined. She needed space, some time alone to decompress and shake off the chaos.

The familiar silence of her apartment greeted her like an old friend. As she stepped inside, the exhaustion settled in, deeper than before. Jolie stripped off her torn, bloodstained clothes. Each piece fell to the floor as she peeled away the remnants of the battle with the succubi. The hot bath she slipped into moments later felt like heaven. She sighed in contentment as the water enveloped her, washing away the grime and the lingering adrenaline of the fight.

For a while, she just sat there, letting the warmth soak into her bones, until every trace of the ordeal had melted from her skin. When her body finally felt like her own again, Jolie pulled herself from the bath and slipped into her sweats.

In a heap of golden fur, Caleb sprawled across her pillow, a single ear twitching in the quiet. The familiar, comforting weight of his presence settled over her like a well-loved blanket. A slow grin stretched across Jolie's lips.

She slid under the covers. The crisp sheets were cool against her skin, but soon they would yield to the furnace of Caleb's warmth. Her arms circled his substantial, breathing mass, fingers sinking into the richness of his fur. "You're the best, Caleb," she breathed. "Good job."

He snorted, and a slow, repetitive thump vibrated through the mattress from the backend of the golden heap. Caleb's tail, a powerful pendulum, swept against the sheets. Contentment filled Jolie with a warmth that allowed her to drift off to sleep.

Jolie woke up to find herself in a strange place. She was sitting in a high-backed chair, surrounded by the scent of new leather. In front of her, a fire burned brightly, casting its warm glow into the darkness. Jolie could feel soft grass under her feet, and she turned to look behind her. The light from the fire didn't reach very far, leaving the rest of her surroundings shrouded in darkness. Despite her amplified senses, Jolie couldn't see any-thing beyond her chair. She couldn't even remember how she got there.

The wind whispered through the leaves, creating a symphony of rustling and swaying. The earthy smell of damp soil filled her nostrils, reminding her of the dream she had the night she found Caleb. Although there was no mist this time, she was certain that she had found the same glade as in that dream. Jolie rose to her feet. The ground beneath her was soft and cool against her bare feet.

"Sikrele?" she called out, her voice echoing through the silent forest. She strained her ears, hoping for a response, but all she heard was the wind and the rustle of leaves.

Jolie walked toward the center of the glade, guided by the faint glow of the fireplace. It was built into the trunk of a massive old tree, its branches reaching toward the sky like outstretched arms. She peered around the trunk, her eyes scanning the darkness beyond the circle of light. But there was nothing there.

"Sit, dear," a voice called out from the shadows.

Jolie spun around to see Sikrele emerge from the darkness. She looked older now, but her dark hair and piercing eyes remained the same. Her white slip was dirty and torn, covered in dirt and leaves; even her skin was smeared with mud. Jolie found herself seated in the chair that Sikrele had gestured to.

The goddess approached the fire and warmed her hands. "You've done well, Vidar," she said, her voice low and gravelly.

The word sounded familiar to Jolie, and she searched her mind for why. Then she remembered. "Mikhail called me that."

Sikrele's head snapped up, surprise flashing in her unearthly eyes. She looked upward at the dark sky, making soft tutting noises. "Yes, yes, he did. I'm not sure how he knew, but he did." Sikrele turned back to Jolie, her head tilting at an unnatural angle as the light danced in her dark hair.

Jolie was overwhelmed by the power she exuded. "What does it mean?"

Sikrele's lips curled into a smile, revealing sharp, irregular teeth. "The Vidar is you," she said, her voice filled with reverence. "You are the chosen one."

Jolie's mind reeled with this revelation. She had always felt different, like she didn't quite belong in the vampire world, but she never could have imagined that she was destined for something greater. "But why me? What am I supposed to do? Why did Mikhail say I couldn't survive?" she asked, her voice barely above a whisper.

Sikrele's head tilted further to the side, as if she were listening to a distant voice. She lifted her nose and sniffed the air, a look of urgency crossing her face. "There isn't time to explain now," she said. "We must go."

The light of the fire gave a soft flicker and then disappeared. Jolie felt the chill of the night wrap around her. Panic set in as she realized Sikrele had disappeared along with the light. Left alone in the darkness.

"Wait!" Jolie called out, her voice sounding feeble in the vast emptiness that surrounded her. "I need more . . . Please . . ." But there was no response, only the silence of the night.

Chapter Thirty-Nine

The Character She Became

The staccato pounding shattered the stillness. A frantic scrabbling against wood announced Caleb's launch from the bed. His entire body quivered, a vortex of fur and anticipation. He whined in a low rumble of impatience, his front paws scraping against the door.

Jolie stood. The worn carpet was a familiar scratch against her bare feet, her footsteps silent as she navigated the short distance to the entryway.

She yanked the door inward, and the scent of freshly baked goods and spiced tea rushed in. Seb leaned in the doorway, his familiar, lopsided grin standing out against the muted tones of the afternoon. Behind him stood two large men, their faces impassive as they hoisted overflowing wicker baskets.

Seb strode past her into the apartment. The sharp scent of granite trailed in his wake. He gestured with a flick of his wrist, his voice low as he directed the men. "Here, on the table by the fire. Oh, and light the fire too."

Coins landed in the porters' hands with a dull clink. His voice boomed as he waved goodbye. "Until next time!" The heavy door swung shut, leaving them alone with the overflowing provisions. Caleb placed his front paws on the table, trying to shove his head into the baskets.

"I have a little service I use when I feel like leaving my comfortable abode," Seb explained as he began to unpack the baskets, tossing treats to Caleb from each plate he removed. He pulled out a teapot and cups, along with the cakes and cookies, and started to set up a small tea party on Jolie's coffee table.

"You heard already? That was fast," Jolie remarked as she helped Seb set up the coffee table.

Seb smiled knowingly as he headed to the kitchen to boil water for tea. "I have my ways," he replied with a wink.

Jolie chuckled lightly at his response. Seb placed the tea leaves in the teapot and prepared plates for the sweets. Jolie emptied the final basket and pulled a large jug of blood from the bottom. She smiled. Seb had thought of everything.

The fire crackled, its warmth bleeding into the couch where Jolie and Seb had finally settled. A sigh escaped Jolie's lips. She relished the scent of Seb's homemade lemon bars and the savory tang of smoked almonds. Caleb lay sprawled in front of the fire, his mouth full of lemon bar, and his tail thumping happily against the floor.

Jolie couldn't help herself. She snagged a lemon bar to nibble between sips from her mug of warm blood. The sharpness of the lemon was muted to her vampire taste buds, but its familiar scent soothed her nerves.

Seb waited patiently for Jolie to talk. Slowly, the story unfolded.

"It's . . . it's good to just sit here," she admitted.

Seb turned, his gaze soft. "You are not alone, Jolie. That's all that matters."

As the evening wore on, the easy banter between them began to fray, replaced by a more somber current. "There's . . . there's something I need to tell you, Seb."

He met her eyes, his own mirroring a quiet readiness. "Anything, Jolie."

She took a deep breath. Speaking Danny's name out loud created a raw ache that made her clear her throat. She felt a familiar prickling behind her eyes. "And then . . ." Her voice caught, a choked gasp. She swallowed hard. She couldn't unleash the full, jagged mess of it all, not yet. She skimmed over the most painful parts.

Seb listened, his expression softening as she spoke. When she finished, he reached over, offering a gentle squeeze of her hand. "I'm sorry about Danny," he whispered. "But I don't think you need to worry too much. From what I've heard, Boden has a way of fixing things." A wry grin tugged at Seb's lips. "A brutish way, sure, but effective."

Seb cut another thick slice of cake and tossed it to Caleb, who caught it effortlessly midair. The sound of Caleb's happy munching filled the brief silence, easing some of the tension.

Jolie's lips curved into a smile. Seb possessed an uncanny knack for knowing precisely when a quiet anchor was more valuable than a flood of words.

"The elders are pleased," Seb announced. "Most of their . . . difficulties have been smoothed over by your hand. And, it seems, they wish to express their gratitude." He dug into his vest and produced a small, drawstring pouch; he sent it sailing toward Jolie.

She caught it, the worn fabric soft against her palm. A faint clinking sound emanated from within. She loosened the cord. When she peered inside, her eyes widened to saucers. The unmistakable gleam of gold winked back at her.

"Gold coins?" Jolie breathed. She shook the bag, the metallic chimes a strange, almost foreign sound. "They're . . . they're actually paying me for this?" A disbelieving laugh bubbled up, escaping her mouth.

Seb simply shrugged and took a sip of his tea. "It's their way. You never know when some extra gold might come in handy," he said nonchalantly. Jolie couldn't quite wrap her head around the concept of being paid for what had happened.

Jolie drained the last of her mug of blood and looked at Seb. "Mikhail called me something in that basement," she said, her voice taut with a hint of uncertainty. Seb raised an eyebrow, signaling for her to continue. "And then, I had a dream about Sikrele again today. She called me the same thing, Vidar. She seemed scared, though. Preoccupied. And then she was gone, leaving me in the dark."

Seb's expression turned serious as he set his cup down and rubbed his hands on his pants. He turned to face the fire, one hand over his mouth as he tapped his index finger against his nose in thought. Jolie watched him, wondering if he would ever speak.

Finally, after what felt like an eternity, Seb cleared his throat and turned to face her. His eyebrows were furrowed in concern as he folded his hands in his lap. "I guess I should just be honest with you. You have a right to know," he began. "When you first dreamed of Sikrele, I was worried about this."

"Worried about what?"

Seb took a deep breath before continuing, "The fae world and the human world exist on a delicate balance, like the blade of a knife. We survive because most humans don't know we exist, and they survive on our good graces. If a war were to break out between our worlds, it would be catastrophic for both sides, as well as the natural world. To maintain this balance, sacrifices must be made. The Vidar is one of those sacrifices."

Jolie pulled her knees into her chest. Her brow furrowed in confusion as she turned to face Seb. "Wait, are you serious? I really have to die?" Her voice was shaking.

Seb shook his head vigorously, his hands waving in front of him as if to physically push away the idea. "No, no, not like that. It's not a physical sacrifice. It's more about putting the needs of others before your own. You are responsible for keeping the humans, fae, even Sikrele and her enemy in line."

Jolie's eyes widened in shock. "Me? How am I supposed to do that? I have no idea where to even begin."

Seb shrugged nonchalantly and reached for another slice of cake. "I don't know either. It's been thousands of years since we've had a Vidar. But don't worry, I'll help you figure it out."

Jolie paused, sipping her blood. "Sikrele has enemies?" Jolie had believed that someone that powerful was completely untouchable.

Seb giggled. "Of course. Sikrele tries to build; her sister tries to destroy. You know, the natural order of things."

Jolie exhaled sharply, aggravation pooling in her chest as she leaned back in her chair. Her fingers massaged her temples as though she could erase the weight of the world from her mind. "What if I don't want to do this? Can't someone else take on this responsibility?"

Seb's expression turned serious as he met her gaze. "If you refuse, the world will fall into chaos. Maybe not immediately, but eventually. The thing about Vidars is that they can't help but help. It's in their blood."

Jolie's shoulders sagged, a heavy sigh escaping her lips. "Let's . . . let's talk about something else, please," she murmured.

Seb's chuckle was a warm, unexpected sound in the tense silence. He reached for a cookie, a triumphant grin spreading across his face. "Of course," he said, his eyes twinkling. He scooped up a generous handful of the crumbly treats and sent a few sailing toward Caleb. "So tell me," Seb continued, his voice laced with amusement, "how did you like those books I gave you?"

CHAPTER FORTY

Born Again Burlesque

Jolie carefully placed her belongings into her bag as the last of the theatergoers filtered out of the building. The Black Cat House had returned to its usual bustling rhythm after the shambles that was the past month. Things were finally settling back to normal. With a deep sigh, she reached for the soft lavender-scented cloth she kept at her vanity. Gently, she wiped away the remnants of her stage makeup, her mind drifting to everything that had happened.

Amidst the drama, something unexpected had blossomed. Jolie had found a true friend in Wyn. At first, she hadn't been sure what to make of her. Wyn's quirks once grated on her nerves. Now, though, they were endearing. Their friendship had grown into something she hadn't realized she needed.

As she sat lost in thought, arms wrapped around her shoulders from behind. Wyn pressed her chin into Jolie's neck; her face lit up with excitement. "Hey! You want to go out tonight?" Wyn asked, practically vibrating with energy.

Jolie smiled, though exhaustion tugged at her. "Not tonight, Wyn. I'm exhausted. You've had me out too late every night this week." She stifled a yawn, half-laughing.

Wyn sighed dramatically, poking Jolie in the side. "Ugh, you're such an old soul."

"I am," Jolie replied with a snicker, leaning in to give her friend a quick kiss on the cheek. "But I'll see you tomorrow." She grabbed her bag, her body already aching for the comfort of her bed. Jolie exited the theater and almost bumped into Maddy; she was surprised the girl had stayed after everything that had happened.

"Hi Maddy," Jolie said brightly. A shocked expression shifted across Maddy's face as she quickly ducked past Jolie and into the dressing room to return the red and gold costume pieces she was clutching to her chest. Jolie chuckled. "Some things never change."

Jolie tossed a wave to Charles as she made her way through the theater. With his after-show checklist held tightly in his hand, he barely registered her passing. Jolie looked up and smiled. Silhouetted against the door stood Boden and Jared.

Jared's head snapped up as she drew nearer. "Jolie," he began. "Need a ride tonight?" He leaned against the doorframe, a pose that was both casual and deliberately inviting. An undercurrent thrummed beneath the simple question.

A tiny, unexpected flutter took flight in Jolie's chest. Jared had been circling her lately, like a curious fox around a tempting hen coop. A part of her, the part that felt the flutter, admitted to a sliver of intrigue, but the more sensible part was already calculating the potential fallout. Shona. The unspoken shadow that always seemed to follow Jared. Jolie couldn't imagine anything worse than stepping into the middle of pack gossip. She wanted to keep things simple, to keep the peace.

"I'm good, thanks," she said with a polite smile. She gave them both a nod and a quick goodnight before stepping out into the cool night air.

The breeze hit her as soon as she was outside. It carried with it the scents of the city. Jolie took a deep breath and felt a calming sense of peace wash over her. It had been a long, exhausting night, but now, alone for the first time in hours, she could finally unwind.

Jolie's worn sneakers smacked against the pavement, each step carrying her away from the familiar bustle of the theater and toward the quiet promise of her new building. Rori and Boden's offer had felt like a lifeline, a fifth-floor unit. It was a haven of safety and belonging, with a balcony that offered fresh air to Caleb. A small patch of sky he could claim when the walls felt too close.

A genuine smile touched Jolie's lips as she recalled the faces that had already become commonplace. The neighbors who'd readily volunteered to keep an eye on Caleb, their offers warm and uncomplicated. It was a community that embraced them. There was also a training facility, right there on the second floor. It beckoned with the clang of steel and the thump of bodies. Angus and Abernathy, their names conjured images of sweat, discipline, and the relentless pursuit of strength. As the chosen Vidar, preparedness wasn't a choice. It was the air she breathed, and Angus and Abernathy had been charged with helping her get ready.

Pushing through the heavy glass doors, the clean air of the lobby enveloped her. "Hey, Jolie!" a cheerful voice chirped. Shona was perched on a stool behind the reception desk. A stack of mail beside her, her smile was as bright as the lit-up elevator buttons.

Jolie returned the wave with a small arc of her hand. "Shona. Everything quiet today?"

Shona adjusted her dangling bracelets. "As a library. Just Mrs. Gable's cat doing its usual opera on the third floor." She winked. "You know, I saw

Abernathy heading to the gym earlier. Looked like he was in one of his moods."

Jolie's lips curved. "That's my cue to avoid him then."

Shona nodded sagely. "Wise move. Have a good evening, Jolie. And tell Caleb I've got a fresh batch of cookies waiting for him."

"I will," Jolie promised, the elevator doors sliding open with a soft hiss. As she stepped inside, the familiar scent of lemon polish, the building's signature aroma, soothed her. Each floor brought her a step closer to that fifth-floor sanctuary.

When the doors slid open, she stepped into the hall and made her way to her door. The moment she stepped inside, Caleb's excited barking filled the air. His tail wagged furiously as he greeted her at the threshold.

The place was smaller than her old apartment, but much nicer. Plump couches and thick, luxurious carpets gave the space a warmth she hadn't felt in a long time. The newly renovated bathroom fixtures twinkled, everything sleek and modern. Not a single scratch or ding marred the furniture, an oddity for Jolie, given her usual state of disorder.

Her eyes drifted to the kitchen counter, where three boxes of fried chicken sat next to a cooler filled with blood packs. The young wolf she'd hired to run with Caleb had gone above and beyond tonight. She smiled, grateful for the small gestures that made life a bit easier. She moved the blood packs to the refrigerator and tossed a piece of chicken to Caleb, whose tail wagged even faster at the sight of his favorite treat.

Just as Jolie was about to run herself a much-needed bath, the intercom buzzed, shattering the quiet of her evening. She pressed the button, her voice anxious. "Yes?"

Shona's voice crackled through the speaker. "There's someone here to see you . . . Detective O'Neil."

Danny. She hadn't seen or heard from him since that night. Part of her didn't want to let him up, but she knew he wouldn't dare try to hurt her here, and she truly needed to know what he wanted.

She looked down at Caleb, as if seeking his guidance, but the dog was too engrossed in his chicken to notice her inner turmoil. With a sigh, she pressed the button on the intercom. "Let him up."

Jolie stood at the threshold of her apartment, her hand gripping the doorframe as she waited for Danny to step off the elevator. She had no intention of letting him inside. Caleb paced behind her, alert and ready for whatever might unfold.

Danny finally stepped out of the elevator, his movements slow and hesitant. He stopped just out of reach, his eyes hard and unreadable. "I'm just here to tell you I won't be coming after you," he said, skipping any pleasantries. His tone was flat, devoid of warmth.

Jolie crossed her arms, then uncrossed them, unsure of where this conversation was headed. "I wasn't afraid of that," she replied, trying to ease the tension hanging in the air. After a beat, she added, "You know I'm not dangerous, right?"

Danny laughed, but it was a cold, humorless sound. "You are dangerous. If I had done my job right, I would've taken care of you before things got out of control."

Jolie's chest tightened with anger, but she kept it in check. This man was impossible. "But now you can't," she said, her voice steady. "Not with the allies I have."

Behind her, Caleb let out a low growl. Jolie placed a calming hand on his head. "You're pathetic, Danny. There's so much you don't understand, and you're too arrogant to even try."

Danny's face remained unmoved, cold as ever. "Maybe. But if I get another chance, if any of you slip up, I won't miss it."

Jolie smiled, but it was a sad, resigned smile. "You should go. You're not welcome here." Without waiting for a response, she stepped back and closed the door in his face.

She lingered there for a moment, listening to the faint sound of his footsteps retreating down the hallway. She had thought she would feel more conflicted, more hurt by this final confrontation, but she didn't. With new friends and family by her side, Danny's disdain and threats held no power over her. Whatever the future brought, she was ready.

About the author

Patience Schoene is a neurodivergent author based in Seattle, where she lives with her husband and rescue dogs. She weaves her background in dance and witchcraft practice into fantasy storytelling, exploring imaginative worlds rich with spiritual depth. When not writing, she can be found knitting, foraging, urban homesteading, or chasing the horizon at the coast.

Also by

The Shattered Moonstone: Brightstar Manor #1, September 2026
Beneath the Guise of Beauty, January 2027
The world of The Black Cat House returns in Fog of Shadows, May 2027

www.ingramcontent.com/pod-product-compliance
Lightning Source LLC
Chambersburg PA
CBHW051212130726

47988CB00001B/63